Praise for

Lauraine Snelling

SOMEDAY HOME

"The story is inspiring and hopeful. Snelling tells a wonderful tale of fresh starts, resilience, loss, and love in this perfect summer read."

—RT Book Reviews

HEAVEN SENT RAIN

"Snelling's story has the potential to be a big hit...The alternating narrators make the tale diverse and well rounded. The premise of the story is interesting and the prose is very moving."

—RT Book Reviews

WAKE THE DAWN

"Snelling (*One Perfect Day*) continues to draw fans with her stellar storytelling skills. This time she offers a look at small-town medical care in a tale that blends healing, love, and a town's recovery...Snelling's description of events at the small clinic during the storm is not to be missed."

—Publishers Weekly

"Snelling's fast-paced novel has characters who seek help in the wrong places. It takes a raging storm for them to see that the help they needed was right in front of them the whole time. This is a strong, believable story."

—RT Book Reviews

"Lauraine Snelling's newest novel will keep you turning pages and not wanting to put the book down...*Wake the Dawn* is a guaranteed good read for any fiction lover."

—Cristel Phelps, *Retailers and Resources Magazine*

REUNION

"Inspired by events in Snelling's own life, *Reunion* is a beautiful story about characters discovering themselves as the foundation of their family comes apart at the seams. Readers may recognize themselves or someone they know within the pages of this book, which belongs on everyone's keeper shelf."

—RT Book Reviews

"*Reunion* is a captivating tale that will hook you from the very start...Fans of Christian fiction will love this touching story."

—FreshFiction.com

"Snelling's previous novels (*One Perfect Day*) have been popular with readers, and this one, loosely based on her own life, will be no exception."

—Publishers Weekly

ON HUMMINGBIRD WINGS

"Snelling can certainly charm."

ONE PERFECT DAY

"Snelling writes about the foibles of human nature with keen insight and sweet honesty."

"Snelling's captivating tale will immediately draw readers in. The grief process is accurately portrayed, and readers will be enthralled by the raw emotion of Jenna's and Nora's accounts."

"A spiritually challenging and emotionally taut story. Fans of Christian women's fiction will enjoy this winning novel."

The Second Half

A Novel

Lauraine Snelling

New York • Boston • Nashville

Copyright © 2016 by Lauraine Snelling
Reading Group Guide Copyright © 2016 by Lauraine Snelling and Hachette Book Group, Inc.

Cover design by JuLee Brand
Cover imagery by Getty Images
Cover copyright © 2016 by Hachette Book Group, Inc.

FaithWords
Hachette Book Group
1290 Avenue of the Americas
New York, NY 10104
faithwords.com
twitter.com/faithwords

First Edition: July 2016

FaithWords is a division of Hachette Book Group, Inc.
The FaithWords name and logo are trademarks of Hachette Book Group, Inc.

The publisher is not responsible for websites (or their content) that are not owned by the publisher.

The Hachette Speakers Bureau provides a wide range of authors for speaking events. To find out more, go to www.hachettespeakersbureau.com or call (866) 376-6591.

Library of Congress Cataloging-in-Publication Data has been applied for

ISBNs: 978-1-4555-8617-2 (trade paperback), 978-1-4555-8616-5 (ebook)

Printed in the United States of America

RRD-C

10 9 8 7 6 5 4 3 2 1

The Second Half is dedicated to all the grandparents who have had to leave their plans and dreams and rear their grandchildren. While there are joys as well as hardships and sacrifices, they are gallant people who step up because they love their children and grandchildren, no matter what.

Acknowledgments

The best research for this book was listening to grandparents who have accepted the role of parent, which has been thrust upon them again. I've talked with people of all income levels and many walks of life. Some of the stories have been heartbreaking, others of people working day by day to help save their grandchildren. The theme is always, "What else could I do? They are my grandchildren." And often, "Why should they have to suffer because their parents aren't doing their job?"

I have heard of churches that are building ministries to help those caught in the parenting grandchildren trap. I hope and pray many more do the same. Jesus tells us to love the little ones, the least of these. One life at a time. One family at a time. All needing year-round help, not just at Christmas.

Blessings,
Lauraine

The Second Half

Chapter One

How could she keep the secret for another whole week?

Mona Sorenson flinched when she heard the special ring that said Ken was her caller. If he asked her any more questions about how she was coming along with his retirement celebration, she might go screaming into the night. She clicked on her phone and into one of her crazy accents. This one always made him laugh. "Miz Sorenson ees not here. Call back later." She clicked off her phone and typed three more lines on the announcement for the local paper. After all, retiring after thirty years on the same job was becoming unheard of. Ken called himself a dinosaur, but she knew the board was scrambling to try to find someone to fill his shoes. She figured it would take two people—at least.

"Jesu, Joy of Man's Desiring" burst forth from her iPhone again. "One minute please and Mrs. Sorenson will be right with you." She clicked the pause button; finished her next two lines, completing the announcement; leaned back in her chair; and, after heaving a big sigh of relief, clicked on speaker. "Sorry, I had to finish this while I had the right words on the brain."

"Finish what?"

"An announcement for the Doran party. You know how she always wants everything perfect."

"Like someone else we know and love?"

"Hush. I have been taking my anti-perfectionist pills, and I am supposed to be all better now."

"Right. What are we doing for supper tonight?" Ken sounded like he was in traffic.

"Supper?" She glanced at her watch. "Is it really that late?"

"Yes, and I am on my way home, and if I need to pick up dinner, you need to tell me what you want before another mile is gone."

"Ah..." She tipped her head back and closed her eyes. "What sounds good to you?"

"Whatever."

"How come I always have to come up with supper ideas?" She scanned her mental list. "Fried chicken from the Chick Hut?"

"Fine with me. Mashed and gravy or wedges?"

"Wedges and coleslaw. Oh, and their grilled French bread, too."

"I thought you weren't eating bread."

"Tonight I am."

"That kind of day?"

"Yes."

He paused. "Do we have any ice cream?"

"You killed the last one last night."

"Okay. I'll pick some up. See you in a half hour or so."

"Thanks." She clicked off her phone. Did he suspect? After all, she'd never been able to pull off a surprise party on her husband in all the thirty-four years they'd been married. He seemed to have an inner radar even if she never dropped one teeny little hint. She thought back to their early years. The kids had never been able to keep a secret for the life of them. Especially not Steig, and here he was now in some hush-hush branch of the army. Wouldn't it be marvelous if he were transferred somewhere within traveling distance where they did all kinds of training for all the branches of the military? He'd said it was a possibility.

She jerked her thoughts away from her elder. How he was managing since his wife walked out on him and their children, she had no idea, but having him closer to home would make his life a whole lot easier. But not necessarily theirs. Back to the case at hand. She hit send and scrolled down to the contracts file. One was ready for Humphrey, the mayor's assistant, who was planning a special event for the Fourth of July, and they had finally worked out the details so she could get started on that event.

Mona loved her job, and she even liked her boss—most of the time anyway. Being a detail person was a good thing when running your own event planning business. It had taken a while, but now she had more business than she could handle. She was hoping Ken would come to work with her part-time, so they could both have time off. He might be ready to retire as dean of students from Stone University, but that did not mean she was ready to retire. She'd reared their two children, gone to work as an editorial assistant, and finally decided what she wanted to be when she grew up. She wanted to be the owner of a thriving business where she could help other people, especially owners of small businesses. Besides event planning, she provided virtual office assistants who also worked from their own homes. The phone rang again, the song the dwarves sang in *Snow White*. "Heigh-ho, heigh-ho . . ." Appropriately, her business number.

"Mona's Professional Services, Mona speaking. How can I help you?"

"This is Sondra Delaney. We spoke the other day; you sent me some information, and I was hoping we could finalize some of this today."

"I see." Mona typed in the woman's name to bring up the file. "The first step is to agree on what you'd like; then I'll get a contract out to you by tomorrow. As soon as you return it, I'll begin." The conversation continued until Mona heard the garage door go up. Ken was home. And she was still working. She'd planned to have the table set at least.

"Excuse me, what was the last thing you said?"

Ken stuck his head in the door. "Supper is on the counter. Ten minutes?"

She nodded and typed some notes into the file. "It looks to me like we have an agreement here. I will pull a contract together tonight, and you'll have it first thing in the morning. I'll include an estimate, and that will be half on signing and the remainder the day of the event. If you have any questions...?"

"Not that I can think of. You came highly recommended. Oh yes, can you...?"

Mona answered a couple more questions, trying to wrap up the call and yet not sound rushed or abrupt. "I see, thank you for calling and I'm looking forward to working with you." She blew out a breath when the call clicked off and switched her business number to voice mail. Scrubbing her fingers through her short, graying hair, she stretched her neck from one side to the other. Even keeping the phone on speaker, her neck and shoulders were tight by the end of the day. Perhaps they could make some time after supper to take Ambrose for a walk.

She glanced down at the mutt snoring at her feet. He'd gone to greet Ken, then returned and flopped back in his usual place. Asleep already. Oh, to be as relaxed as this hound.

She nudged him with her foot. "You hungry?"

One eye popped open and the dog's tail thumped on the hardwood floor. A meow from the doorway said the dog wasn't the only one who knew that it was now past six and supper should be served at six. Hyacinth, the tuxedo cat, spoke again, this time more insistently.

"I'm coming. Why can't Dad feed you?"

"Because I am putting our meal on the table, that's why." Was that a slight edge she heard in his voice?

Mona stood and pushed her rolling office chair back against the desk. Ambrose joined her as they headed for the kitchen, with Hyacinth leading the way, tail straight in the air.

"Sorry. I had another call just after we hung up, and she didn't want to wait until tomorrow since she is leaving on a trip in two days."

"I thought your motto was 'Failure to plan ahead on your part does not constitute a crisis on my part.'"

"I know, but this will be an easy job and good money."

"And you do not know how to say no." His smile took the sting out of his words, but it still rankled. She could say no, but this time she chose not to. *And how many times have you said no lately?* The sneaky inner voice dripped fake sweetness. Sometimes she could entertain herself for extended periods of time with thoughts of how to do away with said voice. Or at least put a lid on it. Amazing how the Critic, as she called that inner voice, could change sides, but more often than not, sarcasm was the tool of torture. A speaker one time had said to train her inner voice to be encouraging rather than judgmental. It sounded like a great idea at the time.

They fixed their plates and took them out into the three-season room, as they called it, where screens thwarted the mosquitoes that had arrived early this year and the blackflies who would zoom in anytime. A light breeze teased the spiky leaves of a giant hanging spider plant, sending all the babies on the ends of the stems to tangling and swinging. Baby spider plants were akin to Friendship bread, in that eventually friends ran or hung up if you said you were bringing them something. Abundant zucchini from their garden brought about the same sort of response by the end of summer.

"Thank you for picking up supper," she said after grace. "I didn't realize how much I needed a fried chicken fix." She bit into the perfectly crisped thigh. Ken preferred the drumsticks, she the thighs, and the next day she had the breasts chopped on her salad. The wings went to whoever grabbed them first.

"I forgot the ranch dressing." Ken pushed back his chair and headed for the kitchen.

Ambrose sniffed the plate but had the good manners to not help himself—at least not as long as someone was watching. Hyacinth zeroed in on the meat and was reaching for it with claws not sheathed.

"No!" Mona waved her extra-large paper napkin and the cat leaped to the floor to sit and begin cleaning her paws, as if she'd had absolutely no intention of helping herself. Royal catness in action.

Ambrose lay next to Mona, nose on paws, tail swishing to greet Ken's return.

"So are you done in your office for today?" Ken asked in between bites of chicken and potato wedges.

"The phone is on voice mail, and I am not going back in there. I thought we could take the two for a walk down along the river trail."

"Sounds good to me. Marit called me today, asked if we could keep the kids this weekend while they go to that resort on Lake Winnebago."

"What did you tell her?"

"To ask you."

Mona shook her head. Some things in life just never changed. "She didn't call."

"Yet. What will you tell her?"

"That she needs to make her plans a bit more in advance. We have the graduation party on Friday night, and you have commencement on Saturday."

"They have to leave Friday, be back Sunday night. I could pick them up from school, we get a sitter here for Friday night, and I'll take them fishing Saturday morning. Then you could work in the garden, order pizza for supper, and let the games begin."

"If you have it all figured out, why didn't you tell her that?"

"Figured she should ask you first—in case something didn't get written on the calendar." The big calendar they set up on the mud entry wall when the kids were little was renewed yearly. "If it ain't broke, don't fix it," a motto they learned to live by years ago and harbored ever since. However, there had been one time when they arrived for a wedding a hundred miles away a whole week early. That was one time back in her pre-organized days, but he still managed to bring that up. As if she did that kind of thing all the time.

She shifted into office mode. "So, you want to call her back to make sure they are coming. Also, you need to call Janey and ask if she'd like to babysit on Friday night. If she can't, see who is next on the list." Strange that grandparents should need a list of babysitters, but this had happened before.

Ken half shrugged and began picking up the supper plates. "I brought ice cream. You want it now or later?"

"Up to you." Her phone rang Marit's song, the familiar opening bars of Sibelius's "The Swan of Tuonela." The tinny ringtone did Sibelius no favors.

"Have you and Dad talked?" Marit asked after the greetings.

"If you mean about this weekend..."

"Yes. I know it's late, but Magnus forgot to tell me."

"So, let him go by himself." Mona flinched at her flippant tone. Marit and Magnus did not get away together without kids that often.

"But, Mom, I want to go. If we don't do something now, school will be out and then life just gets crazier."

"Whatever happened to the good old summertime of lazy days on the river, reading a book, family barbecues?"

"Softball games, T-ball games, swimming lessons, Vacation Bible School."

She dropped her voice. "All clear for next weekend, right?"

"Of course. Have you heard from Steig? When do he and the kids arrive?"

"I'm not sure. It's only a week from Friday. Your dad knows they're coming, of course, but I don't think he suspects the party, at least not yet. But he keeps asking questions, so maybe he is suspicious." Mona rubbed her forehead.

"Don't worry about it, Mom, it'll all work out."

"Easy for you to say."

"That's what you always tell me."

"That's different." Mona never had enjoyed eating her own words.

"And we're on then for this weekend?"

"If we can find a sitter for Friday night."

Marit's voice brightened. "I know; I'll set it up with Steffie to come to your house instead of here."

Steffie was Marit's regular sitter, and the children adored her as much as she adored the three. "Good idea. We have to leave at five, so Dad will pick them up after school and you can drop Torin off here on your way out."

"Thanks, Mom. I'll clear the pickup with the school. I really do need this break before summer hits. And I hate to make Magnus go alone all the time. He's gone so much anyway, what with his job for that new Norwegian energy company."

"Bring plenty of clothes; I don't have time to do laundry. And you know the two will head for the swamp and the pollywogs." Living on the banks of the Yahara River always provided plenty of entertainment for the grands. Once Steig arrived with his two, the five cousins would meld back into the huddle they'd become at Christmas. Brit, at eleven, pretty much ran the show, becoming big sister to all of them. Steig's nearly ten-year-old Melinda seemed destined to rule the world if Brit didn't. Jakey, her five-year-old brother, and Marit's seven-year-old Arne became inseparable. But Marit's Torin, almost five, quiet and thoughtful, pretty much marched to his own drummer.

"Thanks, Mom! I'll check with Steffie and get back to you."

Ken stopped in the doorway. "Walking?"

Ambrose shot to attention, his tail beating a tattoo on her leg. He whimpered in his throat.

"You get the harnesses, please. I need to change my

shoes." She hurried to the bedroom and brought out her gray cross-training shoes with turquoise trim. As she changed into them, Hyacinth was winding herself around Ken's legs, chirping as if making sure she would go, too. They had taught her to walk in a harness when she was a kitten, and while their neighbors were used to seeing the four of them out walking, strangers did a double take. A black dog with a white chest and a tuxedo cat, red harnesses and leashes for both, was quite a sight.

Ken had the two harnessed up, doggy bag in his pocket, and his crusher hat on his head. He and Mona both had their cell phones along as a matter of course. As if anyone went anywhere without one anymore. They picked up the river trail and walked the familiar winding path toward the park up the river. Ambrose took his usual place at Ken's left knee and Hyacinth trotted ahead of Mona. As they neared the third house, both animals kept checking the iron mesh fence line. Neither had forgotten the time a dog had leaped the fence and attacked them. Neither had Ken and Mona. They all still bore the scars, hers of cat scratches as she kept the cat out of the fight between the two dogs. Ken needed stitches in hand and calf, and Ambrose had been at the vet hospital for a couple of days. The attacking dog had been hauled off by animal control, with the owners paying all damages and losing their dog.

They picked up the pace to get by the danger zone, even though the dog that now lived there could no more jump the fence than a porcupine. He would yap them to death if allowed off the porch. And he sure tried from behind their gate. The other family had moved away.

When they reached the milepost, they turned and headed back. Dusk sneaked in through the bushes and spring flowering trees, almost like fog but lighter on its feet. Steam wisped up from the river that was still running high from the spring rainfall.

"Have you given any thought to a vacation this summer?" Ken asked.

"You don't want to go to the North Shore?"

"Not really. I'd like to take a cruise." He tugged Ambrose's leash, drawing him away from a suspicious pile of what looked like horse droppings.

"A cruise where?"

"Up the Hudson River. Mostly people do that one during the fall color, but I'd like to see that country in the summer. You know, stop some places, kind of amble along."

"The cruise company will let you do that?"

"Either that one or the ferry up from Vancouver, BC, to Alaska. We'd take our car on that one."

"How long would we be gone?"

"Two weeks, would be easy to make it three. We could ferry up and drive the ALCAN back."

Mona shrugged. She hadn't thought much about vacationing.

"We will be free to see places besides Wisconsin," Ken continued. "Lovely state, but I really want to explore places we've never been to; do things we've not done before. We'll finally be free to do that."

Hyacinth plunked herself down on the trail and stared up at Mona.

"Come on, you can make it home." Pulled short by the leash and harness, when they stopped Ambrose yipped at her, then ambled back to check out the sniffy news by the side of the trail.

Ken shook his head. "Come on, cat, I'll carry you." He handed his leash to Mona and scooped up the cat. "You need to go on a diet. Don't you know walking is good for you?"

"I wonder what's wrong. She always walks the whole way." Mona studied the feline. "She wasn't limping or anything. She ate her supper?"

"Yes, I guess she just got tired."

Together they started out again, Ambrose giving the riding cat anxious glances.

"See, even Ambrose is worried. Hyacinth, what is your problem?" Mona heaved a sigh of relief when they reached the path up to their house. Having sick kids was bad enough, but at least they could say where they hurt. Animals usually just toughed it out until it was too late. "You think we should call the vet?"

"What will you tell them? Our cat quit walking and wanted a ride? Think how few people we know who take both dog and cat for walks. And there have been no other symptoms." They mounted the cedar steps to the deck and crossed to the entry to the three-season room. Once inside, they removed and hung up the harnesses, and Mona sat down with the cat on her lap to give her a good going over.

At the Steig ring, *Tristan und Isolde*, she dug out her phone and set it on speaker for Ken. "We were just talking about you. So when will you be here?"

"By Thursday, I hope. Thursday afternoon I need to meet with an officer out at the base. I might actually get stationed there."

"An hour away. Will you be housed on the base or...?"

"Nothing is official yet. I'll know more after I meet with the colonel. Can you watch the kids while I do that?"

"We'll work out something." Her mind immediately took off on all the good things about having him closer than Texas. Perhaps for once the military was going to help make his life easier. Ever since Angela left him…Mona still could not comprehend how she could walk out on her kids like she had. Leaving a husband was one thing, but deserting her children? Talk about anathema. Mona and Ken had been totally shocked when Steig called them with the news. They had sensed friction between the two the last time they'd been down to visit, but not something like this.

"Mom, don't get your hopes up."

Mona blinked. "Wh-what do you mean?"

"I mean don't go making plans for the future until we know more."

Ken rolled his eyes. "Don't worry about us. Just be here for the ceremony. We have the other grands this weekend, and we're going fishing. Wish you could be here for that."

"Hopefully we'll find time to go fishing while we're there. Just make sure you have plenty of chocolate chip cookies."

"Call us when you leave, and drive safely," Ken said with a smile. "We'll keep the lights on for you."

Mona shook her head. Ken always said that, so it had become a long-standing family joke. "Hug the kids for me." After clicking off the phone, she stared at it in her hand. "Did you get a sense that he's not telling us something or was it just my worry mode trying to take over?"

"Your worry mode. Let's have our ice cream now."

First Steig, now the cat. Lord, I am putting these into Your hands. Please rap my knuckles if I try to take them back.

Chapter Two

"I sure enjoy having those kids here." Ken turned to Mona after they waved Marit and her family off Sunday evening. He heaved a sigh. "But I sure appreciate them leaving again."

"I know." Mona flopped back in her leather recliner. "I think I'll just enjoy the quiet for a few minutes."

"Aren't we going for a walk?"

"Not tonight. I feel like I've been in a rat race all weekend. I want to sit here, maybe watch a movie, and get recharged for tomorrow. You can go."

Ken collapsed into his recliner. "No, I was hoping you'd say that." He picked up the remote. "I say popcorn and a movie will hit the spot." He brought up the movie menu. "See anything that grabs you?"

"No blood and gore."

"No chick flicks."

He scrolled through the list. "Anything look good?"

He clicked on the Hallmark Channel. "Movie starts in ten."

"I'll get the popcorn." Mona levered herself to her feet. "Iced tea?" "The Swan of Tuonela" came from her phone. She thumbed it on. "What did you forget?"

She listened a moment and said to Ken, "Torin's Bobo Bear. Magnus will be right over."

Then to Marit, "Okay. Any idea where it is? Oh." She thumbed off and turned to Ken. "She has no idea where it is."

"I'll do the popcorn, you find the bear." He made his way to the kitchen, tagged by two shadows. "You guys don't like popcorn." He could hear Mona moving from room to room. "Where do you suppose Bobo is?"

Ambrose wagged his tail and looked over his shoulder.

He smiled. Worth a shot. "Ambrose, go find Bobo." Then he reached up for the box containing the microwave popcorn.

Ambrose returned in a minute with the grungy bear in his mouth.

"Mona," he called, "Ambrose found the bear. Good boy!" He'd just put the bag in the microwave when the doorbell chimed. "Come on boy, you deliver it." Together they walked to the front door, the dog carrying the bear.

"Don't tell me he found it." Magnus looked from Ken to the dog.

Ken looked down at the dog. "A genius in his limited way. Sadly deficient in others. Ambrose, drop it."

Ambrose dropped the bear to the floor and wagged his tail.

"Good boy."

Magnus picked it up and shook his head. "About time Bobo Bear gets put on the shelf."

"Good luck with that."

"Thanks again for watching the kids. Marit and I, we had a good time."

"Glad to hear it. Always good when you can combine some fun with a business trip." Ken watched Magnus stride down the walk, then returned to the kitchen. Good thing he'd not hit start for the popcorn yet. He set the timer and dug the bowl out of the drawer. As far as he was concerned, they could eat it out of the bag, but Mona insisted on the bowl. One more thing to wash. Surely they could find ways to simplify their lives. That would have to be a goal once he retired. The goal list was growing. He waited for the popping to cease and shook the bag before opening it. *Not many old maids*, he thought as he poured the popped corn in the bowl, inhaling the fragrance, the aroma wafting through the kitchen. Glancing down, he saw both animals staring up at him, taking turns licking their chops. He obliged by dropping a couple of kernels. Ambrose sniffed, did a dog shrug, and headed for the family room. Hyacinth crouched down and did away with the treat.

"Since when do you like popcorn?" Her tail twitched at the end. "Anything to make a liar out of us." He carried the bowl into the family room and set it on the lamp table that separated their two recliners.

"I can't believe that Ambrose found Bobo Bear." Mona shook her head while petting the dog. "I wonder where it was."

"No idea. Just in time." Ken leaned back with a sigh. "Thanks for the fish fry supper. Sure tickled the kids after they caught so many fish."

"You clean 'em, I fry 'em." She shook her head as she grinned. "That Arne cracks me up. Making sure you got to eat the biggest fish. He caught it just for you, you know."

"I know. Wish you'd been with us fishing. You and your camera." He dug into the bowl of popcorn. "Someday maybe I'll be able to take Steig's kids fishing. Especially if he gets transferred to somewhere closer."

Mona reached for a napkin and laid it in her lap to fill with popcorn. "Hope I can keep my eyes open long enough to watch this movie."

Ken looked over at her a bit later. The popcorn was down to the unappetizing bits and Mona was fast asleep, Hyacinth on her lap and Ambrose snoring on the floor. Since he'd been floating in and out, he clicked off the TV. "Come on boy, outside." He let the dog out, rinsed out the bowl and put it in the dishwasher, let the dog in, and went to wake Mona. He followed her up the stairs to the bedroom, the pets beside him. The cat darted ahead and leaped up on the bed to settle at the foot, as if someone might take her place.

The nightly ritual brought a sense of comfort and peace. When he went to stand at the open window, he heard an owl hooting and saw the shadow of its flight in the moonlight. Staring out at the river, he watched three deer line up to drink at the river's edge. Nearly a full moon. Three more days at work and he would be free. A lot to clean up in that amount of time. Shame they'd not found his replacement yet so he could train that person, at least in the basics. Sandy, though, his admin assistant, knew all that he did and would keep on working so there would not be a gap. He left the window and crawled into his own side of the bed. Tonight he didn't even feel like reading, so he turned out the light and lay watching the branch patterns waltzing on the rug, thanks to the elm tree they'd planted five years ago. It now reached the top of the house and was filling out nicely.

He turned over on his side and closed his eyes. He huffed a sigh. He'd not set the alarm. Three more days and no alarm. Officially hand over the reins on Wednesday and go home, come in for half an hour Friday to sign pay and honoraria checks, and done. Thursday morning he could sleep as late as he wanted. Maybe he'd run over the alarm with the car. He didn't have a lunchbox to run over. There needed to be some symbol. Ernie had smashed his cell phone with a hammer. Said it felt mighty freeing. After sliding the button on the clock radio, Ken flopped back and tried to close his eyes again. And waited. What was the matter? He never had trouble falling asleep.

"Are you all right?"

"Sorry, I just can't get to sleep." He flipped the covers back and swung his feet over the edge of the bed. "Guess I'll go downstairs and read for a while." Taking his book off the nightstand, he slid his feet into his slippers, grabbed his robe off the end of the bed, and headed back downstairs. At least this way Mona would be able to sleep. He knew if he'd turned the light back on, she'd have been awake. Strange, this was usually her problem, not his. Ambrose padded beside him.

Back in his recliner with the lamp on, he opened to the bookmarked page and skimmed until he found where he left off. Reading the latest O'Reilly book in the middle of the night was a retirement pleasure. He had a full day tomorrow and morning was coming much too soon.

"Ken, are you okay?"

He blinked open his eyes, confused for a moment. "Of course, why?" He stared up at her.

"Because you never came back to bed, and the alarm kept on buzzing and I got worried. This is not like you."

Ken yawned and stretched. "What time is it?" He checked his watch. "Oh...I better get a move on." Slamming his chair back to an upright position, he tried to stand. "Ouch." His right leg felt like it was collapsing, pins and needles stabbed and restabbed.

"Foot gone to sleep?"

"Yes!" He sat back down and flexed his ankle, then toes. When the pain let up, he stood again. "Will you fix the coffee, please? I need to get a shower."

"You sure you're all right?"

"Yes! Ouch!"

"You're late." Sandy Jensen stared at him over the rims of her glasses. "Are you all right? You look like ten miles of unpaved road."

He smiled a little. "Do you have that financial report ready that I asked for?"

"On your desk, and you have half an hour until your meeting with the executive committee. Can you be ready in time? How can I help?"

"Get me some coffee, please, and look up the graduation rate for scholarship recipients. I think they're going to try to trim the aid budget, and we have a National Merit Scholar coming in this fall." He'd planned on doing that himself first thing this morning. He who was always ready for meetings the day before was now fumbling to catch up.

Sandy brought in several pages of graphs and text and laid them on his desk, setting the filled coffee mug down at the same time. "Anything else?"

"Have we gotten any more applications?" He didn't have to say "for my position."

"Three plus the in-house ones."

"Well, at least we meet the legal requirements then." He read through the top page as he sipped coffee. "You have a file with all the résumés?"

She nodded. "Be right back." He finished the second page about the time she returned and set the file folder on his desk.

"Any opinions?"

She cocked an eyebrow. "Is there ever a time I have no opinion?" At his smile, she continued. "They are in order of my preference, but then we've not interviewed them yet. It could be someone who looks gold on paper is lead when you're face-to-face. I can do the follow-up while you're in the meeting."

"Good idea. Book as many of them into tomorrow as you can."

Ken hated leaving important things to the last minute. He also hated the idea of leaving this position with no one else ready to step in. It made him feel like he'd not finished his job. But he didn't want to come back to work after his retirement celebration either. Unfortunately, applications were just starting to come in. On the other hand, when the notice of vacancy goes out late, as this one did, it appears that the candidate has already been chosen, and the vacancy announcement is simply a legal requirement. He would give extra points to those who had theirs in early.

"Did you apply for this position?" he asked when she returned with more folders.

"Nope, I'm not qualified, education-wise."

"A master's degree without the PhD is legal, you know. Not done much, but legal."

"I have no real desire to get one, either. I like being the support crew, I don't like being up in front."

"But you'd be so very good at it."

"You know that theory about being promoted beyond one's strengths? That would be me."

"The Peter Principle. I heartily disagree with you, but I've tried to break down the Sandy stubborn wall before. Let's find you someone you can work with and make them look as good as you make me look."

"Thank you." She glanced at her watch. "You have fif-teen minutes."

"How many years have we worked together?"

"Seventeen." She stacked the file folders in order, set his iPad on top of the pile, and glanced around to make sure she had everything. "I'll call the applicants and start the background checks with a Google search. Anything else? Oh and put your cell on vibrate."

He half shrugged. "Thanks," he said, and did as she suggested. "For something that is supposed to make life easier..."

"I know." She left and sat down at her desk, just in time to answer the ringing telephone.

He went through the printout quickly, ran a high-lighter through the points he would make, gathered the ghastly pile of paper into his attaché case (for the last time?), and walked downstairs to the Harriet Stone conference room. Harriet Stone. He had been intro-duced to the matriarch of Stone University shortly after he arrived and not long before she died. A brusquer, more bristly woman he had never met. He entered the double doors and settled in his usual place at the long oak table. He poked his code into the iPad, swiped to his notes, and laid it aside, then flopped his attaché case open.

First the formalities. Even as the stragglers were still coming in, Dale, the assistant provost, began the meeting with the mandatory but phony words of welcome and thanks, as if they had any choice but to be here. Dale Crespin had married a Norwegian woman, but he had never fully adopted the Norwegian culture with which this whole area was saturated. He did, however, alter his name; Ken happened to know it was originally Crespynocsic. Dale, from Cleveland, Ohio, originally, was one of the few people in town of Polish descent.

Dale glanced at the agenda on his iPad. "Let's tackle finances first. John?"

Across from Ken, their comptroller cleared his throat. "Ken's department is the only one this first quarter that didn't post a deficit. He spent everything he got, understand; no profit, but no red ink. This is a private university with shareholders who get antsy when they don't see at least a modest return on their investment. To come out in the black this year, we're going to have to make some serious and maybe painful decisions about what gets cut."

One by one, each person gave a brief (and sometimes not brief enough) report of the situation in his or her department. Finally, it was Ken's turn.

He smiled at all. "Thanks for your input here, John. John"—he nodded to the other John in the room—"your hard work elevating our academic status is paying off; we have admitted a National Merit Scholar, and four of the ten top students in Wisconsin have opted to come here. Our academic reputation is starting to reflect the excellence of our faculty. We've come a long way."

He looked from face to face around the room at this august governing body. Two women, the rest men. Better than five years ago, when there were no women at all. Maybe Harriet had frightened them off. No, Harriet no doubt frightened men; she had frightened Ken, and he'd known her five minutes, but women were not that easily cowed.

And he realized with a shock that his mind had just completely wandered away from the subject at hand. Totally derailed. That had *never* happened to him before.

He drew a deep breath and cleared his throat. "Since

this is my swan song, so to speak, I would like to make a few remarks beyond the immediate purview of my position as dean of students."

He poked his iPad to wakefulness. "I have here a note from a Stone graduate who is now managing an accounting firm. 'Dear Dr. Sorenson, I made a bold move last week during our annual employee evaluations. I asked the owner why he hired me over twenty-seven other applicants. He replied when he saw that my degree was from Stone, he knew I had the best preparation possible. Thank you, Dr. Sorenson, for your personal guidance and for the splendid instruction I received at Stone.'" Ken looked out from face to face again. "When a student comes here, this is the kind of value she gets from her degree, she or he. We deliver. Our degrees are very highly regarded out in the real world as well as in other educational institutions. Our graduates who go on to advanced degrees can pretty much pick their school, and you well know that not every school can say that.

"But we deliver more than just academics. We deliver student aid and service beyond the usual. Some of these kids are ill prepared for a university experience. We have an excellent record of bringing them up to speed, if you will, and keeping them from dropping out or losing ground. We have the highest retention rate in the state. I also asked Sandy to populate a list of our scholarship recipients and whether they graduated. The graduation rate of our scholarship recipients is five percentage points higher than the rate in general, which as I just noted is very high itself. The figures will be posted on the website this afternoon."

He sat back. "Without a caring staff in student services, we would not be able to achieve what we've achieved. We are now first tier, on a level with Wisconsin's flagship university, and it takes both academics and student services to keep us there. And I hope your new dean of students will understand that."

John Nordlund across the table snorted. "Frankly, Ken, I do not believe in mollycoddling. 'Sink or swim' makes a stronger, better student."

"This isn't mollycoddling, John. A college education these days is incredibly more expensive than when you and I got our undergrad degrees. We have a moral and ethical responsibility to make our degrees cost-efficient, so that our students get the biggest bang possible for their buck." John didn't look convinced. "Besides," Ken continued, "it costs us more to matriculate a new student than to hang on to the students we already have. So student retention is a bottom-line good thing."

Down near the end, John Jenson, the faculty rep, was nodding.

John Nordlund still scowled. And then he asked one of the questions Ken really wished would not be asked: "Damien, you're in the running to become dean of students; what are your thoughts on this?"

At the far end, Damien Berghoff straightened his tie and sat up. "I see good info in both of you. I agree we need students, and good ones fit our bottom line best. But we don't dare lose sight of the fact that we have to make a profit to stay in the game. And perhaps sometimes, the profit motive will have to come first."

They had crossed swords before on this topic, Ken and Damien. His attitude, putting money above kids, was no news to Ken. It's probably why he tended to dislike the man. What troubled Ken most was that Damien had applied for the position of dean of students.

Ken responded, "It's not just our bottom line. Our students have a bottom line, too, and most of them are not out of their teens, so they have less wiggle room."

Damien carelessly waved a hand. "Ken, we all know kids these days are whiners. They expect the world to give them an education, and I cannot see that Stone should finance their supposed entitlement. We have to pay attention to our own bottom line, or there won't be a Stone University. It's that simple."

Ken felt the anger rising inside him faster than he could punch it down. *"Whiners?"* It exploded out of him. "Work with these kids a semester and you'll find out they're not whiners." He glared at John. "And they're not mollycoddled. They're working desperately to stay afloat, and it's a part of our job to help them do that. To stay in school. A high retention rate requires effort from us as well as them."

Damien's smile looked a lot like the Grinch's. "Ken, let's face it. Your attitude of holding their little hands and patting them on the head just doesn't work in the present business climate. In today's academic atmosphere, it's not just about students; it's about attracting alums. Well-heeled alums, especially alums who endow chairs and departments. And to attract them, we have to be able to show them a healthy financial statement."

Fury grabbed Ken's voice and made it roar. "And if they don't graduate, you don't have an alum to impress! You have another failed student who will go elsewhere, if at all. The road to financial stability starts and ends with the *student*!"

Dale raised his hand. "You've both made your points. So has John. Let's get on to the next item."

Ken didn't hear what the next item was or what anyone

said about it. His fury still raged, blinding him. Over and over in his mind he thought about what he should have said, how he might have made his point a lot better. He certainly should never have lost his temper. His mind was kicking itself. And then Dale declared the meeting adjourned, and Ken, for all practical purposes, hadn't even been present. He had been all wrapped up within himself, screaming at himself, ruing the whole morning.

He gathered his papers up more or less mechanically. Dale was still sitting there. Ken closed his attaché case and turned to apologize for his outburst.

But Dale spoke first. "Clever, Ken, fiendishly clever. My hat's off to you. I know you; you've never lost your temper before or even yelled. Ever. Today you were provoking your candidate into a fight, and it worked. We had to know if he could defend his position and stand up for himself, and this demonstrated that. He held on to himself and his ideas even when you were lambasting him. That's about the only way we could tell if he has the stuff to fight, and we all have to have that stuff."

Should he apologize? Not now, not when he had to drive his point home. "Dale, for marketing, planning, budget, you need a corporate wonk. But for dean of students, you need a person with a heart for the students. That's not Damien."

"If not, someone with a similar worldview. Keeping us solvent. Ken, your report was the only one in the black; everyone else isn't getting enough resources to do their job. So your department is logically where we will start to trim a little fat."

And Ken's whole brain exploded. "So what I see as a fiscal responsibility, you see as fat. That's outrageous! Dale, *I* get to pick. Remember?"

Dale's eyes hardened. "As of Thursday morning, you will have no say."

"I was given to understand that I would choose my successor. And I will."

"You can advise. *I* decide." Dale raised a hand, palm out. "I'll give your recommendation full consideration, I promise. But the choice will be mine. The exec committee will have to work with your successor; you won't."

Ken had never felt a fury this hot before. His hands vibrated as he picked up his attaché case. He was so deliciously angry he found himself able to keep a quiet, modulated voice. "I see. In fact, I see more than you think I do. You deliberately delayed posting the vacancy announcement so that candidates would still be filing their résumés for the position after I left the department. And you intend to hire Damien. Period."

"Now, Ken..."

Ken stood up. "Dale, you did not just betray me. You betrayed the student body, and by extension, this school."

"Ken, don't—"

"File a grievance?" he interrupted this devious liar. "That will be the least of it, Dale. Good day." He left.

Chapter Three

Had anyone ever murdered a cell phone? Perhaps some of those accidental cell phone drownings Mona had heard of were really deliberate killings.

The line about not killing the messenger floated through her mind. The woman who had taken up so much of her time on Friday had now decided to not hire her. The venue for the surprise celebration was going to have to be altered. She'd had to turn down Marit's invitation to lunch. They'd not had lunch together for what seemed like months. No word from Steig as to when he and the children would be arriving. This was not like him. That thought brought her up short.

Was it time to start worrying or had she already been worrying and just not aware of it? Worry had dogged her her whole life, as did depression. Perhaps they were both spawn of the same source. Did they come as a package? She had the depression more or less under control. The worry, not so much.

She'd never been so shocked as when Pastor Oliver preached on worry and used the word *anathema*. God didn't just dislike his children worrying, it was anathema to Him. Since then she had come to realize that worry was so sneaky, she could be doing just that and not be aware of it.

Please, Lord, make me aware of worry before it has me trapped had become a daily prayer. For years she had thought she had mastered that ogre, worry. Then she had to confess the sin of pride, too. Sometimes she felt smashed between the two. Awareness. Life was much easier before she became aware.

Okay, Lord, I don't want to worry about Steig, the kids, the celebration, Ken's retirement, and all the other stuff. I want to trust You. Trust that You have this all under control. That none of what is going on surprises You. Trust, such a big word to have only five letters. She closed her eyes. *Lord, I trust You. I trust You, Lord, I trust You, Lord God.* She tipped her head back and drew in a deep breath, held it, and let it out slowly. *Breathe!* That was fast becoming her other favorite word. *Trust. Breathe.* The two worked together.

Glancing at the clock, she caught herself up short. Six o'clock. No wonder Ambrose had come in with his suppertime whimper. Ken was always home by five, unless he'd called and she'd not heard.

She checked her phone and slammed the heel of her hand against her forehead. She'd turned the ringer off so she could concentrate and forgot to turn it back on.

Ken had called, texted, called, and e-mailed. She flinched and hit the speaker on her iPhone. "Sorry, hon, I'm stuck here for even longer than I thought I would be. How come you're not answering your phone?"

She listened to the rest of the messages, each one getting a bit more strained. Hitting reply, she tossed her shoulder-length hair back and waited for his phone to ring. And left a message. "Sorry, I turned off my ringer and forgot to turn it back on. I'll get on supper now and feed the critters. Totally lost track of time. See you when you get here."

She should go back and listen to all his messages, but right now duty called in the form of two four-footed critters who were pacing, glancing over their shoulders to see if she was getting the hint. "I'm coming."

Her inner dialogue continued. *But what about Steig? Lord, I am trusting You.* Learning to trust took moment-by-moment concentration. She flipped her phone on to her music list and sang along with one of the choruses. Anything to keep her mind on track.

Taking out the pet food, she glanced down to see the two, sitting side by side, both sets of eyes tracking her every move. "Thanks, guys, I so need an audience. Would you like to tell me exactly how to do this, as if I've never fixed your supper before?" Ambrose licked his chops, his tail swishing the floor. She set their bowls down, one scoop of canned food on top of kibble, and stepped back. "Okay, you can eat now." She motioned them forward with her hand.

After sliding a premade casserole in the oven, she took out the ingredients for a tossed salad, and after tossing that in the bowl, snapped the last of the fresh green beans. All the while she sang along with the music, anything to keep her mind from thinking on Steig and now on Ken, too. Something happened today that he hadn't expected. When the phone sang his song, "Jesu, Joy of Man's Desiring," she hit the button on the second chord.

"What's happening?"

"I hope to be home in an hour or so . . ."

"You can't talk?"

"That's right. You need anything from the store?"

"No, but are you all right?"

"No problem."

The mystery thickened. Mona upped the music volume

after they disconnected in the hopes of drowning out her initial questions. All her questions; was this just another aspect of worry? Setting the table did not take a lot of concentrated thought, nor did slicing the last of the French bread. *Lord, I am trusting You.*

Marit's song made her punch the button with a smile. When she heard, "Grammy?" she smiled even further.

"What is it, Brit, honey?"

"Can Grampy go fishing?"

"Not tonight. He has to work late."

"Oh, I want to go fishing again. Can you go?"

"Sorry, but after Grampy retires, he'll be able to go fishing more." How he would love to be having this conversation; Brit was absolutely the apple of her grampy's eye. "Besides, you have school tomorrow. How many more days?"

"Twelve."

"Including game day?"

"Yes. Mom said we could have a picnic at the park for supper, and you can come, too. Maybe you want to bring fried chicken and chocolate cake." Brit the micromanager.

"I think we can handle that."

"You better make lots of drumsticks, 'cause Arne likes them best."

"Thank you for the reminder."

"Okay, Mom is calling me. Bye."

Mona clicked off, sure that Brit did not have permission to call. She should have asked; keeping ahead of two extremely bright children pushed her daughter's buttons at times, and the third one looked to be of the same mold.

The sound of the garage door going up announced Ken's arrival, if the two critters standing at the door to the garage, tails wagging or twitching, hadn't already said

"Dad's home." She heaved a sigh of relief and turned on the broiler in the upper oven.

Ken patted his greeting committee, set his briefcase on the island, and crossed the kitchen to kiss his wife. "Smells good in here."

She studied his face. "You look tired."

"I'm beat."

"Or beat up?"

"Some of both. We had issues with the budget. Of course, there are always issues with the budget. Five minutes before I closed down my computer to come home, Dale stuck his head in the door asking about the employee reviews. He thought I ought to do them before Wednesday."

"In one last eight-hour workday?" Mona wagged her head.

"Not even with Sandy and I tearing our hair out will we get this all done. Also, tomorrow I am interviewing candidates..."

"Isn't Damien hoping to step into your position?"

"Yes. I get the feeling he assumes he has it and that all the other interviews are only protocol." He shook his head. "But we'll deal with all that later."

She refrained from asking how he felt. Ken was doing his best to keep his work at work and home life at home. Mona slid the tray of bread under the broiler. "Supper will be on the table as soon as you want."

"Let me change clothes; five minutes?"

"Fine." She watched his back as he left the room. His shoulders slumped like he was carrying the weight of the department up the stairs. Good thing he was retiring while he still had his health and dreams to look forward to. Not like Frank and Josie. Ken's older brother had put off retirement so his benefits would be higher and then died of a heart attack two months after his last day at work, leaving a wife with their dreams shattered. No wonder she was angry, since she'd been after him to retire for years.

"You want to talk over supper or wait until after?"

He sank into his chair. "After, please. Let's talk about anything else while we eat."

"You want to say grace?"

"Sure." He waited for her to settle in her chair. "Heavenly Father, thank You for this food, that Mona is such a good cook, and that today is almost over. Amen." He stroked his thinning-on-top hair back with the palms of both hands and heaved a sigh that sounded like he'd been holding in his breath along with his emotions. Looking around the table, he nodded. "This looks so good and peaceful even."

Mona motioned for him to hand her his plate. "Really hungry or so-so?"

"Really. I didn't realize how hungry until I got out of the car and followed my nose into the house." While she dished up the casserole, he helped himself from the wooden salad bowl. "We should have lettuce from the garden pretty soon. You know, the first project I think I want to work on is the greenhouse."

She knew he meant *as soon as I'm retired*. "We still have more to plant in the garden. The first rows of beans are up, and the radishes are nearly ready." She handed him his plate. "You had a fishing invitation a few minutes ago."

He passed her the basket of toasted French bread, looking at her with a question.

"Brit called to see if Grampy could go fishing."

His grin announced his feelings. "Did you tell her this weekend?"

"No, every minute of the weekend is already planned."

He narrowed his eyes. "Really?"

Oh no! Have I blown it? How to cover this? "Well, think about it; the banquet is Friday night. Saturday the kids will be here, and Sunday we are heading to the cabin." Surely God would forgive her for the little lie. The surprise party that she'd almost alluded to would be Saturday afternoon, and they were going to the resort on Mackinac Island, not just to the cabin like he had planned.

"I know Steig will want to go fishing on Saturday. I'll ask Magnus, too, and Brit, Melinda, and Arne. Hmm, that's too many for the boat."

Mona smiled at him. *Go ahead and plan; they all know better.* "Sounds possible. We'll have the family breakfast at nine or ten."

"We can be back by then."

"You want more goulash?"

"Sure." He handed her his plate. "So, how was your day?"

"Let's just say that my to-do list got rewritten without my permission."

"'Monday, Monday'... Remember that song?"

"Vaguely." She reached for another piece of bread. "I should never make this."

"I know, so good." He dropped a bit of bread to be snapped up before it hit the floor. Ambrose wagged his appreciation.

Mona rolled her eyes. So much for the rule of no feeding the pets from the table.

When they finished eating, Mona asked, "Inside or out?"

"Out." While she took the dishes into the kitchen, Ken picked up the casserole dish and the now-empty salad bowl and followed her.

"I didn't get any dessert made," Mona apologized as she set the coffee to brewing. She put the food away as he cleared the rest of the table.

"We still have ice cream?" At her nod, he retrieved the mint chip ice cream carton from the freezer and set it in the sink while he got the bowls down.

"You ready to talk now?" Mona asked when they were settled in their chairs out in the three-season room, the dog and cat at their feet and the quacking of ducks heard from down at the river's edge.

Ken shook his head as he spooned up ice cream. "I don't know; there are a whole lot of office politics involved."

"As usual."

He half smiled. "As always. Damien feels he is entitled to the job, and I suspect he has visions of climbing the ladder and assuming the presidency one day. But he is very good right where he is, and I wish he would just stay there. He's a numbers and organization person, not a people person."

"If the dean of students doesn't care first and foremost for the students, who will?" Mona thought of all the hours Ken spent talking with not only kids, but also adults returning to school, vets returning home and into school, foreign students who needed a sense of home. This very house had been that for many through the years. In fact, that was one of her concerns about his retiring; he would no longer have immediate contact with the students.

"So what will you do regarding hiring?"

"I don't know." He shook his head. "Apparently I am not the final voice. I will interview everyone, narrow it down to two or three, and let my preferences be known. And why."

"Your opinion carries a great deal of weight."

"I would hope so. I was intending that Wednesday would be my last day, but between interviews and reviews, I suspect that I will still be working into Friday. But I tell you, I will not come home until the reviews are finished and turned in. Just in case Damien does get the job. I don't want him doing performance reviews."

"Why?"

"He's too harsh."

"And he would say you are too lenient?"

"Most likely." He leaned back against the cushion. Ambrose rose and rested his head on Ken's thigh. Ken patted him automatically.

Mona heaved a sigh. Ken had worked so hard all these years to build people, not the department. The letters from grateful students that she'd kept in a file proved the value of what he had done. She had hoped to get them all in a scrapbook, but she'd had to pick and choose or the book would have been many volumes rather than one. She and Marit had finished that part of the project the week before.

Ken scraped the last of his ice cream from the bowl and traded it for his coffee cup, looking out toward the river. "I hope there is a golden boy in that pile of applicants, or golden girl, a candidate who so obviously shines above the rest that the decision will make itself."

"Do you know any of them?"

"I know two. Not golden by any means. I met one of the others at a conference. Not golden, either. If he's the one I think he is, he's lead." Hyacinth leaped into his lap, so he set his cup down, the better to have a hand free for each pet. "Did you hear from Steig?"

"No. I thought we'd call him this evening."

"Are we walking?"

"Let's call him first."

She tapped five, his speed dial number, and with the phone set on speaker, they both waited. When their son's voice reminded them to leave a message, they both sighed. "I left a message earlier. He's not responded."

"He might be on the way here."

"Could be, but I didn't expect him until Wednesday night, so Melinda would not have to miss any more school. It's just not like him to not give me his plans way ahead." There was that worry ogre again; Mona mentally slapped herself. *Stop it!*

"Let's go walk, and then I'm going to read through those résumés."

"Everybody?"

"Why not? Ambrose, get the leashes."

"I'll go change my shoes."

They were nearly home when her cell sang Steig's song. She handed the cat's leash to Ken and clicked on. "Are you all right?"

"Funny you should ask. Is Dad there, too?"

"Yes; putting you on speaker." She held the phone so they could both hear.

"I have some rough news."

Mona felt her heart clench. "You can't come?"

"No, I'm— We're coming. But I got my orders." He paused. "Sorry, Mom, Dad, but I am being deployed to Karachi. Pakistan. Can you keep the kids for me?"

Chapter Four

Only one time in her life had Mona been gut punched. Now she remembered what it felt like.

She handed the phone to Ken and doubled over, trying to get her breath.

"Give us a minute, Steig." Ken managed to sound like their lives had not just taken a whole new direction.

"Is Mom all right?"

"She will be. I think she swallowed wrong."

Mona glared at him. Right now she needed someone to glare at. She sucked in another deep breath and exhaled. All the while her mind screamed unintelligible sounds.

"Sorry to dump this on you both without a warning, but I thought for sure I was being transferred to a Wisconsin base, just like we all hoped."

Mona swiped at the tears that coursed as soon as she heard the desolation in her son's voice. One time they had talked about emergency actions like this, but back then they had been figuring they would help Angela with the children. Not be the sole guardians.

"When do you have to report?" she asked after clearing her throat twice.

"Monday. I would load a trailer with the kids' things, the mover would put all the rest in storage until..." He cleared his throat. "Until I give them another order." He paused. "I don't know anything else to do, Mom. I can't force Angela to take them, and besides, I don't want that woman taking care of my kids, especially not against her will."

"Don't worry, son, we'll work this out. Just give your mom and me some time to talk, and we'll call you back. But the way it looks, you better start packing."

"Thanks, Dad, Mom, you're the best." His voice broke. "I—I can't go AWOL."

"I know. We'll call you back." Ken clicked off the phone and stood staring over the river, a dog on one side, cat on the other.

Mona slipped in beside him, and he put his arm around her shoulders. "At least they can share a room for a while."

"It'll be okay. Probably for a year at the most. Maybe only six months before he is transferred stateside again."

"I thought the military was making an effort to keep families together, not sending the remaining parent to a hot spot."

"Maybe that doesn't apply to Special Forces. You know he is one of their best."

"Right now, I wish Steig was a run-of-the-mill officer, not Special Forces." She blew her nose and stuffed the tissue back in her pocket. "Let's get on home and call him back."

"He knows we'll take the children."

"Are you sure? I feel like I failed him, but somehow I couldn't even breathe." She shook her head. "How can we get all the paperwork done by Monday?"

"What do you mean?"

"I—I'm not even sure I know what I mean. Custodial parents is a legal matter, not just a family one. We have

to be able to make all the decisions, health, school..."
She shook her head, and it kept on wagging side to side.
"This is Monday. He'll be here Thursday. And he has to
report on the following Monday. How in the world...?"
Arms linked, they turned and headed for home. "I keep
reminding myself that God has a plan. That at least someone knows what's going on."

"And I'm afraid I won't be much help. I have to get that
mess at the college straightened out." He heaved a sigh.
"But at least I will be officially free of all responsibility by
the time Steig has to leave."

"Probably a good thing my last almost-a-contract fell
through." And thanks to her advance planning, the celebrations were all in place but for any erupting brushfires.
"I think we should call Marit and Magnus, so they know
from the get-go what is going on, too." She picked up Hyacinth, who was lagging behind. "Come on, cat, we have a
lot to do."

While Ken took care of the animals, she retrieved two
yellow pads and pens, poured them glasses of iced tea, and
settled into her recliner. While waiting for Ken to join her,
she called their daughter and explained the situation.

"How is Steig?"

"I think in shock like we are."

"Not surprising. Ask him if he needs help on that end.
Maybe I could fly down and help him for a couple of days."

"And who would watch your children?"

"Right. Magnus has an overnighter starting tomorrow.
Tell him to call me when the three of you are done talking."

"I will." Mona clicked off the phone and watched Ken
sink into his recliner, sipping iced tea and automatically
petting Ambrose, who took up his place at Ken's knee in

the hopes that if there was any food, he would not be forgotten. Ken looked exhausted, and the week had just begun. "You ready?"

He nodded, his head moving side to side at the same time. "And here I was so looking forward to traveling, seeing more of this country and perhaps a few others. A life with no deadlines, time to do all the things I've been putting off. No more school year." He looked at Mona. "Not raising small children. We already did that."

"It will only be for a year and maybe not even that. We can manage six months. Perhaps Marit can take the two while we do that trip you dreamed of, St. Lawrence or Alaska. We could be gone two weeks in July or August." She didn't add that they'd need to be home before school started. They both understood that. "Ready?"

"I guess." If forlorn had a face, it would look like Ken's.

Mona punched the speed dial. It only had to ring once.

"I'm sorry, Mom," Steig said before anything else.

"I know, but life happens, and we will all work together to make this as easy a transition as possible." She hoped she sounded more positive than she felt. "Now tell me what all we have to do legally."

"I will bring all the paperwork. We'll need to sign those and have them notarized. I'll bring their medical and school records. By the time I leave, you will be their legal guardians until I return and we go back to normal. Hopefully I will then be stationed at Fort McCoy."

"I guess my big concern is what about Angela?"

"She has signed off her rights to the children. I am the legal guardian, so while I will inform her of what is happening, she will have no legal rights. I can't see her even being interested, but I am covering all the bases. If something should happen to me, she cannot come back at you and contest for them."

Mona felt a shudder start at her feet and work upward.

"You will be receiving half my pay and full access to medical, the commissary, and any legal issues, not that I can think of any others, but..."

"And we'll get all this done by Monday?"

"We have to. I had a new will drawn up; you and Dad are the beneficiaries as guardians. I have set up a trust fund for their college expenses."

One year, Steig, all this is not necessary, one year. "Do we need to meet with our attorney, too?"

"This is new and unsettling for us, Mom, but the army is an old hand at it. Single parents deploy all the time. They know how to cover all the what-ifs. I know your will names Marit and me, but we might consider an addendum. I don't see a rush on that, however."

"All right. What time are you planning on being here on Thursday?"

"Depends on what time I can get out of here. Some friends are helping me pack and load the trailer. I am hoping to get out of here earlier on Wednesday, I'll let you know."

"How about if I have Marit sign the kids up for swimming lessons and Vacation Bible School with hers? That will give them something to look forward to."

"All those decisions will be up to you. I think it sounds great. Having cousins close will be good for all of them." He cleared his throat again. "And here I thought I had everything under control. Ha!"

"We'll all manage." Mona said that to make him feel good, of course. Did she believe it? Not really. "After all, six months to a year and you'll be back stateside and maybe even stationed nearby."

"You might expect some pressure from the kids to make contact with Angela. Please don't." His voice paused. "Melinda prays for her mother every night."

Mona sucked in a deep breath. "But Angela has made no effort to talk with the children or see them?"

"None. And no visitation rights. At least this way, the kids aren't being jerked around."

No, just no more Mommy and now Daddy was leaving, too. Oh dear Lord, help us help these two little ones. "Call us when you are ready to leave; we'll all be praying for you." Was that a snort she'd heard?

"Thanks, Mom, Dad. Talk with you soon."

Mona sat staring at her cell phone as if it might have answers for her. She heaved a sigh and shook her head again. "Life sure can change in an instant."

"And as you always say, we don't have control over it." Ken reached across the little side table that separated their two recliners, and she laid her hand in his. "Somehow the mess at the university doesn't seem quite as important as earlier. Good thing we kept the bunk beds up in the playroom."

They had turned Steig's old room into a room for the grandkids, complete with beds; a playpen for when the kids were younger; toys; games; a bookshelf full of books, including those once enjoyed by both Steig and Marit as they grew. Mona had taken over Marit's room for her office, and a bathroom connected the two bedrooms. The physical arrangements were doable. But the emotional ones? There was the rub.

Mona blew out a breath and hit the speed dial number for Marit's cell. She quickly filled her daughter in on the conversation and glanced over to see that Ken had fallen asleep. Good thing someone could sleep. "And that's all I know for now."

"I am so sorry, Mom; I know how you and Dad were looking forward to his retirement. This just isn't fair."

"Since when did life ever promise to be fair?"

"I know, but... Magnus and I were talking about would it be better if we took the kids?"

"Steig has it all set this way for now. Let's not throw any more at him right now. We'll be fine, and if your dad and I can do a two- or three-week trip before school starts, you'll have all five, and we can see how it goes. After all, it is only for a year maximum. Perhaps the powers that be will take pity on his situation and let him come home early."

"Right. We know how sympathetic the military can be. So, let's change the subject. Everything is on track for the weekend?"

"Far as I know."

"And you can't talk because Dad is right there in his recliner?"

"That's right. I'll call you tomorrow. Oh, would you please register Melinda and Jakey for VBS and swim lessons?"

"Of course. Have they had swim lessons before?"

"Good question." Mona tried to think back to the summer before.

"No matter. I'll put them in the beginners, and if they can already swim, it's easy to shift them up to an appropriate level. If you need anything else, let me know."

Mona clicked off, jotted a couple of other thoughts. She needed to clean out the closet in the kids' room. Surely Steig would bring the children's chests of drawers. She brought her chair upright, and taking along her pad, she went upstairs to study the room. The playpen could go to the garage, the stuffed animals in a sling across the corner; she'd seen that done before. Bathtub toys could go into a sling, too. Two children here full-time, not just visiting and going home. Two children who had never stayed with their grandparents by themselves; there had always been parents along. Thanks to Angela, the visits had not been often.

Mona leaned against the doorjamb. How could that woman walk out on her kids like that? She kept reminding herself that they'd only heard Steig's side of this, but no matter. A mother did not abandon her children. Her husband maybe, but not her children. Maybe it was better she had chosen to not see them again. How had Steig explained it to them? Jakey was too young to understand, but what about Melinda? *Dear Lord, how are we ever going to . . .* to what, she wasn't sure.

"How are you and Dad ever going to handle raising two small children?" Marit asked her mother the next day.

Mona stared at her daughter. "Well, moment by moment, the way any other parents manage. It's not like we don't have experience."

"Raising your own children was a long time ago. And you were younger then."

Mona swallowed what she almost said and continued her level stare. "Seems to me we did a pretty good job then, and since this is what God seems to be sending our way, of one thing I am sure. He's not going to dump the kids and run."

"Do you mean Steig or God?"

"Either. This is not a situation to any of our likings, but

this is where we are and we go on from here. It won't be like this is for the rest of our lives, you know."

"But what if something happens to Steig?"

Mona closed her eyes and inhaled a deep breath before puffing it out again. "We could play 'what-if' until Jesus comes again, but that only gets you a headache." She should know; she woke up with one this very morning, feeling like she'd not really slept. The what-ifs attacked from all sides. A dose of ibuprofen had only dulled, not eradicated, the pounding behind her eyes. "Do you see any alternatives?"

"Angela?"

"Would you want to send your children to a woman who ran off and left them?"

"No, but..." Marit leaned her elbows on the table. "I guess I'm just concerned about you and Dad. This is so unfair."

"Fair, unfair. This isn't a ball game with an umpire or a scorekeeper. We make this as easy for Melinda and Jakey as we can. And for Steig. I know this is tearing him apart. After all, we at least don't have to go to some far-off country where people want to kill you."

"He should never have re-upped."

"Easy for you to say. That's his career you're talking about." Mona could feel her vocal cords tightening. The urge to blast her daughter struck like a rattler. She raised her hands, palms out. "Enough. This is going nowhere. If you have helpful suggestions, I'm all ears. Otherwise, enough. My big concern right now is how to pull off that surprise party for your father; or should we just cancel it and...?"

"No, I say go ahead with your plans; it's too good a party to cancel. Did you make the reservations yet for that surprise trip you were going to give Dad in July; you know, the Nordic Fest in Decorah, Iowa?"

"Of course. You have to reserve at least a year in advance for that one."

Marit was silent a moment. "I'm thinking if you have the kids...Look at it from their point of view, Mom. Their mommy and daddy just disappeared, and now the grandparents go waltzing away. I mean, do you think it's good to leave them so soon after they get here?"

"I really hate to have to cancel Decorah. I understand it's a glorious time. Your father could unwind, and...you know."

"So make it a year from this summer. You'll both be free then."

Mona sighed. "I'll think about it. I know you're right, but...But."

Marit slung her purse over her shoulder. "Dad and Steig are taking Brit and Arne fishing Saturday morning as we planned, right?"

"Far as I know." Mona glanced down at her list for the day. "And the party is still on track. If we pull this surprise party off, it won't be just one miracle, but a whole trainload. If he suspects anything, he's not let on to me."

"Maybe that mess at the college is a good thing. Dad's not had time to be nosy." She grinned at her mother. "You always say look for the good in everything."

And sometimes that takes a whole lot of looking. Or waiting.

Chapter Five

Y"ou're going in mighty early." Mona blinked to see the actual time.

"I know. Whatever it takes." Ken shrugged into his blue pin-striped shirt. "This is my last shirt."

"I'll pick up at the cleaners." She glared at the clock again. "Six a.m., the coffeepot hasn't even gone to work yet."

"I reset it. Not sure what time I'll be home tonight." He pulled a tie from the rack in the closet.

"No, not that one. The navy would look better with that shirt."

His glare made her flinch. She should have kept her mouth shut, but he did need to look his best, and the navy was more forceful.

He threw the offending red one on the bed and ripped the other off the rack. For a change, he got it knotted on the first try and emptied the tray on top of the dresser into his pockets. "Call me after you talk to Steig. He said they would leave early." He almost missed her cheek with his kiss, but she wasn't about to mention that. "Are you getting up now?"

"Soon." She puffed pillows behind her back and, once sitting, reached for her Bible and devotional book. "I love you," she called to his disappearing back.

"Thanks." His shoes thunked down the stairs, Ambrose right behind him, she was sure. Hyacinth eyed the door, then changed her mind and walked up Mona's leg to sit on her sort-of lap and chirp.

"I know, you think it is breakfast time, but not for an hour yet. Some of us need to keep on schedule." She flipped to the devotion for the day but before reading, closed her eyes. *Lord God, only You can straighten all this out. Ken at the office and all that mess, safe travel for Steig and the kids, good weather for the party on Saturday, the weather report isn't looking too promising. Please, I want this party to be extra special; he's worked so hard and so long that we all want to celebrate him, as he says, his freedom. Father, You know what You will make happen, please help me keep a lid on the no-fretting kettle. And please, don't let my depression get out of hand. Sometimes I feel like our lives are being shaken in a basket and about to be dumped out in ways we don't expect. All I know for sure is that You know Your plan. And You have promised Your plans for us are for good and not for evil. Please help me hang on to that.* She heaved a sigh and said aloud, "Trust. I know." A song from her childhood floated through her mind. "Turn your eyes upon Jesus, look full in His wonderful face…" She hummed the tune as she paged through her Bible to locate the verses for the day. She'd read the verses and was halfway through the devotional when her phone chimed Steig's song.

She clicked on. "Good morning."

"I hope so. We're loaded and driving down the street to the first stop sign. I'd rather come straight on through, but I'm not sure how the kids will do. They're both back to sleep right now. Who knows how many stops we'll have to make, and there is weather between here and there too."

"How bad? I've not checked anything yet. Your dad just left for work, says he'll do whatever it takes to get everything done that he has to do. All these years of building the quality of his department and now all they talk about is cutting the budget."

"It won't be his problem."

"You know your dad. Those kids, students, whatever the age, mean more to him than the budget. And you can't put a dollar value on caring, even though the dropout percentages show how well he has done."

"Some people can. Just check with Congress."

"I know." Oh, how she wanted to ask him if this wasn't the time to leave the military, but she knew his answer. He had chosen to stay in and being deployed was just part of the package. But then when he re-upped, he'd had a wife to take care of his children. "I'll be praying for you. Call me with progress reports?"

"I will." He clicked off.

Mona tried to focus on her devotions and journal, but all she could think was, *Father, please take care of my two men and their kids.* Both Ken and Steig were caught in a web not of their own choosing. "Lord, I trust You with all of this." She wrote the words large in her journal. *Trust—* such a small word for so much meaning.

Ambrose's nails clicked on the hardwood floor, and he flopped down on the rug by her side of the bed with a sigh and a tail thumping.

"Did he feed you?" When the dog's ears went up and his tail thumped faster at the words, she knew Ken had not taken the time. She stacked her three books on the nightstand and swung her feet to the floor, taking a moment to rub Ambrose with one foot and stroke the cat with one hand. Sighing, she shoved her feet into her flip-flops and headed for the bathroom, where her robe hung on the back of the door. She tied the belt as she headed for the stairs, her animals right beside her. At least the coffee was brewed, the fragrance floating up the stairs.

With the animals fed and her plate of two soft-boiled eggs and buttered toast in hand, along with a refilled mug of coffee, she headed for the three-season porch so she could look out over the river. Mist feathered up from the surface flirting with the sun's rays, shielding the opposite bank but not the houses set back higher. Walkers were already moving along the riverside, some jogging, some walking smartly, most strolling peacefully. She had her cell beside her, but since it was too early to start returning phone calls, she hit the button for Pandora and let the music of her favorite stations fill the room. Hopefully the music would keep her mind focused on something other than Steig and the kids in the car or Ken at his desk at the university. Surely no one else would be in the office yet.

After mopping the last of her eggs with toast, she set the plate aside and picked up her calendar. Marit kept trying to get her to use the calendar on her iPhone so that it would show up on her computer and iPad, but she still preferred to lay her day out on paper first so she could move things around more easily; at least, that was her excuse. All the techno stuff that was supposed to simplify her life often didn't. She wanted her hands to be able to feel her life, to manipulate it, ideally, control it somehow. Swiping a phone simply didn't cut it.

Reading down the to-do list, she checked off a couple she'd already done, added a prayer for Steig's travel, and…"Ouch! Do you have to use your claws?" Hyacinth turned around a couple of times, kneading with claws only partially sheathed, and settled on her lap. Mona held her leather-bound desk calendar higher and clicked on her phone to make sure the phone numbers matched.

An hour later, dressed for the day and in her office, she reminded herself to breathe, thanks to the poster on the wall by the window overlooking their garden and the fruit orchard. Standing in front of the window, she took three deep breaths, letting her air all out and then rolling her shoulders. Tight was one way to describe her chest and shoulders—well, really her entire body, let alone her mind. "Breathe!" This time she focused on breathing and relaxing, stared down at the garden, wishing she had time to go hoe for a while or deadhead flowers. Ambrose looked up from standing beside her.

"No, we're not going for a walk." She shook her head as she spoke and he sank to the floor, his sigh equaling her own. Resolutely, she pulled out her desk chair, sat herself down, and dialed for messages. *Focus* had to be her word for today. Might as well start with the worst first. She pulled down the Hedstrom account and tapped in the number. "Good morning, Mrs. Hedstrom. This is Mona Sorenson returning your call."

"Yes, I was going over the statement you sent me, and it is a hundred dollars over the quote you gave me."

"That is correct. The original quote was for those services listed above the inset subheading 'additional services.' Those services were fully rendered. The services below the subheading are the ones you requested later. The extra hundred dollars covers the envelopes and postage for that list you had me send the flier to, as well as one additional hour preparing the mailing." *Even though it actually took me over two.* Mona kept herself from adding any excuses or offering to cut her bill. "The letter of agreement with my original quote says clearly that additional services will be billed accordingly."

"No, but a quote is a quote."

"I remind you we went over the contract item by item before you signed. In fact I pointed out the clause, as I always do. You agreed to the conditions. You added more after we signed."

"Well, I didn't think it applied to a little thing like that. I certainly won't be using your services again." The line went dead.

Mona cradled the phone. "Well, that's a great way to start the day. Just pay your bill, ma'am, and don't go bad-mouthing me to all your friends. You got more than your money's worth."

Marit's song. No greeting, no preliminaries. "Have you heard from Steig?"

"Good morning to you, too."

"Sorry, but he's been on my mind."

"They left their house at six fifteen, and he said eighteen hours, but you know it will be more with potty, etc., stops. You can't make two little kids sit still that long."

"Tell me about it. I sure hope he has a TV for them. Might keep his sanity."

Exactly what Mona thought, too. "I have no idea. But they usually have travel bags with toys, coloring books, etc. Jakey will be fine, but Melinda..."

"I had the weather channel on. Looks like it might be bad through Kansas. Heavy rain, possibly tornadoes."

"I hope he stops for the night and comes in tomorrow."

Marit snorted. "He always likes driving at night. The kids go to sleep, and he drinks more coffee."

A beep indicated another caller. "Oops. I gotta go." Mona switched to the other caller and pulled her yellow pad in place for notes when she realized this was a new client call.

By the end of an hour, she'd finally gotten calls returned. Now it was time to start work. She pulled out the file for a two-day conference for the local senior assistance association. While the speakers and venue were in place, she had plenty else to do. Playing phone tag was one of the necessary trials of her business. She left messages with three caterers, a printing company, and a graphic artist for the advertising and mailing. Was no one else in their office this crazy day? Her last day before she'd be working around children, too.

That thought made her stomach clench, with burning soon added. She should have had tea for breakfast, or at least not the third cup of coffee. Digging the antacid out of her drawer, she popped two in her mouth and chewed. If her stomach was bothering her, what about Ken? She hit messages on her phone and texted Ken. Hope yr day is going better than y feared. Steig left same time y did. Bad weather in KS. I Love you!!!

When she refiled the conference file, she pulled out the next. A meet and greet for a new business to open up mid-June. Venue set, caterer in place, mailing had gone out but more advertising needed. How to make this newsworthy? She ran down the list she'd already done. The normal stuff. But her motto danced before her eyes. "Deliver more than you promised." A sign on her desk read, IT TAKES SO LITTLE TO BE ABOVE AVERAGE. What in this case would be above average with only three weeks left before the event? They were already doing a silent auction to benefit a local pet rescue. Perusing that list, she pondered. At the same time, her right hand with pencil went into doodle mode. Where was Steig in relation to the storms? She needed to check the weather channel. Her mind took off and left her sitting there, no longer seeing the list. Her hand continued to doodle, only now it was drawing horrid black clouds. She started to stand, to go check the television, but her phone chimed a text.

Weather front moved east, should be ok.

She sank back down and, elbows propped on her desk, scrubbed her hands through her hair. One thing off the fret list.

Three files to go. There would be no seeking new clients today. Perhaps that was best. But the remainder of June would be pretty slim if some things didn't come in. While she was making her goal in May, June would be dismal. And what about July? She had the big Horticulture Society end-of-season convention in late August, so that would possibly suffice.

Here she was helping build other businesses up and letting her own slide. As a friend who was also a business owner said, "Feast or famine." Farmers understand that better than anyone. So far the fields were looking good, but that could change in an instant. She thought back to the Syttende Mai last spring. They'd made it through the festival with all the visitors to Stoughton, and the business it brought in. Everyone enjoyed the celebration of all things Norwegian for which they were famous. She glanced at her calendar. She was on the board and the meeting was next week. She would have children to tend.

Scrubbing her scalp was not sufficient; would hair pulling be any better? Coffee, she needed coffee. But then she'd need more antacids. Somehow herb tea did not sound sufficient. Downstairs she let the animals out; poured herself a glass of lemon and mint-infused water from the jug in the refrigerator door; and, while sipping, started pulling out the Rice Krispies, butter, and marsh-mallow crème. Steig's favorite cookie.

What would they have for supper? Just she and Ken, no kids yet. *You forgot to take the hamburger out!* Good thing for microwaves. They were having spaghetti tomor-row and the sauce needed to cook all day. Another of Steig's favorites. So little time to fix special things for her son. Monday he would be gone, and only God and his su-periors knew exactly where. But someplace where there was shooting going on. She propped her stiff arms on the counter. *Oh Lord, I don't want him to go! Can't You do something about this?* Which burned worse, the tears or the stomach? She slammed the door to the microwave and stabbed the numbers for defrost.

By the time the pan of Rice Krispies cookies was cool-ing in the fridge, the spaghetti sauce was simmering on the stove, and the kitchen put back to order, she had let the cat and dog in; answered six texts from her family other than Ken, but who was counting; and it was already after noon. What was happening at the college? Should she call his as-sistant, Sandy, and ask? Or was she better off not knowing?

She fixed herself a salad with chopped chicken on greens and poured a glass of iced tea. Then with the an-imals padding beside her, she started up the stairs to her office. Halfway up, she turned around and headed for the porch instead. But she didn't have her desk calendar in case someone called. They followed her upstairs to re-trieve the calendar and followed her back down to the porch. She started to sit down when *I need sun* sent her out to the deck. Gathering all her necessities took two trips, but when she sank into the lounger after setting the food, etc., on the low table, she leaned back and closed her eyes in relief.

Breathe! She did as ordered. Three times. As ordered.

Hyacinth jumped up and made a nest between her ankles. Ambrose laid his head on her thigh, eyes and wagging tail pleading for attention. She stroked his head and ruffled his ears. "Sorry, no walk today." He flopped down beside her, a deep sigh causing a niggle of guilt. "Tonight, we'll walk when Dad gets home."

While eating her salad, she checked down her to-do list, crossing off what she'd accomplished. What else had to be done? The kids' room was ready. She still needed to run to the store. The fragrance of cooking spaghetti sauce reminded her to add French bread to the grocery list, along with Popsicles, eggs, and their favorite cereal. (Had Steig allowed the sugary kind? She added one just for good measure.) He'd have boxes from the kitchen most likely and a cooler full of food, too. It wasn't like they were just coming for the week. He'd said he was pulling a trailer. How big a trailer? They'd have to store stuff in the garage probably. What stuff besides the bikes and kid toys?

Winter clothes, summer clothes, school clothes, playclothes. She forced her mind back to the list for today. Groceries. What did the kids like to eat? No way was her kitchen stocked for two small children. When she didn't feel like cooking or got overwhelmed, Ken stopped for takeout dinner. So easy for the two of them. But not with kids. She needed to start planning menus. For every day. She stared out over the river. Not just for visiting, but every day. Food for two children in the house twenty-four hours a day, seven days a week for the next year.

She shook her head. The weight smashed her into the lounger. *I am not ready for this.*

Chapter Six

Ken handed a résumé off to Sandy seated across from him at his desk. "This one looks pretty good, but she's still not our golden applicant."

Sandy glanced at the name. "I thought the same. Worth a shot, though, if nothing better comes along."

Ken picked up the next résumé, paused, and smiled. "Did you ever meet Archer Tarkensen?"

"No, but I've corresponded with him on e-mail. Sounds nice enough. Didn't he retire?"

"He did. Now he picks up a paycheck here and there as a headhunter."

Sandy frowned. "Don't you have to live in a jungle or something to be a headhunter?"

Ken smiled. "A headhunter is a person who knows everybody in a particular field; in this case, Arch's forte is university administration. He knows all the big deans. He worked with many of them before he retired and knows who can do what. I told him about our situation here. He agrees Damien is not the person to fill my position, so he's going to look around for us."

"Look around." She wrinkled her nose. "You mean see if someone is dissatisfied with what they're doing and would like to come do this job?"

"A headhunter doesn't just look for people who want to move. He looks for anyone who would be a good fit. If a person would be perfect for this position, Arch might just sweet-talk him or her into applying here."

Sandy sat back, almost smiling. "That's rather audacious." She shook her head. "Not enough time, Ken."

"That may change." Here was another strong candidate. Middle-aged, PhD in sociology, worked with youth groups, then took a job as associate dean at a small college. He would understand what incoming students need and how to maximize their college experience, and he was well acquainted with academic administration.

Ken's office door swung open so violently they both jumped. Dale charged in and slammed an official-looking paper down on Ken's desk. "An injunction! You're slapping an injunction on us! What the bloody blazes do you think you're doing? Call the judge right now and get it lifted. I mean *now!*"

"Sorry, Dale. You have to talk to my lawyer about that. It's in his hands; I'm not allowed to discuss it."

"Your lawy— No, *you*! Lift this now!"

Ken sat back in his chair, crossed his arms, and quietly looked Dale in the eye. Casually, peaceably, without rancor—well, he hoped that was how it looked. He was feeling anything but peaceable. And rancor was bubbling very close to the surface.

Dale's voice dropped to a purr; its tone was almost threatening. Well, yes, it was threatening. "What's your game, Sorensen? What are you trying to pull here?"

"Talk to my lawyer."

Dale lost the staredown. He wheeled and stormed out, leaving the door open.

Sandy stared at him, at the legal paper. "You really did hire a lawyer and file an injunction!"

"Yes."

"I didn't think our advocacy group had the money to hire a lawyer for just one adjudication. They claim they can only handle group cases."

"That's right."

Her face hardened. "You're doing this out of your own pocket, aren't you? Ken, no! In forty-eight hours, it won't be your problem anymore. Let it go."

He sat back to look at her squarely. "Sandy, have I ever in my career backed down from a fight I felt was important? Ever?"

"No, but..."

"That injunction just bought us another sixty days. Yes, I'll be retired, but I'll be able to keep working on our problem. By then we should find someone. And I can do Rollo's annual evaluation when he gets back from vacation in ten days. One less thing for Damien to get his hands on." He took a deep breath. "I gave my career to this job, and I won't see it defunded and stuffed away on a shelf. It's a line item to Dale and Damien and John. It's academic life and death to the students we serve. Whether they succeed or fail is sometimes in our hands, and we're talking lifetime careers here, not just four years in school. The students. Yes, it's that important, Sandy, that I'm putting my own money into it."

She sat there in silence a few moments. "Who's your lawyer?"

"Remember a mousy little kid in tortoiseshell glasses who had to struggle for every grade he earned?"

She half smiled. "Gerald...Gerald...Wait a minute... Gerald...Leach! Gerald Leach."

"He graduated from Stone..."

"Yes. With honors."

"Right. Went on to law school, and now he's a junior partner in Ross, Vorstein, and Schumacher. He pulls down more than what you and I together earn in a year. And he remembers us."

"But is he good enough to run with the big dogs?"

"He *is* a big dog now."

She sat looking at him without seeing anything, the way people deep in thought do. Suddenly she sat straight up. "Well, since we have a sixty-day reprieve, let's get cracking."

By the time they completed the applications on file, it was near three. Ken glanced at his calendar. Chester Rankin at three. Chet was his last evaluation, except for Rollo. He had not thought he could do it. Dale certainly had not, Ken was certain.

Three came and went. No Chet. Ken filled the time writing letters of introduction for two students and recommendations for three others. Were Damien the dean of students, would he go to all this effort? Do ducks gallop?

He heard Chet out at Sandy's desk and glanced at his clock. Three twenty-two. Yep, that was Chet. Sandy opened his door and ushered their custodian into the room.

Ken waved toward the upholstered chair. "Good afternoon, Chet. Have a seat."

"Sorry I'm late. Had to clean up a mess in the back room. Y'know that little blond girl you hired to file journals? Spilled her milk shake. *All* over. Took forever."

Ken smiled and nodded. "Sorry. Her gross coordination isn't very good. You may not know she has a neurodegenerative disease that has destroyed some of the nerves in her arms and legs. The doctors say she will lead a normal life with, probably, a normal life span, but the degeneration won't get any better. And she's a crackerjack librarian."

"Oh, she was all sorts of apologetic. I just smiled and let it go."

"That's good of you. Thank you." Ken sat back. "Let's see. You're the maintenance crew representative for Stone Hall and also Ashford Hall, is that right?"

"Yes, sir. They gave me Harlan now, too, but Harlan don't take much in the way of cleanup, at least not over summer. Not many people go there when school ain't in session. Mostly just chase the cobwebs off."

"Still, it's your responsibility."

"Yes, sir."

"Three administrative buildings is a huge task. If you have any questions or complaints, now's the time to air them."

"Well, I can't think of any. A couple of the people in the offices, especially over in Ashford, are a little hard to work for, but that's true anywhere you go. So no, I don't have no complaints."

"Hard to work for in what way?"

"Oh, you know, uppity. I don't have any letters after my name and most of them do, so I'm not worth being nice to. You know, like that."

You're not the only person who hates working with them, Chet, Ken thought to himself. *I don't like to, either, and I have half a dozen letters strung out after my name.* "We can get along without labor management people and building inspectors. I'd like to see them get along without a custodian."

Chet laughed out loud. "Never thought of it that way. Yeah!"

"Are you working on that remodel in Ashford?"

"No, sir. I just clean up the plaster dust after they're through."

"Insurance records say you have a wife and three children."

"I do, sir, and those kids are the best kids going. I'm proud of them. They're doing better in school than I ever did, and they're polite."

Ken pondered a moment. Usually, he wrote down evaluees' answers almost verbatim, but not Chet. The man was much wiser and smarter than his poor English would suggest. He could make a recalcitrant furnace work again when it quit and bring defunct kitchen appliances back to life. His gift for repairs saved the school hundreds of dollars a year. Maybe thousands.

"As you know, Chet, an annual evaluation covers all the bases, or tries to. I see that one thing has not changed since last year. I know you start with cleaning Stone here in the morning. I hardly ever see you get to work on time. You're always fifteen, twenty minutes late."

"Yes, sir. Don't know how that happens so much. My day just don't seem to get started right most days. Sorry, sir."

Ken nodded. "On the other hand, I never see you clock out when the day is over at five. You're always working, doing something for at least another half hour or more. Sometimes you don't get out until six."

Chet shrugged. "Sorry."

"Don't be. Technically, I should lower your evaluation for your frequent lateness. But I won't. The way you work until the job is done, the school is more than getting its money's worth. I put in extra myself, and I admire that in others. How long have you been here, four years?"

"Five, sir, come July."

"Ah! Good. Then you're due for an in-grade pay raise. Your supervisor is still Harry Nicholson, is that correct?"

"Yes, sir."

"Anything else?"

Chet shrugged again. "Can't think of nothing."

"Neither can I." Ken stood, so Chet stood. "Chet, would you do me a favor?"

"Why sure, Dr. Sorenson. More'n happy to."

"Take the rest of the afternoon off and go home and relax. I'll call Harry and tell him."

"Well, uh . . ." Chet grinned broadly. "Since that's what you told me to do, I'll do it. Thank you, Dr. Sorenson!" He left.

Ken sat down and picked up the phone. He and Harry Nicholson were old friends—their kids had gone to school together—but he wouldn't tell Chet that. Keep it formal. He opened his lap drawer to look at the phone list and punched in Harry's number.

Harry answered on the second ring. "Nicholson."

"Sorenson. How's your daughter doing with her new job?"

"Hey, Ken! She loves it. Wish I liked my job half as well. How's your kids?"

"Marit's chugging right along, and Steig is deployed again."

"Where to?"

"Karachi."

Silence at the other end. Harry's voice dropped a little. "Pakistan. Well, best wishes and blessings to him from Marge and me both." Another brief silence. "How's Mona taking it?"

"So far, so good. She tends to worry a lot, but she seems to be holding her own well."

"Still, it's always tough. And you're retiring, right? Or retired."

"Semiretired. Winding up some things. Aren't you about ready to hang up your spurs also?"

"I'm going to put in another eighteen months, and then my retirement check will be bigger. You know, it's based on your top three years, and I'm halfway through a pay upgrade. But yes, I'm gonna hang it up."

"Good. Harry, I'm calling about Chet Rankin."

"He in trouble? Not Chet."

"Trouble? No. For some reason I was supposed to do his annual evaluation, and..."

"I thought that was my job."

"So did I, but Dale handed it to me. So I did it."

Harry sighed. "Mine not to reason why, mine not to make reply, mine but to do and die. Something like that."

"Right. I'll write it up and get it over to you. It will glow. He's up for a raise in a month. I want to state for the record he is worth his weight in gold and should start his in-grade at step two."

"I was thinking the same thing. To hear him talk he's a few trees short of an orchard, but he's a whiz at fixing air handlers."

"Same over here in Stone. Incidentally, I gave him the afternoon off."

"Good!"

They chatted a few minutes more, nothing earth-shattering, and hung up.

Ken stared at his desk. What was Dale up to? Something, that was for sure. Ken hated office politics. *Hated* it! But he was actually quite good at it; in academia, you have to be. He was able to hear what was said and what was carefully left unsaid. Who coveted which cause or position. What bells he had to ring to get his way in an important matter. This time, though, when it counted most—funding of the whole department—he could not for the life of him figure out what was going on. Dale had assigned him useless work. Why?

Sandy buzzed him. He hit the button. "Four more candidates just submitted. Do you want to do them today or pick it up in the morning?"

"Do them today. You get off shortly, so let me have them and you can go home."

"Paper or online?"

"Don't bother to print them out. Why kill trees if you don't have to." He swung his monitor around to a better viewing angle as the first flashed onto the screen. But he had trouble concentrating. He simply could not apply himself to this.

Weariness? Exhaustion?

Or was he making the same hideous error his brother had made? Instead of picking up his marbles when he could and going home, Frank had worked on and on past retirement age. And then, when he finally did retire, he dropped dead.

Now here was Ken, hanging on beyond the bitter end when his family was begging him to just quit and walk away.

And if he followed Frank's road, Mona could be raising two small children alone.

Chapter Seven

Go ahead and have supper. I'll get something on my way home."

Mona glanced at the clock. Already seven. "I could bring you a picnic."

"No thanks, I don't want to stop right now."

She could hear not only weariness in Ken's voice, but also a feeling of defeat. Her mother bear came into full force. Right now she could quite cheerfully take on those closed-minded autocrats who only believed in the bottom line. Ken had given his life to that place and this was the way they repaid him? But dumping these evaluations on him right now was the last thing he needed.

There had been talk about hiring him part-time as a consultant after he retired, but as far as she was concerned, they had burned their bridges. If they didn't listen when he was still head of the department, why would they later?

"I wish there was some way I could help you."

"Thanks, I'll call you when I am ready to leave. Oh, any word on Steig?"

"Not since five. They were stopped at a rest area in Kansas."

"Okay. Later." He hung up.

She glared at the phone in her hand, then down at the dog, who scratched at her leg with one paw. "No!"

Ambrose dropped to the floor, his eyes pleading for mercy. Mercy was what they all needed right now.

"I'm sorry, I know you were only trying to help." She puffed out a sigh. A walk would do both her and the two critters more good than pacing here. "Okay, a short walk." The dog leaped to his feet and scrabbled across the tile floor to stand under the hanging leashes, tail waving, tongue lolling. Hyacinth strolled on over and sat down, as if to say, *If you insist, I will accompany you. But only for Ambrose's sake.*

Mona stuffed plastic bags in her pocket, fixed collars and leashes in place, and followed them out the door. At least she was able to give someone pleasure.

They'd gotten down to the river path when her phone announced Marit. Without preamble, Mona announced, "We're walking, your father is still at the office, and the last I heard from Steig at five, they were at a rest stop in Kansas."

"Guess that answered everything. Call me if you hear anything. The kids and I are watching that goofy cartoon feature with a reindeer. Or moose. Something. Magnus is stuck at the office, too. You want to come over here?"

"No thanks. Later." She knew she'd been abrupt, but right now that was all she could manage. *You should just enjoy the walk,* her naggy voice said. Well, easier said than done. She should have stayed home tuned to the weather channel. Or folding that last load of clothes or baking something or...She put both leashes in one hand and rubbed her forehead with the other. Maybe an ice pack on the back of her neck would help. How would they ever get all the paperwork and official legal hoopla done before Steig had to leave on Monday? Where did he have to report? How would the kids adapt? After all, they'd not stayed by themselves with Grampy and Grammy before, thanks to Angela's selfishness. Would Jakey remember them? It was over a year since they had seen them other than on Skype, and his tolerance for that was about a minute. Or less. Melinda, however, loved to chat with them. They'd been six months without their mother now. Oh, those poor kids. How long would they have to pay for the disruption of their family? More than disruption. Destruction? Of course, Steig was doing all he could, but the kids needed a mom. But one who thought more of them than of herself. That they'd never had.

"Okay, kids, I've worried all the way so far, and I certainly didn't intend to. Let's go back; it's my turn to have supper." They both looked up at her as if they understood every word. Her mind took off again. How would the two kids do with the two animals? What if someone was allergic? That thought made her almost choke. At least they were not bringing in pets that needed to be integrated. She had a feeling from something said one time that Angela did not tolerate pets. Or perhaps she was the allergic one. *Please, Lord, no allergies.* She did her poop-scooping job and dumped the bag in one of the trash cans along the path. Walking again, her inner monologue picked up even more forcefully. What could she do to gain some more clients? What a dumb idea; maybe God was trying to protect her with a light client load until their house settled into some kind of routine. One thing would be different from when she was raising kids: Ken would be home to help.

But he wanted to travel, not all the time, but a couple

of times at least. And she liked the idea; get away so he was not tempted to try to help his department. Not that it would be his department after Friday. That led to her running down the list of things for the celebratory dinner on Friday, not that she was supposed to have any responsibilities for that. *Now you're worrying about things for which you have no responsibilities! Stop it!* But really, the surprise party on Saturday was *all* her ball game. *Lord, please change the weather patterns around so we can have it at the park.* Sometimes she hated watching or even glancing at the weather maps.

She unclipped her phone from her waistband and hit Marit's number. "What will the children do if it's storming on Saturday? There is an outdoor area where we can barbecue, but..."

"I have it covered, Mom. I told you I would."

"But they're supposed to go fishing early."

"Magnus made arrangements for something else; not sure what, but he is good at that, you know. All is under control."

"I'll be so glad when this weekend is over..."

"I'll have five kids; going to be a fun time at our house."

"Maybe we better just cancel."

"No! Everything is under control."

Mona sank down on the second step leading to the deck. "Be a miracle if I don't have a nervous breakdown over all this. The mess in Dad's department might be the straw that breaks this camel's back."

"Mom, that is not your problem! Stop worrying!"

"It is mine since it's bothering your father. He's not sleeping, therefore, I'm not sleeping well, and this thing with Steig." She blew out a breath. "I gotta remember that this is no surprise to God, so He has a plan."

"Be nice if He clued you in."

"Yeah, it would, but..." Her stomach rumbled. "I better go eat."

"Kinda late, isn't it?"

"I was hoping your dad would get home, and after he called, I took the twins here for their walk and now I'm starving. Thank you."

"Wish I could help you more."

"I'd say you are doing a hefty share. Bye." She clicked off the phone and hauled herself upright. Now to decide what to have. They mounted the steps; she hung up their harnesses and both animals headed to the kitchen for a drink and a treat. Creatures of habit, that was for sure. After washing her hands, she stared into the refrigerator. Leftover chicken casserole, leftover meat loaf and half a baked potato, a salad with chicken on it, a ham sandwich with chips—why did none of that sound good? She pulled out the casserole, the easiest to fix, then slid it back on the shelf. Surely a sandwich. But all she had was white bread. *Ugh.* Back to the casserole. While her bowl was heating in the microwave, she dug in a box for some crackers and poured a glass of lemonade.

"Okay, kids, the porch or the family room?" Did she want to watch the river or the weather channel or one of the cooking shows she had saved? Food on a tray, she stopped in the family room and, tray on the table, sank into her recliner. Ken did not particularly like cooking shows, so she'd watch one now. She flicked through the list to *Pioneer Woman* and clicked on the longest-waiting episode. She'd learned to keep a pad and paper at hand in case there was a recipe or a tip that she'd want to remember. Tray on her lap, she kicked the recliner back and settled in.

After all, this might be the last evening she had alone in who knew how long, if ever again. *Only a year. You will have children here full-time for only a year, maybe even six months. That is not a lifetime.*

Tristan und Isolde. Steig's song.

Eagerly she thumbed the phone on. "How far are you?"

"Halfway up Iowa, and I really need to stop. The kids can swim off some of their energy at a motel, and I can sit on a recliner with a glass of iced tea and watch."

"Bad?"

"Not really, I know I could push on, but...maybe I'll even go swimming with them."

She could hear him thinking that this might be his last chance to play in a pool with his children for a long time.

"Anyway, we should be there early afternoon tomorrow if we leave at five. Today they slept until after eight." Even his voice sounded weary.

"Thanks for letting me know. Dad is still at work, so you can guess what is going on there. Say hello to Melinda and Jakey for me."

"See you tomorrow. Oh, by the way, she wants to be called Mellie. Wait. Mellie wants to talk to you."

She heard, "Me too, me too," before Mellie's voice sparkled, "Hi, Grammy, we get to see you tomorrow."

"I know, we're all ready. Ambrose will be so happy to see you."

"Jakey doesn't like dogs much."

Oh, great. Mona closed her eyes and leaned her head back. "Why?"

"Mommy said dogs are icky and give you germs."

"And cats?"

"He doesn't like them much either 'cause they scratch."

"Well, I guess we'll just have to teach him that Ambrose

and Hyacinth are good friends and not like lots of other animals."

"I love 'em both. 'Member when Ambrose pulled me and Arne in the wagon and we got dumped out?"

"I do, we all laughed so hard and poor Ambrose couldn't figure it out. We'll have to see if we can get him to do that again."

"I have my bike and Jakey has a three-wheeler. Daddy said we can ride on the path by the river. Do you and Grampy have bikes?"

"No, but that is a good idea. You ask him about that, okay?"

"Daddy says I got to hang up; we just turned in to a motel. I love you, Grammy."

She heard another "Me too, me too," as the phone clicked off. So Angela passed her fear of animals on to at least one of her children. And there was a Norwegian elkhound at Marit's house. They'd better turn Jakey into a dog lover real quick. She texted Steig's message to Marit and added, Stopping in Iowa. Jakey doesn't like dogs and cats.

A few seconds later, one appeared on her phone. Guess we'll have to take care of that. Have I ever mentioned how not sorry I am that she left?

Mona hit the smiley face icon on her phone.

She took her tray into the kitchen, put stuff away, and brought the last load from the dryer so she could sit on the sofa and fold while she watched another episode. Perhaps she should put the Ree Drummond cookbooks on her Christmas list. Ken was always asking her what she wanted for both birthdays and Christmas. But when the time came, she could never think of something. Not that she had a lack of lists anywhere.

When ten o'clock chimed and still no Ken, she went upstairs to get ready for bed. Of course, there was no chance she'd fall asleep until he got home, but reading in bed was about the only thing that seemed appealing. Concentrating took more effort than she had to give. Ken's song. *Thank you, Lord.*

"I'm just leaving the office."

"Don't stop. I'll have something ready for you here."

"Keep it simple; not sure I have the energy to lift a fork." He paused and she could hear him start the car. "I finished the reviews. Tomorrow we interview through the first run."

"Good for you. See you in twenty minutes. Meat loaf and baked potato." She knew those were his favorites.

"Okay. Thanks."

She texted Marit. On his way home.

Marit was a night owl like her mother used to be. Good. Give him a sleeping pill.

Night.

Downstairs she set up his plate and set it in the microwave, fixed a small green salad and a glass of lemonade, and the tray was ready. Letting the animals out for their final run of the day, she stood on the back porch and listened to the night sounds. Frogs from their fountain and the marsh by the river, crickets, and was that a wood thrush's fluting song? Sure enough. They seemed to be arriving earlier these last few years. A great horned owl hooted. Sometimes a pair nested in that old pine tree, in the big hole about ten feet up. Mona could teach the kids to watch for the babies.

So much to share with grandchildren. Melinda, Mellie, was old enough to learn to crochet. Grammy needed to add to the craft supplies kept in two drawers in the family room. Rainy-day activities. Car lights turning into their driveway. "Dad's home!" Both animals ran to her side, or rather Ambrose ran and Hyacinth did her regal stroll, tail straight up.

Mona went inside to start the microwave.

"Thank you," Ken said a few minutes later, when he sat down at the table.

"If you would rather eat in your chair."

"No, this is fine." He bowed his head for grace and then propped his elbows on the table. "How are Steig and the kids?"

"Stopped for the night."

"Good, I was concerned about his pushing on through tonight."

"How…" She stopped when he raised his hand, as if stopping traffic.

"I do not want to talk about work, okay?"

"Sure." She sat down on a chair across from him. When had she last seen such purple shadows beneath his eyes? He appeared to have aged ten years in the last three days. His usually straight shoulders curved. Was his hand shaking, too? She watched to see if the tremor continued. Was he that tired or was something else going on physically? Surely not. She snagged her mind back from galloping off in a terrifying direction. *Worry! More worry!* Why could she not control the urge to fret about things that did not come to pass? And yet, usually her husband was the poster child for a healthy sixtyish man. In fact, no one could believe he really was sixty-four. Even the doctor who had known them for twenty, no twenty-five years, had to check his medical chart.

He pushed his half-full plate away. "Sorry, I just need to go to bed."

"With a serotonin tonight?"

"Doubt I need it, but good idea." He pushed back his chair and used the table to help him stand. "Thank God only two more days and then I am done." He didn't even bend over and pet Ambrose, who sat beside him, chin on Ken's thigh. Tail down, the dog followed him up the stairs.

Please, God, get him through the next two days.

Chapter Eight

"How's Dad?" Marit's voice sounded too cheerful for this time of the morning.

"What are you doing up already?" Mona could smell the coffee. She had set it to start at six.

"Arne woke up with nightmares, and then I couldn't go back to sleep. Is he up?"

"I think he's already left. I went back to sleep." Mona trapped a yawn. "And no, I've not heard from Steig."

"He left at five. Said to let you know, he didn't want to wake you. What time did Dad get home last night?"

"Ten forty-five, almost too tired to even eat."

"And back again before seven?"

"He looks terrible."

"I could strangle Dale and his ilk."

"A slow, painful death like tied to an anthill would be better."

"Mom!" Marit snorted, then chuckled. "Are you going back to bed?"

"No. Too much to do."

"Like what?"

"Baking chocolate chip cookies..."

"Because those are Melinda's favorite?"

"She wants to be called Mellie."

"Oh, really. Wants no part of her mother?" Melinda was Angela's middle name.

"I think so."

"We will certainly oblige. Bye."

Mona moved down her to-do list with the precision of a marching squad, answering the phone, passing on messages, with her headset in place and her hands dropping cookie dough on the pans, mixing more dough, and writing notes when needed. Shame she didn't get this much done every day. All the while her mind flitted between concern for her son and then her husband.

A text from Ken. Steig says he'll be there at 2:30.

She stared at the screen. Why did he text his father and not her? Had something happened he didn't want to tell her about? Were they all right? *More worry! Stop it!* She checked the clock. One hour and ten minutes.

What was most important that still needed doing? Down her list. *Nada.* She pulled the last pan from the oven, turned it off, and slid the peanut butter cookies on the rack to cool while she washed all the utensils. With the big rosemaling tray of both kinds of cookies and the Rice Krispies bars in the center of the island, she headed upstairs to change clothes. Her pants were wearing floured handprints in spite of her apron.

Two twenty. Steig was remarkably punctual. If he said two thirty, it was rarely two twenty-nine or two thirty-one. Well, perhaps not *that* punctual, but close enough. Back downstairs to set glasses on the island along with napkins. Ambrose barked his "Dad's home" welcome at the moment he heard a car drive into the garage. Along with the two four-footers, she stepped into the garage as Ken was climbing out of the car. "You came home early. I can't believe this." Wrapping her arms around his waist, she hugged him close.

"I couldn't miss greeting the kids, I just couldn't. So I said I'd see them tomorrow and left."

"You really did?"

"I'm here, aren't I?" He reached down to thump Ambrose on the ribs and greet Her Highness.

The sound of a car turning in their driveway brought them and the animals outside.

Steig honked the horn. Ambrose leaped and barked. Hyacinth headed for the door to the laundry room, and Mona gave up trying to sniff back tears. She locked her arm with her husband's, and together they waited for the SUV to roll to a stop.

"Grammy!" Mellie squealed, and bailed out of the car almost before it stopped rolling.

"Mellie, be careful." Steig shook his head as he smiled at his parents. Then he leaned in to unlock his son from the car seat. He swung Jakey up in his arms. "See, you remember Grampy and Grammy. And that's Ambrose who is so excited to see you both."

Jakey locked his arms around his father's neck and buried his face in his shirt collar. "No! No dog!"

Steig hugged his dad with his spare arm, and Mellie switched from Mona to her grandpa. Mona patted Jakey's leg as she hugged her son.

"You are really here and all right?"

"We're good, Mom. And seeing you makes good even better. Jake..." He stopped and, looking into his mother's eyes, shook his head. "It'll take time. Overload with too much change."

Keeping one arm around Steig's waist, she decided to give Jake whatever space he needed. "Surely you can hear the cookies calling from the kitchen? There's a whole big tray."

"Chocolate chip?" Mellie grabbed her grandma's hand and swung it as they headed for the kitchen. When Mona nodded, Mellie cocked her head. "And Daddy's Rice Krispies cookies?"

Mona nodded again. "And I heard that a certain little boy likes peanut butter cookies the very best. Now, who do you think that could be?"

Steig jiggled his son. "Who is it that always wants peanut butter cookies?"

"Jakey likes peanut butter on everything." Mellie spread her spare arm wide.

"Uh-uh." Jake looked up at his dad. "Not eggs."

Ken snorted, making them all laugh as they trooped through the garage and into the kitchen. "I wouldn't like peanut butter on eggs, either." He made a face and reached for a cookie. "Here, Jake, see if this one is okay."

The little boy studied it and half turned his head. He looked at the cookie, up at his dad, then back to his grandpa. Apparently it would not bite or poison him. He reached for the cookie.

"What do you say?"

"Thank you," he mumbled around a mouthful of cookie.

Mellie scrambled up on the stool to better reach the cookie tray. "That's lotsa cookies, Grammy." She studied the cookies and took a browner, crunchier one. "This is the best kind." She handed her daddy a bar. "You better eat them before Aunty Marit gets here. She can make her own."

Mona choked on a laugh at the seriousness of her granddaughter. When had she taken over watching out for her father? After pouring the lemonade and passing around the glasses, they all headed for the screened porch. Steig tried to put Jake down, but he superglued himself to his father, cookie crumbs tumbling down Steig's shirt. Mona set the cookie tray on the coffee table, along with the pitcher.

"Hadn't we better start unloading?" Ken asked.

"Let's just sit and visit for a bit. What a drive." Steig settled Jake on his lap. "Hey, Mellie, how about another cookie for your old dad?"

Mellie looked up from petting Ambrose. "You're not old...much." But she fetched him two bars. "One for each hand."

"Me, too." Jakey reached out.

Hands on her hips, she stared at her brother. "You have to get your own."

Steig smirked. "In some ways, Mom, she's just like you." He sobered. "The pictures we have of you when you were ten; you and Mellie look a lot alike. Angela resented that; that Mellie didn't look like her, like her side of the family. Both kids."

Staring at Ambrose, Jakey curled in tight against his father. "Go away, dog."

"Ambrose won't hurt you." Mellie wrapped her arms around the black neck and got a quick lick for her efforts, making her giggle. "Don't be a baby."

"I'm not a baby. I don't like dogs."

Mona and Ken swapped glances and smiles.

"Then don't act like one." Mellie smiled at her grandma. "Where's Hyacinth?"

"Probably under the bed. She'll come out after a while."

"I could go get her," the little girl suggested hopefully.

"You could try, but she'd just run away. She always does this when new people come."

"She forgot us?"

Mona shrugged. "Most likely. Just give her time." Time was something they had an abundance of.

Steig looked at his father. "So you got them all straightened out?"

"Almost. I finished the reviews, did three interviews this morning, and will do two more tomorrow. There are two who really look possible."

"And neither are absolutely wonderful?"

Ken nodded. "Not our great golden hope, no. It takes a lot of time."

"I'll bet. It sounds easier than it is."

From the man who has had to do a lot of letting go. Mona watched her son. Surely there were new lines on his face, and he looked almost as tired as his dad had. Maybe he could get a good night's sleep while he was here. They did not need to stay up late talking, or at least she hoped they didn't have to.

He finished the bar. "Thanks, Mom. Think I'll just sit here and soak in the peace." He patted his son's back. "Been too long." Jakey snuggled into his father.

Ken kicked back his recliner. "Think I'll join you."

Mona resisted the urge and stood instead. "Come on, Melinda, er, Mellie, we'll go weed the flower bed."

Mellie took her hand. "Come on, Ambrose, you can help."

Mona noticed that Jakey was carefully watching the dog leave. Teaching him dog love was going to be a big challenge.

Outside, Mona hooked her garden apron with her gloves, trowel, and clippers around her waist, grabbed a bucket, and they knelt down by the curving bed. "Now, these are the weeds and these the vegetables. See that?

That's lettuce and a row of carrots right behind them."
While the lettuce was nearly ready to pick, the carrots had
feathery tops but no carrot yet.

"Can I have a digger, too?"

"You sure can. But your fingers work best for these
weeds. We'll pull them before they get big, then throw
them in the bucket."

"I saw a goat eating weeds. The lady said they keep
grass down, too, so you don't have to mow. Maybe you
should have a goat."

"I don't think they allow goats here; chickens and rab-
bits but no goats."

"Do chickens eat weeds?" Mellie dumped a handful in
the bucket.

"They do, but if they are loose, they eat the good plants,
too."

"Maybe we could have chickens."

Down inside, Mona smiled. Already Mellie was saying
we instead of *you*. "You talk to Grampy about that." Mona
already knew his opinions on more pets than Ambrose and
Hyacinth. "But later. I think he's sleeping."

"I know. I really want a pony. I rode one at the park."

Mona smiled. "I wanted a pony when I was your age,
too."

"Did you get one?"

"No."

"Why?"

Mona could hear her father on the matter of horses.
"We lived in town, no pasture for horses or ponies."

"Why?"

Mona rolled her lips together. "Because that's where we
lived. Like here."

"You have a big yard."

"We do, but not enough space for big animals." She leaned back on her heels. "Looks like we're making progress, wouldn't you say?"

"I think more cookies would be good."

"Let's finish this bed, and then we'll have a cookie break."

"Can I eat the lettuce?"

"If you want, but you will want to wash it first."

"Does Ambrose like lettuce?"

"Not particularly." She watched as Mellie lay back on the grass with her head on the dog's ribs. Ambrose licked her cheek, making her giggle. She reached over her head to pat him, then kicked one bent leg up in the air three times, then the other.

"I'm doing my exercises."

"Do them for me, too."

Mellie sat straight up. "I can't do them for you."

"Oh."

Mellie giggled and flopped back. "Texas is brown, not green like here. Daddy said you get more rain here. Why?"

"Because Wisconsin is more north, Texas is in the south."

"More snow, too, huh?"

Mona kept on digging and dropping weeds in the bucket. *Guess the guys all needed naps.* She thought about waking them but figured sleep was more important. The time passed pleasantly. She turned to smile when she felt a hand on her shoulder.

"I'm about done, Mellie."

"Grammy, Daddy's going to leave, huh?"

"Yes, he's being deployed again."

"And we're going to stay here?"

"That's right."

"Go to school here, too? I'm in fourth grade this year. What is fourth grade like here, do you know? Will I find any friends?"

"I'm sure you will. And you'll have Brit." Mona pulled off her gloves and sat cross-legged instead of kneeling.

Mellie frowned. "Your knee just popped."

"Yep." She reached over and snagged the little girl, drawing her down into the sort-of lap, then wrapped her arms around her, chin resting on the top of Mellie's head. They sat that way for a little while. Ambrose scooted over to lay his head in the little lap. Mellie reached up with one hand and patted Mona's cheek. *Thank You, Lord, for moments like this.*

They both looked up when the screen door opened and Steig stepped out onto the porch.

"Hi, Daddy. Come sit by us." Mellie patted the grass.

"You got room?" He yawned and stretched his arms over his head. "I put Jakey down on the sofa. Dad's still snoring." Jumping down the three steps, he sat cross-legged like his mother. "We should start unloading."

"Magnus will be over later. We can wait for him."

"You have no idea how much stuff is here." He tweaked Mellie's nose. "Kids just need a lot of stuff."

She giggled and changed laps. Ambrose came to sit by Steig, tail swishing the grass. "We could go down to the river." She looked at her dad. "Want to?"

"We could, but we have to unload so I can get the trailer turned back in today."

"Oh. Maybe we can go down to the river tonight."

"Maybe." He hugged her tight and made her giggle.

Mona caught the look in his eyes as he kissed the top of her head. Talk about a breaking heart.

"Come on, let's get your bike out, and you can ride on the driveway while we unload." He rose to his feet without putting her down. "Oof, you're getting big."

"That's okay." She patted his upper arm. "You got lots of muscles."

Together the three of them walked over to the rear of the trailer, where he put his daughter down and dug in his pocket for the keys. "See what I mean?" he said when he swung the doors open.

"Oh, good, you brought chests of drawers."

"Easier than packing the stuff in boxes. This way I just bungeed the drawers closed and put that dolly to work." He pulled the two-wheeled upright dolly out first since it was on top. A pink-and-purple girl's bike was next. "There you go, kiddo."

"You made a rhyme," Mellie said accusingly. "I thought you didn't like poetry."

"I did." He pulled out another two-wheeler with training wheels. "Neighbor insisted we take this for Jake. So far he likes his sidewalk bike better, but I'm sure you'll all be riding your bikes along the river trail." He paused. "You did get bikes?"

"Not yet, but we plan to. Lots of stuff got put on hold these last weeks. Garden came first." She turned to Mellie. "How about wheeling this into the garage, off to the side where the garden supplies are?"

Mellie did as asked and ran back to drag the red wagon in next. "Did you bring the Slip 'N Slide?"

"I did, it's here somewhere." He turned to his mother. "Maybe we better back Dad's car out."

"I'll get the keys to my car. We'll put stuff up by the back wall until we can put it all away. Ken talked about putting those steel shelves along that wall."

"Did he buy them yet?"

"No."

"Tell you what, we get this unloaded and I'll pick up the shelves when I return the trailer. No sense moving this stuff more than we have to."

They had only made a dent in the load when Ken joined her in the garage. "You should have wakened me."

"Why? You needed the rest. You still look haggard. Steig got up about half an hour ago. Is Jake still sleeping?"

"He was when I left. Catch me up out here."

"Steig plans to buy shelving when he returns the trailer. We're just stacking stuff out of the way now."

Ken nodded in his noncommittal way. Mona only hoped he did not feel guilty about failing to get the shelves yet. He had so much going on already.

Mellie paused with a big box of dolls. "Hi Grampy. Grammy and me weeded the flowers." She stacked the box on others.

"Good for you. Grammy needs all the help she can get." Ken headed for the trailer, where Steig had the dolly loaded again.

Mona and Mellie started on the SUV. "You carry your travel bags in, and I'll get the suitcases."

"Okay. Where should I put them?"

"In the family room by the bookshelves. You know where the games and things are?"

"'Kay."

Steig slammed the trailer door and lifted the rear door on the SUV. "I think all this should go upstairs."

A wailing scream reverberated through the house and out the garage. "Daaaddyyyyy!"

Steig charged into the house, Mona right on his heels.

Jake was crunched up in a corner of the sofa, sobbing and shaking.

"Jake, easy son, what is it? What's wrong?" Steig scooped him up.

He clung like Velcro to his daddy's neck. "The c-c-cat! The cat is going to hurt me! She hates me!"

Steig settled down on the sofa with Jakey in his lap close against him. "Okay, stop crying so you can tell me what happened." He grabbed a tissue and mopped the tears. "Blow." That done, he continued, all the while rocking his son and making comfort sounds. "Now what happened?"

"The cat."

"I get that. I don't see any bite marks or scratches or anything. Jake, I think you're fine." Steig looked up at his mom. "Nothing."

Mona asked, "Did the cat bite you?"

Jakey shook his head.

"Scratch you?"

Another headshake.

What was going on here? "Where was the cat?"

Jake pointed to the first cushion on the sofa where he'd been sleeping, half on that one and half on the middle one. Instantly he curled up inside his daddy's embrace again.

Mona cleared her throat, and when Steig looked up at her, she nodded. "I bet that Hyacinth just jumped up on the sofa to see who was there. Is he really that terrified of cats?"

"Beats me. Maybe just the shock. I'll work on him and the cat before..."

He didn't have to finish the sentence. The *before* was enough to make his mother blow her nose.

Chapter Nine

I waited as long as I could!" Marit reached up to hug her brother.

Steig snorted. "Figures. The work is about done."

How Mona loved the lighthearted banter these two had engaged in their whole lives. Marvelous children. *Thank You, Lord.*

Marit playfully elbowed Steig in the ribs. "Who's this you're holding? Sure doesn't look too happy."

"Jake, you remember your aunty Marit and your cousins, right?" He waved an arm toward the other kids who were already pulling out the outside toys.

"Hey, you guys. Come say hi to Jakey." Marit patted his leg, but he immediately hid his face in his father's neck. "Oops. Not a happy camper?"

"Not right now, woke from a nap to see the C-A-T." Steig rolled his eyes. "Fill you in later."

"Magnus called to say he'd meet us here, so we came on over." She looked at her mother and motioned to where her dad was unloading the SUV. "He okay?"

"Yes, I'm fine." Ken smiled as he answered. "I just decided I needed to be here greeting my family more than..."

"Duking it out with Dale?"

"Let's say, I did all I could for the moment."

"You gave up?"

"Not really. I'd rather term it as gaining wisdom." While Ken's smile was wide, somehow it didn't reach his eyes. "Grab some of that stuff; all this goes upstairs."

Marit looked at her mother, who shrugged. "You put it at the bottom of the stairs, and I'll get my steps in today going up and down." Mona glanced over at Jakey to see him watching her, thumb and forefinger in his mouth. But he hid again as soon as she smiled.

"Hey, Brit, would you please get the grocery bags out of the car?" Marit took two black plastic bags full and headed for the house. "The tossed salad is in the big green bowl. I can smell the spaghetti sauce from here."

Later, with the guys gone to return the trailer, including Jake, who had yet to leave the safe refuge called Dad, Marit and Mona finished carrying the last of the kids' belongings up to the bedroom to join the stack in front of the closet doors. "I thought military people traveled light." Marit dropped her bag.

"Usually the movers do all this." Mona leaned against the wall. "I was hoping both chests of drawers would fit in the closet, but that left no room for hanging anything up. Then I could set up shelves along that wall with baskets to hold toys and such."

"When things settle down, we can redo the closet and make it more efficient."

"Right."

"Come on, Mom, things won't always be this chaotic. It wasn't when we were kids."

"And chaos comes and goes at your house."

"True, but..."

"Mom!" Brit yelled from the bottom of the stairs. "Arne is bleeding."

Marit rolled her eyes and started for the door. "How bad?"

"He skinned his knee, but the blood is running down his leg."

"Where is he?"

"Outside."

"He can't walk?"

"He doesn't think so." Brit sounded like an exasperated big sister.

"Tell him to get in here so we can clean it up."

She ran for the door. "Mom said to get in here right now!"

"You could have waited until you got outside," Marit muttered as she turned toward the bathroom. While Marit got the first aid kit, Mona went on into the kitchen to see her sniffling grandson come limping in from the garage. "What happened?" She patted the stool and he climbed up. Handing him one tissue for his nose, she used another to mop up the blood trickling down into his sock. "What did you do?"

"Ambrose and me were chasing, and I fell over him on the gravel. He felt real bad. He tried licking the blood, but Brit pulled him away. He was trying to help." He sniffed again. "It hurts, Grammy."

"I know, and scrubbing that gravel out is going to hurt worse. But not for long. We have to get it clean. Maybe we should use a scrub brush on it."

His eyes saucered. "Really?"

"No, silly, Grammy's teasing." She turned to Marit, who plunked the plastic box of first aid supplies on the counter.

"I don't know, a brush sounds like a good idea to me."

She looked at the knee. "Let's get you up on the counter with your leg in the sink. Maybe the running water will be enough so that we can forget the brush."

"Mooooooom."

Marit looked at her mother. "Are they born saying mom that way or is it learned?" Scooping up her son, she set him on the counter, his leg straightened out over the double sink.

"Got me. But all kids seem to get it." Mona adjusted the water to cool and set it to run over his knee. "You really got a scrape all right." She looked down to see Ambrose staring up at her, as if pleading to make everything all right. "Look, Arne, he's so sorry."

"I know." He scrunched up his face. "Ow! Mom!" A tear leaked out of his clenched eyes.

"Hang in there. I need to make sure this is clean." She turned off the water and wiped the knee off with a gauze pad. "You got a flashlight, Mom?"

Mona pulled it out of the drawer, flipping on the light over the sink at the same time. She held the beam right on his knee. "Looks good to me."

"Bleeding like that helps." After drying off her son's knee, she applied salve and a big square bandage. "That's big enough we could draw a face on it."

"Yeah, do it." Arne leaned forward.

Mona pulled a Sharpie out of the kitchen junk drawer and drew a smiley face on the tan plastic. "There you go."

He swung his legs out over the edge and slid to the floor. "Come on, Ambrose." Swiping a cookie off the tray, he grinned at his mother. "Thanks, Grammy, Mom." Stuffing the chocolate chip cookie in his mouth so the others wouldn't see it, he slammed out the screen door.

"Don't slam the door."

Arne peeked around the edge of the door he opened again. "Sorry." This time he very carefully closed the door so it barely snicked.

Marit cleaned up the mess, all the while shaking her head. "Kids."

If supper that night was a portent of things to come, life ahead wouldn't by the slightest stretch of imagination be peaceful. Five kids, only one of whom was not talking, five adults, only one of whom was not laughing. Or shushing. Or practicing the rolling of eyes.

Mona enjoyed the chaos in a way—so much life, so much vibrancy. But a nagging thought forced itself into the back of her mind: *What will this do to your tendency to depression? It's going to weigh on you, this constant churning. You won't be able to just walk away from it. Can your nerves handle it?* Maybe not.

When the majority was finished eating, only Torin being a slow eater, Marit pushed back her chair and raised her arms. "Okay, enough! We will now have thirty seconds of silence." Someone snickered, someone else snorted back, and laughter burst all around the table. Even Jakey smiled, almost.

"So much for order." Magnus had become an expert eye roller since he met Marit.

Mona leaned back in her chair. "Can I get anybody anything?"

"Ice cream?"

Arne's request spread through the ranks to become an instant chant.

Steig adopted his military voice. "No ice cream until the table is cleared and food put away." He turned to his mother. "There is ice cream, isn't there? Otherwise we'll have to go find some."

"Is this house ever without ice cream?" Mona smiled at her son, who at times could be the biggest kid of all. Or at least he used to be. Had he lost his exuberant youth in the last year?

"And cookies." Torin was the quiet one of the bunch, at least so far, but at four he could still do a lot of changing.

Steig stood, Jake still on his arm. "Okay, kids clear the table, dishes in the sink for Grampy to rinse and put in the dishwasher. Moms put the food away, Magnus and Steig go for a walk."

An instant of silence, and laughter broke out again. "Not fair."

Steig looked at Magnus. "Sounded like a good idea to me."

"The dads dish up the ice cream after you heat the hot fudge sauce. And you can't do that until we have counter space, so..." Mona wiggled her eyebrows at her husband. "Oh and Magnus, please get the ice cream out of the outside freezer so it can soften a bit."

Ken stood with a groan. "Come on, kiddo." He prodded Brit on his right. "Now!"

Brit picked up her plate and silverware.

By the time they were ready to dish the ice cream, only one glass had spilled and one plate with food hit the floor. Ambrose leaped to take care of that before Marit could get through the congestion to pick it up.

"Okay, we are eating ice cream either outside or on the porch, take your pick." Marit held her ice cream scoop like a baton.

Arne, first in line, piped up. "Outside."

Ken pleaded, "Porch."

"Okay, kids outside, adults in the porch room." She and Mona dug into the ice cream, and Ken manned the hot fudge dispensing.

Seated in comfort on the three-season porch, Mona looked at her son, whose shadow had decided to go outside with his sister, Mellie, taking care of him. Steig relaxed into his papasan chair. "Thanks, Mom, Marit, for such a fine meal. Been a while since we had all the fixings."

"One-dish meals?" Mona asked.

"Yeah, or takeout. Thank God for their sitter, who cooks for us at times."

"Being a single parent must be the pits."

"On one hand, but there is no more dissension. That's worth some nonhealthy meals, not that Angela liked to cook much."

"You are sure she cannot come after the kids?" Marit asked.

"She can try, but legally she signed herself out. My army lawyer made certain it's airtight. She doesn't want them; she made that clear, and that creep of hers made sure of that. She had the choice of him or us, and she chose him."

"The kids seem content."

"Mellie never mentions her out loud, and poor little Jakey reverted to babyhood, like needing diapers at night again." He turned to his mother. "There are night pads in one of the bags so the bed stays dry. The counselor said this was normal; he'd grow out of it soon."

"So you've been working with a counselor?" Ken set his bowl on the coffee table.

"My chaplain. He's become a good friend and, of course, understands the military. He says to tell you hello and thank you for agreeing to take the kids. I knew I was facing deployment again, but I figured down the road, and if we were all settled up here, the transition wouldn't be as rough." He raised and dropped his hands. "World affairs don't cater to families, that's for sure."

"Have you thought of leaving the military?"

"I plan on going the whole route. I love what I do and I'm good at it. And basically, the military has been good to me."

Just your wife that wasn't. Mona and Ken exchanged one of their glances. She knew he felt the same way she did. How to keep from hating a woman who would walk off and leave her kids was taking more than she thought it would. God help them if that woman tried to get back into their lives.

"Sometimes forgiveness is an ongoing sacrifice, but I am too aware of how not doing so can destroy your life. I saw it in action."

"Meaning Angela?" Marit asked.

Steig nodded. "That's one of the things Roy has been hammering into my head."

"Roy." Mona frowned.

"My chaplain. He doesn't like honorifics like pastor or reverend because not all faiths use them. And he has to serve everybody. He says, 'Do not let bitterness take root, and not forgiving leads right into bitterness.'" He glanced sideways at his mother. "She hurt my kids."

"Physically?" Ken asked.

"No, emotionally. Far worse."

Mona heard the door to the garage open and Ambrose's nails ticking on the tile. "They're coming in."

"Mom?" Brit called. "Torin's all wet."

Marit rolled her eyes. "They're probably all wet."

Jakey clung to Mellie's hand. "Daddy, I got wet."

"What happened?"

"I was filling Ambrose's water bucket and the hose..."

"Leaped out of your hand and splashed everyone?" Marit stood. "Come on, Magnus, let's take these three home."

Jakey whined, "I didn't mean to."

"Right. Is the hose still running?" Magnus asked.

"I turned it off." Arne grinned at his dad, as if he'd saved the day.

Mellie handed her little brother to their father. "He likes the dog now."

Ambrose shook, splattering water everywhere.

The kids shrieked, the adults laughed, and Steig bent down to pick up his now smiling son.

"I need to warn you, this guy is a water baby, never happier than when he is soaking wet. Mud pies are his specialty." He poked Jake in the belly. "You like mud, huh?"

Jake nodded. "I am wet."

"On that note…" Magnus motioned his family toward the garage door and out to the cars parked in the driveway.

"See you tomorrow." Marit grabbed her purse and the bag with her now clean bowl. "If you need me, call."

"We'll be working on all the paperwork in the morning."

"You want me to come pick up the kids?"

"I'll call you if need be. I hate…" Steig scrubbed the back of his neck with one hand and sighed. "Time is so short."

Mona knew he meant his time with his children. "I know. But the official retirement hoopla this Friday won't last too long. The banquet starts at seven, but we have to be there for the cocktail party before. There's a table reserved for our family even though Ken has to be at the head table. I thought we could drop the kids off at your house earlier. Let them settle in."

"Brit thinks she is old enough to attend Grampy's party."

Ken chuckled. "I wish she could. I wish they all could. Well, what I really wish is that none of us have to go."

"You got your tux?" Marit arched her brows.

"Yes."

Mona smiled at her daughter with a slight nod. They all knew how Ken despised formal anything. She patted her husband's arm. "You look really handsome all dressed up."

"I look like an emperor penguin. Feel about as stiff as one."

"Come on, kids, out." Magnus herded them out the door.

They waved them off outside the garage and returned to the house, Jake back in his father's arms. "I'll get them down, and then we can at least start." He headed for the stairs. "Come on, rug rats. Bedtime." He poked Jakey. "Get you dry."

"Bath?"

"Not tonight. Looks like you already had one."

Mona watched them go upstairs. Too soon putting kids to bed would be the grandparents' job. She should go up, too, so she learned the secrets that would make this easier. *Tomorrow. We'll do that tomorrow night.* No, Saturday night. Two nights to get all the details down. The thought of Steig actually leaving hit her in the solar plexus, nearly dropping her to her knees. How would they manage?

Chapter Ten

Dear God, how will we manage without him?

D
ear Ken stared at his son, who was pointing out something on the stack of paperwork in answer to Mona's
question. Deployed again. They had thought his last tour
in Afghanistan would be his last overseas tour ever. Ken
grabbed his mind back from wandering to pay attention to
this process that was changing all their lives.

A friend from church had reminded him that God was
giving them a chance to make a real difference in the
lives of their grandchildren and their son, too. While his
head knew that, his mind did not really understand and his
heart wanted to scream, *Stop, you can't do this, we can't
do this...Lean not unto your own understanding.* He'd
been leaning on that verse a lot lately.

Marit, bless her heart, had come and taken the kids
back to her house, so quiet reigned in this one. Only on
day two and he'd already realized quiet went into hiding
when the kids woke up. So much for sleeping in as part of
the beginning of his retirement. He'd not planned on that
for every day, but some healing time right now would be
in good order.

"Okay, Dad, your turn." Steig pushed the file of papers

over to him. "Sign all the places Mom did. Those green flags help."

"I feel like we're signing our life away." He looked up at his son. "I know this is not forever, but..."

"Yeah, the *but* does us all in. I wish there were some other way, but short of bailing on the army right now, this seems to be it."

"I know. Life doesn't always go the way we want. Or plan." *Or dream.* Ken signed the first page and flipped on through. Why was it he seemed more concerned about problems with Angela rather than Steig in a land of flying bullets and exploding shells and bombs? Not that he'd voiced either. Steig had no other answers, nor did Mona.

"Iced tea anyone?" Mona pushed her chair back from the kitchen table.

"I'll take coffee if it's made," Steig said.

"Ken?"

"Iced tea." At least the stack was diminishing. "We have to get all this notarized?"

"Yes, so we all need to go." Steig checked his watch. "What time do you need to be all gigged out and at the college?"

"Five. For the cocktail party." He rolled his eyes. If he had his way, he'd leave for the North Shore tonight. "I need to be at a staff lunch at twelve thirty."

"Then we better hustle. I'll explain the medical stuff later."

They took two cars so Ken could drive to Madison for the celebratory lunch. "Like I want to do this," he muttered as he backed into the turnaround.

"Just get through it is my motto for the day." Mona leaned her head against the seat. "One step at a time." She reached over and patted his thigh. "Try to enjoy all the festivities. After all, they are honoring you and all your years of helping thousands of students get into and out of college with degrees in hand and a better future. Ken, you have made such a difference in so many lives. Keep that in mind rather than all this garbage of the last week."

"I'm trying."

"I know you are. It'll all work out."

He flashed her the best smile he could generate at the moment. It wasn't much.

Ken was surprised that notarization did not take long. The bank manager, Emma, laid out all the papers on a long table behind the bank counter and mass notarized them, pointing to where their signatures went and using a stamp instead of the old embosser Ken remembered. She recorded them by hand in a logbook. Done.

As they left the notary, Steig said, "I promised the kids we'd go up to the park this afternoon, so I'll drop you off at home, Mom." He gave his father a surprise hug. "You're going to do fine tonight."

Ken hugged his son back. "I'd rather be fishing."

Steig grinned. "I know. I'm just glad the rest of us are not required to wear a monkey suit to this gig tonight."

"No worse than a full-dress uniform."

"True." Steig smirked. "Not! You don't look like a penguin in class As."

Perhaps all the mayhem of getting ready kept him from worrying about the evening, but once he and Mona were in the car driving north, he felt like he was halfway through a marathon, not that he had ever been a marathon runner, but he'd talked with a lot who were. Soon he would be in the homestretch.

Put the last week behind you, he ordered himself as they entered the VIP party. *Sufficient unto the day is the evil thereof.* Tonight he would celebrate. He patted Mona's hand on his arm and squeezed it against his side.

"We'll get through," she whispered. "I'm praying for you."

He smiled. "You know me all too well. These people think this is the end. But thanks to that injunction, I'll be back at it Monday, the last hurrah."

"Slaying dragons?"

"Perhaps. There are some dragons out there just begging to be slain."

Other than wanting to wipe his hand on his pant leg after shaking John's and Dale's, he still had his smile in place by the time the crowd began to thin. Wallaver in physics left early; he always left early, but at least he showed up. There was Merril Stark from geology. He had to be nearing retirement. Smartest man in Wisconsin and deaf as a post. Harlan Norlun, professor of linguistics, was surely close to retirement, too. He stood in the corner with a cocktail in his hand, schmoozing a woman. Some people never change.

Ken's eyes got hot after a few comments, and he realized he would indeed miss some of these people—Harlan, Merril, Chet, Jonah. People he worked with, tussled with, helped out over the years. Thirty years was a long time of friend building. Not that he'd never see them again, but everyone knew it would not be the same.

"We should have worn our bunads," Mona said as they followed the crowd from the cocktail party to the banquet room for dinner.

He chuckled. "Yes, that would have been fun. But warm as it is tonight..."

"Your bunad would not have been hotter than a tux."

"But yours would have, all those petticoats and the heavy woolen waistcoat."

They had both purchased their Norwegian bunads when they visited Norway ten years earlier, went whole hog, and got the especially fancy festival outfits. Each different area of Norway had its own color and design of festal wear. Of course, Ken had carefully worked out exactly where his branch of the Sorensons came from, so that they might have properly authentic bunads.

The truth be told, in the beginning he had fought the idea of getting one, but Mona insisted, and she had been right, as usual. Since Stoughton had such a plethora of Norwegian celebrations, they wore them much more than he had thought they would. As active as they were in the Sons of Norway lodge and on the various boards for celebrations, Mona had sewn simplified bunads for Marit and Steig when they were growing up, and now she was outfitting the grandchildren as well.

"We need to get a picture of our whole family in bunads." She didn't add *before Steig leaves*, but the phrase was glaringly there. It ended so many things said these last few days.

He pulled into valet parking, and the young man gave Mona a hand out of the car.

"Congratulations, Mr. Sorenson, I hope you have a grand evening." The young man paused. "Thank you again for helping me get through that freshman year." Most of those on the valet parking staffs throughout the area were university students earning pocket money.

"You are welcome, Jeb." Good thing the lad was wearing a name tag. While Ken recognized the face, names were not so easy. "Keep up the good work." Ken held his arm out for Mona.

"See, I told you," she whispered as they traversed the walk to the entrance.

A threefold collage with pictures of his years at the school greeted them when they entered, with Sandy on hand inviting people to sign the guest register. "Looks like it's going to be standing room only," she said with a wide smile.

Ken nodded toward the collage. "You did that?"

"Well, a lot of us worked together. I got as many students and former students in on it as I could. You'd be surprised how many of them couldn't come because they're in the field collecting data for their doctoral dissertations. No, I guess you wouldn't be surprised."

A curved-top wooden chest on the table in front of the collage said CARDS.

Ken smiled and gently ran his fingers across the lid. Smooth, perfectly shaped. "Who made the chest?"

"Head of the art department—what's his name, Brian Vigness," Sandy replied. "He's a woodworker, too, you know. I know you always dreamed of taking up woodworking when you retired. Old Mrs. Lund from home ec did the rosemaling. She's in a nursing home now, but she insisted she was going to do this for you. And she's obviously still the best there is. We wanted something that would last for you and have meaning."

"It certainly does." Ken turned to Mona. "Did you know about this?"

"The collage, but not the chest. That is really beautiful."

"Enjoy your evening, sir," Sandy said as she greeted another couple. Her grin took any sarcasm out of the *sir*.

A six-piece string ensemble played light classical music. A few were seated already, and the room was rapidly filling. He heard someone mention they would open the

doors to the extensions when the program began, as there
had been too many requests for dinner tickets to fill them
all. Someone was beckoning him toward the front, but
everyone wanted to shake his hand and share some memory, so it took a while. He left Mona at the family table
right in front of the head table, stepped up onto a low
dais, and slowly made his way around to the step. When
he looked back, Steig, Marit, and Magnus had joined some
friends with Mona.

President Osler greeted him with a three-hand shake.
"Well deserved, my friend, well deserved. You'd think we
had a rock star here." Marian Osler, the president of Stone
University, was graying, but she moved smoothly, athlet-
ically, like a thirty-year-old. And her handshake was firm
and no-nonsense.

"Hardly. But I'll tell you, this blows me out of the
water." They looked out over the gathering.

"All the years you've invested are showing you the pay-
off. Not everyone gets to see something like this in their
lifetime."

Bill Pepper, the master of ceremonies for the evening,
stepped to the microphone. "If you could please take your
seats." Amid laughter and many comments, folks did as
asked.

Ken looked down to see Mona give him an okay signal
with a wide smile.

"Welcome, everyone, as we gather to honor our retiring
dean of students, Ken Sorenson." Applause made him
stop momentarily, then continue. "Pastor Oliver, will you
please lead us in a blessing?"

"As the pastor of Celebration Lutheran Church, where
Ken and his family have attended all the years they have
lived in Stoughton, I am honored to be with you all

tonight. However, my wife made me promise to not do a sermon, so let us pray. Lord God, we come to you tonight in honor of a man who has served this university faithfully all these years. Thank you for the many lives he has blessed and therefore made richer because of his caring. We ask your continued blessings on him and his family as they step into the next stage of their lives. Bless this food and this evening and all those gathered here to celebrate. We pray in Christ's holy name, amen."

The conversation level in the room rose as the waitstaff brought beverages around and everyone started with their rolls and salads.

While the food was served, the chorale sang several songs and a young man made the grand piano sing and dance before the ensemble continued with music of Ken's college years. His college years! This had to be Sandy's doing; she so often kidded him about the music back in his college days. He still remembered one exchange vividly: Sandy said, "Ken, your music was deep; they sure don't write lyrics these days like they did then. I mean, just think: 'Peanut, peanut butter. Peanut, peanut butter. I love peanut butter, creamy peanut butter, crunchy peanut butter, too.' Doesn't that just resonate?" And his response was, "Sandy, that song was way before my time, okay?"

Why did they not have Sandy up here at the head table with him? She ran the department and made him look good. She was as much a part of his world as the computer on his desk.

You couldn't fault the celebratory meal—prime rib with baby red potatoes. And ice cream for dessert; that was *so* Sorenson. Was the menu Sandy's doing as well?

At the close of dinner, they opened the doors to the extensions while the tables were cleared. The drama department presented a spoof skit on Ken's dealing with a distressed student, which caused waves of laughter as the young man playing Ken hammed it up.

The MC introduced several speakers who had won the right to speak, always reminding them they had five minutes to share something about Ken Sorenson. Ken smiled through pain; this was just plain embarrassing. He remembered well the girl speaking on behalf of the students his department had helped. She had been quite a pill when she arrived, belligerent and impatient. Now look at her, a school administrator who had just won an award for excellence.

Finally the president was introduced and she stepped up to the mic. "Tonight we honor Ken Sorenson's years of serving our university. It was still a college when he began his career here, teaching sociology, then moving into the dean's chair. In that job, he molded the department into a true service for students. Anyone who came to him received whatever help needed, in ways beyond the typical of advice or financial aid, and often a shoulder to cry on. Ken finds solutions, he thinks outside the box, and he dreams big for his students and this university. Whoever becomes our new dean has a mighty big pair of shoes to fill."

She went on to tell a couple of stories that happened through the years, one of them bringing laughter, the other near tears. "So, tonight we honor Ken, all the while knowing we cannot say thank you enough." She nodded and two men carried the trunk up on the stage, its rosemaling bright in the overhead spots. "Since no one on the board could see any value in a gold watch, we searched for something memorable and in keeping with Ken's life. I heard tell he wants to learn the woodworking craft, so we

filled the trunk with appropriate tools to get him started."
She motioned Ken to join her. "Accept our gratitude, and
I pray you not only enjoy your well-earned retirement, but
you can continue to make a difference as you go through
life." She hugged him as he stepped up to the lectern, and
together they opened the trunk.

Ken wagged his head. "I have no words. What an original gift." He raised a small sander and set of chisels in
the air for all to see. "Thank you. I will truly enjoy using
these." He glanced at a note in the chest. "And I see here
that Dr. Vigness has already agreed I can have private
lessons until the next class session starts."

"I hope you have a few words to share." President Osler
handed Ken the microphone, stepped back, and sat down.

"Only a few?" They laughed together, and Ken stepped
back to the podium. He looked around the room, nodding
and smiling as if he spoke to an audience of this size every
day. The applause finally settled down.

"Thank you for coming tonight, for all your comments,
for your contributions both tonight and to this university.
Stone University is a forerunner in many departments,
and yes, we set the standard for student services. If someone wants to come here badly enough, we will make a way.
One program I am especially proud of is for our returning vets. Most government programs are usually with the
state schools, but you will find many veterans attending
here, some of them with horrendous injuries that we do
our best to help accommodate. We are privileged to work
closely with the University of Wisconsin, and while we are
not an affiliate of Norwegian colleges and businesses, we
work closely with them, too. All that to say that we serve
students of all ages, all backgrounds, and many ethnicities.
I believe God has blessed us mightily because we are will-

ing to go the extra mile, share our cloak, if you will." He paused and looked down at his family and then around the room. "I am honored to be a part of a university so alive and growing..." He took in a deep breath. "And I pray that growth in serving continues."

Applause broke out, and table after table of guests rose to their feet.

"Thank you." He raised his hands. "Thank you." He smiled around the room again, this time praying he could hold in the tears burning the backs of his eyes. As the audience sat down, he continued. "Thank you. Thank you. I promise I won't do a list of those I'm in debt to, but my family is here, and above all I thank my wife, Mona, and both Marit and Steig, who are graduates of this university." This time he had to blink several times, and when they sat down again, he said, "In closing, I want to repeat the words of one of the greatest scholars of all time, Sir Isaac Newton. 'If I have seen further, it is by standing on the shoulders of giants.' May each of us be giants to pass the torch along. And now, may the Lord God bless us all and continue to shower us with His favor. Thank you."

Bill finally got the crowd to sit down again. "Thank you, Ken. We will miss you here." He looked at the audience. "Thank you for coming, and if you'll let Ken and Mona through, they have asked for the privilege of standing at the door. Good night."

Chairs clanked and rattled and skidded, putting up an amazingly cacophonous roar for being mere chairs. Ken stepped down off the dais, took Mona's hand, and the two made their way to the door.

"You were phenomenal," she told him at the doorway. "I am so proud of you I could pop every button I own. You are an amazing man." They turned to greet those lining up. It took over an hour, but Ken managed to say good-bye to nearly everyone there. The sheer number of people astounded him.

When President Osler and her husband shook hands with him, she leaned close to Ken. "Come back to the Holmdahl Room a moment, will you?"

Now what?

Mona smiled. "I'll wait for you here."

"You can come with me. You are my life." He kissed her forehead.

The cleanup crew were pushing brooms, gathering up tablecloths into a big canvas bin, and reconfiguring chairs for the next day's events. Ken led Mona through and around and among the busy scene.

No one was in the Holmdahl Room when they entered, but President Osler arrived moments later. She was smiling. "Your children put your chest in the car for you. And while you were shaking those thousands of hands, I had a chance to talk to Steig and Marit a few minutes. You realize, the only time I ever talked to them before tonight was when I shook their hands and handed them their diplomas."

Ken chuckled. "That's been a few years."

"Hasn't it!" She sobered. "I had several callers a few days ago. Dale Crespin and John Nordlund."

So that's where this was going. Ken nodded. "And they complained bitterly that I had filed an injunction."

"Can you tell me why you did so?"

"Yes. To counter their sneaky moves with a sneaky move. They support a candidate to replace me that I do not support. They tried to sidestep me and weasel out of a letter of intent giving me the say in who will replace me."

"Office politics at its finest."

"Office politics, but I would certainly not call it finest. I doubt they remember the full content of their letter of intent in which they made the written promise, but I'm using it for my legal basis in opposing their move. Unfortunately, I am now emeritus, before the decision was made. This injunction puts the whole process on hold, giving me time to fully review applicants."

She nodded, pausing a moment. "Fiendishly clever. Who would you say is best qualified to hold the position?"

"My office assistant, Sandra Jensen. But she won't accept it."

She nodded again and studied the floor a moment. Then she looked him in the eye. "Ken, frankly I didn't like Dale and John trying to make an end run on the sly, you might say. Politicking privately. That's why I wanted to hear your side of that injunction business before making any decisions."

"If you don't like end runs, you don't like my move."

"Oh, but I do now that I know the reason." She turned to Mona. "Mrs. Sorenson, when I ask your husband something, I know that he will give me a straight and honest answer. That's a rare commodity these days. Ken? Your answer satisfies me. I have made up my mind."

"About...?"

"Your successor."

Ken licked his lips. Where should he go from here? "Do I know the person?"

"You do, very well. Sandra Jensen."

"Sandy... But... but she said... *Sandy?*"

"You put student services on its feet and made it the best. She can keep it there." She cleared her throat. "Normally, I leave it to the board. You may not even have known—or thought—that as president I have the authority to preempt the board. Dale and John knew and tried to get me to use it, completely sidestepping you. So I did, but not as they intended."

Ken was so flabbergasted he felt dizzy. This whole day was...was...was surreal. "Dr. Osler, that is the best, the finest thing you could possibly do to keep this school in top tier, with a first-class faculty and first-class student body. Each depends on the other. I...thank you. And I am grateful for your wisdom and farsightedness." He pressed his lips together. "Dale and John won't like this. Their candidate, I'm sure you know, is Damien Berghoff."

"Yes, they extolled him in the highest terms. In fact, they were so complimentary of him that I grew suspicious. The 'Methinks he doth protest too much' thing. I have not made the decision public yet; I hope you'll keep it to yourself."

"Of course. Does Sandy know?"

"I told her this evening. She promised silence as well."

Ken drew in enough air to loft the Hindenburg. The sudden release of pressure had unhorsed him. "Dr. Osler, you've greatly eased my mind at a time when many other things are weighing on it. Thank you."

"So I hear. Your son is a single parent being deployed overseas. Heavy for you in many ways. I will be praying for Steig's safety and your grandparenting adventures."

"Adventures. Dr. Osler..." Mona suddenly moved forward and embraced the president of the university in a massive bear hug. "Thank you! I cannot begin to tell you how much this all means to us."

The president was smiling broadly. "Go in peace, both of you."

Ken turned Mona aside, and they walked out into…
rain. And from the size of the puddles, it had been raining
awhile.

Headlights approached. Ken's car pulled up in front of
them, Steig driving.

Sandy stepped out of the shadows from behind them
with a big plastic bag. "Your well-wishes cards. If I were
you, I'd put those cards in a safe place until you have time
to go through them. Don't question, just trust me."

"If you say. Sandy…Sandy, I thought you refused to
take the job. I am absolutely stunned that you accepted,
and so very, very glad. But why did you?"

"When I learned you were putting your own money
into legal steps, I began to see how very much this means
to you and how important it all is." She cackled. "You
know that headhunter you hired to find your perfect replacement? Archer Tarkensen? He claimed I'm the best
candidate; he's the one who finally talked me into it."

Chapter Eleven

"I'm sorry." Through the kitchen window, Mona watched rain and wind whip the treetops. "The weather is worse this morning than it was last night."

Ken nodded. "I know. Bucking waves on the lake is not conducive to fishing enjoyment, nor is getting soaked."

"Maybe tomorrow?" Steig held his coffee mug with both hands.

Ken shrugged. "According to the weather map, it is supposed to move on about noon. Maybe we can go this afternoon."

Mona caught Steig's raised eyebrows and shrugged. She had already talked with Marit and the party was officially moved to the Sons of Norway hall. Magnus and crew were ready to move the grills to the covered area outside. If they could pull this off, it would indeed be miraculous. Good thing they'd not planned on using Ken's grill.

But now what could she do with Ken since they couldn't go fishing? That had been the perfect cover. Options: Give up and tell him of the party. Put a sleeping pill in his coffee so he slept the morning away. She couldn't think of a third option.

"Daddy?"

Morning quiet just flew out the door.

Steig turned. "Good morning, sweetheart. Is Jakey still sleeping?" He bent down and lifted her to join him and Grampy watching the rain sluice out the downspouts.

"I was real quiet." She wrapped one arm around his neck. "Can't go fishing, huh?"

"Maybe tomorrow."

"Or perhaps this evening. Fish bite in the evening, too." Grampy smiled at her. "You ready for breakfast?"

She shrugged. "Is Grammy making pancakes?"

"How did you ever guess?" Mona crossed the room and turned the griddle on. "You want chocolate chips in yours?"

Steig shuddered. "Not mine, that's for sure." He poked his daughter in the belly. "But you do, right?" She giggled and nodded at the same time.

Mona turned the hash browns in one skillet and checked the bacon in the oven. "Five minutes. Someone want to set the table?"

Ken turned to the cabinet. "Juice?"

"Of course." This morning she was serving all Steig's favorite things. One more day after today. How would they bear to see him off when the van stopped at their door to take him to the base? They'd said five a.m. Monday morning. She jerked her mind back to the smoking griddle and poured the batter for six pancakes, then sprinkled miniature chocolate chips on one. After turning off the kettle of hot water warming the syrup, she turned with a smile; at least she hoped it was in place. "Two minutes, you better get to the table." After dishing the hash browns into a bowl, she handed Ken that and the bacon platter to set on the table. Flipping the pancakes as soon as they were popping bubbles, she grabbed another platter.

The others took their places at the table just as "Daddy!" echoed down the stairs.

"I sure hope the cat didn't go in there. Mellie, did you close the door?"

"Yes. He has to get over this. Hyacinth won't hurt him. Besides, I want her to sleep with me."

"You sound all grown up. Don't get in a hurry, okay?" Steig hugged her with both arms.

Mona slid the pancakes onto the platter while Steig headed for the stairs.

"I think today and tomorrow we better do cat conditioning." Ken took the platter. "Looks like only one has brown dots."

"That's mine." Mellie held up her plate. "How come you don't like choco-pancakes?"

"Ah." Ken shrugged. "Just don't, I guess. But Grammy made it for you." He took two and put the remainders on Steig's plate. "You want hash browns, sugarcheeks?"

"Sugarcheeks!" Mellie grinned.

"And bacon?" At her nod, he scooped both onto her plate. "Eggs, too?"

"No thank you."

Steig sat down in his chair with tousle-headed Jakey, thumb and forefinger plugging his mouth, on his lap. "Looks great, Mom." He dropped a kiss on his son's head. "You can have part of Daddy's."

Jakey shook his head and turned his face into Steig's broad chest.

Mona stepped to the table with another platter, this time eggs fried, cooked medium splattered just the way her family liked them. She slid two on Steig's plate and two on Ken's. "More pancakes ready in a minute. Jakey, you want pancakes?" She got another headshake for her trouble.

After breakfast, the adults spent a good part of the morning finishing off their discussion with Steig while the kids watched TV.

"Now, if something happens and I don't come back..." Steig held up a hand as Mona sniffed. "I know, but we have to be prepared." He pulled more papers out of a file folder. "Here is my will; the kids are the beneficiaries with you two as guardians, and Dad, you are the executor, as we discussed. All this is on file with the army. I talked with Marit and Magnus, and they agreed to become guardians if something happens to the two of you. As you see here"—he pointed to a green flag—"I staggered the benefits for the kids so they don't receive a huge chunk of money on their twenty-first birthdays. Their educations will be pretty much paid for, especially with army benefits."

Mona tried to listen carefully, but her mind fought to run off with concerns about the surprise party and pleas that none of this was necessary. Steig would return in a year or less, and their lives would revert to the retirement Ken dreamed of. They'd not had time to go through the cards yet, but that box was stashed upstairs in their closet.

Marit's song chimed. Mona thumbed her phone on and put it to her ear as she turned pancakes. Marit's strong voice: "I know Dad is right there so just listen. All is in order for the party. Don't worry about a thing, we have a marvelous crew. We even have entertainment for children of all sizes, although I don't expect a lot more to attend than ours. Now, Magnus is going to call Dad and ask for his help on buying something for the garage and no one else can come with. You and Steig get to the hall, and we'll be there already. Got it?"

Mona nodded. "Sounds good to me. Yes. Put me on the

list, please. Thank you for calling." She heard Marit giggle as they clicked off.

Steig glanced at her to catch her slight nod. "Any questions or other things you can think of?" He lifted a manila envelope. "The medical cards and records are in here, including vaccination records. This one has Mellie's school records. As you can see, I have all of this in this file box; some of it needs to go into your safety box or open another in their name. We set up the bank account yesterday, so that is all taken care of. My checks will go directly into that account, usually on about the fifth of the month. With the online banking, I can keep track, too. I'll have my laptop with me, and I told Mellie we would Skype every Thursday night."

Ken thought. "Will that work with the time difference?"

"I'll make it work."

Ken's phone sounded like a duck quacking. "Hey, Magnus, what's up? Sure, since we couldn't go fishing, we can do that. Okay, I'll be waiting, but I could meet you there. All right, see you." He looked at Mona. "Magnus wants some advice at Home Depot. He'll be here in a couple of minutes. You need anything there?"

"You might want to pick up another set of those garage shelves," Steig suggested.

"Okay, Mona?"

"Yes, we can use them if we can find someplace to put them. Nothing else that I can think of." She started gathering the files off the table. "I'll call you if so. Hand me that file box, please, Steig." *Keep it cool, nothing to indicate we need to get ready and out that door in about fifteen minutes.* As soon as Ken left, she roared into action. "You look fine, I have to change, Magnus is stalling, then will take Ken to the party. The kids need different clothes on."

She grinned at her son. "So far so good—I hope. I so want to pull off a surprise."

"If he's had an inkling, he's not mentioned it to me." He headed for the family room. "Come on, you two, we need to dress for Grampy's party."

They all flew around and were out the door in twenty-one minutes and on their way.

The parking lot of the hall had only a couple of cars since they'd asked everyone to park on the side streets. Steig dropped her and the kids off at the door and drove to park.

"Daddy!" Jakey started to tear up, but Mellie held his hand. "Daddy had to go park. He'll be right back. Come on, this is Grampy's party."

"Where is Grampy?"

"He'll be here soon." Mona checked her watch. "Come on, we have to go hide."

Ken followed Magnus out of Home Depot. Together they loaded the cartons and two-by-fours into Magnus's pickup.

"Sure appreciate your help. Someday I'll know enough." Magnus smiled at Ken.

"Took me a while, too. I'll help you install it anytime you want. You want to come in for coffee?" He slid into the passenger seat beside Magnus.

Magnus checked his list. "Oh no, I forgot to pick up Marit's extra pots at the Sons of Norway hall. She loaned them for some ladies' do. Then I think she has lunch ready for everyone." He squinted at his paper. "At least I think that's what this says. I'll swing by and get the pots right now since we're closer to there. You in a hurry?"

"Nope, I am officially retired and I don't have to hurry anymore."

"Good luck." Magnus parked right near the front door. "You want to come help me find them? Last time I had to tear the kitchen apart. I sure don't know my way around in there."

"Sure, why not." Ken studied the exterior of the hall, the fake pillars that marked the entry. "You know, this old building could do with a paint job. Look. Flaking. I'll have to write out a recommendation for the board." The two men walked up the three steps, and Magnus swung the door open for Ken and stepped aside. *Age before beauty, as they say.* Ken went in.

"SURPRISE!" over fifty voices hollered at once.

Ken grabbed the doorframe, hand to his chest. "Wh-what in the world?" He searched for Mona, shaking his head all the while. There she was, grinning like a mule chewing thistles.

She came over and grabbed him around the waist. "Surprise!"

"How did you ever pull this off?"

"Either you really are surprised or you are an Oscar quality actor."

Marit joined them.

Mellie ran up and grabbed his hand. "Are you surprised, Grampy?"

"Yes, I am surprised. Addled. Shocked."

"Good." Mona took his hand. "Come this way." They pushed open the doors to the main hall now full of decorated tables; a banner that said HAPPY RETIREMENT, KEN stretched across the front of the room.

"Okay, chefs, back to the grills." With that, some of the men clapped Ken on the back as they hastened out.

"No wonder I smelled barbecue when I got out of the car."

"They put the ribs on a while ago."

"As if last night wasn't a huge celebration." He looked around, seeing some folks who'd attended the retirement dinner and lots of others from church, the Sons of Norway lodge, neighbors and friends, along with the relatives within driving distance. He stared at Mona again. "This is the first time you ever pulled one off. How did you do it? I had no idea."

"That's the best thing you could say to me." Mona's face nearly split grinning. "I've tried ever since I met you to surprise you with something and I never could." She heaved a big sigh and spread her arms wide. "But we did it, all of us together." Someone started applause, and it ricocheted around the walls. "And now, you go greet your guests, and we'll get this dinner ready to serve. Party on!"

By the time they returned home late that afternoon, they all collapsed around the seats on the porch. Steig kept his sleeping son on his lap and his daughter tucked into his side. "That was one amazing party." He grinned at his dad. "This town does indeed know how to throw a celebration."

Ken looked at Mona. "Please tell me we are done partying, at least for this weekend."

"We are done." Mona did not open her eyes, her body sunk deep into her kicked-back recliner. "Needless to say, I am done in."

"Why should you be any different than the rest of us?" Marit asked from a padded lounge chair, her arms dragging on the floor. "Please, Dad, don't go retire anymore, at least not for a while."

He smiled. "I have nothing else to retire from. It is all retire to now."

"Now that is a great line." Mona looked at her husband in the neighboring chair. "Retiring to?"

"Yep, I heard someone say that people who retire from don't live long, but people who retire to have a full life ahead. Figured it made a whole lot of sense." He heaved a sigh, looking at Mona. "How you pulled that surprise party off is way beyond me. Maybe I've been so involved on the job these last two weeks, I missed any signs."

"Give it up, Dad, there were no signs." Marit waved a triumphant thumbs-up at her mother.

Ken looked at his son-in-law. "You were in on it, too?"

"Of course. But we will be doing that remodel on the mudroom. I promised before winter. One of the things you are retired to."

Mellie straightened up from her father's side. "Grammy, I'm hungry."

"Didn't you eat at the party?"

She nodded solemnly. "But that was hours ago."

"Spoken like a true Sorenson." Steig grinned at his mother.

"You know what would have made these two days absolutely perfect?" Ken looked up at the ceiling.

"This wasn't perfect?" Mona's voice squeaked, her eyes wide.

"If Mom and Dad had been here to celebrate, too."

"True, but I think a big celebration was going on in Heaven, too. After all, you have a lot of friends and relatives up there, watching the earthly goings-on."

"I know, but Dad was so proud when I became dean of students. That his son had *made it* like that."

"He's always been proud of you and your education, you know."

"I know. But just thinking."

"Maybe pizza?" Mellie looked up at her dad. "Even Jakey likes pizza."

Magnus heaved himself to his feet. "Marit, you go order and I'll call the kids in, then get the pizza." He winked at Mellie. "Thanks. I love pizza."

That last Sunday with Steig was the shortest day of Mona's life. Soon after everyone was up, dressed, and fed, it was time to undress, bathe, and get in bed. At least it seemed that way to Mona. She deliberately, over and over again, forced her mind back to the now. No thinking about Monday allowed.

When she went in to kiss the children after Steig said good night, Mellie whispered, "Daddy leaves early, huh?"

"Yes."

"We get to say good-bye, right?"

"Yes, we will all say good-bye." She leaned upward and kissed Mellie's cheek, not easy from a top bunk.

"But he'll come back, he promised."

Mona nodded. She kissed sleeping Jakey like the touch of a butterfly. And closed the door so Hyacinth could not get in and set off another screaming frenzy. She leaned her forehead against the door. *Please, Lord, please.*

Monday morning the sun was yet to rise when the army van pulled into their driveway. Steig carried his duffel bag on one shoulder and his son in his other arm. He dumped the duffel on the ground.

"Good morning, sir." The driver saluted smartly and picked up the duffel.

Steig returned the salute. "Stow this bag, too." He took another bag from his father and hugged first his dad and then his mom, still holding his son. "I love you."

"We'll be praying for you, Lord willing you come home soon." Mona didn't bother to even try to mop the tears.

Steig knelt down to hug his daughter.

"Don't go away, Daddy." Jakey locked his arms around his father's neck. "Don't go."

"I have to, son, that's my job, but I'll see you soon on Skype and I'll come home as fast as I can." He clutched both of them to his chest. "You be good for Grammy and Grampy." He stood. "I love you all so much. God bless." He turned and stepped up into the van as Ken scooped Jakey into his arms.

"Don't go Daddy! Daaaddyyy!" Jakey shrieked, and tried to pitch himself out of his grandpa's arms, reaching after the already-moving vehicle as if he could drag it to a stop and bring his daddy back.

As if anyone could.

Chapter Twelve

"Come on, little man, let's go look for worms." Ken stood up from the table after lunch. Mona smiled as she watched him move. The man was a pied piper with little kids, college kids, ugly-tempered academics...

"Will Daddy be there?"

"No, but worms are really wiggly, fun to play with." Ken held out his hand. "You can dig in the dirt, too."

"Dirt?" Sitting on his grammy's lap, Jakey wrinkled his nose as he studied his grampy. His finger and thumb popped out of his mouth, and he slid to the floor.

"Can I come, too?" Mellie looked up from the game she was playing on the iPad.

"Of course."

"Thank you," Mona mouthed. Perhaps she could hide out in her office for a while. Why had she not planned for such contingencies as a small child's grief at his father's leaving? Good thing Ken had decided to remain home. She watched as Jakey reached for Grampy's one hand and Mellie took the other. As soon as they got involved, she'd go out and try to catch a good photo for Steig.

Just the thought of what he was going through made her blink a few times. *Comfort him, good Lord.* As the screen door closed behind the four, since Ambrose had decided to join them, she stood and stretched. With a glass of iced tea in hand, she headed upstairs. Chore one—check for messages, taking notes all the while so she could prioritize. Then, starting with number one, she put on her cheerful face and voice and started in. At least problem solving for her clients took her mind off her son.

She had one call to go when she heard laughter from the garden.

"No, Jakey, don't eat it!" Ken sounded like he was about to expire in laughter.

Ambrose barked and Mellie was giggling so hard that Mona's curiosity won over one more phone call. Even though this one might turn into a new client. She headed down the stairs and out. Ambrose charged over to greet her, yipping his delight at her joining them. She followed the laughter trail, iPhone at the ready. Ken sat cross-legged on the grass with Jakey holding up a very wiggly worm. Mellie was digging in the well-aged compost heap, obviously searching for more.

Ken took Jakey's hand in his, whispering something that made the little boy grin up at him. Mona snapped the photo, then moved closer for another one.

"Grammy, Jakey almost ate the worm." Mellie dropped the shovel and danced over to join Mona. "I didn't find any more."

Mona took a couple more pictures and sank down on the bench under the maple tree. "Oh, this is so lovely." A breeze teased her hair and kissed her cheeks. "To think I was working when you all were having such fun out here."

"Go show Grammy."

She watched as Jakey cupped the worm in both his hands and came to stand in front of her. "What do you have there?"

"A big worm." He opened his hands and giggled as the worm wiggled in his palm. "See, Grammy?" He looked up at her. "Fish eat worms, not me."

"I'm glad to hear that. What are you going to do with the worm?"

A puzzled look met her question. He stared at the worm, which was about to flip out to the ground. Jakey grinned. "Give him to you." He dumped the worm in her lap. "You eat it."

Mona looked up to see Ken and Mellie laughing, she with both hands spread over her mouth, as if to keep the giggles in. "Well, I guess I'll have to take the worm inside to help me eat the cookies."

Jakey spun in place, almost dumping himself on the ground. "I want a cookie!"

"How about then you put the worm back in the compost while Mellie and I go find the cookies?"

"I help you."

"Take care of your worm first." She placed the worm in his hand.

A short while later they gathered around the umbrella-shaded glass table and helped themselves to the last of the cookies and a plate of sliced apples.

"Is this coffee break time?" Ken asked.

"I guess you could call it that. As you know, around here folks take a coffee break whenever they feel like it."

"A perk of retirement?"

She smiled. "Nope. I got lots of work for you to do here."

"I suppose you have a list."

"Several, in fact, arranged by location: garage, yard..."

"Grammy, can I have another cookie?" Jakey asked.

"Of course." She passed him the plate. "And some apple?"

She passed him the other plate as well, barely keeping from chuckling at the look on his face.

"I guess." He took a slice.

"Jakey doesn't like apples," Mellie announced to no one in particular.

"I like applesauce."

"That's cooked apples." Mona looked a question at both the kids. "Try this apple; it might be sweeter than others." Vaguely she remembered Steig being quite particular; he only liked apples of the tart and crunchy variety.

Frowning, Jakey picked up an apple slice two-fingered, eyed it suspiciously, and touched it with his tongue, then put it down quickly.

"I don't like it."

"You have to take a bite. At least one bite."

Reluctantly, he picked up the apple slice and carefully took a tiny bite. "There." He tossed it back on the dish.

Mona knew when she was licked. She had, after all, said "one bite."

Another battle loomed; now if they could only change his fear of the cat. His father had worked with him on Saturday and Sunday, so at least now he didn't mind the cat being in sight. There was hope. And obviously the best way to victory is through stealth. But what way to go?

She pondered that question as she fixed dinner a while later, Hyacinth now curled up in her favorite chair at the kitchen table that from now on would be set for four. Once the sandwiches were made, she went to the door and called for Mellie to set the table.

"Is there time for Jake and me to walk down for the mail?" Ken finished hanging the garden tools on the wall rack.

"If you hustle. Do you want salad with your sandwich?"

"Sure." He looked down. "You want salad, Jake?"

"He doesn't like salad," Mellie threw over her shoulder as she climbed the three steps.

"I do, too!"

Uh-oh, rebel in the ranks, Mona thought.

"You do not. Every time Dad tries to get you to eat it, you won't even try it because it's *green*."

"Well, I'll put some on everyone's plates. Green things are good for you." Mona smiled at her granddaughter. "You know where everything is now, right?"

"Guess so." She stared at the cat, who stood and arched her back, more a stretch than a defense move, then looked to Mona for attention.

"What made Jakey so terrified of cats?"

"Mah— Our mother did not like cats. At all. One time at the neighbor's, a cat scratched Jakey because he was rough with it, and she got all upset. She wouldn't let us go back there anymore." She reached for the napkin holder on the counter and pulled open the silverware drawer. "Just forks?"

"That'll work. I think Grampy is going to have to build a stool so you can reach the cupboards." *And then I'll have it to trip over in the kitchen.*

They finished setting the table, and she sent Mellie out to see where the guys were.

Picking up Hyacinth, she stroked the cat's head so the motor started. "How do we get that kid to like you, huh?" Hyacinth slitted her eyes and upped the purr power. "Well, I can tell you one thing, we're not getting rid of you; you lived here first." When she heard the guys coming in the deck door, she patted the cat one more time and set her outside on the step. "Try to stay away from him, okay?"

Hyacinth sat looking out over the yard, tail curled around her legs, the picture of an innocent cat.

Mona raised her voice to the kids. "Wash your hands good."

Mellie called, "We are."

When they were all seated at the table, Ken asked, "Who wants to say grace?" No answer. "Mona, how about you?"

"Ah, sure." She'd been waiting for one of the children to volunteer. They all joined on the amen, but this made her wonder if the kids did say grace before all their meals and that jerked her thoughts back to Steig. How was he? Where was he? He should have flown out by now. To where? *Lord, keep him safe.* From now on that would be part of grace, including their daddy in the prayers.

Tuning back into the conversation, she heard Jakey ask, "Grampy, when is my daddy coming back?"

"I don't know, but I'll tell you as soon as I find out."

"Do we Skype tonight?"

"No, Thursday. This is Monday." Mellie could sound mighty grown up at times.

"Tomorrow is Tuesday?" Jakey asked.

"Good for you, little man. So you know the days of the week?"

"I learned it in school."

"Preschool," Mellie corrected.

"School!" His jaw set.

Mona and Ken swapped looks. Fortunately, she'd forgotten to put the drinks on the table. "Do you want milk or lemonade?"

Mellie looked at her. "Well, it *was* preschool. He goes to kindergarten this year, and I'll be in the fourth grade."

"Oops, something I just remembered. Your birthday is in two weeks." Anything to change the subject.

Mellie nodded. "But Daddy won't be here." Her voice sounded so matter-of-fact, but her chin quivered.

"Your birthday?" Jakey spoke around a mouthful of bread and tuna salad.

"Don't talk with your mouth full." Mellie threw off the order as if she did so every day.

He stuck out his tongue, coated in his last bite.

"Ooh, ick." She made a face to match. "Graaaammyyy!"

For sure, the honeymoon is already over. Mona shook her head. She had thought it would last longer than this. "Milk or lemonade?"

She brought her and Ken lemonade and the kids milk. "After we eat, you can mark your birthday on the calendar, and we can think about a party."

"Cookies?" Jake asked when they were done eating.

"Sorry, we ate all the cookies. How about a Popsicle?" At least she had bought a bag of them at the grocery. She'd have to learn to shop all over again, taking the kids' likes in mind.

"Jakey likes green. I like red."

"I like banana best." Ken joined the discussion. "They're yellow."

"Grampies don't eat Popsicles!" Both kids stared at him.

"Why not? I like Popsicles." He reached for their plates. "Mellie, do you know how to load the dishwasher?"

She shrugged. "Sort of."

"Well, we are now going to have a lesson on dishwasher loading. Jake, you can learn, too."

"And then Popsicles." Mona thanked him with her eyes. "Outside." Her phone chimed that she had a text. She stood. "I'll go in the other room to stay out of the way of dishwasher loading. How about wiping the table off, too?" Maybe it wasn't going to be so bad if Ken really pitched in, too.

Mona was glad she'd not checked the message in the kitchen. Steig. Boarding now. Will let you know more as soon as I can. I love you all. Thank you. No wonder they picked him up so early. She texted back, All is well. Love you back. God keep you, and went out to her favorite room so she could see the river. And let the tears fall.

This was not the way it should be. She and Ken should be on the road halfway up to the ferry to Mackinac Island, where she had reserved a suite with a view of the lake and the mainland for them to enjoy for two whole weeks. Hiking, fishing, taking photos—all the things he loved to do. She was going to take her crocheting and a stack of three books to read and others on her iPad in case she ran out. They would eat out, no cooking for two weeks; visit friends; and possibly even take some classes if interesting ones were being offered. Ken had thought they were going to the cabin where the guys and sometimes the women went fishing on Green Lake. She'd wanted to surprise him again, but this trip was not to be—at least not right now. She would call and cancel the reservations. Tears flowed again.

She wiped them away. "Tears are an absolute waste of time and energy."

When she didn't hear any kitchen noises, she headed up the stairs to return the last phone call. While dialing the number on the landline, the only phone set up for business, she reminded herself to smile. The first rule of business calls—smile, even if you didn't feel like it. A smile made a big difference in telephone communications; she'd learned that lesson well. And taught it to others.

When the woman answered the phone, they exchanged pleasantries, realizing they had met some time ago at a

Rotary meeting and Mona had shared her business card, another of those rules she had taken to habit.

"I see congratulations are in order, according to the spread in the paper."

"Really? We've not even had time today to read the paper. Thanks for letting me know."

"You'll be impressed. They did a splendid job."

"Glad to hear that. Now, how can I help you?" Mona listened to the woman with one ear and for the kids with the other. She'd not had to do that for many years—well, not really, because when Marit's brood came, she got a chance to practice. But when they were here, she was not trying to run a business at the same time.

"We're starting a nursery/preschool at our church, and we are hoping we can hire you to help us with the publicity and to plan a grand opening. So, I would like to meet with you privately first; then if you will draw up a proposal, we will take the next step."

"What kind of a budget do you have for this stage of your dream?"

"I assure you, this is more than a dream. Another committee is working with an architect so we can make sure to meet the codes, not as a new facility but as a remodel."

This was catching her attention. "And you plan to open after the first of the year?"

"Yes. Someone in our church has bequeathed this to the community. They were a highly thought-of couple in business and have laid out specific guidelines regarding budgets for setting this up and then maintaining it. Hopefully our school will be paying its own way before two years are out."

"All businesses hope for that. When would you like to meet?"

"Would next week be all right?"

"Let me explain the ways I work the fee situation. On a project like this, I need to be on retainer with the first month paid in advance and will require hourly payment due on the first of the month for any hours billed beyond the monthly retainer." Since she'd never anticipated a project like this, she was basically flying blind, but some business advice she'd read had talked about retainers. "Our first meeting will be gratis. What would you like me to bring?"

"Possible suggestions for a campaign and then can we brainstorm? I will e-mail you all the info we have so far."

"Good. Once I am on retainer, I will gladly meet with your planning committee and go to work. We have basically seven months to make this happen." She could feel a bubble of excitement starting in her middle.

"I know, but this whole enterprise is a surprise for all of us. Their stipulation was that it happen ASAP. I think that is what we are all committed to. How about we meet at Dorothea's? Are you available for lunch on Thursday?"

Mona checked her calendar. "That will work. Can you please give me your contact information?" She typed it in as Carole with an *e* answered her questions. "Okay, I will meet with you on Thursday, May twenty-eighth, at noon at Dorothea's."

"I'll make reservations. Feel free to call me if you come up with more questions."

After they hung up, Mona sat staring at her computer screen. A great project that would make a difference. Only two questions: Was she capable of handling a project this size?...And the next question left her feeling just a wee bit sucker punched. What about the grands?

Chapter Thirteen

"Time for bed, you two." Mona tried to sound like they'd been doing this for years.

Jake looked up from his Legos. "I want Daddy to put me to bed." He returned to what he was doing.

Mona and Ken shared a sad glance. If only they were waiting for Steig to return tonight. "Okay, guys, see the clock on the mantel above the fireplace?"

They looked where she pointed and nodded.

"You have ten minutes, big hand from the two to the four. Then I will start the bath running while you pick up your Legos, Jakey, and Mellie, you put your book back on the shelf with a bookmark in it. They are in the drawer here." She removed one and laid it out for her. "Got it?"

Jake kept on with his Legos. Mellie nodded.

Mona wished she had asked Steig about bedtime procedures. Those two nights as she watched him do it were not enough. Surely he had a routine. He lived by routines. Until Angela left. That thought made her flinch. So many things she didn't think to ask him. Dreading real confrontation, she was so tempted to just let them stay up until she could see they were tired. She used to allow her kids leeway in the summer. She stuck her crochet hook in the ball of yarn and tucked it into the quilted bag she kept by her chair. *Lord, help us.* Ken continued reading his book as if nothing was going on.

She thought back to the years when Steig and Marit were these ages. Ken was the one to read to them before bed. Okay, so change of plans. She went to the bookshelf in the family room, then called, "Mellie, could you please come help me choose a book for us to read?"

When the little girl smiled up from beside her, Mona asked, "Your daddy read to you kids, right?"

"When he could. Or our babysitter did."

"Okay, we are going to have story time before getting ready for bed. See any on there you've not heard?" She pulled off *Charlotte's Web.* "How about this one? We loved this story."

"We have the movie."

"Did you like it?"

She nodded.

"Good, then let's read it unless you have one you'd rather."

Mellie shrugged. "We saw it a long time ago." Together they returned to the family room.

"Look at the clock, Jakey," Ken said softly.

Jake glanced at the clock and, studiously ignoring his grandfather, continued to search out another Lego and attach it to the structure he was creating.

Mellie picked up her book, bookmark in place, and set it on the shelf. "Grampy said it was time; Jakey, put your Legos in the basket now!" He kept on, as if he couldn't hear her. Mellie stomped over to him and nudged him with her foot, and not gently. "Come on, Jake, you know what to do. Put them away."

She sounded so much like her mother that Mona flinched. She looked at Ken with raised eyebrows.

He pushed himself out of the chair and knelt by his grandson. "Here, just for tonight, I'll help you so we can start our new book sooner." He started to put some in the basket.

"No, I need that one for the wheel." He took one of the pieces back out and set it in the pile beside him.

"Jake, it's time for bed."

"But I'm not done."

"You can finish tomorrow. We can work on it together, how about that?"

Jake studied the truck he had half built, testing it by wheeling it along the carpet.

Mona watched the struggle and breathed a sigh of relief when Jakey started picking up pieces and filling the basket.

Ken smiled at him. "Good boy, now why don't you put the one you are working on right on top so you can go back and finish it?"

Jake hesitated, then dug into the basket for another Lego. Ken snatched it out of his hand, tossed it in the basket, and stood up, bringing Jakey with him. The little boy struggled briefly and gave up.

Ken nodded and carried him away from the Legos. "Let's go read our story."

They all settled on the sofa, Mellie snuggled close against her grampy, and Ken picked up the book from the coffee table. "Ah, I remember reading this before, but it was a long time ago." He settled Jake in his lap and opened to the first page. "'Where's Papa going with that ax?' said Fern to her mother as they were setting the table for breakfast."

Mona allowed herself a smile. Victory, more or less.

At the end of the first chapter, Ken closed the book and

laid his cheek on the sleeping boy's head. "I say, skip the bath and put him right to bed."

"I say you are very wise."

"Wait." Mellie looked peeved. "You didn't put a night diaper on him."

"Perhaps he'll be fine tonight."

"No, he won't. And he's dirty and his clothes are, too."

Mona nodded. "You're right, but we don't want to wake him up. Come on, Mellie, let's get you a bath."

"Can I have bubble bath?"

"You sure may." Mona held out her hand. "And you get to choose what kind."

"I never had bubble bath at home. But I like them." She frowned. "I think I do."

They walked hand in hand to the bathroom and Mona pulled her bath bottles out of the closet. She was glad now that this was one of her little pamper splurges.

Mellie smelled all three of the bottles, settled on lavender, and Mona dumped in a bunch.

Mellie watched the fragrant foam pile up. "Thank you!"

Mona hugged her close. "You are so welcome. Do you need help washing your hair? You don't need to if you don't want to."

"Tomorrow?"

"And tomorrow we will all get ready for bed before story time. How does that sound?"

"You and Grampy, too?"

"Yep."

Mellie giggled as she shed her clothes, then felt the bathwater, the giggles floating like the bubbles. "Perfect!" And climbed in.

"I'm going to go get my jammies on, but I'll leave the door open a bit in case you need me." Hyacinth met her at the door. She returned to the lavender-scented bathtub. "Mellie, Hyacinth is asking may she come supervise."

"I never had a bath with a cat before."

"She doesn't like water much, and she really dislikes bubbles. But she likes to observe, and if you talk with her, she might even answer." Mona lowered the toilet lid, and Hyacinth jumped up and sat down, watching Mellie as if assigned to her rightful job. "Call me if you need me."

Mona met Ken in the hallway. "You got him down?"

"I took off his shorts and his shoes; those were the dirtiest. I think he's like his dad, can sleep through anything."

"I certainly hope so. I can't figure out why I am so tired." She followed him into the bedroom. "We didn't get our walk in today—well, since the kids arrived."

"Tomorrow. There's always tomorrow."

Sometime in the deepest dark of night, a piercing scream woke them. They both bailed out and dashed to the kids' room. The screams were from Jake, thrashing in his bed, and from Mellie: "Jake, shut up! Quit it! Jakey!"

"What's wrong, buddy?" Ken sat on the bed and gathered Jake into his lap. Jake just kept thrashing and screaming.

"He's not awake. He wakes everyone in the house up, but he doesn't wake up," Mellie said matter-of-factly from the top bunk. "Ever since she left us."

Mona reached up to pat her. "Does he have them often?" *She never calls Angela Mommy. It's always she.* That thought was worth thinking about when she was more awake.

"Sometimes. Daddy says it's night terrors. He says I don't have to worry, so I don't." And she rolled over with her back to them, but she shuddered a little sob.

The screaming and thrashing began to subside.

Ken continued to hold him close. "I'll stay in here for a while with him; you can go back to bed."

"Thanks." Mona returned to the comfort of her pillow, but she could not get back to sleep. *Lord, how do we help these children the very best?* And then she amended her fervent prayer. *Okay, I'm not so much concerned about how best. Now I'll settle for How Can We Do It at All?*

But this time, prayer was not enough. Her brain was racing at freight-train speed, coming up with hideous scenarios and questions.

What if Steig was killed in the line of duty? Or by friendly fire, for that matter. It happened. Her mind dwelled on a casket draped in the American flag and flying home for the last time.

Night terrors? She knew nothing about them. Obviously Steig knew something about them. She would also add that to the list of things to ask Steig on Skype Thursday. But how many other problems and dangers did she simply know nothing about? They lurked out there, scowling ghosts of ignorance about things she had to know.

What if the night terrors everyone was so casually dismissing were actually symptoms of a much deeper problem? They were frightening, for Mona as well as for little Jake. Maybe Jake, being the most vulnerable person in this hideous situation, was crumpling beneath the weight of worry and abandonment. And what if there was nothing they could do for him to keep him from crumpling completely? Or turning to drugs when he got older, as so many do? Or any other self-destructive behavior...?

What if Angela decided to reenter the picture? Steig said she could not reach the children legally, and besides, she preferred her new life with the lowlife she had latched on to. But what if that lowlife walked out on her or if she walked out on him even? Then she might crave the affection children can provide. And if she had the resources to mount a legal fight...after all, she was the mother, and the courts seemed to prefer seeing mothers regain their children.

Mona and Ken weren't getting any younger; the health of either one of them could implode at any moment. Could Ken carry on alone if Mona were hospitalized or bedridden? Could she, if it were Ken who cratered?

"No, Mona! Look what you're doing!" She said it out loud.

Intense worry usually opened wide the barn doors to depression. Her states of severe depression had all begun with runaway worrying, and as it always turned out, the worries and fears had been groundless.

But these fears were not groundless. These what-ifs had a solid basis in reality. Things like this happened all the time; just listen to the news for a day or two.

She needed to nip these worries in the bud. But they would not nip. Already they had planted themselves into her thoughts with roots of iron. Probably they were not new; probably they had been at the back of her mind all the while, growing. Growing. And now suddenly they were exploding.

Activity. She had to get active somehow. But it was the middle of the night. She got up and padded softly, barefoot, to the children's bedroom door to peek in. Ken was stretched out in Jakey's bed with Jakey nestled tight against him. They were both sound asleep. She closed the door.

Hyacinth meowed a question as she walked to the kitchen. How do you tell a cat that you're teetering on the

edge of a dangerous bout of depression? She set her vial
of pills out to remind her to take it in the morning. Maybe
it was time to see the doctor.

She quietly continued down to the basement, to her
corner of the basement, turning on the light. The basement never got too hot and never got too cold. A single
vent in the ductwork that sent warmth from the furnace
up to the rooms was enough to keep the basement fairly
comfortable in the winter. In summer it needed no help.

Mona stood beside a punching bag now. It was not the
same hard, heavy regulation bag Marit had used, a huge
beast that seemed to be made of wood. This punching bag
was softer than regulation and had more give to it. It was
made for a child or an older woman, not a powerful young
man or woman.

When the high school faced a lawsuit if it didn't afford
equal opportunity to both girls and boys, the school board
said, in effect, "All right. We'll open all the classes to both
boys and girls. You watch; the girls will all still take girl
courses and the boys will still take boy courses. Nothing
will change."

The first semester the new rules took effect, Steig defied that attitude by signing up for cooking ("Nothing will
change, huh? Besides, I'm going to be baching it for years
after high school," he said; "I'm going to want to eat well").
Privately to his dad, he added that taking cooking with
eighteen pretty girls, and he the only boy, didn't sour the
pot at all.

And also in defiance, Marit took up boxing. Ken seemed
somewhat dazed that his own daughter would...would...
but Mona was tickled. She even bought Marit a punching
bag and gloves so that she could practice in the basement.

Marit, in turn, had purchased this for her mother a

few years ago so that Mona could vent frustrations. Would this help ward off worry and depression? Marit hoped so; Mona desperately hoped so.

Now she slipped into the gloves, tightened her fists, and poked the bag. She jabbed it with the other fist. She upped the pace, punching, punching harder. She must be quite a sight, balanced on the balls of her bare feet, in her pajamas. *So what?*

The bag moved away from her, trying to evade her punishment. She soon had the rhythm going, though. *Puppa, puppa, puppa, puppa, puppeta, puppeta, puppeta, puppeta . . .*

She broke a sweat now. Her brain was still trying to worry, but it was having a harder and harder time keeping track of all those fears. When all else failed, the punching bag was saving her. In half an hour or less, worn-out, she would go back upstairs and crawl into bed and fall asleep.

But the fears and worries would still be there; they would return. They always did.

Chapter Fourteen

The only time Mona managed to pull a complete surprise on him was that party Saturday. And it was a
lulu. Ken smiled to himself, bringing back the many memories. He sat in the Adirondack chair out by the fresh dirt
pile Mona planned to spread on the garden. The kids were
tackling it with buckets and shovels. And he thought of the
beautiful chest, his gift. Jakey was a little too young yet to
introduce to whittling and carving or building furniture,
but perhaps Mellie might get interested.

And if his instincts served him correctly, Mona was
planning another surprise of some sort. Most likely, it
would have something to do with the getaway to Green
Lake they had talked about. He would keep an ear to the
ground. He loved the cat and mouse they had developed
over the years—she planning surprises, he detecting them
in advance. But then, maybe she did not love it nearly as
much as he did.

"Jakey, put that down!" Mellie swatted her brother's
knuckles hard, making him drop a handful of dirt. He
yowled, got up from his dirt pile, and came running to
Ken. Ken gathered him in and settled him on his lap.
Good grief, the kid was dirty.

"Mellie, come here, please."

She got up and came over to him.

"Who said you could boss your brother around like that?"

"Mah— Our mother. She said I'm oldest so I have to take care of him."

"From now on, Grammy and I will take care of him. Not you."

"But she said I have to. She doesn't have time."

"Mellie, listen to me. Grammy and I are taking over. You do not—"

"But he was going to eat it. The dirt."

"If he actually eats dirt, you tell us. You do not yell at him, and especially, you never hit him, ever, nor is he allowed to hit you. No hitting."

"But he might eat dirt."

"I understand. We'll be his caregivers and worry about his diet. You don't need responsibility like that yet. You just concentrate on being a little girl."

"He's not supposed to eat dirt."

Ken deepened his voice. "Grammy and I, Mellie. Not you. Understand?"

Pouting, she wandered back to the dirt pile.

Ken gave the boy an extra hug and put him on his feet. "Jakey, as dirty as your hands are, sticking your finger and thumb in your mouth like that is equivalent to eating dirt. I suggest you shouldn't."

Jakey stared at him. "Uh kwivel?" he asked around his fingers.

"What?"

"Wha's uh kwivel?"

"Jakey, please take your fingers out of your mouth. They're dirty and I can't understand you."

He popped his fingers out of his mouth. "What's uh kwivel?"

"Uh kwivel...? Oh, equivalent. It means the same." Down inside, Ken sighed. He was accustomed to talking to academics, not small children. He was going to have to considerably alter his vocabulary.

"Oh, okay." He returned to the dirt pile.

"Ken?" Mona called from the porch. "Telephone."

He got up and headed for the house. Was this part of some sort of ruse? He was getting too suspicious. He smiled at her and said, "Thank you," as he accepted the phone. "Hello?"

"Ken? Sandy. Ken, I'm really sorry to disturb you, but I have knots here I can't untie. Could you come in for half an hour? It shouldn't take any longer than that."

"Certainly. I've been handling my grandson, so I'll have to wash up first. I'll be there shortly."

"Thanks, Ken. I'm really sorry."

Now what? He was retired; he could look sloppy at last. Still, he tidied himself up a little—what the kids called business casual—in case he had to meet with muckety-mucks. Sandy sounded distraught.

He climbed into the car and started for Stone University. What kind of leverage did he have, anyway? Probably not much anymore. And Dale and John seemed relieved that he was out of there. Maybe now they were trying to drive Sandy out. Would they ever do such a craven thing? *In a New York minute.*

He parked in what had been his usual spot and headed inside. How fortunate that Sandy biked to work; her reserved space was available today. He pushed through the doors into his old, familiar office.

"Oh, thank heavens!" Sandy leaped up from her chair.

"Here. I'll show you." She hustled over to the side table where she had papers laid out. He watched over her shoulder.

She picked up a letter from the provost's office. "Damien filed a formal grievance claiming his credentials were better than those of the appointee. Me."

"We pretty much knew he was going to do that."

She nodded. "So I called the legal department, and they said his grievance has standing." She was studying his face, looking for hope.

He thought about this a few moments. "Because Damien is the sort who would do this, I prepared a little in advance. We have sixty days to respond. I'll get Gerald on it. I think we can squelch the grievance and justify choosing you."

"You think. You don't know."

"No, I never know what the legal department is going to come up with, or the board, for that matter. But if you are replaced by Damien, we can kiss funding good-bye."

"That's what I'm afraid of. That's why I took the job. Ken, I have no idea what I'm doing here."

"You've been doing it for years."

"The paperwork, not the thinking. The planning. Smoothing out wrinkles."

He gestured toward the other stacks of paper. "What else do we have?"

"Remember Jasmine, that girl who needed financing?"

"The Kiwanis Club pledged to pick up her tab."

"That's the one. Well, Kiwanis says they sent a check, and Greg says Stone never got it, so they're withholding her grades. But she's applying for an internship and needs her transcript."

"Did you call the bank?"

"They won't talk to me. I'm not authorized."

This one he could handle. He walked over to her desk, picked up the phone, and punched in a number from memory. "One ringy-dingy...two ringy-dingy..." The old *Laugh-In*. Their guest one week was Billy Graham, and at the end, they gave him space to make his Gospel pitch. He smiled at the thought.

"Greg Thorsen, how may I help you?"

"Greg, Ken Sorenson here. I need a favor." He put the phone on speaker so Sandy could hear.

"Anything for the good buddy who saved my butt by taking over my Sunday school class. What can I do for you?"

Ken explained the situation. Greg asked him to hold for a few minutes. Ken muted the phone for a moment. "Greg is a fellow church member and a good building contractor. I helped him out of a tight spot once. He's also the local Kiwanis president."

"I'll bet you don't realize how valuable your many connections are. I don't know anyone in Kiwanis, and you know everyone in all the service organizations."

"I'll have to make you a phone list of people who could be helpf—"

"Ken? I just talked to our treasurer, who has the inside scoop. The check never cleared, and the university is assuming that Miss Pine intercepted the check and kept it. Theo is going to cut a new check and stop the old one. Do you have Jasmine Pine's address and phone number? We can ask her to pick it up and hand deliver it so that she can get her transcript out of purgatory."

"Wonderful. Jasmine and I both thank you, Greg. She's an excellent student who simply needed a little boost. All As except two Bs. Magna cum laude."

Sandy had already pulled Jasmine's record. She handed it to Ken, he passed on the information, Greg and he chatted a moment, and they hung up. She wagged her head. "So simple if you know whom to call."

"You had several other things on that table. Let's get them done." He stood up. "Oh, and while I'm thinking of it, please put together a file of all the correspondence between us and Damien and another file with his full dossier."

"I'll do that today. All right, here's that Fisher boy who got arrested last month for possession, remember?"

When Sandy said she had knots she couldn't untie, she had been understating it. Ken was unable to untie all of them, but they took care of most. Sandy was so apologetic, too. But she was learning quickly; she would do fine once she found her footing. He finally got out of the office at past three.

He was ravenously hungry. He could go home and Mona would...No, she was busy. He sat a moment at the wheel, one foot on the ground. He got out and went back into the building.

As he approached Dale's office, Dale was just coming out. He looked at Ken; his face fell, and then he carefully arranged it into a smile. "Surprised to see you here, old friend."

"I'd like to talk to you a moment."

"I'm sorry, I have a meeting in just a few minutes; perhaps tomorrow."

"Library board over in Sutton. Yes. You meet there every month. I'll walk you over."

Dale sputtered, but what could he say? Ken fell in beside him, and they left the building together.

Better make this quick. "Sandy is handling things well;

I stopped by there, of course. But she has a much heavier workload than she ought to have this early in the summer. I was looking at some of the things she is doing, and quite a bit of it looks like make-work. Things that are not really necessary or that should be done by other departments. Things I never had to contend with."

"I don't know how that could be."

"It couldn't be that you and John are dumping your problems on her, trying to overwhelm her, could it?"

"Of course not." Dale walked faster.

"John should have taken care of the problem with Jasmine Pine. Instead he plopped it on Sandy's desk. There are several other tasks of like nature."

"I'll speak to John, but I don't think...uh..."

Ken pushed harder. "I filed that injunction for two reasons. One is, I want to keep the department intact with a head who knows the students. The other is so that you know I will use legal leverage whenever I have to."

Dale stopped abruptly and turned to face him. "Are you threatening me?"

"By no means. I'm pointing out realities." Ken kept his face relaxed and pleasant, even though down inside he was boiling. Yes, Dale knew what was going on and was no doubt a party to it. Better than most people, Ken could read body language; it was necessary for understanding students and avoiding being scammed by those who thought they saw a money tree with low-hanging fruit.

"Well, I don't..." Whatever Dale was thinking, he left it unspoken and started walking.

"Dale, I have inside information." That was nothing more than Ken's reading of Dale's body language. "You are trying to force Sandy out so you can put Damien in. To the detriment of the department, to the detriment of the many students who so desperately need the department. I am not going to let that happen, Dale. You can cooperate with the department and work with Sandy as you worked with me, or you can learn the hard way. It is your choice. Enjoy your library meeting." He stopped.

Dale stormed on up the steps into Sutton. *Congratulations, Kenny, old boy. You just made an enemy.*

No, not really. Ken probably always had that particular enemy, but the enemy was just now showing his true colors. He turned aside to the student center.

No one was in the food court now; the spring students had left and the summer students had not yet arrived. In fact, about half the food kiosks were closed. The Thai booth was open. Pad thai would taste mighty good just now. Or he could go home, build a simple sandwich, and relieve Mona of their babysitting chores. Or...

He just stood there, uncertain. He could untie knotty problems, but he could not direct his own footsteps. Were these child-rearing responsibilities going to be more than he could handle?

Chapter Fifteen

A re you sure you can handle all this?" Ken was leaning against her office doorjamb, watching Mona juggle three folders, a legal pad, her phone, and a split computer screen on a desk that wasn't big enough to handle all that. Maybe she should get a bigger work surface. Ken had that side table in his office, and it came in so handy.

Mona paused and stared at him. "Why not?"

"Because we have children now. This looks like a really big, complicated project, and while you don't have a lot of others going right now, maybe it's because God is trying to keep us sane."

"So we are to give up our lives because we now have two children?" She shook her head. "I don't think so. Ken, this is what I do, and I'm very good at it. I know I'll have to pace myself more, but things will lighten up when school starts..." She rolled her lips together. "I know I can handle it all."

"But I guess what I am really asking is if this project will be the best for all of us right now."

She studied the floor a moment. "It will keep me sane." She looked up at him and half smiled. "And that is kind of the same thing."

He nodded and lurched erect. "I'm going to fix coffee. You want some?"

"Too late, I'd never sleep." She paused in her busyness to gnaw on a cuticle.

Ken turned toward the kitchen, then turned back. "You know, I've noticed that when you chew your cuticles, it's usually a sign of you feeling overloaded. That concerns me because it's opening the doors for depression to sneak back in."

"I've been doing better since the antidepressants kicked in."

"True, but sometimes you'll go gung ho on a big project like this and then collapse when it's done. You know, post-project letdown. I get it all the time."

"I'll keep an eye on it, all right?" She tried to sound cheerful, but his comments irritated her. She knew all about it. A couple times the big D, as they called it, had blindsided her. No one could figure out what triggered it, and that was the fear.

He left. He returned. He snickered. "I was going to ask you from out in the kitchen, but as I opened my mouth, I remembered the children. I suppose they are sleeping. Would you like herb tea?"

She smiled. *Let sleeping dogs lie.* He had a point; this continual childcare was going to take getting used to in ways she'd never thought of. "Yes, please, that would be lovely. How about the peach? Oh, and I think I will move out to the family room." She scooped up her work and went out to the three-season room, settled into the papasan chair, and went back to making notes on one of those yellow pads that she bought by the case.

He disappeared into the kitchen. Back he came. "I'm having ice cream; you want some?"

"Make it a small bowl, please, not your normal size."

"Chocolate syrup?"

She leaned her head back against the padding, feeling weary. "Yes, but I better not. The last few days have not been good to my diet. Oh, go ahead. Thank you."

She could almost read his mind when he glanced down his front. No paunch, but since the gym he usually went to was near the university, he wouldn't be going there anymore. He should probably be a bit careful, too. "I'll think about diet tomorrow."

"Or next week, Scarlett?"

She returned to her notes, hoping he would get the hint and let her work. She could go back to her office, but she liked his company and the songs of the crickets and frogs. Especially now that the children were in bed, hopefully to sleep all night, the house was quiet. The teasing made her want to see *Gone with the Wind* again. She closed her eyes and leaned back in the chair. How many years since she had read the book? She remembered that she had read it at least three times, maybe more. They would definitely have to watch the movie again. She looked up with a smile as Ken set her sundae on the table beside her. "Thank you."

He settled into his chair with a sigh. Hyacinth jumped up in his lap and Ambrose settled down beside him. "Thanks, guys; I know you think you'll get some, but not until I'm done."

"This is good. Thanks." Fudge syrup over peppermint chip ice cream. "Good idea." She studied her notes for the preschool presentation while she ate. Surely she could handle it all; the trick would be to not take on other jobs until this was completed. She picked up her Day-Timer calendar and flipped through the months ahead, counting her other jobs first. Four for sure and two maybes. One was a yearly thing she'd been doing for the last three years. Piece of cake. She set her ice cream bowl on her lap, and Hyacinth immediately changed allegiances, landing on her extended legs with perfectly sheathed claws. "Good girl. Have at it." She had really cleaned up the chocolate syrup so it would be safe for the critters.

"We didn't go for a walk today, either." Ken paused his spoon. "I was planning on it." Ambrose perked his ears at the word *walk*. "Nope, sorry, fella, not tonight."

"Mellie's birthday is next week. Shall we do her party here or at the park?"

"Here, I'm into easy right now. It'll just be us and Marit's bunch, right?"

"What do you think of hiring a blow-up jumping thing?"

"I think that is a totally unnecessary expense. Remember, I'm not getting a paycheck anymore, and it'll take a bit for my retirement to kick in and I won't get Social Security for another year and a half."

"The thought of going on a budget is not exciting."

"I know, but you agreed." Ken had always been the money manager in their house, and while he was not stingy or tight, he referred to himself as inordinately frugal. "I'll get one together, and we'll go over it. I sort of had one, but things like groceries and gas will probably change, along with the electric bill."

"Steig said to use part of his money for food and living expenses, remember?"

"I know, but..."

Mona waited before asking, "But what?" She pretty much figured what he would say, saving for an emergency.

"I want to put part of that income into a savings account for them, and we have to keep a backup plan for emergencies."

"There is already an account started with automatic deductions, did you forget that?"

"That's for their school expenses."

"Since most of his wages are going into the bank, with no other expenses like house and car and such, I don't see what the concern is."

"He'll need money saved up for when he gets home for housing and all the rest of daily life. I've been thinking of putting his SUV into storage."

"Really? Why? We can park it in the garage."

"For now, but when winter comes, we are going to want both our cars in there."

"True. You sure are thinking ahead, not that I'm surprised." She stroked the cat, the purr motor starting immediately. "My big concern right now is getting Jakey to accept the cat. Not fair to her to banish her outside or in the garage so much."

"I figure he'll relax just by having her around. Mellie is working on this, too. After all, it's only been two days since Steig left." He stood and picked up their bowls. "I forgot to make the tea."

"That's okay." Mona tried to stifle a yawn but failed. "I'm ready for bed."

"I think I'll work on the books for a while. You go ahead. Perhaps I could sleep in tomorrow. That was one of the things on my list to do in retirement."

Mona snorted. "Longtime habits are hard to break."

She gathered her things, left them on the desk, and slogged upstairs. One of the signs of depression is excessive weariness, and here she was, so weary she couldn't think. That worried her a lot. Worry. *Give it to God and quit worrying!* But she worried anyway. She couldn't help it.

She prepared for bed and crawled under the covers.

And lay there. She was weary and yet not sleepy. That was mighty dumb. But . . .

Mellie was yelling, "Jakey, no! Stop it!" Jakey was yelling, "You stop it! I want Daddy! Stop it!"

Mona leaped up and ran out into the hall just as Ken came bounding up the stairs. Together they rushed into the children's room.

Mellie had grabbed Jakey by two handfuls of pajamas and was shaking him violently as she screamed, "Stop! Stop!" And Jakey was yelling just as uncontrollably. Ken wrapped his arms around Mellie and dragged her backward. She started to pull Jakey out of the bed, but Mona grabbed him and drew him in against her, breaking Mellie's grip. Shocked beyond words, Mona flopped to sitting on the foot of Jakey's bed, pulled him into her lap, and wrapped her arms around him. He sobbed wildly, loudly. "I want my daddy!"

Ken was just as tightly wrapped around Mellie. He turned around and sat at the head of Jakey's bed, pulling her in against him, pressing her head to his chest with his free hand. She was vibrating, shaking. Mona watched her contorted face for some clue; she could see none. Mona rocked gently back and forth, trying to soothe Jakey and feeling so totally helpless.

It took long minutes for the children to quiet down to simple sobbing.

Ken drew a deep breath. "Mellie? What was going on? What happened?"

She hiccuped and sobbed. "I don't know how to say it."

"Okay." Ken sounded so calm. "Can you tell me what you're thinking?"

Another shuddering sob. "It's Jakey's fault. He ruined everything. Now he's gonna ruin it again."

"How so?" Ken's voice was so gentle, quiet.

Mellie just sat there a moment. "He made Mommy leave, and he doesn't understand. Now he's going to make you leave."

"Whoa. I'm the one who doesn't understand. Can you explain it?"

A few more sobs and a sigh. She licked her lips. "Mommy told us she couldn't stand us little kids anymore and she was leaving. When I asked her why, she said that; she can't stand us. But Grampy, I was being really, really perfect. I tried very hard, and I was really perfect. Jakey was the naughty one. Jakey made her leave by being naughty."

Mona gaped. What mother could ever tell her children that?

Ken purred, "I see. And you are afraid that Grammy and I might leave."

"Mommy left. Daddy left. We don't have anyone, and when you can't stand us anymore, you'll leave."

Ken nodded slowly. "Perfectly logical." He unwrapped his arms from around Mellie, sat her upright, and took the sides of her head in both hands. He aimed her face straight at his and looked her right in the eye. "It's logical; it's a pretty good deduction, in fact. But Mellie, it's completely wrong. Your daddy has to do what the army tells him to do. It's called military discipline. But Grammy and I will not leave you. Do you hear me?"

Mellie shuddered another elephant-sized sob, but she was looking at him.

Ken repeated, separating each word, "We will not abandon you. We love you and Jakey, and we will not leave you or let you come to harm. You are safe here until your father returns."

"But Jakey..."

"Jakey is a very small boy being a very small boy, just like his father when he was growing up. There will never be a day we can't stand him or you, and you are safe here." He took his hands away from her head. "Do you understand?"

"Mommy said..." Another sigh. "Never?"

"Never. Now. Why were you yelling at Jakey and shaking him?"

"He was crying and saying he wanted his daddy, and he didn't like this bed, he wanted his own bed, and I was afraid he'd wake you up and you'd be mad."

"Ah." Ken drew her into another hug. "Thank you for thinking of us, but from now on, remember, when you or Jakey need something, we don't mind waking up. In fact, come get us. And please don't shake him anymore. That's as bad as hitting."

"But he won't behave."

"That's our problem. And we will never leave you or stop loving you."

Mona felt completely drained. Sick. Actually sick. Horrified. Would these children be warped forever by their mother's cruelty?

Jakey twisted around to look at her. "Is it Thursday yet?"

Finally, finally, Thursday evening arrived. Ken, Mona, and the children waited eagerly for Steig to call. Marit came over at nine, leaving Magnus and the kids at home.

They sat. And waited.

"How did that meeting with the school people go today?" Ken asked.

"Very well. I think I have the project. And they seem very cooperative. Eager."

Marit frowned. "Is this Carole Bergstrund's board?"

"You know about that project?"

"I teach special-needs kids, remember? Everyone in the school knows about it. Mom, are you going to handle that okay with two little ones?"

"Your father asked the same thing. Why? Are you worried?"

"Just asking."

They sat. And waited.

"Can we have ice cream afterward?" Jakey asked.

Mona smiled. "I think that can be arranged. We'll celebrate."

They sat. And waited.

Marit finally said, "It's past ten. I'd better go home. Let me know, will you?"

"Of course."

"Jesu, Joy of Man's Desiring" began to play, Ken's cell. "Hello? Oh, hi Bert. No, why?" He frowned and sat back to listen, grunting now and then.

"Maybe we can have ice cream tomorrow night. Time for bed." Mona stood up and motioned to the children. She herded them upstairs to the bathroom. She slipped Jakey's clothes off and shook out a fresh night diaper.

"Don't want to wear those anymore!" Jake pushed them away.

"I don't blame you, but…" Mona paused. "I know. When you wake up dry three mornings in a row, we can put them away. But you have to be good about putting them on between now and then."

"Why didn't Daddy Skype tonight?" Mellie looked up at her grandmother with sad eyes about to brim over.

"Wherever he is, he is in a different time zone than we are, and that might be causing problems."

"A time zone? Like when it's later at Virginia Beach than it is here, so we can't call Daddy's friend Edward?"

"Yes, military people go all over the world. Tomorrow we'll have to get a world map out and talk about time zones. Perhaps we should go shopping for a globe."

Usually the idea of shopping perked Mellie right up. Not tonight.

"I hate the military," she muttered.

"I understand, darling girl, but your daddy is proud to serve our country in the military, and we are proud of him. That is what he has chosen for a career, and he is very, very good at what he does. We just need to pray that God will keep him safe. Perhaps he'll be able to Skype tomorrow."

"Tomorrow can we write him a letter?"

"We most certainly will." Mona wrapped an arm around her granddaughter and rested her cheek on her head.

"If he Skypes after I go to sleep, will you wake me up?"

"Of course we will, and we'll keep the laptop right by the bed—just in case"

Ken was off the phone when Mona came back downstairs. "Lodge troubles?"

"Yes. Bert wants a meeting tomorrow evening to work out some financial problems."

"You want a cup of tea or coffee or iced tea?"

"I guess." He scrubbed both hands over his head. "I think I want out of this job, too."

"Lodge elections won't be until fall. You've been the lodge treasurer for how many years?"

"More than I care to count."

"You could probably ask to be released, but why?"

"I guess I'm feeling the pressure here. I'll be fine in the morning."

From upstairs came that now-familiar wail.

Ken sighed as he stood. "I can't wait till he grows up."

Friday at noon, Mona got out of the car as the children tumbled out and ran into the kitchen. She lifted their parcels out of the trunk and followed them in. "The shoppers return!"

Smiling, Ken met them at the kitchen table. "What treasures do you bring?"

Mellie dug into a bag. "I got a new bathing suit. The one from last year is too short."

"Look, Grampy. Look. Look." Jakey found his package, a set of Legos with which to build an airplane. "Look."

"That's going to be a lot of fun, Jakey."

"And we got this." Mona set a twelve-inch globe on the counter.

"This is excellent! It has a time indicator up at the top here, where the Arctic is. Look, Mellie, now we can find out what time it is where your daddy is stationed."

She scowled at the globe.

Ken gave it a twirl. "Here is North America, and here is the United States. Wisconsin is right here, see? So we'll follow this longitude line up until we can set the time indicator to nine at night. Now we find Pakistan, which is..." He turned it to the Indian subcontinent. "...Right here. What does the time indicator say?"

Mellie climbed up on a stool to read it better. "Seven. No, eight. In between."

"Seven thirty. And the indicator is white, meaning daytime."

She sat back. "So if he calls at seven thirty in the morning, he talks to us at nine, bedtime?"

"Exactly."

"Maybe he doesn't know that, and he calls at the wrong time."

"That's possible, but I'm pretty sure he knows. He's traveled a lot."

"Grammy, did you know that?"

"I knew there's a big time difference; he's almost halfway around the world."

Mellie laid a finger on Pakistan and rotated the globe slowly, seeking Wisconsin. She found it, too. Steig's daughter was one smart girl. Her face melted into a sad, sad look. "That's so far." She murmured, "So far," and slogged off upstairs.

Friday night passed with no word, as did Saturday. Marit took all the kids to the community swimming pool, and the first thing Mellie asked when she came through the door: "Have we heard from Daddy?"

"No, but I don't expect to during the day. Maybe tonight."

"Oh."

"You want to help me make supper?"

She shook her head and made her way upstairs, as if climbing them took all her strength.

Jake clambered up on a kitchen stool. "Can I help?"

"Maybe you and Grampy can set the table." She glanced at Ken to see him shrug.

"You need us right away? I was hoping to set up the watering in the garden. If we don't get some rain pretty soon..." He tousled Jake's hair. "Come on, buddy, we need to find some stuff in the garage."

"We could go find worms and go fishing."

"I think maybe we could do that; how about off the dock?"

Jakey grinned, near to splitting his face. "Maybe Mellie wants to go fishing, too."

"Maybe she would. Come on, let's dig out the sprinklers first."

As Mona slid the homemade macaroni and cheese in the oven, she heard a door slam upstairs. Mellie did not slam doors. Mona made her way up the stairs. When she stepped into the room, she sucked in a breath of shock. Every game piece from all the games on the shelf were strewn about the room. *Oh Lord, give me wisdom.* Had she been younger, she might have been furious, but now all she could do was try to stop the tears.

"Mellie…what…?"

The little girl stood in the middle of the room, sur-rounded by her mess. "You lied to me! He's dead, isn't he? Daddy's dead!" As Mona strode forward, Mellie ducked away, her arms wrapped around her head.

"Oh, you poor baby." Mona grabbed an arm and pulled the little girl in against her. She hugged tightly, rocking sort of, until Mellie stopped struggling. Then Mellie sim-ply melted against her, sobbing. Mona sidled a couple steps to reach the tissue box with a free hand. She handed one to Mellie and used one herself.

"No, Mellie," Mona purred, "I will never lie to you. Your father is okay. He just missed his Skype, but he would never do that on purpose. He must have a good reason. Remember, I raised him. I know him so completely, I usu-ally know what he thinks. And I'm sure of his love for you.

"But…" She left the rest unspoken and simply clung. Finally she lifted her head.

"I—I'm sorry, Grammy, I'll clean it up, I promise."

How to handle this? Screaming temper tantrums she could understand, but malicious behavior left her bewildered. *Lord, oh, do I need wisdom now.*

"Later, when you feel better. How about we go downstairs, and you can break up the lettuce for salad? Then we'll talk about what to do, okay?"

"Do you hate me now?"

"Hate you? Why, heavens no. I could never hate you."

"She said she hated me, that I was a spoiled brat, and she didn't want to see my face again."

"I'm sorry she said that. But that is her fault, not yours or Jakey's. Let's go downstairs and get the supper on the table. Grampy and Jake are supposed to set it."

Mellie sniffed and almost giggled. "Jakey doesn't know how."

"Then it is time he learns. We'll let Grampy teach him while we whip cream for the dessert." She stood and held out her hand. "I made Jell-O. Guess what kind."

"I hope red." Mellie stepped back and blew her nose again. "Hyacinth licked my cheek. Can she sleep with me if she wants?"

"Once we get Jake over being afraid, we will see." Hand in hand, they walked down the stairs.

Chapter Sixteen

Birthday parties took more effort than he ever thought they would, but then Ken generally wasn't in on the planning stages. "So why can't we just meet at the ice cream shop, order a cake in advance, and that's it? I know they have a party room."

Mona gave him one of those looks. "Really."

He wasn't sure if it was a question or a statement, so he let it lie there. "Would be easier than packing everything up, hauling it to the park, unloading, setting up, party, clean up, reload, get home, unload, and put stuff away."

"You really think you could get away with this?"

"Okay, then, the pizza parlor. Bring the cake and presents…." He paused for a moment. "Maybe they would put candles on a pizza or we could." The look on her face did not bear much hope for his suggestions. He sighed. "All right, what is it you and Marit have hatched?" He knew it was going to be a whole lot like his scenario of all the steps. "If you didn't want my opinion, why did you ask?"

"Good question. I guess because now that you are retired, I thought you wanted to be involved in planning some of our events. We have to do something special because this is her first, and I hope only, birthday with neither her mom nor her dad in attendance. And if we don't hear from Steig pretty soon, I'll need to go downstairs and beat the snot out of that punching bag."

"Better than throwing toy pieces all over the house."

She lightly punched him on the arm, shaking her head. "I felt so sorry for her. I've sure been praying for God's wisdom with these kids."

"Why is it so different from when our kids were young?"

"First of all, we are a lot older, and sometimes my get-up-and-go just doesn't get up, let alone take off and leave me behind."

"But we are wiser and more patient. And you don't have to do it mostly alone while I'm at work." He held out his arms, and she walked into them, cushioning her cheek on his chest.

"You might not be the best party planner, but you are a mighty good man and I am so grateful to be your wife."

"Hey, you are the party planner by choice. Remember, that is your business." He laid his cheek on her head. "What can we do with five children and four adults? Think back to some of the early parties, which you always made into an event. What can we redo?" He paused a moment. "Maybe we should ask Mellie what she wants to do?"

"Good idea." She hugged him and stepped back. "We'll ask her when Marit brings them back. In the meantime, let's go work in the garden for a while. I want to get the tomatoes transplanted."

As always, they bought tomato plants when they were seedlings, planted them in pots up to their leaves, then did another transplant into a bigger pot, repeating the plant-to-the-leaves process. They always had fantastic tomatoes because the roots grew out from the buried stalk each time. But it didn't work for corn. At all. At times, Ken wished he'd gone into horticulture. Maybe now that he was retired...

"We could still have a frost."

"Then I'll cover them. Watching the forecast will be your job." Together they headed outside, both dog and cat trailing. "If you dig the holes, I'll do the rest."

"And we need how many holes?" He glanced over to where the tomato pots were lined up against the south side of the garage wall. "I think next year we'll put a hotbed in where the pots are now. Then we can start lettuce, cabbage, and some of the hardier seeds earlier."

"I thought you were talking about a small greenhouse."

"I was, but..."

"But what?"

"I guess—I guess I want to not be tied down just in case we can travel during springtime. They say Holland is amazing in the spring. And Butchart Gardens in Victoria." He lifted the shovel off the rack and grabbed a pot with the other hand, heading for the remaining empty spot where the dirt was ready and waiting for him. "You get the cages, please. They're hanging in the shed."

By the time they finished, dusk was sneaking in, mist spiraling up from the river as the air cooled.

Mona watered the seedlings one last time and they put the tools away, Ken carefully scraping the dirt off the shovel as he always did. His father had taught him how to care for his tools well.

"When does your wood-carving class start?"

"Tomorrow night. There are two of us beginners he's going to start privately so we can catch up to the regular class. Apparently his course started three weeks ago. I figured I'd wait until the next class started, but he wanted to do it this way, so..."

Ambrose barked and, tail flagging, headed for the drive-way where Marit's car was just turning in.

"So much for quiet around here." He halfway flinched at the look Mona shot him. But after all, he was entitled to his opinion. Maybe they'd go to bed early. Working like this in the garden with Mona was one of the things he'd looked forward to in retirement. As in not only in the evenings, but also during the day—in the middle of the week—whenever. He followed her out to greet the family.

Marit rolled down her window. "I promised everyone ice-cream cones at the shop. Come on with. My treat."

"Let me go wash my hands first; we'll be right back." Mona glanced at him and he nodded. "I'll put the animals in."

"You don't have room for us," Ken said to Marit once they were ready. He looked at the loaded van with two booster seats and five kids...

"Sure we do. Big kids in the back, one of you up here, and one between the seats there."

"I'll take the middle seat." He grinned at the two grand-sons. "So I can keep you from fighting."

"Grampy..." They were learning to turn that word into three syllables like they already did *Mom*. He flipped the fold-down seat back in place and slid in. "How did you earn ice-cream cones?"

"The boys picked up and put away all the toys and books and stuff in the right places, while the girls helped in the kitchen."

"The kitchen, eh? And what did you girls do?" He spoke to those in the rear seat.

"I unloaded the dishwasher and scrubbed the cookie sheets and stuff." Mellie spoke first.

"And Mom is teaching me to sort the laundry and get

the washing machine going. Did you know if you put too much soap in, the suds can run right out the top?" Brit finished.

"Hmmm, I wonder how your mom learned that lesson?" He poked his daughter on the shoulder.

"You don't have to remind me, I told them the whole story. What a mess that was, but we had a sparkly clean laundry room by the time I got it all cleaned up." She turned the van into the parking lot. "Okay now, everybody, two scoops and you have to decide quickly. Looks like a busy night."

"Saturday always is busy here. We could have had ice cream at home."

"But not all the flavors, Grampy." Brit patted his shoulder. "What kind are you going to have?" Marit and the children bailed out of the car and aimed for the ice cream parlor.

Ken decided to just wait in the car; he had plenty of ice cream at home. And he made a mental note to buy both sugar and plain cones at the store. He crossed his arms over his chest and prepared to watch the traffic go by. There was always visual entertainment at the ice cream parlor.

Brit appeared at the door. "Please come in, Grampy; it's not the same without you."

How did one resist a plea like that? He followed her in. *They probably just want me to pay. I think for a change I'll stand my ground.*

"What'll it be, sir?"

"One scoop Jamoca Almond Fudge in a sugar cone."

Brit looked up at him over the cone. "How come you always get the same kind?" She licked around her cone, catching the drips.

"Because it's my favorite, but Grammy doesn't like it much, so I never buy it for home." He took his cone and thanked the young man, at the same time digging in his back pocket for his wallet.

"The bill is already paid, sir. Enjoy your ice cream."

"Oh. Thank you." He turned to look at Mona, who shook her head.

Marit whispered as she herded the troops out the door, "We don't just invite you along to pay, you know. We like your company." She raised her voice. "Careful, everybody, so you don't drop your ice cream. Torin, settle down. Jake..."

"Too late," Ken murmured so only Mona heard him.

Jake stood staring at the blob of ice cream on the sidewalk, screwed his face up, and started to wail.

"What did I tell you, buddy?" Marit crouched in front of him. "Wouldn't have happened if you'd not been chasing Torin."

"I want more ice cream."

"What did I tell you?"

"But I didn't mean to."

"I'm sure you didn't, but you need to listen and do what I tell you." She took out a tissue and mopped his eyes. "Now you can go ahead and eat your cone. There must be some ice cream down in it, and next time—listen up." She stood and headed for one of the benches.

It was all Ken could do to not hand his cone to his grandson, but he well knew this was what the pros liked to call a teachable moment.

Mellie heaved a dramatically heavy sigh and stood in front of her brother. "I'll share mine with you, but you can't hold it."

"Want my own ice cream." He took two bites from

Mellie's cone, grabbed it, threw it on the concrete, and stomped on it.

All the kids froze, eyes swiveling to Marit. Ken and Mona stared at each other. If this were a college student, how would Ken handle it? Was this his problem? After all, he was in loco parentis, but he had no idea how to respond.

Thank God, Marit took over, but then, she was not just a teacher, but a teacher of special-needs children. She no doubt knew how to handle tantrums. "Everybody, go ahead and finish your ice cream; use the wipes in the car to get the sticky off. Jake, here's a paper napkin. Please pick that up and throw it in the trash. You cannot leave here until you do."

His glare could have started a bonfire.

The standoff lasted as all the others climbed back into the car, finished their ice cream, and wiped their hands. Ken waited beside the car door.

"Come on, Dad, we'll all wait in the car where we can be comfortable." Marit said it loudly, no doubt to make certain Jakey heard. Her tone of voice sounded as if tem-per tantrums like this happened every day and this was no big deal. Jake would have to learn.

When Grampy climbed in the car, Jake's eyes widened. He stared at the car full of his family, down at the smashed cone still in the paper wrap, and back to Marit. A big fat tear trickled down his cheek, glinting in the lights above and from the windows.

The stubbornness in his face defied description.

"There's no use all of us wasting time. Mom, if you'll stay with Jakey, I'll drive the rest of us back home and return for you." Marit leaned forward in the driver's seat as Mona slid out. The engine roared to life. In fact, Ken noted, Marit was gunning it a little extra.

"Nooooo!" Jakey wailed. "No! Don't leave me!" He bent over, picked up most of the cone, dumped it in the trash, and ran to the open car door.

Ken lifted him into his seat, and Mona handed him a wipe before she got back in. Marit backed out and tooled out into the street. What a battle of wills. How his daughter managed to stay so cool through it all, Ken would never know. One thing he did know; he couldn't have done it. He reached forward and patted her shoulder, leaving his hand there a moment. "Well done."

Back at their house, Marit drove in and stopped. "We're heading on home, church tomorrow but no Sunday school. Need to get baths and all that. Thanks for coming with." Marit added, "By the way, Mom and Dad, don't worry about Jake's tantrum or his thumb-sucking. With all he's gone through, he's doing well."

"Guess we're seeing your expensive college education in action, teacher." Mona sounded as proud as Ken felt.

"I think so. Night."

"Thanks for the ice cream," Ken called. The two kids dutifully followed Ken's example and walked with him and Mona to the house, waving as they walked.

Ambrose thwacked him with his tail, and Ken leaned over for the ritual greeting, no matter how long or short a time they'd been gone. "Where's your buddy, or are we going to hear a scream from the kid again?"

Later with the kids in bed and the other two in their normal places—Hyacinth on Mona's lap and Ambrose snoring beside the recliner—Ken exhaled as if from his toes.

Mona looked up from her laptop. "That bad?"

"I'm in need of a break, and they've not been here two weeks yet."

"Bible School starts Monday, so you'll have that time alone. Unless, of course, you are planning on assisting at VBS?"

He felt his eyes widen. "You're kidding, right? You didn't volunteer me for something?"

"No, but they always need help, and grandpas are always in big demand."

"Not this grandpa. And I told Magnus tomorrow I would help him put up those shelves and some other stuff."

She nodded. "I had forgotten that. You want tea? Iced is in the fridge, but if you are thinking hot, I'll start it. I need to do some other things in there anyway." She set her laptop on the coffee table.

"Hot, some of that chamomile mix. Thanks, hon."

He could hear her banging around in the other room but didn't even have the energy to offer to help. They hadn't walked for a week now, and the week before the kids came, they walked every evening if not in the morning. Even with all the craziness at the office, they'd taken time to go walk. *This has to stop or I will have to join the gym. Or walk by myself.* That might be the answer until they got some kind of a routine going here.

"Here you go." She set his steaming mug on the coaster waiting for it. Setting her own mug down, she collapsed into her recliner and kicked it back.

"Thank you." He inhaled the fragrance. "Did you put cinnamon in here? Smells good."

"I read that cinnamon is good for something that I can't remember right now but thought I'd try it."

He broached a subject he dreaded. "How's the planning coming for that preschool project?"

"I think I have the proposal ready to put in final form. I meet with her again this week."

He studied the tea in his cup. "I don't have a very good feeling about this."

"Why? It's my chance to do a big job that should be fairly easy, make lots of contacts. It's all good."

"Did you work in a contingency clause?"

"No. Good point." She picked up her pad and pen and made the note.

"I treasure the fact that so far, I have not heard you downstairs beating that punching bag to bits." He looked at her with raised eyebrows. "Right?"

She grumbled the answer, but at least it was affirmative.

"I really don't want you to slide back. Do you?"

"They haven't even signed the contract yet. They said they weren't ready. So maybe I won't even get the project."

"Maybe not." *Lord, please keep her from this. All I see is trouble if she takes it on.*

Chapter Seventeen

S o you and Magnus finished the project?"
"We did and all the shelves look mighty fine. Made me think of places here where we could add more shelving." He shook his head. "So much stuff moved in."

"Just think, much of their belongings are in storage."

"Grampy?" Mellie leaned against his legs. "Do you think Daddy will Skype tonight?"

Mona held out her arms from her recliner, and Mellie squeezed in beside her. "I'm sure he's someplace where he can't Skype. You know, here in America we have all kinds of cell phones and phones and radios and TV, but there are parts of the world that don't have anything like that. Maybe he's in one of those parts and doesn't have a working phone."

Jakey climbed up in Ken's lap. "I want to see Daddy." His forlorn little voice made Mona fight back the tears. She looked at Ken, and he half shrugged, his eyes as sad as she knew hers must be.

Ken cuddled the little boy into his chest. "He would if he could. I know he is even more sad than we are."

Mona laid her cheek on the top of Mellie's head. How to make two children understand something adults had a hard time with? She wished she were in the rocking chair.

Cuddling was more comforting in the rocker. Her mind flipped back to when her own two were little kids. Marit loved to cuddle in the rocking chair and be read to. Steig had a harder time sitting still, even when he was so tired his eyelids fluttered. He was so afraid he might miss out on something.

"How about we skip baths tonight and get into our jammies for Grampy to read to us?"

Jakey scrambled off Grampy's lap. "Whoo-hoo, no bath. 'Mon, Mellie. Hurry up!" He headed for the stairs.

"You need help?" Ken asked.

"Grrrrr-aaaaaam-pyyyyyy." Three syllables said in unison.

Mona and Ken rolled their eyes and shrugged at each other. "We better get ours on."

A few minutes later, they were gathered back on the leather sofa, animals at their feet as if ready to listen, too. Mona looked from Hyacinth to Jakey, who was snuggled under Ken's arm, totally oblivious to the cat.

Jakey pointed to the bookmark. "Grammy marked it."

"Well, I'll be flummoxed; she did, didn't she?"

Mellie jerked upright and stared at his face. "What does fl-fl- mean?"

"Flummoxed means, ah . . ." He looked at Mona. "You're the word person."

"You're the one with the PhD. But it means, ah, surprised, shocked, amazed, overwhelmed." She almost shook her head, her grin inviting one in return.

"See, Grammy is right. All of those things."

"Then why didn't you say so?"

"Because flummoxed is a fun word. Say it."

Dutifully the children did as he asked. Jakey giggled. "There's an ox in it."

"You're right! Smart kid." Grampy and Jakey high-fived.

"Can we read the story now?"

"We most certainly can." Ken flipped open the book. Mona picked up her crocheting, and they all lost themselves in the spider and the pig story, as Mellie called it.

Later, after the children were tucked in bed and prayers said, Mellie clung to Mona's hand. "If Daddy Skypes or calls, you will wake me up, won't you? Please? Anytime, not just on Thursday."

"Me, too," Jakey said sleepily.

"Of course." Mona and Ken both nodded and gently closed the door, leaving it open a crack, guiding the animals with them.

At the breakfast table in the morning, after a cereal discussion, Mona looked at Mellie and asked, "Since your birthday is coming up soon..."

"Friday."

"I know. What I want to know is what you would like to do for your birthday."

"See my daddy."

"Oh, honey, I know that, but we have no control..."

"I know, but Grammy, I want to see him so bad."

"Me, too."

Ken raised his hands in a time-out T. "Okay, before we have a big crying time, let's think of party ideas. Is there something special you would like to do?"

"Ride a pony."

"Our friends had ponies and horses, and we got to go see them lots of times." Jakey held up all ten fingers.

"Half of Texas has horses, but here in Wisconsin, it's a bit different." Ken looked at Mona. "Didn't you plan a children's party once, and someone brought in a pony for the kids to ride?"

Mona nodded. "I did and I will most certainly look into that. At that party, the farm owner brought the pony to the party, but usually the party has to go to the farm. Seems to me that the farmer raised ponies, and it's spring, so perhaps they might even have a colt or two."

Mellie's eyes shone. "Baby ponies are so cute." She flew off her chair and threw herself at Mona. "Oh, Grammy. That would be fantastical."

Mona hugged her back, her heart twanging from this little girl using a word her daddy had adopted when he was this age. "Okay, I'll see about Saturday so your cousins can come, too. But your birthday is on Friday, and you get to choose the menu for supper. Anything you want."

Mellie stared up at her, obviously thinking hard. Index finger on her chin, she chewed on her bottom lip. "Cake, chocolate cake and ice cream."

"What kind?" Ken asked, fishing his singing phone off his belt.

Mellie decided. "Strawberry, that's good with chocolate cake."

"Okay, that's the dessert, what for the meal?"

"Hot dogs!" Jakey jumped in.

"No! This is *my* birthday. You can choose hot dogs for your own."

Ken dropped his napkin on the table as he stood up. "That was Sandy; she needs some help again."

"Oh, rats, I was hoping you and the kids could work outside so I could get some of my work done."

"We can watch a movie," Mellie suggested.

"*Nemo*! We want *Nemo*!" Jakey beat a tattoo on the chair legs with his shoes.

"No! Not *Nemo*," Mellie snapped. "I want *Frozen*. You can be the monster."

"I am the shark!" He bared his teeth and growled.

Ken dropped a kiss on Mona's forehead. "I'll call you as soon as I have an ETA for home. Come on, you two, give Grampy a kiss. And you do what Grammy asks." He looked directly at Jakey. "Without arguing." The kids followed him to the door, tailed by the dog and cat. They waved him good-bye and returned to the table, where Mona was making a list.

"How about you clear the table, Jake? Mellie, you put the food away, while I get something out for supper. Any suggestions?" Cooking was not the problem. Always trying to decide what to make—now that was the struggle.

"Hot dogs."

Mellie poked her brother and shook her head.

"For dinner then?" He looked at Mona with puppy dog eyes, as if he would just die for hot dogs.

"Why not?"

"He always wants hot dogs," Mellie said with a long-suffering sigh.

"He can have hot dogs, and you and I can have something else, you know."

"Really? We had hot dogs lots with Daddy."

"I know, your daddy has always loved hot dogs. Come on, Jake, let's get the table cleared. What is that cereal bowl doing on the floor?"

Ambrose sat down, tail feathering the floor, and licked his chops.

Jake picked up the bowl. "See, it's all clean now."

"Ah, sorry, Jake, Ambrose and Hyacinth do not eat from our dishes."

"But he was hungry."

"Ambrose had his breakfast earlier. He will always eat

whatever we give him, but people food is not always good for dogs."

Jake stared at the bowl. "Not even milk and cereal?"

"Dog food is best."

"Dog food is icky." He set the bowl on the counter.

Mellie turned from putting the jam and the milk in the refrigerator to ask, "How do you know?"

"I ate one."

"Jakey!" Mother Mellie barked.

"Only one, it was icky."

Oh, good grief, how do I keep up with him? "Don't eat any more, you got that?"

"I won't." He dropped the last of the silverware into the sink. "Can we watch the movie now?"

"Beds first and pick up your room. Any toys out in the family room? I'll wipe the table off while you get started."

A couple of minutes later, she peeked in their room. Mellie was at the head of her upper bunk bed, pulling up the covers; Jake was sitting on the floor putting a Lego man of some sort together, bed all rumpled.

"Okay, Jake boy, I'll help you one more time. You have to fix your bed."

"I did."

"Let's try again, a little bit harder. Pick up the Legos and..."

"Don't wanna do the bed. It's too hard."

Mona sighed. "Well, you must try."

He got up, tugged on the blanket, and sat down again with his Legos. "Can't."

Making a bunk bed was not easy, Mona would agree. If only there was space in the room so he could get on the other side. Could they make do for a full year? Mellie should have a room of her own. That meant moving out of her office; that used to be Marit's room. For short-time stays, the one bedroom was fine, but long term, like this?

"I'll help you, baby." Mellie used her big sister tone.

"Not a baby," Jakey yelled back at her.

"Are, too, baby, baby." The singsong would make anyone yell.

Mona barked, "Mellie, that's enough."

"Well, he is, can't even fix his own bed."

"He has to learn how."

"Andy always fixed my bed. I like Andy." Jakey tugged at a corner of his blanket.

"Who is Andy?" Mona helped him pull the sheet up. "Now you do the comforter."

"Our babysitter most of the time."

"Oh, Andrea?"

"Yeah."

"Okay, beds are made. Now finish putting your toys away."

Jakey growled, "Don't want to put them away," his lip sticking out.

Mellie shoved her books onto the shelf. "The rest are Jake's."

"You have until I get my bed made to get them put away." Mona left the room. She continued ruminating on the room situation as she did her bed and picked up the bathroom. She had told Steig to put the kids' beds into storage because they had the bunk beds here. Good thing that bed could be taken apart for two singles. She and Mellie could go pick out new bedding. Or was there some in those black garbage bags waiting in the corner of the closet?

Jakey was still sitting there, surrounded by Legos, when she returned.

"I told him to, but he wouldn't listen to me." Mellie had taken a chapter book up to the bed and lay on her stomach reading.

"You two want *Nemo* on now?"

Mellie shook her head. "I'd rather read."

"I want *Nemo*." Jakey hopped up.

"But you can't come down and watch movies until the Legos are put away."

"Don't wanna put them away!" There was that lip again.

"Your choice. Come downstairs when they're back in their bin."

Mona went to her office. Could she get anything done? *Maybe.*

A few minutes later she heard music in the living room and went down there. Jakey had *Nemo* up and running. Mona silently envied the ease with which small children could adapt to electronics. Mona was not adapting gracefully. "Oh, good. So the Legos are put away."

Jakey, on his tummy on the floor, was obviously too wrapped up in the opening credits to respond.

Mona jogged upstairs and checked; she came back down. "Go put your Legos away, Jakey."

"I don't wanna."

Mona desperately needed Ken now, but he was busy at the university. *So much for retirement*, she thought. *Very well.* Punishing the punching bag surely made her strong enough for this. She knelt beside Jakey, scooped her arms around him, and stood up, hanging on to him.

He squirmed and shrieked, "No! I don't wanna!"

She hauled him upstairs, afraid that any second he would pull her off-balance, even though she gripped the handrail, and they both would tumble. She put him down in the middle of his Legos.

He twisted to his feet and started to bolt for the door, but she caught him by an arm. She gripped it like King Kong gripped Fay Wray. "Don't. Even. Think. About it. When the Legos are put away, you can come down. I'll leave *Nemo* on for you."

"I hate you! You're mean!"

Mona kept her voice soft and even, although his words pierced her right to the soul. "Hate me if you want. But you must learn to cooperate. I love you, Jakey." She left, his mournful wail ripping her heart apart.

The door opened; she poised to grab, but it was Mellie. "I can't read with all that howling. Can I lay on your bed?"

"You may. I'm going to work in my office for a while."

"'Kay."

Mona started at the top of the calls list. The first was from Carole Bergstrund regarding the preschool project. Ken's words nagged in her mind. He'd not made comments about the projects she'd been hired to do before. But then, as he said, they'd not had two small children in the house before, and this one would take up a lot of time, more so the closer to the opening date. *Lord, what would You have me do? No answer, no indication.*

Shouldn't she be cutting poor Jakey some slack? The child had been through so much, and she was just making his situation worse. Was there some other way she could resolve the issue? And she should do it herself rather than hand it to Ken. She had never been a just-wait-until-your-father-gets-home kind of mother.

Look, her worrying was already interfering with her business. *Cut it out, Mona! Get your mind back on your work!* She dialed Carole's number.

Carole answered on the first ring. "Oh, good! I got hold of you just in time. We have an emergency meeting this afternoon that you really ought to be part of. It concerns financing. Try to get to the Stoughton Library at one."

"I'm sorry, I can't do that." She could not expect Ken home for several hours yet.

"But we need your input. Whatever else you're doing can wait."

"No, I cannot leave the house for several hours yet. I'm sorry."

"We'll pay you, of course."

"It is not a matter of money. I cannot."

"Very well. Have a good day." She hung up. She sounded kind of huffy.

Why could Mona not bear to say, "I have my grandkids here and cannot come?" But she couldn't. Just when she thought she knew herself, some new quirk showed up.

On the one hand, she deeply regretted that this might make her lose the account. On the other hand, it really irked her that Carole assumed she could just drop everything and go. If that was the way the whole account was going to go, she didn't want it. Even without Jakey and Mellie, she could not always simply drop what she was doing and run.

Lord, I'm feeling so torn and buried. Please help me make sense of this strange new life I fell into. And I beg You, don't let me fall into depression again.

Chapter Eighteen

Ken finished shaving and toweled his face. Monday morning. Except for keeping two lost little children from fighting and/or killing each other, he didn't have much to do today. A day to himself, more or less? How novel. He slipped into a pocket tee and headed downstairs.

The phone rang as he entered the kitchen. He saw Mona at the stove doing breakfast sorts of things. "I'll get it." He picked up the receiver. "Sorenson residence."

"Ken, Sandy. John just called a finance meeting, and Dale has a big sheaf of papers. I feel trouble brewing."

"I agree. I'm leaving right now." He replaced the receiver. "Mona, there's an emergency at the university. I have to run; I'll get something later."

"Oh, dear!" She wheeled. "Anything dangerous, did anyone get hurt?"

"Not physically. Financially, very dangerous."

"Financially..." She looked just plain peeved. "Again? You're supposed to be retired, remember? Breakfast is almost ready. You can at least eat first."

"No. I'm sorry. I'll call later." He hustled out the door as she was shouting his name, spreading it into two syllables—"Ke-en"—like the kids. She was not pleased.

Neither was he. Sandy hadn't said so specifically, but it was obvious that she, the dean of students, had not been invited to this meeting. Not only was it a major breach of etiquette, but also it was a breach of ethics.

Traffic was heavy already today. It was as bad as living in a city. Well, probably not, but it was irritating. He could drive only as fast as the car in front of him, and that was five miles under the limit. The traffic was getting on his nerves big-time. *Ken, you can't think quickly unless your nerves are settled; you know that.* He must get himself under complete control now.

Breach of ethics. *Hm.* That might be a good weapon to use if they did anything underhanded with the budget. All the deans were supposed to be participating, and if they left Sandy out of it, that might be cause for protest, perhaps even a suit. The first suit Ken filed made them sit up and take notice.

Here was another possibility. If they excluded Sandy, he might put Gerald Leach, their lawyer, on permanent retainer, and he could represent the dean of students. They might not think Sandy should be there, but they didn't dare exclude her lawyer.

That would cost a pretty penny, but...

Traffic ground to a standstill. Of all the times...

Where was the closest place to get off this road and onto back roads? Ken knew them all; in fact, at this time of morning, he probably should have gotten off I-39 to start with. He mentally kicked himself for not doing so. He was going to have to get his brain back into university mode and fast. Traffic began moving again, inching along, a lethargic caterpillar on tranquilizers. He finally reached an exit and scooted off, one in a long line of cars who had the same idea in mind. He arrived in the visitor parking lot forty-five minutes later than normal traffic would have allowed.

He was frustrated, angry, and that would not do. *Get hold of yourself, Ken!* He parked in one of the very few slots left and laid his permanent parking pass on the dash.

Where was the meeting? He had no idea, so he headed for Sandy's office. It was locked.

Should he wait, or should he prowl until he found the meeting place?

It was probably the Stone Room upstairs. Barge in; that would be a nice surprise.

He couldn't see the elevator from here, but he knew the long, heavy sigh when the doors slid open. A moment later, Sandy came around the corner.

She said nothing. He said nothing. She unlocked the door, and he followed her inside, closing it behind him. She flopped into the desk chair, so he took the side chair; the wingback was just as comfortable as his desk chair. Former desk chair.

Her eyes were red and wet. "We're dead." She took a deep breath. "You're not dead. You escaped the massacre barely in time."

He had to be supersharp for this. "Talk to me."

She shrugged under the weight of the world. "I'll start at the beginning. As soon as I called you, I grabbed everything out of my out-box and ran after Dale as silently as possible. I lost him at the elevator, but I saw he got off on the fourth floor, so I ran up the stairs. I saw him go into the Hostmark Room."

"Not the Stone Room?"

"Not where we normally meet, no. I entered right behind him, and you should have seen John's face. First, he was startled, and then he was furious. He actually blurted out, 'What are you doing here?' I know, I just know Dale was thinking about chasing me back out, but I suppose he knew he didn't dare. I said, 'This is an executive meeting and I'm dean of students. Is there a problem?'"

Ken smiled. He could just picture the scene.

"I asked, 'Will we wait for John Macy?' and Dale said, 'No.' So I said, 'He's usually the first one to come in. He must not know about it,' and I stared right at John Nordlund. We all knew John M. was ready to side with you."

Ken laughed aloud. "Beautiful! Just beautiful. You let them know you were onto their shenanigans, but you didn't say anything accusatory."

"They went around the room as always, and when they came to me, I spread the out-box papers in front of me. I said, 'My show-and-tell,' and picked up a letter to a junior in engineering. 'This young man went to the bursar's to drop out. They sent him to me. His mom had a hysterectomy but is basically bedridden from a serious infection. She desperately wants him to stay in school, but he has to take care of her and his brothers. So he and I put heads together and worked out a plan where he works in the herbarium in return for tuition; this is the letter confirming the agreement. He's going to be a great engineer in a couple years. And he is one of over two dozen students we've helped in the last couple of weeks.'"

"Nicely done, showing a positive outcome with a human face instead of just spouting statistics."

She looked so weary and sad. "But my pitch didn't make any difference. They're phasing out the aid aspect of the department. They said students will have to find outside aid and scholarships, that we can't afford it anymore. They have to keep the department because it's written into the structure. But they're diverting the funds, and without sufficient funds, we're sort of hollow. Just standing around staring at the wall."

"There may be legal avenues. I'll talk to Gerry. I doubt John or Dale will change their minds without a legal shove in that direction."

She nodded. "Incidentally, my future is assured. After the vote, and as the committee was breaking up, John sat down beside me and leaned in. Then he laid a hand on my arm. 'Now, Sandy, you are probably worried about your future, that you might end up without a job. Please don't be. Regardless whether you remain as dean of students, you'll have a place in this university. Maybe over in procurement. But you'll have something.' Those were his exact words, but I did not repeat them to you condescendingly enough. He talked to me as if I were a high school freshman! I was so repulsed I wanted to break a chair over his head, but I knew I didn't dare burn that bridge, so I just took it."

Ken studied her a moment, then stood up and crossed to the main bookcase, his old bookcase. "I understand your favorite celebratory drink is San Christoff Sparkling Cider."

"San Chris— What?"

He pulled the bound student aid reports from 1993 to 2002 off the shelf and tossed them aside on the floor. Yep, it was still there. He pulled the bottle of sparkling cider out from the space behind the reports, crossed to his desk, got the cork puller out of the bottom left drawer, and went to work.

She gaped. "What . . . ?" She twisted around to stare at the blank space on the shelf. She twisted back and watched him pull the cork. "You mean that was there all this time?"

"I got the primo, you'll notice, not the less expensive stuff. It was going to be for some special occasion, but it's worth pouring now." He picked up her coffee mug, dumped the coffee out into the queen palm beside the window, and poured sparkling cider nearly to the rim.

"Wait. Here." She handed him the spare mug out of the right-hand drawer.

He poured himself a libation and settled into the wing-back chair. He raised his mug. "A toast to the woman who has what it takes and has never realized it. You did us proud."

"But I couldn't cajole them into giving us the money we need."

"As I've so often told Steig and Marit, 'Whether you win or lose may be controlled by someone else, but only you can do the very best you can.' You did the best you could. That deserves celebration."

She smiled and sipped, then took a healthy swig. She stared at nothing a few moments, then asked, "So how's it going on the home front? Quite a change for you two."

He wished she hadn't asked that, because she was too good a friend and colleague for him to get disingenuous. But he didn't want to dump on her when she was under such a black cloud already, so he shrugged noncommittally. "We're trying, and they're trying; we'll get by."

She didn't ask anything; just gazed at him.

The silence became unbearable and he dumped. "Jakey's having a hard time of it, and Mellie has buried herself in her books. She's a good reader; she told me she took a test her teacher in Texas gave her, and she reads at eighth-grade level. But that's not adjusting, that's escaping. And they don't have enough to occupy them all day. I guess Mona and I have lost that touch."

"Mona and you did a pretty fine job of raising responsible adults."

"Thank you. But this is different."

"You have to remember that Steig and Marit never had to deal with abandonment. Abandonment by both parents yet."

"Steig didn't abandon them. He..."

"Ken, I know Steig better than those kids do. I've been in your home and around your whole family for nearly a quarter century. And you know Steig better than I do. You changed his diapers and taught him to use a fork. And you taught him to man up. You and I know absolutely that Steig will not willingly abandon his children. If he has to drag himself through a minefield, he'll get back to his kids."

"So why do you say...?"

"Those children have known Steig less than ten years, Ken. You tell them they can trust him, and Mona assures them they can trust him, but their experience tells them otherwise. He's gone. If he's gone a year, that's ten or twenty percent of their lives. They don't yet possess our assurance that he's trustworthy, especially when their mother walked out."

Ken nodded slowly. Of course Sandy was right. He thought again of the tears and sadness as Mellie tried to deal with her loss. Abandonment. In her eyes, that was exactly what it was. No calls, no Skype. No Daddy. And no Mommy. And Jake, only five, having to handle the same unspeakable loss; no wonder they were not the perfect angels that Steig and Marit had been. Usually. Well, sometimes.

Child psychologists would be quick to say that to a child, relationship is everything. Adults might be distracted by pretty toys or fancy belongings, but to children, family is everything. Everything. These two children had just seen their family, the most important thing in their lives—the only real thing in their lives—shatter irreparably, and there was nothing they could do about it. The insight almost brought Ken to tears.

"I don't know what I can do to help you and your family, Ken. I'm at a loss here, but I'll keep you in my prayers. And I'll try not to ask for help so much. You don't need this job on your plate, too."

"I can't just see it disappear, either. I've had a vested interest in it for far too long to see it evaporate."

She smiled. "I won't let that happen. Now that I've been at it firsthand, I see the difference it makes. It's my fight, too, now, Ken."

Ken finished his cider. Her words comforted him more than she could know.

She poured herself another mugful. "I'll talk to Gerald Leach. See if our law counsel has anything to offer."

Ken stood up. "Our help getting him through school means that much to him. Besides, I don't think he likes John's department very much. Apparently they gave him a difficult time. Well, Sandy. Hang tough."

She came around the desk to give him a hug. "You hang tough, too."

Ken left.

Now what? He ought to get home soon. The traffic by now would have smoothed out. He could go I-39. He walked across campus to the parking lot.

Bless her, Sandy had given him immense insight into the children's needs. He still didn't have any idea what to do, but at least he could see more clearly what they were battling. He could glimpse the depth of their sorrow.

The road had cleared out considerably; not that many people were entering and leaving Madison at this time of day. He passed a Cracker Barrel, which reminded him he had eaten no breakfast, savored no coffee. Should he get breakfast at home, assuming Mona was in a mood to let him back in the house? No, it was almost lunchtime. So he turned around the block and went back to the Cracker Barrel.

He bought a paper at the restaurant door and took it in with him. The smiling hostess seated him in a booth and plopped the menus in front of him. Should he have breakfast or lunch? Something brunchish would be the most appropriate. He settled on a cheesy omelet, received his coffee and sent in his order, and opened the paper.

Steig didn't express much respect for newspapers or for news in general. "Same things happening to different people and the same people doing goofy things." That about summed it up.

You are so right, Steig.

Where was he? Ken wondered. Special Forces are elite, so Steig was serving with the best of the best, but where? Obviously, it was nowhere with adequate cell service. Carefully Ken scanned the international news page, looking for mentions of deployment, transfers, or hot spots. That didn't mean much, of course, since the army could be sending Steig to someplace that was not a hot spot yet. Nothing jumped out at him.

He found the crossword puzzle and folded the paper open around it. He reached in his breast pocket for a pencil. *Nuts.* He had not put a pencil in it before he left. *Oh, well.*

"Excuse me, sir. Your omelet."

"Thank you." Ken smiled and put his puzzle aside.

The waitress smirked, although it was mostly a smile. "Pen?" She held one out.

Ken accepted it. "Why, thank you. That is most thoughtful."

"I'm a cruciverbalist, too." Smiling, she left.

Now Ken had even more to think about. Here was a woman in a job that one usually associated with limited education, using the word *cruciverbalist*. Obviously, her world was much larger than one would expect. And the children came back into his mind. For the next six months to a year, Mona and he would be their caregivers and teachers. They could merely babysit, or they could widen the children's horizons in ways that Steig, when he returned, would not have time to do.

Travel. Where could they travel? Travel broadens one's horizons. Either this was a very tasty omelet or he was hungrier than he'd realized or both. Travel. Mona and he had full custody, but it would probably involve considerable legal hassle to take them out of the country. Somewhere stateside.

Historical areas? They were pretty young to appreciate Gettysburg or somewhere like that. Natural areas? They'd love seeing any wildlife that popped up, but mountains, lakes, and canyons? Not so much. The hash browns were good, too.

That left museums. And museums were increasingly catering to youth. There was his answer. Go down to Chicago for a couple days, spend at least a day at the Field and another at the Museum of Science and Industry, an afternoon in the planetarium. He wouldn't mind seeing Chicago again himself. Milwaukee would be good, too. It had enough to fill a two-day visit.

And then his idle dreaming stopped short. Mona was all

wrapped up in her business. She would never travel far or for an extended trip. He began to resent her business, and that was ridiculous. But—well, there it was.

Her business was helping her stay on top of her chronic depression, too. The kids were going to encourage depression, so he'd better not ask her to travel. Some of her really depressed swings had been murder to live with, punching bag or no.

She was emotionally fragile. Would her tendency to depression rear its ugly head when she tried to take care of two children who were just as emotionally fragile?

Ken could see no rainbow in the clouds ahead.

Chapter Nineteen

Find a pony farm. Find a pony farm. Nothing in the phone book. Mona googled pony farms/Madison, WI. Bingo. West of their area about ten miles. She looked over their website, Clauson's POA's and Norwegian Fjord Horses. "Rent a pony" was listed among their services. She punched in the number.

She explained what she was looking for, and the woman from the farm chuckled.

"This age is our favorite kind of birthday. We already have one party in the morning, so could you arrive, say, two? We have a party room with a freezer if you want to bring ice cream, and we have a special surprise for the birthday child." She gave the cost. "And that includes the children meeting some of our stars, and we can include a buggy ride with one of our Fjord horses for an extra ten dollars. I can e-mail you the contract, you e-mail it back, and then you may pay that day when you arrive. There is a list on the contract of all the things you can bring."

"You certainly do a good job of making this as easy for your visitors as possible."

"Years of experience, my dear. My name is Beverly, and I will be your greeter."

"See you on Saturday, and I'm so grateful we can do this on such short notice."

"We had a cancellation; that's why."

Mona hung up and leaned back with a smile. This was a gift of God, she realized; a cancellation just when she needed the pony farm. *Thank You, Lord!*

Now what to buy for her present? Which reminded her of the black garbage bag that held birthday and Christmas presents for both of the children from their daddy. Their son had always been so well organized, but this was beyond believable. *Lord, keep him safe wherever he is. These kids need their daddy so desperately.*

Every evening Mellie's prayers for her daddy grew a bit longer, often ending with tears leaking into her pillow. Every evening Jake asked, "Daddy Skyping tonight?" And Ken responded with, "Guess we'll just have to wait and see. He'll Skype if he can."

Mellie's school year had been nearly over when Steig brought her to Wisconsin, but the local school was not. Wednesday Marit picked her children up after the final half day at school, and with all the cousins and Grammy in the van, they headed for a picnic up at the park. While the lake was still too cold for swimming, the kids played in the creek, and even Jake wore mud from head to foot by the time Marit called them back for lunch.

"Wash your hands at the faucet and let's eat. Grammy and I are starving." She smiled at Jake. "And I brought hot dogs just for you." At Arne's groan, she shook her head. "Don't worry, son, we have peanut butter and strawberry jam sandwiches for you and anyone else who wants one."

"What are you today, short order cook?" Mona asked as she dug a hot dog out of a thermos and stuck it in a bun for Jake. "You put what you want on it." She knew his father usually still did those things for him, but she figured he was old enough to decorate his own hot dog—along with a host of other things, like choose his own ice cream flavors and dish up his plate at the supper table.

"Just for today and a proper school-is-out celebration. Tomorrow they are on their own."

As soon as everyone was eating at the table, she and Marit moved their folding chairs into the shade and settled in to eat and chat. Giggles grew in intensity.

"What's going on up there?" Marit tried to sound menacing, but Mona shook her head.

"Nothing." Standard answer meaning Mom should probably go check.

With a sigh, Marit got out of her chair, and as soon as she saw the sight, she stopped and sighed again. "All right. Torin, Jake, do not put anything more in your mouth until you chew what you have." Their cheeks bulged like two busy chipmunks. "The rest of you, knock it off; Brit, you know better."

"You always blame me."

"You're the eldest; you should be setting an example." As soon as the two lost their fat cheeks, she gave them all the stink eye and returned to her chair and her iced tea.

A couple of minutes of peace and someone asked, "Can we go back to the creek now?"

"Has everyone finished?"

"All but Torin, and he's always the last one."

"Okay, the rest of you clean up, and when Torin is finished, you can head for the creek."

Multi-toned groan. Brit went into big sister mode and rapped out the orders. Within a few minutes, the table was indeed cleared and they were off to the creek.

"Every home needs a place for kids to dig and a creek

running through it. Best child sitters in the world." Marit sipped her tea and closed her eyes. "Hear the laughter? They are having such a great time, and it doesn't cost a dime."

Mona caught her up on the surprise at the pony farm party, and Marit grinned at her. "Good job, Grammy. I bet you put that place in your file for future kid parties."

"I sure did. I'll take pictures, or rather you'll take pictures and we can put them in the file, too."

"Did you tell her what you do? Maybe she'll knock a bit off the price if you will send families her way."

Mona shook her head. "Naah, her prices are rock bottom already."

"Still…"

"To change the subject, I know I've asked before, but is there any chance you could come work for or with me for a while?" She went on to describe the proposal she put together for the preschool. "Your dad is really against me taking this on because of our two new family members."

"He's afraid all that will send you back to the punching bag?"

"Or worse." Mona looked toward the creek from where she could hear children's chatter. "Should we go over there and check on them?"

"You realize he may be right?"

"I know. But this is a really big project, the kind of thing I dream of doing."

"I know, but…"

"You have your hands full, too."

"I mean, I could help you once in a while, but not on a regular basis. You could advertise for an assistant."

"I've thought of that. But training a helper…" She shook her head. "Maybe I need to put what I want on hold and hopefully pick it up again when Steig returns." She tipped her head back and stared up into the branches of a maple tree that come fall would burst into a magnificent flaming beacon. But right now it was just getting into full leaf. Was she like that tree that needed time before the glory? "I've prayed and asked God to guide me in this, but He seems to be off dealing with other more important things."

"Someone I know once told me that times like this He was saying, *Wait*. That person who shall remain nameless even gave me a few verses to back it up. Verses like 'Wait upon the Lord' and 'Be still and know that I am God' and…"

"You know how much I hate eating my own words?"

"I do. You gave me a ditty for that. Remember? 'Oh, dear Lord, make my words so sweet, when I have to eat them, 'twill be a treat.'"

Mona tossed the bits of ice left in her glass at her daughter. "Think about it, okay?"

Marit brushed the ice off her shirt. "I will pray with and for you. That you will do what is best for all concerned." She glanced at her watch. "We better round up the animals and get them washed off so they can get back in the car. This has been pure delight."

"Saturday will be too."

Marit nodded. "And VBS starts Monday. Can Dad help?"

Mona grimaced. "We'll have to see. The time he is spending back at the job gives me a pain in the backside. They can hire him as a consultant if they need him that bad."

"Are you surprised?"

"Not in the least." Together they folded up their recliners, repacked the baskets, and carried them to the car.

"Have you mentioned how you feel?"

"Not in so many words. What good would it do?"

"If you phrased it carefully—at just the right time." Even Marit's face looked a question mark. Mona shrugged and shook her head, sliding the last of the baskets into the back of the van.

"Mooooom!" Brit's voice carried from the creek. "Come see."

Together, mother and daughter ambled over to the small creek that tinkled merrily to the lake.

"See our boats? Grammy, you get to be the judge. Go stand at that rock where the creek goes into the lake, and whichever boat gets there first wins. Mom, you stand here and yell 'go' when we are lined up, okay?"

"Good idea!" Mona looked at each of the kids with their leaf boat in hand.

"See, Grammy, I put a sail on mine." Arne showed her. He had used another leaf as a sail on a boat made of two or three leaves tacked together with tiny sticks.

She looked at Marit, who nodded and shrugged. This kid had been blowing their minds since he was three. Ken always said he was an engineer in the making. She made her way to the rock some twenty feet away and turned with a wave.

"Okay, get your boats ready."

All six lined up in the creek, ready to set their boats down.

"On your mark, get set"—Marit chopped with her arm—"go!"

Boats on the water and the cheering began. They took to the banks and followed their bobbing crafts. Arne's boat caught on a piece of wood and bobbed a few times until it spun around and kept on going, now way behind the others. Brit's leaf tipped over but kept on in the current. Mellie's boat took the lead, then caught on a rock. Brit's floated on ahead but was listing to the side more with every swirl. The kids yelled for their boats, the adults laughed and clapped. Jake's boat sank lower and lower until a swirl caught it and whirled it on. But by the end, only Torin's and Mellie's boats were still in the race.

Mona threw up her hands. "Tie! The boats are tied!" She clapped for the winners. "And everyone else did a fine boat job. Mellie and Torin get two scoops at the ice cream shop on the way home. So load 'em up and let's hit the road."

"After you wash up at the faucet!"

All the way back to town, the kids talked about the boat race and what they would do on the next one.

"Actually, I hadn't planned on ice cream." Marit glanced at her mother.

"I figured the winners needed an award, so this is my treat. Oh my, but that was fun. They were so creative."

That evening after supper, the four of them headed for the river walk with the animals on leash. Jake rode his three-wheeler, and both kids explained the boat race in detail to Ken, then Jake said, "I sure wish you had been there, Grampy. You really missed out."

Ken glanced at Mona, who was nodding along with the kids. "I do, too," he answered.

"So, Grampy, I thought you retired." Mellie slid her hand into his and looked up at him. "Doesn't that mean you don't work there no more?"

"Anymore," Mona corrected automatically.

"Anymore?"

Ken nodded slowly. "That is what retired is supposed to mean, but sometimes one should help a friend out. I think we got it all straightened out today."

"I sure hope so," Mona muttered for his ears alone.

❈   ❈   ❈

Saturday wore a cloud cover that looked an awful lot like rain.

"But they predicted sun." Mona grumbled as she flipped the switch on the coffee and removed breakfast fixings from the refrigerator.

Ken checked his phone. "This is supposed to blow over by ten." He returned to his paper. Flipping the corner down, he whispered, "Does she know?"

"Only that the party is at two." The night before, they'd had a birthday dinner of spaghetti with *crispy bread* (as Jake called French bread under the broiler), red Jell-O salad, and ice cream. Mellie had opened her present from her daddy and immediately lost herself in book one of a series about horses.

"Someday I get to have a horse," she announced later.

"Now where would we put a horse?" Ken had asked.

"At a stable." Her answer sounded like every horse-loving girl got to stable her horse. Ken smiled at the memory.

"What are you making?" Ken asked Mona.

"French toast with syrup, or applesauce if you'd rather."

"I want applesauce," Jake announced, climbing up in Ken's lap.

"Where's Mellie?"

"Reading her book."

"Will you go get her, please?"

Jake slid to the floor and, dragging his blankie, yelled from the bottom of the stairs. "Mellie, breakfast! Grammy said."

Mona shuddered. She turned to Jake. "I asked you to go get her, not call her."

"Oh." He climbed back up in Grampy's lap and leaned against his shoulder. "Can we go walk again tonight?"

"I hope so. That was nice, wasn't it?"

"Uh-huh."

Mellie slid into her chair just as Mona set the platter of French toast on the table, then brought both the warmed-up syrup and the applesauce. "Applesauce, thank you, Grammy."

"Can I have both?" Jake asked.

Ken rolled his eyes. "You really want both?"

Jake nodded. "The applesauce on first and then the syrup, just like Mommy liked hers." He ducked at the look Mellie sent him.

Ken and Mona exchanged a look of sadness, then Ken wrapped his arm around his grandson. "That's okay, Jakey boy. You can have your French toast any way you like it."

"We don't talk about her," he mumbled, tears brimming and about to run over.

"I understand. You want to fix it yourself?"

Jake shook his head, so Ken spooned out the applesauce and ran a drizzle of syrup over the top.

"There you go. Now, let's have grace and we can dig in. After all, we have a big day ahead."

After they silently finished eating, Mellie turned to her grandma. "Grammy, what should we wear to my party?"

Mona appeared to be thinking deeply, then nodded. "I think jeans would be best. And a T-shirt."

"Me, too?" Jake popped up. "I like shorts."

"I know, but today I think you better wear jeans." She grinned at the two studying her, hoping for clues, she suspected. "That's all I'm going to tell you."

"T-shirt! But it's raining," Mellie whined.

"Weatherman says nice day by noon."

"And the party is at two?"

"Right, but we'll need to be in the car by one fifteen. We are taking both cars today."

"Cousins?" Jakey asked.

"You got to have cousins for a party," Mellie said as if they'd always had cousins at their birthdays.

Both kids were waiting by the door by one. As predicted, the sky had cleared and they climbed in the SUV giggling with excitement.

Jake looked over the backseat. "What is all that stuff back there?"

"Party stuff, silly." Mellie helped him buckle into the car seat.

"Everybody ready?" Ken asked.

When Mellie read the sign where they turned in a long driveway, she shrieked and giggled. "We're going to a pony farm. Look, Jake, all the horses and ponies out in the pasture. Will we get to ride one?" Her words tripped over each other as she plastered her nose to the window. "Oh, Grammy, this is the best birthday ever."

They parked next to Marit's van, and all the cousins bailed out at the same time, Mellie and Brit dancing in place as they watched a lady with boots and a Western hat come to greet them.

"Welcome to Clauson's pony farm. I'm going to give you kids a tour while your moms do what they need to do."

"This is my grammy and grampy," Mellie said, turning to look at each one with a huge smile.

"All of ours," Brit clarified.

"Ah, I see. Well, you can call me Miz Beverly and I will be your wrangler for today. And if you will tell me who the birthday girl is, I have a special hat for you that you can take home and keep as a souvenir." She held up a red Western hat with sparkles on it.

Mellie's eyes rounded. "Oh, for me, I mean this is my birthday party!"

Miz Beverly set it on the child's head. "Now, don't you look purty? Okay now, you follow me and I'll give you a tour of the farm first so you can meet our family, and then we'll head on over to the corral where you can all ride, just not at the same time." She turned and beckoned them. "Come along now. Your moms can set up the party while you ride."

Marit gestured. "You go. You wanted to see the operation."

"You can handle this alone?"

Marit smirked. "I'm a big girl now."

"And she has her daddy to help her." Ken stepped in beside her.

Magnus joined the party. "I want to see what they have here."

Miz Beverly paused beside the first pony pasture. "Here is our newest member. Her name is Shadow for short, but her mama isn't going to let her come visit with you yet. She was born three days ago."

As Mona snapped some photos of a terminally cute gray baby pony, she realized that she and Mellie would both want photos of this party—Mellie for memories and Mona for reference as well as memories. This would make a great event attraction.

Two other ponies joined them at the fence, sticking their noses between the wooden boards. Beverly showed the children how to feed a treat from a flat palm and soon the carrot pieces disappeared, leaving contented ponies and giggling children. Mona took pictures, including a close-up of Torin's little hand feeding nibbling pony lips.

They gave carrots to several of the Norwegian Fjord

ponies in another field. Mona had seen articles and pictures, but she had never seen one up close—short, stocky, and incredibly shaggy.

Magnus smiled. "The only ponies of this breed I've ever seen are in Norway."

They walked through the long pony barn with stalls on either side, and Mona noted that the barn was clean, airy, and smelled fresh. Yes, she would bring children's parties here.

They met the family of barn cats, including a lovely little calico miss who sat picturesquely on a hay bale with her tail curled around her paws. Jakey cringed, pressing against Mona, and would not look at them.

And all the while, they were accompanied by the fluffy mottled-gray farm dog, who obviously had decided Jake could become his best friend. When they stepped back out in the sunshine, two of the golden Fjord horses were hitched to an open carriage big enough for all of them. Mellie was helped to the place of honor up by the driver.

The party preparations must have been completed, for Ken and Marit joined them. She frowned at Miz Beverly. "Are those horses strong enough to take all of us? It's such a big carriage, and all these people..."

Miz Beverly laughed. "Oh my, yes. Pound for pound, these ponies are the strongest horses in the world. Hop up there; the load is not too heavy."

And so they all climbed in, including adults, and rode all around the farm, crossing a bridge over the flowing creek, down a tree-lined path under a canopy of rustling branches overhead, and eventually back to the barn.

"Now we get to ride?" Mellie whispered.

Miz Beverly nodded. "Now you get to ride. We have three ponies saddled and ready. Have you ridden before?"

Mellie nodded. "But only in a circle that led the ponies."

"Today you will have one of our helpers with you but there will be no machine. See the corral over there? That's our riding corral for beginners." She climbed down and opened the half door for the rest of the party. "Pony riders over there, please. Moms and dads over there." She pointed to a separate building over near the parking lot. "One of my helpers will meet you there and be your host."

The more she looked around, the better Mona liked this place. The place was neat, orderly, and spacious. She paused to watch the budding horsemen in the far corral. Mellie, already aboard her steed, was wearing a riding helmet. *Good!* This operation made safety a top priority.

By the time the children had all ridden, enjoyed their cake and ice cream, and were headed home, Jake had fallen asleep almost before they cleared the entrance.

Behind Mona, Mellie took off her hat and studied it. "Thank you, Grammy and Grampy, for the best birthday ever."

Mona twisted to smile over the seat back. "I'm so glad you liked it."

"Miz Beverly said they give riding lessons at the farm."

"I know." Mona caught the raised-eyebrow look Ken shot her.

"Maybe someday I could take some lessons out there."

"We'll have to see." Mona stretched across and patted her granddaughter's knee. "We'll send the video to your daddy, too. He'll be so proud of you."

A tear meandered down Mellie's cheek. "I wish he could have come, too."

"So do I, Mellie, so do I." If only they would hear from him. *Perhaps tonight, Lord, please let him contact us.*

Chapter Twenty

W hat's the matter, honey?" Ken poked his head in the
kids' bedroom doorway Sunday afternoon.

Sniff. "Nothing." Mellie wiped her eyes.

Ken crossed to lean his arms and chin on the upper
bunk where his granddaughter lay on her stomach, open
book in front of her. "Is it a sad story?"

She shook her head.

"You can tell me."

A hiccup caught on her sigh. She sniffed again and
mumbled, "Daddy didn't call me on my birthday."

"Did he say he would?" He stroked her back.

She shook her head. "He said he'd try, but Grampy, I
always talk to him on my birthday. If he's not home, he
calls me."

Ken closed his eyes. *Lord, give me wisdom here.* "Remember, he might not be near any telephones. Lots of
places in the world don't have phones like we have."

"He always has his cell phone. He said so." She chewed
on her bottom lip. "Something musta happened. He might
be hurt real bad."

"He could be, or he might be out of cell service. You
know how our phones go out sometimes when we are

camping far from a town or fishing out on the lake. The cell tower doesn't always reach everywhere."

"But he *said*!"

"And when Steig says he'll do something, he tries his very best to do it. He's always been like that, Mellie. Remember, I've known him his whole life. He's true to his word. That's why I am absolutely sure that he would call if he could, and he will call as soon as he can." He blew out a breath.

"That's what Grammy said, too," Mellie said quietly.

"Well, Grammy is pretty smart and always right. Right?"

Mellie nodded slowly.

"You want to go for a walk with me?"

"Can I ride my bike? Just us?"

"Yes and yes, unless someone else asks to go along, like a certain dog or a cat."

"Or Grammy. What if you and Grammy rode your bikes, too? Jakey could ride in the kiddie seat on your bike. We could go farther that way." Her eyes sparkled through the tears.

Going for a bike ride right now hadn't been in his plans, but oh, well. He had to admit it was a good idea for cheering up a sad little girl. "Let's go see."

She stuck her bookmark in her book and scrambled off the bed, dropping to the floor. "We can go faster that way, too."

"That's for sure." He stuck his head in Mona's office only to find it empty. Their bedroom the same. He heard Mellie pelting down the stairs. Where were Mona and Jakey? He found them in the kitchen, where she was giving Jake a lesson on how to peel a potato. He watched from the door. Talk about concentration. Jake stared at the potato as if daring the skin to ignore his peeler. When he finished it, he splashed it in the water bowl and announced, "One done."

Mona asked, "How many more to go?"

He counted from one to six carefully out loud. "Six."

"Good job." She glanced over to Ken in the doorway. "Mellie just flew through here out to the garage, saying something about a bike ride. Care to fill me in?"

He explained the conversation.

Jake let out a whoop and his half-peeled potato splashed more water on the floor. "I want to go!"

Mona shook her head. "We have to finish peeling the potatoes first, so I can put them in with the roast."

His brow turned black. "But…"

"I'm ready, Grampy," Mellie called from outside.

Mona called back, "If you can wait long enough for me to put the vegetables in with the pot roast, we can all go."

"You can help me peel the potatoes." Jake looked up at Ken with a pleading smile. He held out a potato helpfully, in case Ken hadn't noticed the jacketed potatoes on the counter between them.

Mona dug in the drawer and handed Ken a peeler. "Are the bike tires up?"

"Maybe I should go check them." He sat down on a chair next to Jake. "All right, buddy, let's peel fast."

Mellie stopped in the door to the garage. "Can Ambrose go?"

"Not if we're all on bikes." Mona dumped carrot peelings in the compost bag. "Would you please get us each a water bottle, Mellie, and put them in the bottle brackets on the bikes?"

"Okay." Mellie snapped crossly, "Hurry up, Jake. You get to ride in your kiddie seat on Grampy's bike."

"I want my own bike!"

"You're too slow. We're going on a *real* bike ride." She headed back out to the garage where they kept the bottles of water in the other refrigerator.

A pout formed, and Jake stared at his grampa. "I want my bike. I'm a big boy!"

He shrugged. "I know you are. You can always stay home, you know."

"Don't want to stay home!"

"Then be glad you can ride with me." He got an idea. "How tall is the wheel on your bike?"

"I don't know."

"Say, this high?" Ken held his hands fifteen inches or so apart. "And Grammy and Mellie and I ride bikes with wheels this high." He spread his hands wider; it was probably twenty-eight or thirty inches instead of twenty-six, but he needed the emphasis. "With bigger bikes, we can go faster. See? Now, peel your potato or we'll never get to go."

With the animals left in the house and staring out the big window as if they might cry, and all the cyclists helmeted, they finally pedaled out the driveway and, at Ken's instructions, turned left on the street that bordered their land.

"Where we going?" Mona asked.

"It's a surprise," Mellie answered.

Ken shot his wife a shoulder-shrugging look, which made her chuckle. "Okay, single file here until we get to the bike path."

She frowned suspiciously. "How come we're not down by the river?"

"Decided to do something different." Ken glanced over his shoulder. "How you doing back there, Jakey boy?"

"Faster, Grampy, let's go faster."

They rode the city streets until they could turn to the city park that had a playground at one end. Ken parked his bike by a picnic table and lifted Jake to the ground. "Okay, go run off some of your energy. Grammy and I are going to sit right here and watch you." The two kids ran to the swings and Ken glugged from his water bottle, then leaned back against the table edge and rested his elbows on the wooden table. "It's warmer than I thought."

"We're not used to pedaling bikes yet this year." Mona copied his actions. "I'd planned to work in the garden for a while."

"We can do that after supper. All of us."

She licked her lips. "The kids start Vacation Bible School tomorrow."

Between Sandy's problems at the university and keeping these two occupied, Ken had forgotten all about VBS. "Are you going to help?"

"I've baked cookies, and I will deliver the kids, but then I want to come home. I need to get some work done in my office. You have anything else planned?"

"Not during the day, but I start the carving class tomorrow night, five to eight. Thought I'd spend the morning sharpening my tools and getting ready."

"You could deliver the kids on Tuesday?"

"I guess." Why did he have the feeling she was leading up to something? "Okay, what?"

"Just that Marit would really like you to help, for a couple of days, anyway. It lasts for two weeks."

"I thought I could go fishing. Lars asked me at church today if we could go Tuesday morning, early."

"And?"

"And I said I would. Then I'd like to spend the rest of Tuesday in my shop."

"But after you take the kids?"

"All right." He took another swig of his water. "But I'm not staying to help."

She shrugged and cocked an eyebrow.

He found himself getting angry. "No matter what Marit promised anyone. She volunteered for the job, but that didn't include grandparents helping. You want to go, you go."

"Grandparents day is next Monday. I promised we'd both be there for that."

"Fine." He got up and meandered over to where Mellie was calling, "Push me higher, Grampy." Grumpy Grampy is what he felt like at the moment. And why not? He had waited years for retirement, when he could do something for Ken Sorenson for a change, instead of for everyone else in the world. So far he hadn't been able to do a single thing that he actually wanted.

He gave Mellie a shove. He pushed Jakey. At least he was making someone else happy. The giggles of his swingers tickled his ears. He remembered pleading the same thing when he was a kid. But his grandfather was not the swing-pushing kind. Besides, he was always working on his farm. His grandfather had built a tire swing that entertained the visitors—young kids and sometimes the older ones. Maybe he should rig up a tire swing at the house. The lower limb on the big elm should work. He'd stop at the hardware store for rope tomorrow. And old Coffee at the tire store always had a couple beat-up tires for cheap, maybe even a big farm truck tire. He'd have to put up two; this pair would never peacefully take turns on one. Suddenly his tire swing project was looming huger and huger, just like everything else he tackled lately. On the other hand, tire swings were a good place to daydream away the summer hours.

He turned when Mona called, "Time to head home so the roast doesn't burn."

"Already?" Mellie quit pumping. "But we haven't played on the jungle gym yet."

"Or the sandbox," Jake chimed in.

"Too bad. The boss has spoken, and I don't want burned roast, do you?" He grabbed Jake around the middle and brought him to a stop. "Come on, buddy, we'll come back here another day." Hand in hand, the two headed for the table and the bikes. When he looked back, Mellie was twisting her swing around, her lower lip out beyond her nose.

He paused. "Come on, Mell, we'll be back."

She left the swing but dragged her feet all the way back to the bikes, giving her grandmother a resentful look.

Mona looked from her glaring granddaughter to her husband, who gave her a shrugging, raised-eyebrow look. "Okay, kiddo, what's the pout for?"

"I don't want to go home yet. We just got here." When Mellie whined, it was a world-class nasal, moaning whine. You had to give her her due; she had it perfected to a T. Ken was going to have to consider carefully whether to call Mellie on her instant whine whenever she didn't get her way or just blow it off. After all, the kids' home was shattered.

"I'd rather stay, too, but I'm hungry, and we have to get everything ready for tomorrow tonight, meaning baths, reading time, and..." Mona swung her leg over her bike. "Packing the cookies."

"They're already packed, and I didn't get dirty today and..."

Ken firmed up his voice. "That's enough, Mell. Get on your bike and let's get going." While the girl did as told, her face shouted what she thought of the whole thing.

Back at the house, they parked the bikes in the brand-new rack by the back door and followed their noses to the tantalizing fragrance wafting from the oven. Mona washed her hands and gave orders as she dried them. "You two kids wash your hands first, then set the table. I'll make the gravy, and Ken, you put that bag of rolls in the oven when I take the roaster out, then turn it off. Then you can fill the glasses, milk for the kids and iced tea for us."

"Yes, ma'am." Ken grinned at her as he saluted.

Jake copied him precisely, then looked at his grandpa. "Why'd you call her ma'am? Her name's Mona."

"He was being funny, or trying to." Mona opened the oven door and waited to let the heat out a bit. She set the roaster on the stove and lifted the lid. "Ah, perfection."

With the food all on the table, they took their places and Ken said, "Mellie, I think it is your turn to say grace."

"Dear Lord, thank You for this food and please keep my daddy safe, amen."

When the food had been passed around, Mellie looked at Mona. "Daddy always said his mom made the best pot roast anywhere. You think they have pot roast where he is, wherever he is?" Her voice trembled on the last.

"I don't know, sweetie, but this was the first supper he always asked for when he came home."

"Even better than hot dogs?" Jake looked up from mashing his potatoes.

"'Fraid so, buddy." Ken smiled at his grandson. "But he used to think hot dogs were the best, just like you do."

"He liked peanut butter sandwich with pickles on it." Mellie made a face.

"Funny, but he always liked that, dill pickles rather than jam." Mona made a face like Mellie's. "Not for me."

Later, after all was done and the kids were in bed and prayers said, Ken and Mona kissed them each good night.

"Do you think Daddy will Skype tonight or maybe call?" Mellie's usual whine was now a melancholy, wistful moan.

"I don't know, honey," Ken answered her.

"If he does, you'll come and get me, won't you?"

"I will for sure."

"Can I read for a while?"

"Not tonight. You have to get up early tomorrow."

She rolled over to face the wall, her grumble muffled in the actions.

As always, they shut out the light and left the door partway open. They always had a night-light in the hall for bathroom runs. As they made their way downstairs, Mona trailed her hand along the rail. "I wish I knew what to answer her."

"That's the problem, there is no answer."

The next morning, Ken handed Mona a cup of coffee and asked her, "What are you working on that is keeping you from helping at VBS?"

"A few things for the preschool project." Mona put down the coffee to pour water in a kettle to make the oatmeal.

"I thought you changed your mind."

"No. I've prayed about it, and God does not seem to be saying no, so I will go ahead with it." She measured the oatmeal into the hot water, added salt and Craisins, and set it carefully on the burner, before turning to him. "I know you are not happy about my decision, but my company is important to me and I want to give it my best shot."

"I don't think you—"

"Grammy, what are we having for breakfast?" Dragging his blankie, Jake stopped in the doorway, as if sensing something was wrong.

Mona scooped him up, and after a big hug, she set him in Ken's lap. "I think we are about due for a celebration. This makes three days that Jake has gotten up dry. What did I say we would do when you reached three days?"

"Don't need diapers anymore."

"Right!" She crossed to the calendar on the refrigerator door and put a star on today. "See, there."

"Good boy, Jake." Ken hugged him close. "Where's Mellie?"

"Reading."

"Figures. Now, I am going to put you down, and you are going to go up the stairs and tell her she has five minutes before breakfast, okay?"

"Do I gotta get dressed first?"

He looked at Mona. "What time do you have to leave?"

"Starts at nine. Eat first, then dress."

Jake slid to the floor and charged up the stairs.

Ken got up and fetched the cereal bowls from the cupboard to set on the table. "Should I make toast?"

"Please."

The slight feeling of frost in the kitchen didn't melt until she left with the children at 8:40 a.m.

Ken poured himself another cup of coffee and sat down, dog and cat beside him. "Why is she being so stubborn?"

Ambrose cocked his head, tail sweeping the floor. Hyacinth wound around his ankles. Elbows on the table, Ken finished his coffee. He was glad for her work under normal circumstances. In fact, he encouraged it. It was a benefit to the community, pleased her and kept her occupied, and possibly it even kept depression at bay. But these circumstances were not normal. Like a huge storm cloud, the threat of her depression loomed over him.

He really had a bad feeling about this.

Chapter Twenty-One

I am going ahead with this because I believe this is what I am supposed to do. Take the next right step." Mona said the words aloud and firmly, not sure whom she was trying to convince. What if God was talking through Ken? Now that was a new thought, although she knew right away she should probably have thought of it earlier. She parked the SUV in front of the garage.

A touch of self-pity made her pause. "I so want to do this project and do it well. I've dreamed of leading a campaign for something major, and this is right up my alley." She slapped the palm of her hand on the steering wheel and grabbed her purse. Go ahead until she felt God stopping her. After greeting the animals, she headed upstairs to her office. She needed to edit the packets she had prepared for each of the committee members that included a proposed calendar from August until two months past the grand opening. She'd already circled January 5 on her calendar for the grand opening. November 4 was also circled as the beginning of registration.

She could hear a grinding or something down in Ken's workshop. Slowly but surely, he'd been collecting tools over the years so he could have his dream of woodworking. He'd been fixing and building simple things like shelves for the toy baskets through the years, but now he would start a carving class.

Ken's getting his retirement dream. Why can't I use these years to build this business? I'm not putting blocks in his way. This is my dream.

Whoa, girl, that sounds more like "Woe is me."

Well, it is woe is me. I want my dreams, too.

Ignoring her dueling inner conversation, she sat down at her computer to read through the materials again. Finally she printed them out and took the pages to her chair with a footstool, the place where she usually did her best thinking. Red pen in hand, she prayed first to find every mistake and after that to read aloud to hear how it sounded.

Ambrose barked as a car drove up to the door. *Already? Oh no!* She hadn't printed out the materials yet. Mona stared at the clock. The kids were home from VBS, and no lunch was ready. They would be famished. She'd have to finish later. All five kids burst through the door as she cleared the last stairstep and headed into the kitchen.

"Grammy, see what we did!" All five were giggling and shouting at once. Ambrose barked to help them out.

She raised her hands, eyes wide. "Help, I'm being attacked."

"Better you than me." Marit set her purse on the table. "Do you have something for lunch or...?"

Mona oohed and aahed over all their treasures. "Looks like you had a great time."

"We did," Brit answered for all of them. "Our class is making a play. You and Grampy will come, won't you?"

"Of course we will. Now how about all five of you go run

around the outside of the house five times, and by then we should have lunch ready."

The boys headed out, laughing and shouting. Mellie looked at her. "We're not having hot dogs, are we?"

"Nope, grilled tuna fish sandwiches. Why don't you two go down to the basement and tell Grampy we're making lunch; then you can run out the doors down there?"

"Okay." She and Brit charged off.

Marit sank into a chair and blew out a cheek-rounding breath. "What a morning."

"All went well?" As she talked, Mona poured her daughter a glass of iced tea, then hit the pantry for tuna and pickles, grabbing a bag of chips as she went by. She plunked the cans of tuna and the can opener in front of her daughter. "Here, surely you can handle that."

"Jakey doesn't seem to like VBS much and needed a little redirection. A theme this year is 'what pets can teach us,' and today was cats. Not the best topic for our cat hater."

"I was hoping he would get used to cats by now." Mona chopped sweet pickles and onions for the tuna salad. "Grilled or not?"

"Grilled sounds mighty good. We've not had that for a long time."

Mona dug out the big circular electric grill that she used to make lefse and set it on the counter. "Faster than the stove for this many." They could hear the kids shouting as they ran. "That should wear them down a bit."

"Genius idea. How did you do on *the* project? I assume you're going ahead with it, Dad's approval or no?"

"I am. I feel so strongly this is a gift with a trail I need to follow. I'm praying that if I am off track, God will stop me."

"I thought you and Dad had a deal that if one strongly disagreed..."

"We'd stop and rethink."

She looked up and closed her eyes. "It just seems to be such a perfect opportunity, one I've dreamed of." She heard Ken on the stairs and shrugged. "What do you want to drink, Ken?"

"Iced tea. You want to eat outside?" He smiled at his daughter. "So how did the morning go?"

"Well, one bump on the head that swelled up during recess, two little girls crying for their mommies, and one teacher with a migraine who had to go home, and, ahem, Jakey. Other than that?"

"That's all?" He shook his head as he snagged his now-full glass off the counter and grabbed the dishcloth to go out and wipe down the table. "Thanks for the drink, hon."

He must have worked the stiffness out down in the woodshop. Breakfast that morning had been a rather silent affair, even though they'd apologized to each other later. But asking for forgiveness and totally letting go were two different things. Especially since she was going ahead with the project.

"Here, you butter one side; the grill is hot enough." She could hear the kids outside telling Grampy about their morning. While she did sandwiches on the grill, Marit got out the paper plates and napkins, then poured the chips into a bowl. "Plastic glasses?"

"Please, raspberry drink is already made in the fridge. Call the kids to wash their hands."

"Grampy is taking care of that at the faucet outside." She pulled a tray from on top of the fridge and started setting supplies on it.

After lunch, the cousins left. Ken nodded to his grandchildren. "Once you get the lunch stuff hauled into the kitchen, you two can come help me in the garden for a while and let Grammy have some time off."

She raised her eyebrows at him, then smiled a thank-you. From her upstairs window a while later, she heard him below.

"I cut the handles off these hoes so you can manage them more easily, so now we are going to learn how to use them."

"In the garden?"

"Right. This is a faster way to kill the weeds."

Mona went back to her project, and when she had it all finished and packed in her briefcase, she straightened up her office and headed downstairs, curious as to why it was so quiet. She found Ken and Jake asleep in his recliner and Mellie reading out on the deck, curled up in a chair in the shade with Hyacinth on her lap and Ambrose stretched out snoring in the sunshine.

"What a marvelous idea. I think I'll go get my book, too."

"This is such a good story."

"Glad to hear that. You want something to drink?"

"Raspberry ice."

Mona was going to remind her, "please," but for some reason didn't. *How can I take time to read when I have so much to do?* Mona banished the thought, sliced some cheese to go with crackers, and set them on the low table between the loungers out on the deck. Then fetching her book, she sank onto the lounger and took a sip. "Ah, bliss."

"Thanks, Grammy." Mellie grinned at her grandma. "I like just us." And she tucked a piece of cheese between two crackers. She handed that one to Mona and fixed another, then the two bit in—and giggled.

That night when Ken had his tools all packed and ready
to go out the door, Mona kissed him good-bye. "Have a
good time."

He nodded with a smile. "I will." He hugged both kids,
who grinned up at him. "And no popcorn, you hear?"

As he went out the door, Mellie shouted, "We're not
having popcorn, we're having kettle corn. And a movie!"

Tuesday morning, Ken left the house at four thirty to go
fishing.

"Catch lots," Mona mumbled as she drifted back to
sleep.

The alarm clock, her blessing and her curse, woke her at
six thirty. She would be making her presentation today to
the preschool board; better get up and get going. She heard
the children downstairs already, so she dressed quickly,
wearing black slacks and a cream tank, with her pink jacket
ready to slip into just before she walked out the door.

Mellie was pouring milk as Mona entered the kitchen.
"We were hungry."

"Is this going to be enough for you?" She eyed the
counter, cluttered with the milk carton, the chocolate
syrup dispenser, the peanut butter jar and peanut butter
smeared in odd places, the cracker box, lots of cracker
crumbs, both the strawberry jam and the grape jelly, and
half a loaf of bread.

"We get a snack at Bible school." Mellie finished
spreading strawberry jam and slapped her peanut butter
and jelly sandwich together.

"Grampy told me to behave better, but I don't like cats.
He said I should suck up and take one for the team. What
does that mean?" Jakey took a bite of his cracker with
peanut butter.

Mona had never really used that particular reference. So she made up something. "It means to behave even when you don't feel like it or even if you don't like cats."

"Is Grampy taking us to Bible school today?" Jake licked his fingers off.

"He said he'd be back." Her purse and briefcase waited right on the chair seat. *Come on, Ken, you said . . .* But she knew that at times if a wind came up or something, fishermen did not get back when they planned. She checked the clock. Five more minutes was all she could give him. She was just herding the kids to the SUV when he parked right beside her.

"Come on, kids, jump in. Sorry, we had to wait to load the boat."

"Thanks for making it. See you later. My appointment is in half an hour." She always liked to arrive at least ten minutes early and sit in the car to collect her thoughts.

"I've got fish to clean so we can have a fish fry for supper."

"Sounds good." She waved them off as he backed out. At least now she wouldn't be rushing to get there on time. Here she'd thought the years of juggling kids, jobs, and VBS were over. Little did she know. But it was only for a year, right? They could manage for a year. When school started, they'd get in a routine and she'd have more hours to work on her business. *Lord, You know that I really want to do this project. You said to ask for what I want, and You would answer. Please let me do well today.*

She turned into the church parking lot to see that construction was well under way on a building on the back part of the property. One story, lots of windows, and a breezeway connection to the main church building. If that was for the preschool, this church had gotten behind the idea and supported it fully.

Getting out of her car in the visitor's parking slots, she followed the sign that said OFFICE OFF TO THE RIGHT. A receptionist looked up when she entered the room.

"If you are Mrs. Sorenson, the group is meeting right around the corner. I'll show you the way."

"I am, and thank you. Is that building under construction for the preschool?"

"It is. The first block in what we hope will be a private school here on our campus."

"That's a big dream."

"God honors big dreams."

Oh, I hope so!

She stopped in front of a door where laughter could be heard from the room inside. "Here you go. They're expecting you." She opened the door and ushered Mona inside. The ladies were seated around an eight-foot table with coffee cups and crumb-decorated napkins in front of each.

"Oh, I'm so glad you're here." Carole Bergstrund rose to meet her. "The coffee is ready, and there's still coffee cake if you'd like."

Mona declined with a smile. Right now she didn't feel that feeding the butterflies would calm them down any.

Mrs. Bergstrund introduced the five women, and Mona smiled a greeting to each. "Please, we saved the head of the table for you. Can I get you anything? Water even?"

One woman smiled and said, "We're so glad you're here. Can't wait to hear what you have to offer."

Mrs. Bergstrund nodded. "Since I already gave them

your background, why don't we get right to it. We have another presenter coming in an hour and a half. Will that be enough time for you?"

Swallowing her surprise, Mona smiled and nodded. "I have packets for each of you so we can all be on the same page in our discussions." She handed them to Carole to pass down and took her seat. "I need to start with a couple of questions. First of all, are you still on track for registrations starting November first and grand opening on January fifth?"

"Construction is a wee bit ahead of schedule, and all the interior furnishings are on order. One of our women"— Mrs. Bergstrund pointed down the table—"is an interior decorator, and she is handling all the interior furnishings. This is just as exciting as building a new home."

Another woman added, "Meeting all the city codes is one of the major hurdles, but there, too, we are on track."

"That's marvelous. If you'll open your packets to the first page, I have included an overview of all the stages of marketing and promotion. In all actuality, those are two separate fields but often combined. That includes a timeline. Now, all this is up for discussion, so if you have any questions, please ask." When they all nodded, she launched into her well-planned introduction. Mona knew they were following her from all the head nodding and notes being written on the pages. She concluded in fifty minutes and asked again for questions, although they had felt free to ask during the hour.

"I have one," the interior designer said. "I thought you were a one-woman office, and this looks like a heavy load. How can we know you can meet your deadlines?"

Mona kept a smile in place while the thoughts galloped through her head. What kind of question was that? Almost rude really. "I have never missed a deadline in the four years I've been in business. I listed some references on the last page if you would like to check on my performance." After fielding a couple more questions, she went into her closing remarks. She touched on the contract that said the increments she expected to be paid in, pointed out the references, and smiled at each of the women. "Thank you for the opportunity to prepare this for you."

"Fine job, Mona," Mrs. Bergstrund said, and they all nodded. "So very professional. We have two other presenters today, so we'll get back to you as soon as we've made a decision, which will be within the next couple of days."

She thanked them again and headed for her car. She'd done her best, and now it was in God's hands. As she backed out of her slot and headed toward the street, she reflected on one thing she had done absolutely right: avoided the PowerPoint and provided hands-on material that they could refer back to. She believed God was in charge, of course, but it would be hard to keep from second-guessing all she'd done. Another one of the character traits she was trying to overcome.

Ken was at the outside table and faucet set up just for fish cleaning. "How did it go?"

She shrugged. "I didn't realize they were having other companies give proposals today, too. That was a bit of a shock. I left my packets with them; I included some pretty original ideas in that, which someone else could put to work."

"Second-guessing, eh?"

"I guess. Trying not to. I really realized how bad I want this when they said there were two others. Wouldn't it have been more ethical to mention that up front?" She went on to tell him about the building and the dreams for more school room. Standing back far enough to not get splashed, she finally ran out of information.

He dried off his hands. "I'm going up to change. I'll pick up the kids. Do we need anything at the grocery store?"

"I thought Marit was bringing them home."

He grimaced. "She called and asked if I would pick them all up; something going on there that she had to deal with."

"So I need to make lunch for all five, right?"

"Well, six. She should be here before too long."

Mona dragged herself up the stairs. Right now she would like a few hours to herself to unwind and make any notes in case they did hire her. Or rather, to be prepared when she needed to begin the project. *Think positive, Mona, not negative! No Monday-morning quarterbacking. You said you were leaving this in God's hands, so do just that!*

Why was it so much easier to say than to do?

That night after the kids were in bed sleeping and she'd located the flashlight that Mellie snuck under the pillow, she and Ken were enjoying a cup of tea before bed when the doorbell rang.

"Who could that be at this hour?" Ken looked at her blankly as he got up to answer the door. Her stomach churned a bit. She got up and followed behind. He checked the peephole and opened the door.

"Sir, are you Kenneth Sorenson?" The man wore the army dress uniform with official-looking epaulets and a broad spectrum of medals on his chest. Another man in uniform stood beside the first, but he wore a clerical collar and a cross.

"I am. How can I help you?"

"May we come in?"

"Of course, sorry, no idea where my manners went." Ken stepped back and ushered them into the entry.

"Is this your wife?"

Ken waved a hand. "My wife, Mona."

The fellow dipped his head toward her and returned to Ken. "Major George Paget, U.S. Army Special Forces. Is Captain Steig Sorenson your son?"

"Yes, he is. What is this about?"

Mona started to shake so hard her teeth chattered. She crossed to stand by Ken, who put his arm around her.

"I regret to inform you that Captain Steig Sorenson has been listed as missing in action."

Chapter Twenty-Two

Would the scene never stop replaying in her mind?
Mona gave up, scooted to the edge of the bed, and got up carefully to let Ken keep on sleeping. Good thing someone could sleep around here. She felt like the sandman kept dragging more sand through her eyes as she stuck her arms in her summer robe and picked up her flip-flops to put on downstairs. With a sigh, Ambrose rose from his bed and padded down the steps beside her.

Fixing tea rather than coffee in the hopes she might be able to go back to sleep eventually, she settled into her recliner. Hyacinth had given up the comfort of her spot on the foot of the bed and now leaped up to nestle beside her. Ambrose sighed again, then settled on the floor beside the chair. Protected by her armed guards, Mona sipped her orange spice herb tea and let the scene play again. The ringing of the doorbell, the two men entering, the horrendous news they had to deliver. The chaplain reminding them, perhaps three times, that he would be there for them. To call him with questions. He would be the liaison between the military and the family. After they left, she and Ken were more shell-shocked; the grieving and fear had yet to attack. The worst had happened. No, not the worst; at least there was a chance that Steig was still alive.

MIA, they had assured her and Ken, was just that. Missing in action. They would let the family know immediately of any change.

Then the horrors took over. Steig lying dead somewhere, Steig bleeding and horribly wounded, Steig as a prisoner of war, being tortured like they had seen of prisoners online and on TV. The tears started in a trickle but soon nearly drowned her. *Lord God, protect my son. Please let him live and bring him home to us.* Like all tears, they eventually stopped, and after mopping them up, she rested her head against the cushions. Ambrose licked her hand, a whimper more than a whine of consolation, his tail gently fanning the air.

She tried constantly to avoid imagining scenarios. They almost always turned ugly and fed her tendency to depression. Sometimes they even triggered her depressions. She couldn't help it; they wouldn't banish. And now, of all times, she must avoid depression. Those two little children needed her like never before, and she would be useless to them if one of her major depressions hit. *Lord, help me!*

By now her tea was cold and she felt chilled, her only warm spot her tummy, where Hyacinth had curled up. "Lord, how will I bear this, this nightmare of all nightmares?" With a start, she realized she was nearly shouting. "Sorry Lord, but how will we tell the children? When will we tell them? What am I supposed to do? Tell them and send them off to Bible school? Help us."

Surely the news would not be on TV or the Internet yet, but it would be soon. Steig was a local boy—in fact, something of a local hero. The reporters might even show up on their doorstep soon. She couldn't let the children learn accidentally. She would call Marit, too. But not in the middle of the night. Three a.m. Hyacinth got up, and Mona dug in the basket beside her chair, pulling out a crocheted afghan, and threw it over herself.

Would going back up to bed work, or would she just wake Ken?

Lord, what are we going to do?

Seek my face. The words seemed to float in and around her.

"I am seeking Your face. I know of nowhere else to turn." The tears burned again.

Trust me. Are you going to trust me?

"Right, trust You. Who else can I trust? You know I have always put my children in Your hands." She reached for her Bible that always lay beside the lamp. Flipping to the Psalms, she turned to Psalm 91, but the tears again blurred the words. Her memory took over. *My refuge and my fortress, my God, in whom I trust.* All she could say or think was *Lord, I trust You. Lord I trust You.* The phrase *dark night of the soul* seemed perfectly clear right now.

"How will I get through this?"

A very present help in time of trouble...where was that? A psalm. She thumbed back through. There. Psalm 46:1. *God is our refuge and our strength, a very present help in trouble.*

A sob caught in her throat and made her cough. "Oh, Lord God, let it be so. Help me!" Hyacinth purred against her leg. The warmth of the afghan penetrated and, between the exhaustion, the comfort of the words, and the hour, calmed her enough that she drifted off.

She woke to the fragrance of coffee brewing. The cat and dog were both gone, most likely to their dishes in the kitchen. Six thirty. How had Ken gotten to the kitchen without her waking? When she tried throwing off the cover, she knew why. Not only her mind but her body

did not want to respond. She recognized the feeling—
total exhaustion. How could it be? She'd not done anything physical. Besides cry. That inner voice reminded her
it woke up when she did. Or probably had never gone to
sleep. She forced herself to her feet and, wrapped in the
afghan, made her way to the kitchen.

Ken turned from pouring his coffee, handed her the full
mug, and reached for another. They sat down at the table,
both propping their elbows to hold the mugs up to sip.

The silence got too heavy to carry. "I figured we'd call
Marit at seven. She should be out of the shower and
dressed by then."

"I agree. But the kids could be down by then." Ken
stared straight ahead. "How do we tell them?"

Mellie and Jake. *Yes, how?* Marit would be straightfor-
ward. Although Ken, Marit, and she had discussed this
eventuality, the discussion was only in the most general
terms, more along the line of wounded or dead. Not MIA.
Even the acronym sounded ominous. "How about you go
call Marit, and I'll keep the kids in the kitchen? Then we
tell them together. You cuddle Jake, and I'll hold on to
Mellie."

Ken nodded, cocked his head. "Here comes Jake."

"I better start breakfast. I'll fix some strawberries to put
on cereal." How could such a simple thing sound so insur-
mountable?

Jake, in his Spider-Man jammies, blankie in hand,
climbed up in Ken's lap, like he did every morning. Ken
kissed the top of his head. "How's my buddy this morning?"

"We goin' fishing today?"

"Not this morning, maybe this evening."

"'Kay."

"Is Mellie awake?"

"Reading. Grammy, can I have peanut butter toast for breakfast?"

"With cereal and strawberries?"

"'Kay."

"You want to get the toaster out? Grampy has something he has to do."

"'Kay."

Ken nodded his thanks, let the boy slide down his legs like he liked, and pulled his cell off his belt on the way out to the garage. Mona had the strawberries ready for serving when he returned. "She'll talk with you later."

"All okay?"

He grimaced. "She's managing. Jake, let's go get Mellie and get you dressed."

"Breakfast in five."

Jake scrambled up the stairs, pulling off his top as he climbed. "Mellie, hurry up, Grammy said five." His ultra-soprano yell echoed through the house.

From somewhere up there came, "I'm coming."

They were about finished eating when Ken and Mona exchanged a warning look. It was time.

"Kids, we have something important to tell you," Ken began.

"Daddy called?" Mellie dropped her spoon.

"No, but we found out why he hasn't. Let's go in the other room." Ken led the way, and they gathered on the sofa as if they were going to read. Jake climbed up on Ken's lap, and Mellie sat between her grandparents in the circle of Mona's arm.

"Last night . . ." Mona choked.

Ken picked it up. "Last night your daddy's commanding officer came to tell us that your daddy"—he stumbled but regained—"is what they call missing in action. That means that no one knows where he is and they have not heard from him. But the commander will let us know as soon as they can find out what happened."

"Did my daddy go to be with Jesus?" Mellie asked.

"We don't know. We do know that right now he cannot call us or Skype us, but he will as soon as he gets found."

Mellie gripped Mona tighter. "Are they looking for him?"

"Oh, I'm sure they are. They want him to be safe, too."

Mona's thoughts took off on her. At the back of her mind, she heard, sensed, *Trust me.* "We pray for your daddy every night, don't we?"

"Uh-huh."

"And we ask God to keep him safe?" Mona could feel Mellie nodding. "Then we will keep on praying, and Jesus said He would answer our prayers." *Please, Lord, don't let it be no.* "So we must be very brave."

"Daddy said if something happened to him, he would call us as soon as he could."

"And he will. Your daddy always keeps his word." *And so does our heavenly father.* Mona knew she was reminding herself and would need to keep on doing that. Every time fear snuck back in, only the name of Jesus could drive it out. *Trust Him. Lord, I trust You. But my trust is so fragile and momentary.*

"Let's pray for your daddy right now," Ken said. "Lord God, thank you that Steig is in Your hands and You are holding him safe."

"Help Daddy get found so he is not missing in action. Make him better if he is hurt." Mellie's eyes were squeezed tight shut.

Jakey added, "And make him come home to go fishing with Grampy and me."

"Thank you, Jesus, that You are right here with us."

Jakey looked up. "'Cause Jesus is right here in my heart." He pointed to his chest. "Daddy said so."

"Yes, Jakey, He is right here in all of our hearts." Ken heaved a sigh. "Help us, Lord, to get through the days ahead." He hugged Jake and gripped Mellie's hand. "And we all agree." They said the amen all together.

Mellie looked up at Mona. "You will tell me as soon as you know something?"

"I will."

"Even in the middle of the night?"

"Yes."

"Or if I am at school?"

"If I can."

"You could come and get me."

Mona turned and put a hand on both sides of Mellie's face. "I promise I will let you know as soon as I can."

Mellie stared into her eyes, then nodded. "Okay, Grammy. Daddy always said his mommy and daddy would take care of us, but Grammy"—her eyes filled with tears— "I miss him so much."

"Me, too, baby, me, too." She reached for a tissue for each of them. "And when you have questions, you come ask, okay?"

"Okay, Grammy, I will."

Ken glanced up at the clock. "We better hurry, or you will be late for Bible school." Both kids bailed off their laps.

"Ten minutes," Ken said. "The car leaves in ten minutes."

When the kids pounded up the stairs, Mona clenched

her husband's hand. "You sure are a good grampy." She sniffed. "And an even better husband and daddy." She chewed her bottom lip. "We're going to get through this, right?"

"We sure are. Jesus said so. And that makes it so!" He held up their clasped hands. "One day at a time."

"Sometimes one moment at a time is about all I can manage." Her head suddenly felt so heavy she wouldn't be surprised to see it plunk on the floor.

"How about you go up after we leave and sleep for a while?"

"I look that bad?"

"Let's say I can tell when you are nearing the end of your rope."

"What about you?"

"I got a pretty decent night's sleep. You didn't."

"Thank you."

After she hugged and kissed the kids and Ken good-bye, climbing the stairs took every ounce of energy she could dredge up. Falling on the bed, she didn't even remember pulling up the sheet and light blanket.

Something tapping? What was that noise? Mona fought to resurface. Finally her eyes opened enough to see that the light coming in the window was now from the west, and she sat up, realizing it was Mellie at the bedroom door.

"Come in, sweetie." Even her voice didn't sound right.

"Grammy, are you all right?" Mellie stood in the door.

"I was just sleeping." Mona spread her arms wide, and Mellie flew into them.

"I thought you went to be with Jesus, Grammy..." The sobs obliterated any further conversation.

"No, no. Oh, Mellie, no. Grammy was just terribly tired, that's all, and Grampy let me sleep. I'm getting up right now and…" She glanced down to realize she never had gotten dressed. "You go on down, and I'll get dressed and be right there. Is Grampy making supper?"

"He said to tell you that supper is almost ready. I set the table." She sniffed again and took the tissue Mona handed her. She started toward the door and turned back. "You are coming?"

"Let me get dressed. I'll hurry."

Knowing there was no time for a shower to help get her fully awake, Mona splashed cold water on her face, pulled on a pair of capris and a T-shirt, slid into sandals, and made her way downstairs, following the voices coming from the kitchen. *Lord, please get my mind in gear. I feel trapped in whatever I was dreaming.* Just as she hit the main floor, her mind caught up. Steig was MIA. If Ken had heard anything, surely he would have called her. Her eyes sent him the question as soon as he looked up, and he gave a minute shake of his head.

"Can I do anything to help?"

"No, sit down, we're all ready." Ken pulled out her chair, and as she slid into it, he kissed the top of her head.

She smiled from Jake to Mellie sitting on the opposite sides of the square kitchen table. "Now, how did Bible school go today?"

Ken took his chair and made the time sign. "Let's have grace, and then you can catch Grammy up on the news." They joined hands. "Jake, your turn to say grace."

The pause stretched until Jake started. "Dear Jesus…" He sniffed. "Please take care of my daddy and bless this food. Amen." The last words came in a rush.

Mona squeezed both their hands. "I love you, Jakey and Mellie, and don't you ever forget it."

"Me, too." Ken's voice rasped, quite unlike his usual tone.

Jake looked at Ken. "I sure am hungry, Grampy."

"You are always hungry, Jakey."

Ken and Mona tried to keep straight faces. Ken rolled his eyes, and Mona shook her head—and gave up. *Ah, Lord, thank you for laughter.*

"Pass your plates, please."

"What are we having?" Mellie looked dubious.

"I forget what this said on the wrapping. I just grabbed a package out of the freezer and stuck it in the oven. Smells good." He wiggled his eyebrows at Jake.

Jake studied the serving dish a moment and announced, "Tonight we are having meatball and bisketti."

"Jakey, it's spaghetti," Mellie said as if putting up with her little brother was a horrid chore.

"Oh, really?" Ken looked down at the plate. "Well, so it is. Grammy, you want to pass the lettuce wedges as I dish up the..." He looked at Mellie. "Spa-ghet-ti? Right?"

Ken managed to keep the dinner conversation light, getting both kids to fill Mona in on the *big* event at VBS.

"And Grammy, he bleeded all over his shirt, and..." Jakey sucked in a breath.

"Who had the nosebleed?" Mona asked, trying to sort through the story.

"I-I don't 'member his name, but two big boys smashed into each other playing dodgeball and..."

"Is he all right?"

Mellie took over and Jake nodded right along with her. "Aunty Marit brought an ice pack, and they took him to the clinic, and he came back before we left, and his nose was big, but it stopped bleeding."

"So what did you do all afternoon?"

"We helped Grampy in the garden and had Popsicles, and he said we could not go wake you up, no matter what!"

"Can we go for a walk after supper? With Ambrose and Hyacinth, too?" Mellie asked.

"Not Hyacinth," Jakey said firmly.

"Yes, Hyacinth," Mona replied gently. "She's part of our family."

"We sure can." Ken looked at Mona. "We'll clean up in here while Grammy gets ready. And then we can go walk."

Mona nodded. "Sounds good to me."

How could everything seem so ordinary when their whole world turned upside down last night?

Chapter Twenty-Three

Remember what the chaplain said. If we have questions to feel free to call him?"

Ken glanced up from his newspaper with a nod.

"I've been making a list." She handed him a sheet of typed questions. "If you have more to add, do so. I am going to call him."

"What about Pastor Oliver?"

"He's not in the military." Mona watched as Ken read through the list. "What do you think?"

Ken nodded. "If we can meet with him while the kids are at Bible school."

Mona found his business card and punched in the phone number. When he answered, she identified herself and nodded. "Thank you. Ken and I are wondering if you could answer some questions for us." When she finished the call, she held the phone for an instant, sucked in and released a deep breath, and said, "He'll be right over. I'm going to text Marit and ask her to take the kids out to lunch or over to her house until I call her." She took another deep breath and sniffed, fighting back the tears that seemed to wait right at the back of her eyes, ready to attack at the slightest break in her defense.

"Good idea."

The doorbell rang as Mona finished fixing a tray with iced tea. That was fast.

The doorbell had sent Ambrose into full-scale announcement mode. She brought the tray into the living room as Ken shushed the dog and opened the door. He ushered Chaplain Bernov in, keeping one hand on Ambrose's collar. "Thank you for coming so quickly. We had assumed we would need to make an appointment. Ignore Ambrose. He's all bark and no bite."

Chaplain Bernov smiled. "He's a Lab, what can you expect?" He reached out, palm down, and let Ambrose sniff his hand. "Yes, Ambrose, I have dogs, too, so you have lots of good stuff to sniff."

Ambrose wagged and whimpered, welcome written all over him.

Ken waved a hand. "We thought we might sit out on the deck, if that's all right with you."

"Sounds delightful."

They followed Mona and her tray outside and within minutes were comfortably seated around the shaded table.

"What a lovely retreat you have out here. A view of the river and the trees. I'm sure this place gets plenty of use." He nodded his thanks and helped himself to the cookies Mona pushed his way. "Now, you said you have a list of questions. I'll answer all I can."

Mona burst out, "Is there any word on Steig?"

"None that I've heard, and I will be one of those notified immediately with any news."

"But someone is looking for him?"

"I would assume so."

Mona's face must have registered her consternation, because he added, "Understand it is not as easy as we might think. If someone gets lost hiking in the forest, the proper agencies launch a search. Because Steig is in Special Forces, where he went and why he went there is classified information." He raised a hand. "But we have not found bodies, either, so that's good news."

Ken had not touched the cookies. "I've been watching the papers closely, looking for military operations, hot spots—possibilities, you might say. Could he be a hostage or prisoner of war?"

"I suppose it's possible." Chaplain Bernov smiled. "However, we've not heard any gloating. Usually if hostages are taken, someone brags to the media immediately. That someone may not be the actual party who took the hostage, but that doesn't stop the bragging. Two of their unit went missing, Steig and another Special Forces man. If these men are still alive, they know how to go under to survive. That's part of their training, and both of these men are known for their resiliency. They will not do anything stupid to hurry things along."

He reached over and patted Mona's hand. "The waiting and staring at the unknown is the hardest part of being a military family."

"God keeps asking, 'Are you going to trust me?'"

"And your answer?"

"What are my choices?"

"I see." His smile made her feel warm and known.

"Who or what else is there to trust? He alone knows what is going on, and I know He is in the answering prayers business. I know that whatever happens, God will not let us go and we will get through."

"Well said. But the moment by moment is rough."

"It is." Ken's voice sounded bleak. "But we have to keep chins up for the kids."

"True, but they need to know that you hurt like they do. The pain and fear are so real and so very human."

Mona snagged a tissue; she'd come to keeping tissue boxes on every table. "Can I ask some procedure questions?"

"Of course. Ask away."

"If he is severely wounded..."

"You will be notified, and he will be airlifted to the nearest hospital, given emergency treatment, although first aid would be done immediately. If he is able to speak, we will set it up so he can talk with you. If he is unconscious, one of the staff will tell you all they know."

"No surprises?"

"Not if we can avoid it."

"I assume then that he will be sent to base hospitals?"

"Right. All will depend on the severity of the injury."

"And if they find his body?"

"The coffin will be shipped home with full military honors. I know that is not much of a comfort, but..."

"If he is too severely wounded to come home or at least stateside, will we be able to go to him?"

"That is a possibility." His gentle smile made Mona blink again. Right now the load was so heavy, she felt like a huge hammer was driving her right into the ground.

"Is there anything we should be doing for the children while we wait for news?" Ken asked. "Everything happened so fast before Steig left, and we thought we'd be in touch. It's been a long time since our kids were so young."

"Have you been over to the commissary yet or set up appointments with the doctor there for preschool exams?"

Mona and Ken both shook their heads. "I never thought to do that yet. I mean, August is not even near."

"Sometimes it is hard to get in; I've learned to think way ahead. You have all their medical records?"

"Yes, Steig made sure all the paperwork is in order."

"You have all their medical cards and such. And have you checked his bank to make sure his check was deposited?"

"No."

"But your name is on all the banking? If I were you, I'd follow up on everything to make sure it is in place."

"Thanks for the advice; we'll take care of all of that. Any other advice for now?"

"I know, school. I wouldn't wait; I'd go to the school where they'll be going and take in all their records and get them signed up. Summer is flying by, that's for sure." He drained his glass. "Feel free to call me whenever you need me."

"Thank you. Do you live here in Stoughton?"

"Yes, I pastor the First Methodist Church on the highway just east of town. I know your pastor well, fine man of God. I know you are in good hands with him."

"Chaplain . . ."

"Please call me Len. What were you going to ask?"

"Thank you. Are there any support groups for grandparents who are now parenting their grandchildren?"

"Not that I know of, but I'll check around. That would be a good thing." He pushed his chair back and stood, extending his hand first to Mona and then Ken. "I pray we hear something soon."

After Ken showed him out, Mona refilled their glasses and moved over to the lounge. "I better call Marit. But I'd really like to sit here and enjoy the quiet."

"I've been thinking."

Why did such a simple statement destroy the peace of the moment?

"Okay."

"You know we planned to do some traveling this summer."

"Right."

"Remember all those trips we took to help our kids experience as many different things as we could expose them to?"

"I am not going canoeing and fishing up at Lake of the Woods again. Sorry, but I have to draw the line somewhere."

Ken snorted his laugh. "That was some trip all right."

"And we were plenty younger. Up to the fishing cabin is as close as I want to be to camping."

"I was thinking more along the lines of Chicago. The museums there, the zoo. We could spend a couple of days there. I don't know if they've ever been."

She leaned back against the cushions. Right now it felt like getting smacked with a two-by-four. In the middle of her forehead. She knew it might be good for the kids to distract them. But how could she take time off if she was given the contract for the preschool? She would have to, that's all.

"We gave our kids the best education we could, and I think that now we need to do the same for our grandchildren."

"I agree but…" She stared at her fingers that really needed a manicure. Prolong this, let him talk his idea through. And perhaps she'd be able to work around it all. "Have you thought of when?"

"I was thinking along the idea of July. I know they are registered for swimming lessons after Bible school. But we don't have to wait for weekends since I'm retired."

But I'm not. I didn't plan any of this, and now I'm caught in a web not of my own making.

*If you go ahead with the preschool project, that will be
your own making.*

Sometimes she wished she could strangle that bullying
voice, even if it was correct. But God hadn't told her yet
to quit, so perhaps this whole thing was His idea. She had
sure felt that in the beginning. An answer to prayers for
success, a business of her own, one that would use all her
talents. She took hold with both hands and dragged her attention to what Ken was saying.

"You want me to go ahead and set this up?" he asked.
"I know you used to do all the travel arrangements, but I'd
like to do this one."

More power to you. "So let me get my calendar." She
dragged herself up the stairs. Yes, this was a great idea,
but why right now? Of course, she hadn't been offered
the project yet, and perhaps this would be taken out of
her hands. *Lord, I do want what is best for all of us, but
I hadn't planned on this many of us. I was hoping Ken
would help me in my business.* She picked up her calendar
and flipped to July. Only the one project to finish, so if she
didn't take on anything new, she could do it.

Back downstairs, she showed him her calendar.

"So, I can go ahead?"

"Have at it. I need to let Marit know that we can pick
up the kids or she can bring them home. Remember that
the play is two days away. Hard to believe two weeks has
gone this fast. Did you get the mail yet?"

"No, I was going to do that when I went for the kids."

"We'll go get it. Come on, Ambrose." She snapped his
lead on at the door, and the two headed across the lawn.
She stopped to check on the flower bed across the front
of their property. The daisies were budding, as were the
irises. She had planted mostly perennials in this bed just

filling in with a few annuals, zinnias and marigolds being her favorites. She bent over and deadheaded a couple; then she and Ambrose crossed on the stone path to the mailbox. Ambrose whined and wagged his tail; the neighbor's dog was up at the fence.

"No, you don't need to go greet her." She pulled the bundled mail out and slammed the door. The mailbox needed to be painted again. She hadn't painted for a long time; would she be able to do it again? Able, yes, but could she find time? Rather than flipping through the mail, they headed back to the house.

Ken met her at the door. "Come on, let's go get the kids."

"I wasn't planning on going."

"Oh, come along, you and Ambrose both."

Ambrose perked up and turned to look at the door.

"Oh, all right." Mona laid the mail on the center island. "But you know with all of us there, someone is going to suggest ice cream."

Ambrose leaned toward the door. He loved ice cream, too.

Once they were in the car, Ken turned to her. "This is the way I pictured retirement. We could just jump in the car and go do something on the spur of the moment. My life has been so planned for so long, I am treasuring freedom."

They dragged the two from cousin playing and stopped for Popsicles after at the little store to eat on the drive home.

"So, how was Bible school today?" Ken asked.

"I got all my verses just right," Mellie said, catching a falling piece of Popsicle. "I get an award for memorizing all my verses."

"How was yours, Jakey?" Mona asked. She and Jake had worked on his.

He heaved a sigh. "Okay. Teacher had to help me."

"Jake has a hard time memorizing anything." Big sister bit again.

"Was that a kind thing to say?" Mona asked.

Mellie stuck out her bottom lip. "It was true."

"Maybe, but you have to remember he is only five and you just turned ten."

"I got three right all by myself." Jake's lower lip matched his sister's.

"Good for you," Ken said as he pulled into their driveway and parked. He opened the rear for Ambrose to jump out.

In the house, Mona set her purse on the counter and picked up the mail. When she flipped to the third piece, she let out a shriek. "Oh, Ken, kids, come quick. Hurry!"

Ken burst through the door. "What's wrong?"

"Nothing's wrong." She mopped her tears and waved a big envelope at all three of them. "It's from Steig!"

"Daddy wrote to us?" Mellie jumped up and down and even made Jake giggle as they danced together, spinning around.

"Daddy's coming home."

"Come on, let's go sit on the sofa, and we'll read this together."

"Hurry and open it." They all plunked on the sofa, and Ken took out his knife to carefully slice open the top. Several letters fell out in Mona's lap. She picked them up. "Here's one for Jakey, one for Mellie, one for Grampy, and for me, and one for both of us."

"Read mine first!" Jake waved it in the air. "Grampy, cut it open."

Ken did so and with Jake on his lap read the letter. Steig had written in big letters so Jake could help read it.

Dear Jake,

I hope you are having a good time with Grammy and Grampy. I can see you and Ambrose playing. You do what they tell you to, and when I get home again, we'll go fishing first thing. I love you, son, and want you to have the best summer ever with your cousins. And when school comes, you'll make new friends. Love, Daddy.

Jake held the letter in both hands. "I want to read it."

"I'll help you later. You know some of the words. But now let's read Mellie's."

"I can read my own."

"Of course, read it aloud."

Dear darling Mellie,

I miss you so, and I hope you are helping Grammy and Grampy. I'm sure Grammy will teach you how to cook so when I come home you can make supper. I can't believe that you are really ten years old now! Do you like the books I found for you? I thought you would, since they are about horses. Maybe you'll get to ride a horse again this summer. Be good and do what Grammy and Grampy ask you to, without pouting. That's my big girl. I'm sure Aunt Marit is signing you up for swim lessons. You learned a lot last summer, so when I get home, you'll be swimming like a fish. Love from your daddy.

She laid her letter down in her lap and looked up at Mona. "Can we write another letter to him? Even if they can't find him, when they do, there will be letters for when he can read them."

"We most certainly will. In fact, I think we should do a letter a week, and we'll put them in a package to surprise him."

"Now read your letter, Grammy." Jake grinned up at her.

Dear Dad and Mom,

I cannot begin to tell you how grateful I am that I know my children are safe and being not only well cared for but loved. I can see you all in the kitchen or out in the garden. I'm sure you've been on bike rides, and perhaps by now Jakey has caught a fish or two.

Mona leaned over and tweaked his nose.

I'm hoping you will find a pony for Mellie to ride, as that is the desire of her heart. I hear that is true for most girls her age, but we all know Mellie is special. Maybe someday when I get home again, we'll be able to buy her a horse. In the meantime, thoughts of all of you together make my days much more pleasant. I pray for you all every night, just like I know you do for me. I'll write again as soon as I can. Love from your fighting son, Steig.

Ken checked the postmark. The letter had been mailed over a week before, but he still had no idea where it was from, as it had the military stamp on it.

He pocketed the letter that had just his name on it as Mona did hers.

"He wrote to us! Bet he doesn't have cell service. Can we go on a bike ride now?" Jake asked as he slid to the floor. "All of us on our own bikes."

Ken reminded him, "That means we won't go as fast or as far."

"I know but I want to ride, too."

Ken looked at Mona, who gave a faint nod.

"Let me get something planned for supper; I forgot all about it."

"Hot dogs!" He bounced up and down.

"No! Not hot dogs again! Something else." Mellie paused on her way to the stairs. "Can I go read while you decide?"

"What would you like for supper?" Mona looked at the three of them.

"Anything but hot dogs." Mellie took the stairs up two at a time.

"Fried chicken," Ken said. "And I'll go get it when we get back."

"Sold." Mona gathered up the letters and put them back in the envelope. "I'll be ready in five minutes." She headed for the stairs, knowing what she really needed was a few minutes alone, and the only place where that seemed to happen anymore was in the bathroom. She paused at the bathroom door, then went on to Mellie's room.

"I heard you sniffling. What's wrong?"

"The date on the letter. It is way *before* those men came and told us Daddy is gone. Jakey thinks he wrote; he did, but it was…when he was still…when we still knew he was…"

"I understand what you're saying. Yes, the letters were mailed before he disappeared."

"So he…" Mellie shuddered a huge sob. "But Jakey thinks…"

Mona took Mellie's hands in hers, her left hand and the right hand holding a crumpled letter. "Mellie, please don't pop Jakey's bubble. He's happy for the moment. This has all been as hard for him as it is for us. Will you let him be happy for a moment?"

She sighed and nodded. "I won't explain to him."

"And I suggest you don't throw your letter away, even if it's old."

Another sigh, miles deep. "Oh, I won't. Grammy, I'm sure he's dead. I just know he's dead. And this is the last thing I'll ever have from him." Her face looked not just sorrowful, but despondent. *Dear God, she has given up hoping.* And how could Mona offer any when she wasn't sure of it herself?

Mona patted her hands. All she could say was, "Good girl."

She hurried to the bathroom, shut the door behind herself, and flipped the lock. Staring into the mirror, she blew out a breath, and, arms propped on the sides of the sink, she let the tears come. *Lord God, help Mellie. I cannot. And Lord, save my son. Please, Lord, save him and bring him home to us. Only You know where he is. Guard him as only You can do.* She washed her face in cold water, grabbed a headband from the drawer, and fitted it in place. *Please, Lord God.*

Chapter Twenty-Four

Some things hit like the proverbial ton of bricks or an earthquake, but some things sneak up on you like a vicious hunter stalking its prey. The attack caught Mona by surprise.

"But Lord, I thought we beat this thing." She fought to open her eyes to see the new day, but the effort was too great, let alone getting out of bed. Instead of fighting, she sank back into the darkness.

"Mona, I'm taking the kids to their swimming lessons. I told them you were feeling sick."

She nodded. Sick didn't begin to cover it. Would that she were throwing up and her heart was dancing an erratic Zumba. Instead of this heavy infusion that deadened not just her limbs, but her mind. Only her tear ducts seemed to work as she felt tears leaking back to her ears. Turning over felt high as a mountain peak, and she could no longer climb. Surely she had nodded—hadn't she? At least she could hear, since that took no visible effort.

Ken had suggested the punching bag, but she really had thought she could beat this monster on her own. After all, she could recognize the symptoms. *Stupid pride.* Short of grieving a son still MIA, fearing and desiring the preschool project, taking on two grandchildren, and her husband retired and gung ho to travel, could that all be sufficient trigger? At least her mind was working again, not like two or three hours ago when she usually got up.

The next thing she knew Ambrose leaped up on the bed and sat pawing her arm, one whine per swipe. Ambrose never got on the bed without an invitation. She felt Ken sit down on the edge.

"Okay, how can I help you?" His voice was gentle.

He used to go off to work; he rarely saw me like this. Or did he ever? She forced her eyes open.

"Are you taking your antidepressants?" he asked.

"The pills don't kick in right away. I feel so groggy. There were nightmares, like I didn't sleep all night but kept running from something, not even sure what."

"You were sound asleep when I got up; not even the coffee fragrance roused you."

She scrubbed her fingertips through her hair. "I need a shower, perhaps that will help."

"I'll start it."

She wanted to yell at him to go away, but she knew he was trying to be helpful. Instead she stumbled into the bathroom. Standing under the beating water helped. At least coffee sounded palatable now. Once out, instead of blowing her hair dry, she just pulled it back with a hair-band, settled a sundress over her head, and slipped her feet into summer sandals. Makeup was not an option.

"I hope you made this extra strength," she muttered.

"I did. That's why I'm drinking iced tea. I'm going out to work in the garden, but I'll fix you something to eat first." He shook his head when he saw her grimace. "You need protein. I'll put those leftover strawberries over cottage cheese, how does that sound?"

"Thanks." She watched as he set the bowl with a

piece of peanut butter toast on a tray. He added a glass of iced tea.

"Come on, you're eating outside."

Obediently she followed him out the door. The sun felt warm on her back as she settled at the table with an umbrella. Dutifully, she picked up the spoon and took a bite of her meal, whatever meal of the day it was. She loved summer strawberries, and cottage cheese always tasted good, but this time she had to force herself to swallow it, using a swig of coffee as a chaser.

Feeling Ken's gaze on her, she looked up.

"What is it, Mona? What has sent you into a tailspin like this?"

Tears instantly clouded her vision. "He's not coming back. They say Steig is MIA, but it's been a week and he's not coming back."

"You don't know that, only God knows that. Why give up when we don't know?"

"Ken, it has been almost two months since we heard from him. If he were alive, he would have contacted us by now."

"We got those letters."

"All written before he disappeared. I tried punching the bag, but all I got was sore arms. How can I—we keep on going if our son is dead? Surely I would know; somehow my mother's heart would know, and I think that is where this came from."

"Maybe you give up this easily, but I will not believe he is dead until I bury his body at the cemetery. We say we trust that God is in control. What has happened to your faith? You say you trust Him." Ken twirled his glass in the ring of water that had run down its sides. He looked back up at her. "We cannot give up! Not today, not tomorrow, not until we have actual proof. And we have to keep up hope for those two children who are in our care."

"Speaking of the kids, where are they?"

"They got back from their swim lesson, and now they're at Marit's. She's concerned about you, too. She says you need to go see your doctor."

"I have an appointment for a mammogram on Friday, and my yearly physical is next week. Soon enough to see her." She ate a bit more of her food. It didn't taste quite so much like crumpled newspaper. Perhaps being out in the sun was helping. Or maybe talking with Ken was helping. "When are they coming home?"

"After swim lessons tomorrow. They asked to spend the night. And yes, they have their jammies and such."

She felt so out of it. Life was proceeding normally and she wasn't. "How are your plans coming for the trip?"

"Still checking on events in Chicago. I'm thinking we could do one trip in July and perhaps a few days up at the fishing cabin in August. We can take the canoes up, too. Marit said maybe we can all go up there for a week or at least a few days. Magnus will be in Norway for a week or ten days, and we could go then. You have always loved it up there, too."

"I know." But right now the idea of planning and packing seemed beyond possible. "What dates are you thinking for the Chicago trip?"

"I want to go during the week, not on the weekend. I'm thinking the third week. We'd drive there on Monday, one day for the Museum of Natural History, one for the zoo, and another for the aquarium. They opened a new exhibit, *Wild Reef*, several years ago. I'd like to see it. I'm looking at the event calendars to see if something else might be appealing."

Mona ate some more and drank her coffee. The peanut butter toast had sufficient crunch to make her mouth happy.

"So the kids won't be home tonight?"

"No. It'll be just us. How about we go work in the garden for a while?"

"I think I'll go deadhead the pots and the front yard; maybe I'll get some more ambition."

"The leaf lettuce is big enough for salad for supper. I'll pick and wash, and you make that dressing that's so good."

Even before Mona could finish up the deadheading, Ken handed her a lovely washed leaf of lettuce as if it were a royal present. The first of the produce of their garden deserved a special celebration.

"Are the radishes ready, too?" Mona nibbled on the lettuce. "Sure beats anything from the store." She picked up her bucket of spent blossoms and took it over to dump on the compost heap. She hadn't finished, but it looked better and she felt better. Maybe if she'd just gotten up and outside this morning, she might have felt better then, too.

But thoughts of Steig bombarded her again as she made her way into the house. *Lord, You said You'd protect our son. Whatsoever we ask in Your name. But now he is MIA, and I know the only one who knows where and how he is is You. This walking in the unknown is horrendous. I cannot bear it.* With each step, she felt the weight of the cloud push her downward, like a pile driver on a riverbank. Leaden feet, leaden heart, leaden soul. Once inside, she collapsed on a stool at the counter. *Breathe!* came the voice from within. *Breathe!* She did as commanded. Once, twice, three times. As she felt the tension leave her shoulders, she felt herself straighten, and with the next breath, her shoulders let loose of her earlobes and a lightness of being trickled in through the cracks like sun seeking entrance through the tiniest tear in the drapes.

She got up and fetched the vinegar and sugar from the pantry. She set the ingredients on the counter and paused for another breath. *Steig loved this salad, this dressing, this time of year, Lord above, this life. He cannot be dead. God, would I not know if my son were indeed no longer of this earth?*

Blindly she poured the ingredients in the jar, tightened the lid, shook it, and set it on the counter. Carefully. Precisely. "My son is not dead. He might be missing in action, but he is not dead."

She removed the chicken breasts from the refrigerator, poured Italian dressing in a plastic bag, and added the chicken breasts. Supper for just the two of them. Ken could grill them all, and she would make chicken salad with the leftovers. Who was Ken talking to outside? Glancing out the window, she saw their neighbor from across the street. He and Ken used to go fishing together. Perhaps they could again.

With supper preparations under way, she headed upstairs to check her messages and clear some things off her desk. Strange she'd not heard from Carole Bergstrund on the preschool project. They'd said they'd get back to her. Should she call or just wait? *Call.* She located their number, tapped it in her cell, and hit cancel. The timer downstairs was blaring.

Mona woke that night with tears soaking her pillowcase. After mopping her eyes and flipping the pillow over, she drifted back to sleep, praying the nightmares would not return with their clouds of sadness.

The alarm made her jump. She hit snooze and rolled

over. Ken was already up, the coffee said so. *Go back to sleep, get up.* At least when she was sleeping, she couldn't think.

"Come and get it!" came from the foot of the stairs.

"Coming." How could he sound so cheery?

Ambrose met her at the foot of the stairs, as if he'd not seen her for days. Hyacinth, tail straight up but for a slight bend at the tip, preceded her into the kitchen.

"I see your court is in place."

She petted the dog and picked up the cat. "Can we eat out on the deck?"

"Yes, of course. You grab the coffee mugs, I'll put the rest on a tray."

Set up on the deck, she sank into one of the cushioned seats. Sunlight slid between the leaves and branches of the maple tree to dapple the fresh green grass.

"Thank You, Lord, for food, for Your provision, and for taking care of our Steig. Bring him home to us. We thank You and praise Your name."

Mona sniffed and added her amen.

"Did you bake the muffins?"

"I did."

"You made the muffins?"

"Well, Betty Crocker and I or whoever created the box."

Mona shook her head, took a muffin, and passed the basket. She sniffed it. "Orange?"

"I guess. It said I could add walnuts, but I couldn't find them, so I put in pecans."

Mona shook her head. "You know there is a bag of muffins in the freezer and another of biscuits?"

"No, but I shall look next time."

She took a bite of the scrambled eggs. "What did you put in these? Delicious."

"Half-and-half."

"I cheerfully turn over breakfasts to you."

"Not so fast, this was an experiment."

As they sat sipping their second cups of coffee, she leaned back to look up through the branches. "We need to eat out here more. Thanks."

Just as Ken picked up the tray to return things to the kitchen, her phone sang. Her heart leaped in *what if . . .* then settled back into regular rhythm. *Marit.*

"How come you didn't return my call?"

Guilt stabbed her. "When did you call?"

"Dad didn't tell you I called?" Her voice danced with accusation.

"He said you were concerned and that the kids were staying overnight at your house."

"Are you sick or . . . ?"

"Felt like it, but I'm better now."

"Get real, Mom, the depression is back."

Mona felt herself stiffen. "I'm dealing with it."

"When do you see the doctor?"

"Next week for my physical. Aren't you being a bit over-bearing?"

"Someone better."

A soft answer turns away wrath. This didn't sound like Marit. "Okay, what's bothering you?"

"Probably the same thing that is bothering you." Marit did an audible inhale. "Sorry, Mom, but you're scaring me. You can't go down like last time, not with the kids here. They're worried about you—well, at least Mellie is."

"What happened?"

Her voice dropped. "I'll tell you later."

"They're there now?"

"Uh-huh. Talk later."

Mona laid her phone back down. Marit was right, Ken was right, they were all right. *Don't let the depression get to you.* Far easier said than done.

"What did she want?"

"To yell at me."

"Marit doesn't yell."

"Felt like it. You didn't tell me she wanted me to call her back."

"I told you she called."

"Right. I just realized I have a mammogram this morning. What's on your agenda?"

"Woodshop, fishing with Bert this evening. Thought I'd take Jake along, Mellie if she wants to go."

"Thanks for breakfast."

At nine, she left a message for her doctor, asking for a renewal of meds. At ten, she checked in at the radiology center.

"We have the new machine in place," the nurse bubbled. "This is so much better than our other—3-D technology, they say it reduces callbacks by ninety percent. We can detect cancer far sooner. We've been waiting for this."

"I hope it doesn't squish like the old ones."

"Well, you have to admit our other machine was far more gentle than a few years ago."

"True." Mona stepped into the changing room and slid out of her blouse and bra. *Just get it over with.* No one liked to be flattened between the plates. Even so, digital beat the old way.

She stepped next to the machine, did what she was told, and breathed again when allowed.

The technician told her to relax, checked the monitor, and came back. "I think we better do this again, just to be sure."

"Did I breathe wrong or something?"

"I just like to be really thorough."

They repeated the procedure. Mona watched carefully to see any sign of concern on the technician's face.

"You should hear by noon tomorrow," she said.

"Really, I don't just get a letter in the mail?" She paused. "What did you see?"

"The mammogram will go to radiology."

"But…"

The technician shrugged. "Thanks for keeping your appointment."

They'd always sent a letter before. A squiggle of doubt nagged at her.

Okay. More than just a squiggle.

Chapter Twenty-Five

Ken's wolf was taking shape. Sort of. He stepped back from his bench to get a better view of his first big carving project. For the class, Brian had purchased a number of roughouts—pre-carvings, which had the big chunks of excess wood cut away already. All the carver had to do was the final shaping. Brian had a good point; it's hard for a beginner to visualize the finished piece if it is still buried in the wood.

Ken laid down the half-inch chisel and picked up his seven-sixteenths gouge. The hardest part, Brian claimed, was carving around the ears without breaking them.

Why was he feeling so angry? Why was he asking that question when he already knew the answer? Mona had descended into another one of her deep funks, and it was her own stubbornness that put her there. He could not help but be upset by her refusal to lighten her load before this depression business started. She didn't even let off steam at her punching bag; she claimed she could handle it. Well, she couldn't. Now they were both going to end up doing damage control. He'd tried to talk to her about it when she got back from her appointment. But, as always, the discussion didn't resolve anything. She'd gone to garden, and he retreated here.

He gave his gouge a gingerly push behind the wolf's ear.
"Grampy."

The sudden voice in the silence made him jump; the
gouge cut deep into the ear itself. Fury leaped up inside
him, and he knew he mustn't let it show. He turned.
"What, Jakey?"

The boy stood in the shop door, but it was Mellie behind him with the hangdog look.

"She has to fess something," Jakey blurted.

"Jakey! You weren't supposed to say that!"

Obviously, his carving time was shot. It sounded like
he'd better put this fire out right away. Reluctantly he laid
down his gouge. "Come over to the steps there and have
a seat." He scooped up a stepstool and plunked it down in
front of the stairs. They sat and he sat facing them. "Okay,
now what's all this about? Mellie?"

She licked her lips. "I heard you and Grammy arguing."
She waited. Nothing. She went on. "I was hiding and listening. I shouldn't have."

He frowned. "Is that what you're confessing?"

She nodded. She looked so miserable that it made him
feel sad.

"That's not so terrible. Is there more?"

"I shouldn't have been sneaking. When you and
Grammy are arguing, I get scared because Mommy and
Daddy used to all the time."

Ken pondered this a moment. Realizing that Steig's
home life must have been a kind of nightmare didn't help
his sadness and anger at all. "You don't have to be scared.
It's not about you. It's a little noisy here, but it's safe."

"But you said about the kids...that's us..."

Jakey chimed in, "You and Grammy don't yell at each
other, you just talk. Mellie said it was an argument, but

it didn't sound like one. She said, 'What am I gonna do,' and I said, 'Grampy says always tell the truth. If you tell the truth, maybe he won't get mad.' And she said, 'He's already mad.' So she made me come with her because you like me, and maybe you won't spank her if I'm here."

"Spank her...?" *For listening?* "Let's go up into the house."

They climbed upstairs to the kitchen, and Ken opened the back door. He called, "Mona? We have a problem here."

Mona came in through the door and closed it behind her, pulling off her gardening gloves. Her eyes were all red and wet and puffy. Good, in a way—crying gave vent to at least some of her doubts and worries.

Ken explained, "Mellie here is frightened because we were arguing. I want to reassure them both that it's all right and that it's not about them. And we're not going to attack them or anything."

She gasped. "Attack? Oh, dear, no! It's not you. Your world is all torn up; we understand that. It's not you."

"But you said..." Mellie looked so confused and forlorn.

Ken looked at Mona. "Perhaps some ice cream will be the oil to soothe troubled waters."

"Good idea. I think we have some cookies, too." Mona reached for the cookie jar.

Mellie looked dubious as she climbed up on a stool. "Are you sure you aren't mad?"

Ken smiled. "Oh, I'm mad at all kinds of things, darling. But you're not one of them."

It took the child a moment of concentration to figure out what he had just said, reminding him once again that he was going to have to adjust his speech. He was talking to small children, not college kids; although some college people acted like small children, including some professors.

Mona put the ice cream carton and scoop in front of him. As he dug into the hard ice cream, she set out bowls and spoons. This pleased him. At least she was functional and not curled up in bed all day, as occasionally happened. She settled at the counter with her own bowl of ice cream. "Your grampy and I were talking about something else the other day, Mellie. And I talked to Miz Beverly on the phone yesterday."

"The lady at the pony farm!" Mellie brightened.

"We set up a schedule for a series of beginner riding lessons. I put them on my calendar." *Good.* She didn't mention that when Ken and she discussed riding lessons, they agreed that the distraction would help Mellie deal with her fear for her daddy.

Mellie bobbed up and down on her stool, pumping her fists. How could she do that? Ken envied the strength and flexibility of youth; he was starting to lose his.

"I don't wanna." Jakey stared at his ice cream a moment, then took another bite.

"You don't have to if you don't want to. This is mostly for Mellie. Remember what your daddy said in his letter?"

Ken asked, "Why don't you want to, Jakey?"

"Horses are big and they smell."

"It's a good smell!" Mellie snapped. "And they have to be big to carry grown-ups around. Or pull wagons or things. Grammy, this is great!"

Ken nodded. "Jake, I understand now why you don't like horses, but cats are little and they don't smell. Why don't you like cats?"

"They scratch and bite."

"Some dogs scratch and bite, but you like Ambrose."

"He's different."

"So is Hyacinth. She won't scratch or bite, and she's little and she doesn't smell."

Mona chided, "Ken, you're expecting him to use logic. He's five."

"Remember when Steig was five?"

"You mean the commercials around Christmastime?"

Ken smiled and explained to the kids, "When your daddy was your age, Jake, he and I would sit watching Saturday-morning cartoons, and we'd pick apart the commercials logically. He was actually very good at it. Pretty soon he was analyzing how they used a low camera angle to make a dinky little toy look big or how kids would be shown playing with it and laughing when it wasn't all that interesting to play with...We had a great time." *And Steig still looks at life—and commercial pitches—analytically.* Ken should sit down and do the same thing with these kids.

"Mommy says cats are dirty."

"Is Hyacinth dirty?"

Jakey frowned. He studied Hyacinth a moment as she sat in the doorway grooming herself. "No. She's clean."

"I agree." Ken kept his voice casual, but inside he was jumping up and down with delight. Jakey had inherited his father's natural bent for examining life critically. All he needed was to be encouraged in it. Ken scraped the last of his ice cream out.

Mellie asked, "May I have some more?"

Before Mona had a chance to argue about spoiling her appetite, Ken said, "Sure." He wanted this teaching moment to continue. He dug out another scoopful. The ice cream was softening up slightly.

Mellie took her bowl back. "Thank you." She scraped off a spoonful. "Mommy doesn't like horses, but Daddy does. But we couldn't have a horse because Mommy would have to take care of it when Daddy deployed. I promised her I'd take good care of it, but she said no."

Ken agreed. "They're a lot of work every day." Surreptitiously, he glanced now and then at Jakey. The little boy was studying the cat when he wasn't scraping up the last of his ice cream. Did Mona see it, too?

Mellie stared more at nothing than at her ice cream. What was going on in that pretty little head? "I so wish we could find out about Daddy."

"So do we, honey. So do we." Mona looked ready to cry again.

"I think he's dead. Do you think he's dead? I mean, is that what you really think?" She looked at Mona.

"I pray for him all the time. So does Grampy. And we both know God answers prayer. So no, not dead. I believe your daddy is still alive somewhere. I also know that God knows where he is because God watches over all of us and that He will take care of him."

Ken added, "And I believe that also. We both pray to God to keep him safe."

"I pray for Mommy and Daddy every night, too." Jakey pushed his bowl toward Ken and looked at him hopefully.

Ken chuckled, "Sure," and served Jakey a short scoopful.

Mona still looked near tears. "I am learning to trust that God knows the situation and will bring your daddy back to us. I trust God for that."

Mellie pondered a moment. "You usually say 'God's will be done' when we pray."

"That's right."

"What if it's God's will that he just kill Daddy off? What about then?"

Ken's mouth dropped open. Suddenly this teachable moment felt more like damage control, and he had no idea how to respond.

Mona got up to retrieve a tissue from the other end of the counter. She blew her nose, and tears were coursing down her cheeks. "I guess we'll just have to wait and see."

The phone rang.

She grimaced; it was probably supposed to be a smile. "We'll clean up. You answer the phone."

He nodded, snatched up the kitchen handset, and carried it into the other room, looking at the phone screen. It was Sandy's cell. What else was going to go wrong today? *Ken, for crying out loud, don't adopt Mona's negativism.*

"Hey, Sandy."

"Ken, I'm in the procurement office, my new workplace..." She began to talk. And talk.

He said nothing, mostly because there was nothing more to say. There was nothing more to do. He listened to the sadness in her words just as much as he listened to the words. They spoke a few more minutes, he thanked her, and they said their good-byes. He thumbed the phone line closed and just stared at it a moment.

So Dale had won. He wandered back to the kitchen pretty much in a daze.

Mona frowned at him. "Ken? Who was it?"

"Sandy." He flopped onto a stool, laid the phone aside, and sank forward to lean his elbows on the counter, his face in his hands.

Mona laid a hand on his shoulder. "What?"

Ken drew a deep breath and sat up. "I built a legacy, Mona, an important and useful legacy. It helped to make

Stone University a much better place, a splendid educational institution. My department helped the students get through, helped them become successful. And now the worst has happened, and that legacy is gone. Rather than fight over who would head the department, they simply gutted it. Pulled Sandy off to do a clerical job in procurement and put in a minimum-wage wonk to answer the phone and direct everything financial over to John's office. The department I built, all the work I did, has disappeared forever."

Chapter Twenty-Six

"How do we help these children when we are falling apart ourselves?"

Mona stared at the face in the mirror the following morning. Red eyes from weeping, weeping from being angry and afraid and wanting to hide. Beating the bag just made her arms hurt; it used to help her feel better, but now she and Ken were arguing and the kids were terrified and there were no answers. It just kept getting worse and worse. And here she thought she had beaten the depression that had been so debilitating. Pride, that's what happened. How could they have forgotten that the children might hear them?

She soaked a washcloth in cold water and applied it to her face. While it almost helped, perhaps an ice pack would be more effective. She dipped and wrung out the cloth again, still to no appreciable avail. Water dripped down on her top, reminding her of the call to come back for another mammogram. She'd never had that happen before. She'd done a manual breast check like they taught at the center, but she'd not felt any lumps. Nor pain. Surely it was an error. Surely. But the technician explicitly said they now had far fewer recalls because of the superior analysis of the machine.

Closing her eyes, she tipped her head back, then took a couple of deep breaths in an attempt at keeping her thoughts under control. The verse floated through her mind. "...Take every thought captive." Sometimes this was far easier than at other times. Like right now. Just the thought of cancer could throw her into total panic. Her mother had died of breast cancer. Granted, that was twenty years earlier, and there had been amazing changes but... *You haven't told Ken.* That thought piled on top of the other. Guilt and fear, two close cousins who loved traveling together.

She applied the cold cloth to her face again; anything was better than nothing. Another thing she was trying to learn. Life was not black and white, either/or. All or nothing. What her father always said. Black and white to the bone. Stiff elbowed, she propped her hands on the counter and dropped her head forward. *Breathe! And again!* After the third inhale and release, she pulled out a tissue, blew her nose, and reached for the face cream. Step one: Tell Ken. Step two: Fix supper. Step three: Apologize to the kids. Putting herself in their shoes made her cringe even more. They'd surely seen and / or heard their parents fighting. And Mom left them. Deliberately walked out of their lives. And now their dad was gone, too.

And Grammy and Grampy were arguing.

Lord God, please protect them and help us to let go of our own fears and frustrations to help them deal with theirs. Forgive me for thinking of myself first and being stubborn as to what I want. I don't know what to do or where to turn, but I know You do. I've got to remember that. Slamming the washcloth in the sink did not help, so she squeezed it out again and hung it on the towel rack.

A whimper snagged her attention. Both Ambrose and

Hyacinth sat in the doorway. Ambrose whimpered again, his tail barely wagging. Even the dog and cat could tell things were bad. She sniffed and knelt down in front of them. "You are far too perceptive." Doggy kisses, purrs, and rubs of the cat persuasion could be an amazing antidote to the blues. She fluffed ears and smoothed their faces. "You are the best and I thank you. How about some treats?"

They spun and headed for the stairs, Ambrose checking over his shoulder to make sure she was coming. Treats for the four-footed family reminded her that treats for the senior member of their pack would not be amiss. "Where's Dad?" she asked.

Ambrose looked toward the stairs to the basement, then took a few steps that way.

"Okay, thanks." She delivered the promised treats, then filled glasses with iced tea and made her way down to the daylit basement that housed Ken's woodshop, their stationary bike and treadmill, and the laundry room. A game room took up the remainder of the space. She stopped in the doorway. Ken had his back to her, sanding something held by clamps to the workbench.

"You ready to take a break?"

He turned and blinked. "I didn't hear you come down."

"You were concentrating." She motioned with the tray. "Inside or out?"

"Outside. I need some fresh air."

"You don't have your fan on?"

Ken had installed an exhaust system to catch the dust made by working with wood and tools. It vented out the side wall. He dumped the collection bag in the compost when needed.

"Guess I forgot." The four of them padded outside to

the shade created by the deck overhead and sat down at the table and chairs. "Nice out here, isn't it?" He mopped the sweat from his forehead. "I was so engrossed I didn't even realize I was hot."

She handed him his glass. "The critters reminded me it was treat time."

He looked at her over the rim of his glass. "Something's wrong."

"You know me too well." She wiped the rim of the glass with one finger, then looked back to her husband. "I have to ask you to forgive me for my bad attitude and the way I've been picking fights."

"Who's to say you're the one setting up the fights?" He shook his head. "Of course I forgive you and ask that you will do the same for me. Too much, it's all been too much lately."

"For me, too. Only I run and hide under the covers."

"I've felt like that. Going fishing helps me, but I've not even been able to do that much lately."

"I love you, Ken Sorenson. I know I've not said that very often lately. Anger took over. I really don't like myself when I act like this."

"Join the club." He sipped his tea. "Thank you for taking the initiative here." He reached for her hand. "In spite of the way I've acted, I love you now and forever. Please don't ever forget that."

She nodded. "I have another confession to make."

He squeezed her hand. "Okay."

"I have to go back for another mammogram, more tests."

"They found something?"

"She was pretty noncommittal. I go tomorrow."

"When did you learn this?"

"Yesterday afternoon. I thought it was no big deal, and then the thoughts took off. Then they called this morning about another test. Just the word *cancer* terrifies me."

"Me, too."

"All the memories of Mom came flooding back and—and I lost it for a while."

"You want me to go with you?"

"If you don't mind."

He shook his head. "What time?"

"Ten, after we get the kids to the pool for lessons."

Ken huffed out a breath. "Will you tell them?"

"Not now, but Ken, we have to apologize to them for scaring them with all this arguing. They're trying so hard to be brave, but they're little children. I'm sure Steig had no idea what kind of burden he was laying on his eldest when he said she should take care of her little brother."

"And for them to be brave. So easy to say, but…" He paused. "After supper, let's do the sofa together, and then we'll go for a walk and talk."

That evening, with all of them snuggled on the sofa, Ken started. "Grammy and I have something really important to tell you."

"Is my daddy gone to heaven?" Jake asked.

"Oh no, no, this is not about your daddy, this is about us here." Mona hugged Jakey, who sat between her and Ken, and Mellie tucked under her arm on her other side.

"We need to ask you to forgive us for getting mad at each other. We are so sorry. Sometimes we say things when we are angry that after we get over it, we wish we'd not said. It is not your fault Grampy and I got angry."

Ken nodded. "We love you both more than we can say.

But that's what's bad about fighting. We have to talk about things without getting angry and blaming."

Mellie was staring at her knees.

Mona continued. "We are a family, and we have a lot to deal with right now. But we stick together. And get through it together. No one hides or runs away."

"Like Mommy?"

"Hush, Jakey, Daddy said..."

"It's okay, Mellie. Sometimes we have to talk about Mommy and Daddy, too. They are part of our lives. Your daddy didn't know what was going to happen, and he was trying his very best to make things easier for his two kids who he loves more than anything else."

"I want my daddy to come home." Mellie's voice sounded like a little girl lost.

"We all do. So we'll keep talking about him and praying that God will bring him home again. And if you don't understand something, we'll figure it out together."

Mona hugged them both, as did Ken.

"You're squishing me." Jake's giggle brought more giggles from the rest.

"I think we need to go for a walk along the river," Ken said.

"All of us?"

"All of us."

Jake ran for the leads and Hyacinth's harness.

Mellie cuddled closer. "I love you both."

"And we love you. How about getting some shoes on, not the flip-flops?"

"'Kay."

Mona grabbed the mosquito spray, did all arms and legs, and away they went. When Ken handed Jake Hyacinth's lead, the little boy did not object.

❖   ❖   ❖

"One step at a time," Ken said that evening after the kids were in bed and he and Mona were getting ready for bed.

"Like for the mammo?" Mona sat down on the bed to take off her slippers.

"Yes, especially that, but for all we've talked about today. We have to trust that God is indeed in control, and we cannot afford to worry about what is going to happen with each of us." Ken sat down on the other side. "Me and the mess at Stone, you and your preschool job, and your tests tomorrow, Steig, the kids, all of us. The burdens are too big for us to carry, so we have to let Him carry them for us. Otherwise, I don't know what will happen to us."

"Waiting is hard."

"Now, that's the truth for sure." He slid under the sheet and light summer blanket. "I keep asking for wisdom for us."

"Thanks. I hope there are no nightmares tonight, either in there or here."

"Amen to that."

Breathing deep the next morning was all that kept Mona from the shakes or running screaming from the clinic. Clinging to Ken's hand helped, too. *You usually handle things so much better than this,* she chided herself. But right now she had cooked-spaghetti knees, and they weren't holding her up too well.

"Mona Sorenson?"

Mona used both arms to push herself up from the chair and followed the scrubs-dressed woman down the hall, a different one than she'd been in the other day. "Will the tests be the same?"

"Pretty much, but more views and more localized." She motioned to a curtained cubicle. "Strip to your waist, and put on that sexy top on the table. Got to look good for the machine, you know."

In spite of herself, Mona smiled. Levity was always a help. "Open in the front?"

"Yes, ma'am. Sexier that way."

"Just wondering, as I've never been much of a one for showing cleavage."

Nodding and grinning, the escort said, "Good one. I'll have to remember that. Some women come in here so terrified, I try to set them at ease. Thanks to machines like this, we can detect so early, cancer doesn't have a chance. You are smart to keep up your yearly visit."

Feeling more encouraged, Mona did as told, waited only a few minutes, and followed all the instructions as precisely as she could, anything to get all the needed information.

"You can get dressed now," the technician said with a smile.

"You've done enough of these, surely you can give me some information."

"I'm sorry, but I can't. The law requires a licensed radiologist to give the reports. They'll call you within twenty-four hours if you need more tests; otherwise, they send a letter." She paused and smiled. "Watch your mailbox."

Relief felt like stepping into a perfect bubble bath. "Thank you."

Telling Ken the story made her smile all over again.

"Well, that is good news. She's rather clever, I'd say. How about I take you out to lunch to celebrate?"

"I'd love to, but we need to pick up the kids at the pool. Marit had something she had to do."

"Oh, well, it was a good idea. Are they all coming to our house?"

"No, Marit's sitter Steffie will take the cousins. Remember, Mellie has her first real riding lesson this afternoon."

"That's right, I totally forgot. Well, I'm sure she'll have fun and you, too; you've always liked horses."

Have fun. Easier said than done until the medications kicked in completely. Mona would have to pretend to have fun, though, for Mellie's sake. Mona kept that in mind as they drove through the gate at Clauson's farm.

Jakey sat scowling and did not look out his window. "Isn't this the most perfect day ever?" Mellie beamed.

"I don't like horses." Jakey pouted.

Mellie leaned forward, straining to see every horse as they drove to the stables, where Miz Beverly was waving at them. Mellie was out of the car before the wheels stopped.

Ken, Mona, and Jakey got out. Jakey insisted, "I don't wanna ride horses."

"Good to see you again." Miz Beverly waved toward the slim young girl beside her. "Mellie, this is Miss Dixie, our best riding instructor. She loves horses and she loves kids. Starbright is waiting for you. She really loves to be groomed, so you will make an immediate friend."

Miss Dixie led them to a stall halfway down the barn. "Now, the first thing our new riders learn is putting on a halter, cross tying, grooming, and how to put on bridle and saddle."

"All that?" Mellie's eyes grew rounder.

"And then you get to mount up and ride. Mrs. Sorenson, I suggest you learn right along with Mellie since someday you may indeed have a horse of your own."

"Oh, Grammy! Please!"

"I don't wanna ride." Jakey hung back, his lip out and his arms crossed.

Miss Dixie smiled. "We don't make anyone ride. Just if they want to. Let me introduce you to your new friend, Starbright." She gave instructions on how to approach a horse, enter the stall, and buckle on the halter and a lead rope.

By the time they had brushed the deep bay coat to a gleam, picked hoofs, and finally tacked up, Mellie was beaming like she was having the time of her life. "Oh, Grammy, isn't she beautiful?"

"She sure is."

"You've done a good job, both of you." After making sure the helmet fit, Miss Dixie had Mellie lead Starbright out to the round pen, showing her the best way to hold the lead rope, hovering close but not too close. Mellie led her beautiful Starbright around, stopping, starting, turning around, and going back. Finally they stopped at a mounting block with Miss Dixie giving instructions that helped Mellie crawl up into the Western saddle.

Mona leaned on the metal fence and watched her granddaughter concentrate. The three—Miss Dixie, Starbright, and a happy little girl—moved out into the arena. Mellie rode and reined as instructed, but Miss Dixie kept a close hold on the lax lead rope.

Watching her ecstatic little granddaughter helped lift her own spirits. Well, a little. She looked toward Ken and Jake. Ken was watching from the fence, but Jake was sitting with his back against a fence post, still pouting. He had been pouting all day, Marit said.

She heard Mellie ask, "Can we go faster? Please?"

"No. When you can keep complete control at a walk and maintain a safe, steady seat, we'll advance. You're doing very well, Mellie. See how you are starting to move with the horse? You're not just sitting there anymore. That's excellent."

Mona and Ken had talked about this horsemanship course being more than just teaching a little girl how to ride. She glanced over at Ken, and he was looking at her, smiling, nodding. Mellie was being provided a distraction, a thing at which she was excelling, something to occupy her mind and heart.

Now to find something for Jake.

Chapter Twenty-Seven

Ithink they are getting tired of me asking for information about Steig." Sitting around the kitchen table, Mona looked from her husband to her daughter and back. "Or rather all of us." She knew Ken had called and written, and Marit said she had, too. They all got the same answer. *We will inform you as soon as we hear anything. You will be the first to know.*

"I asked the chaplain if there is anyone else we can contact." Ken half shrugged. "He said he would give anything to be able to give us some kind of news, but there is a huge silence out there. He said this is not unusual with MIAs, especially those in the elite corps like Steig."

"What did he mean by that?" Marit asked. "Is there more to this that we don't know? This isn't making sense."

Marit looked at her father.

Ken grimaced. "I'm sure there's much more to it that we don't know, but that's just it; we don't know."

"Unless they really aren't searching for them." Mona voiced a thought that had visited her more than once. "You know, out of sight, out of mind."

"He's a valuable investment, too much money pumped into his training. They'll search for him." Mona glanced at Ken, always thinking of the investment angle. He had done that with his students, too.

Marit sighed. "Or he was killed during some covert operation, and they can't tell us because it would blow the cover. We have to trust that God is hearing our prayers and keeping Steig safe from harm. I know that if I don't keep trusting Him, I will go—well, I don't know what would happen, but I'm not about to try to find out."

"One day at a time, actually hours and minutes. We are choosing to live in the moment, not looking ahead to what might happen. Like Pastor Oliver said more than one time, we are living in the here and now because that is where God meets us and leads us. Not tomorrow or the next week."

"Easy to say, Mom. Not easy to do." She pushed her chair back. "I better get home before Magnus and the kids do. Begging out of the movie didn't mean I'd be gone when they got back."

"He said he'd drop our two off here first; he knew you were coming over here?"

"He did, they didn't."

"I wish we could have gotten something accomplished."

"Well, we got the next packet of letters ready to mail to Steig. He's going to find a whole duffel full when he gets back."

Mona refused to think, *If he gets back.*

Marit paused at the door. "Mom, you heard anything on that preschool campaign?"

"No, I've been meaning to call them but..." *But it took more energy than I have lately.* While the depression appeared to have somewhat let up on her mind, she still constantly felt far more tired than she should. That, too, was a symptom of depression.

"Well, I'm sure grateful that mammo turned out to be false." She left with a wave.

"Since she brought it up, what about your preschool project?" Ken drained his teacup.

"It's their call now, but they haven't made contact yet. They'd better hurry; we have to get it going if it will meet their time frame." She hated this wait-till-the-last-minute-and-then-make-demands pattern, and so many clients did it.

"We leave for Chicago in three days."

"I know, I just feel so torn." She would not say she would rather wait for Carole Bergstrund's call, but she dreaded it, too. Look how simple their life was and how simple it could have been now had Steig not called that day.

Ambrose barked his welcome and ran to the door.

"I know, boy, the kids are home."

The dog watched eagerly while the kids waved good-bye and ran to the house.

"Hi, Grampy; hi, Grammy; hi, Ambrose. We had popcorn, a big box." Jake used his hands to show a monster box of popcorn.

"Each of you?" Ken asked.

"No, we shared. Uncle Magnus bought two boxes and extra cartons so we wouldn't spill passing the boxes back and forth." Mellie retrieved a glass and poured herself a drink of water. "Torin spilled most of his, so I shared mine."

Jake wrapped his arms around Ambrose's neck. "We didn't bring you any, sorry. Grampy says you don't like it."

"So, how was the movie?" Mona asked.

"The best. So funny." Jake launched into telling the story in fits and starts, with Mellie correcting him.

"It was a funny movie," Mellie finished. "But I still like *Monsters, Inc.* the best. We could watch that one again; we brought it from home." She stopped. "Texas, I mean." Mellie headed for the stairs and the haven of her bed.

Mona considered. She coveted that spare room that was her office. Yes, *coveted* was the word. Everything in one place, her records and files at hand; she could not picture how she would manage her fledgling business without a proper office. *But.* Always there was that but. Mellie was ten now. She needed her privacy, and you do not get privacy with your little brother in the room.

Lord, give me strength to do this and appear happy while I'm doing it.

She trudged upstairs to the children's room. "Mellie?"

Mona found her, with a tear-wet face, propped against her pillows, writing on a pad of paper. "What are you writing?"

"A letter to Daddy." She scrubbed her fingers under her nose and sniffed again.

"I figured as much. Are you telling him about your riding lesson?"

"I already wrote about that." She motioned to her paper. "About the movie. And asking him to please write to us or, best, come home."

"I hope you told him we all want that. Right now, I have an idea, but you have to help me. Would you like your own room?"

Her eyes got wide. "You mean without Jakey in it?"

"Without Jakey. We can put my office downstairs and move you into that room."

She bounded off her bed. "Oh yes! Then Jakey can't keep me awake talking and crying because he can't go to sleep!" She stopped. "But my bed's in here."

"The top bunk lifts off to make twin beds. Your bed will go with you."

"Perfect!"

Mona called Ken, and together they moved her office furniture out into the hallway; Mona could deal with it tomorrow. "Let's strip your bed since we have to take it apart anyway. Will you get new bed linen from the hall closet, please?"

Mellie ran out.

Ken paused from lifting off the mattress. "Are you sure this is best? All they really have is each other, and now we're separating them."

"I don't know if it's best. Ken, I don't know anything anymore."

"You and me both."

They pulled the set pins and lifted down the bunk bed, toting the bed and dresser into Mellie's new room. Mellie carried one of the drawers with her underwear still in it; she was getting stronger, it seemed. Ken set the nightstand up beside her bed as Mona brought the clothes over from the closet. She still had office supplies in the closet; she could take them downstairs tomorrow.

Jake was just as delighted as his sister. "Now Mellie can't boss me around and tell me to shut up all the time."

Mellie flopped on her bed. "Look! I don't have to climb!" She carefully stacked her books on her nightstand. "I finished these books. Can we go to the library tomorrow? I want some books to read on the trip. I told Daddy we are going to Chicago."

"You'll miss your riding lesson next week, you know."

"Maybe I can have two lessons the next week." Her eyes pleaded for a yes.

"We'll ask Miss Dixie if they have an extra space."

"I wish you would ride, too, Grammy. Just think if we could ride out in that big pasture. And they have riding trails all around. When Daddy comes home, I'm going to ask him for a horse. Maybe we can buy Starbright. She's a rescue horse. Miss Dixie told me all about her. She was really skinny when they got her, but she's all fleshed out now."

Mona nodded and smiled and listened to Mellie dream. Best of all, she was back to saying "when Daddy comes home," not "Daddy's never coming home." *Oh, my darling granddaughter, you are far braver than I was at your age.*

"How about coming down for dessert, unless you are hungry for real food, too?"

"Can we have peanut butter and jam?"

"Crackers or bread?" She smiled and held out her hand. "I saw an app on the Internet that I want to show you."

Mellie bailed off the bed, tucking her paper and pen into the drawer of the nightstand. "What's for dessert and what app?"

"Surprises both."

"Brit and I played *Minecraft* on their computer. I didn't do so good 'cause that was my first time playing." She looked up at Mona. "I don't like computer games so much."

"Good. I'd rather play board games with people at a table, not on the computer."

"Me, too."

After they were all served, Mellie and Mona took their plates into the family room to the computer. "I found a program on drawing horses. I used to draw horses all the time, and I thought you might enjoy it, too."

"Oh, good. Can we do it together?"

"I don't see why not. I think we have some pencils and

drawing paper in my craft supplies." Mona brought up the app, and together they watched the first five minutes.

Mellie was beaming again. "Yes, let's do this." She paused and glanced at Mona hopefully. "We could put it on your iPad and take it along in the car." There it was again, that innate skill for electronics that children possess.

"We can and we will."

Sometime in the wee hours, Ambrose barked Ken and Mona awake so they heard Jake crying. Rushing into his room, they found him covered in vomit, as were the sheets on the bed. While Ken went for cleanup supplies, Mona felt his forehead. "Bring the thermometer, too, please."

"I—I'm sorry," Jake moaned as she removed his jammy top.

"Honey, you can't help being sick. Here, let's get you into the bathtub to cool you down." She carried him into the bathroom, set him on the toilet, and started tepid water, then finished undressing him.

Ken appeared at the door. "I stripped the bed."

"You stay here, and I'll get out clean sheets."

"Grampy..." Jake started heaving again. "My head hurts."

"Tummy, too?"

"So hot."

When he stopped barfing, Ken set him in the bathtub. "Let's wash you and maybe you'll feel better."

Back in his bed, with a bath towel protecting the sheet, Jake flopped against the pillow. He sipped water and promptly threw up again, but this time Ken had a bowl at the ready.

"I'll stay here with him, and you go back to bed," Ken said softly.

"We'll call the base clinic first thing in the morning." Mona checked the clock. "Not that morning is so far away." She stroked Jake's hair back. While the water had cooled him somewhat, she knew he was still far hotter than he should be. Taking his temp again, she was right: 102 degrees, far too close to the danger zone.

"I'll get some ice chips; perhaps he can keep that down." Returning with a glass of chips and a spoon, she found Jake sound asleep and Ken lying beside the ill child. Perhaps the worst was over.

Mellie rubbed her eyes as she met Mona in the hallway. "Grammy, what's happening?"

"Jake woke up vomiting, but he's asleep now. You go on back to bed. If you feel sick at all, you let me know right away."

"'Kay." She wrapped her arms around her grandma, who hugged her back. "Will Jake be all right tomorrow?"

"I hope so." Mona led her back to her bed and tucked her in. "You go back to sleep."

By morning, Jake had not kept anything down, but no one else had any symptoms. Mona called the doctor's office, scolding herself that they'd not made appointments with the base doctors as the chaplain advised, new patients and all that rigmarole. She'd planned to but somehow kept putting it off. She explained the situation to a nurse who took the call and answered her questions, including length of time since the onset.

"And his temp has not abated?"

"Not even with cold cloths."

"Does he complain of pain anywhere?"

"Head and tummy."

"You know, I think you better bring him in immediately, be on the safe side. As soon as you can. I'll call the gate and tell them to expect you. Give me your names again. And bring your papers, please."

Mona did and agreed to bring the medical records. Next, she called Marit and asked her to come get Mellie.

"I'll be right there. Good thing you called before Magnus left."

Mona headed upstairs to get dressed and met Ken in the hall.

"He has diarrhea now, too. And he's too weak to sit up."

"Let's clean him up and put a diaper on him for the trip; we still have some of his overnight diapers. We'll wrap him in a sheet and take a blanket and bowl with us." What in the world was going on with him?

They took turns staying with him and dressing, then, as soon as Marit came for Mellie, bundled Jake and Mona in the backseat with all the supplies, and Ken drove the interminably long road to the base. Mona held Jake in her arms, prayers bombarding heaven as she fought the fear that threatened to drown her.

"How is your grandson, sir?" The young soldier at the gate asked.

"Getting worse."

"I'm so sorry. Follow that jeep over there. He'll get you the shortest cut to the hospital. The nurse said to send you there."

"Thank you." Ken gunned the SUV as the jeep threw gravel moving out. When they reached the emergency entrance, two young men met them with a gurney. One reached in the backseat to take Jake.

"We'll take him now, ma'am. We're all prepared." With Jake belted on the rolling bed, they headed for the door, Mona right on their heels, while Ken went to park their car.

A woman with a clipboard stopped her at the swinging door that now cut off her view. "Please, Mrs. Sorenson, I know you are frantic, but right now they can work faster without you there. Here comes Dr. Washington to ask you what all has happened, and meanwhile, I'll get the paperwork in place. This is your grandson, right?"

"Yes, and we are his legal guardians. Here are copies of the guardianship materials. And all medical records, of course."

"Good." She stepped back, and a man who looked barely old enough to be in college introduced himself.

"Please tell me what happened."

She told him all that occurred and what they had done as concisely as possible, clenching her hands together to keep them from shaking. And she realized you can talk about something even while praying inside.

Ken came in and stopped beside her. "We thought he'd caught a flu bug or something simple, like kids do."

"A reasonable deduction." He glanced at a chart. "You called here about seven?"

"Yes, because we could see he was getting worse. I figured he was dehydrated by then," Mona added.

"Wise move. We'll let you be with him as soon as we can, so for right now, please help Dahl there get her paperwork under control."

Waiting took forever. Ken alternately paced and stared out the window. Mona called Marit to say what they knew and asked her to call the prayer chain. Something was seriously wrong with Jake. But they had no idea what.

Chapter Twenty-Eight

All the signs point to intussusception, but we will do an MRI to be sure. You can see him now, but he is pretty woozy from the meds, so don't be alarmed if he doesn't respond like he usually does."

"Would you please repeat that word you said?"

"Yes, intussusception, a collapsing of a portion of the bowel. If this is the case, we will do surgery immediately before it causes further problems. A kid like him will bounce back fairly quickly, but we'll be keeping him here for a few days at least. As soon as we know more, we'll bring you up to date, too. Dahl has papers for you to sign, permission for surgery being one of them. I'll keep you posted." As the young doctor left by one door, Pastor Oliver entered the waiting room from the hall.

He immediately put an arm around each of their shoulders. "What a shocker."

Ken nodded while Mona blew her nose. "He said intussusception, a portion of the bowel collapsing in on itself. If the initial diagnosis is accurate, they'll go in and remove that section."

"I take it this isn't potentially fatal."

"If not dealt with quickly, it can lead to worse complications. He'll be here a few days."

"And we can't tell Steig." Mona's tears ran again in spite of her tissues.

Pastor Oliver nodded. "I see. Good thing we all know and absolutely believe this is not a surprise to God. He always has a plan." He looked directly at each of them, waiting for a confirmative nod. "And the Holy Spirit is right here with us and will never leave."

"Like Jakey says, pointing more to his tummy. 'Jesus is right here in me,'" Mona reminded them.

"Ah, the faith of children."

A nurse came through the door. "You can see him now, come with me." She led the three of them through a maze of curtained cubicles past the nurses' station and finally pulled the curtain back to where Jake lay, head propped up only a little, connected to tubes and machines that hummed or clicked, with screens that transmitted information if one knew how to read them.

Ken and Mona moved to the side of least apparatuses. Mona took his free hand. "Jakey, Grammy and Grampy are here. Can you hear me?"

Jake's eyes fluttered but didn't quite open. They'd have missed the tiny nod had they not been watching so carefully.

"He's not in any pain right now, and all his vitals are good. As soon as they do the·MRI, they will most likely take him directly to surgery. They are preparing the OR now."

A man in blue scrubs pulled back the curtain. "Excuse me, but we are on our way to the MRI." He pushed a gurney up to the bed.

"We'll take good care of him, I promise." The nurse motioned them to step out of the way. When Jake was transferred and ready, Mona leaned over and kissed his forehead, as did Ken.

"We love you, Jakey; see you when you wake up again." Mona leaned against Ken as they watched the gurney being pushed down the hall and through two swinging doors. *Lord, how do we get through this? I know, trust You, and I do, but this is so hard. On the other hand, where else can I go? He is so little.*

The three of them returned to the waiting room. "Have you eaten anything yet?" Oliver asked.

Ken and Mona looked at each other and shook their heads. Who'd even thought of food?

"Let's go to the cafeteria. We can talk there, too."

"I want to wait until they tell us he has gone into surgery." Mona glanced around like she was lost. "Did I leave my purse somewhere?" Ken pointed to the strap on her shoulder. Mona rolled her eyes. "I think they call this discombobulated."

"Or grief stricken." Oliver motioned them to the chairs. "Let's go sit in that corner and pray together. That will help us all." Once they were seated, he took both their hands. "Lord God, You promised to comfort the afflicted, that Your peace passes all understanding. Right now, we need both comfort and peace, the assurance that You are indeed right here and overseeing the doctors and nurses, all who are caring for Jake. Lord, fill them with Your wisdom that far surpasses even the best training. Jake is Your child, as we all are. Waiting is so terribly difficult, but we know that You can and will help us through this period. Lord, we give You all the glory as You pour Your peace over and into us, this place, these people. We will keep our eyes on Your face, Jesus. You will not let us go." He squeezed their hands. "Amen."

"Thank you." Ken looked up as some other people came into the room and took over another corner. One woman sat by herself, knitting needles flying. "Not a lot of people in here."

"The front waiting room is full. I checked for you there when I came in."

"Marit called you?"

"And the prayer chain. Our family is stepping up to the plate. Once you know what is happening, I will let them all know."

The nurse returned. Mona glanced at the clock, surprised than almost an hour had passed.

"The MRI showed the location of an intussusception, so they are now moving him to the OR and sedating him. The surgery will last between an hour and an hour and a half. The doctor will come to see you to explain what they did, and at the same time, Jake will be moved to the recovery room, where we watch him very carefully as the anesthetic wears off. We will make sure he is not feeling pain, and as soon as he is awake, we will come for you. He will be moved to the ICU, and one of you at a time can be with him there."

"You are being so helpful. Thank you." Mona sniffed. Someone being kind made her even more weepy.

"I'm taking them to the cafeteria for breakfast, but we'll be back in an hour." Oliver stood. "Thank you."

"If you need anything or you have questions, please ask."

The three of them followed the signs to the cafeteria. "Have you even had any coffee yet?"

"I don't know how we got along without it, but..." Mona filled three cups at the coffee machine right by the door and set them on a nearby table. Their orders arrived swiftly, but once they sat down, a wave of exhaustion nearly knocked Mona off her chair.

Ken reached for her hand. "Are you all right?"

"I will be." Hands shaking, she added cream and sugar to her coffee, making Ken's eyebrows arch. "Should help faster this way." She kept an eye on the clock as they ate. Ken and Oliver discussed the idea of forming a support group for parenting grandparents to be opened to the community as a service of the congregation. To think there was even a term for what they were going through. She left half of her scrambled eggs and toast but had another cup of coffee, black like usual this time.

Back up in the waiting room, Mona's phone began to sing "The Swan of Tuonela." "Marit." She caught their daughter up to the minute, said not to come right now, and yes, she would call as soon as they met with the doctor. Tapping the red button, she slid the phone back in the outside pocket of her purse. "She's calling the others, said Mellie is frantic."

"Why didn't you talk with Mellie?"

"She was outside; they are all riding bikes. She'll call when she gets in." The clock moved in slow motion or had stopped moving altogether. An hour passed. She could play a game on her iPhone, but hadn't thought to put her iPad in. *Who would?*

Inching closer to another half hour. Had something gone wrong? No, the nurse said it could be longer than an hour. She reached for Ken's hand.

A man in green scrubs with a mask dangling around his neck came through the door. It was not Dr. Washington. "Sorenson?" They all stood. "Jake did well through the surgery. We removed the intussusception and stitched him back together. He won't be eating for a day or two, but he's on a drip now and we'll probably start liquids in the morning. See how his body accepts that, then soft food, and if the bowel is working properly, he can go home in three, maybe four days."

"Thank you, what a relief. Can we stay here with him?" Mona squeezed Ken's hand, the dread lifting like fog when the sun comes out.

"One at a time in the ICU, but we'll most likely move him to a room tomorrow. I know you don't live nearby."

"It was a fast hour this morning."

"I'm sure it was. One of the hotels near here offers special rates for families with someone in the hospital. If you have no further questions?" He looked at each of them.

Ken asked, "Can his sister visit? She's ten."

"Not today, and he'll feel pretty rocky tomorrow, but after that, he might enjoy entertainment. Ask your nurse. She'll fill you in about life in our hospital."

"Thank you."

"So now we wait again?" Mona felt so weary.

"But at least we know he's through the roughest part." Ken sank down in a chair and scrubbed his hands through his hair. "Do you realize this is a first for us? We've never had a child operated on or ill in a hospital. We forget how blessed we've been."

"Now, the clinic or the urgent care, that's another matter." Mona sat down, too.

Oliver checked his watch. "I'm sorry, but I need to hit the road. Call me immediately if there is a change for the worse."

"Of course, what a comfort you have been." Mona stood and hugged him. "We'll keep in touch. Any words of advice, feel free."

"Hmm, I'll keep that in mind. My kids think I am far too free with advice, so this feels real good." He hugged them both and headed for the elevator.

When they saw Jake an hour later, he blinked at them, tried to smile, and drifted off again.

"His vitals all look great. We'll come for you when he is in a bed."

"How long might that be?" Ken asked the nurse.

"Maybe another hour or so. We do have an available bed in ICU, but barring complications, he'll be on the pediatric floor in the morning."

Mona leaned over and kissed his cheek. "I love you, Jakey boy," she whispered. Was that a nod she saw?

"I'm going down to buy him a balloon or two in the gift store," Ken announced. "We can tie them to the foot of his bed. You want anything?"

"A candy bar sounds good."

"Baby Ruth?" His smile looked tired, but his eyes broadcasted relief. "I'll get myself one, too."

She watched him walk away. His step was jauntier again, too. She picked up a *Better Homes and Gardens* magazine. She never took time to read many magazines, so this was a treat. Her phone sang Marit's song.

"Grammy, is Jakey okay? I mean . . ."

"Yes, he won't be feeling too good for a while, but the surgery is over and he's waking up again. The doctor was very positive."

"Aunty Marit told me what was happening. How come he got sick like that?"

"Sometimes things like this just happen. We really don't know why, but we can sure be happy the doctor could fix it."

"When can I come see him?"

"Maybe tomorrow, for sure the day after."

"We could play games on your iPad. Can he walk around?"

"Oh yes, they'll have him up and moving probably by

this evening. There will be a TV in his room tomorrow. You all keep praying for him, but don't be afraid. He's going to be just fine."

"You're sure? Not telling me something because I'm only ten?"

"Yes, I'm sure. If something else happens, I promise to tell you right away."

"I sure wish Daddy was here. And we can't even let him know Jakey is in the hospital." Tears clouded her voice.

"Me, too, honey; me, too."

"Tell them Jake likes green Jell-O and Popsicles best."

"I will. Popsicles will probably be the first thing he can eat. Good thinking."

She sounded plaintive. "Can we still go to Chicago?"

"No, I'm afraid not. He won't be well enough for a while yet."

Silence. Then, "I miss you, Grammy. Will I have to stay here with Brit and the boys?"

"Yes, for now."

"Will you stay there all the time?"

"We'll see. I love you, Mellie, and I am so proud of you. I can't say how much." Mona sniffed and blinked. "Marit will bring you home to get what you need. Grampy will probably come home this afternoon to feed the animals and pack me some clothes. He'll call you."

Sniff. "'Kay, I guess. I didn't think I'd miss Jakey—he's so naughty—but I do. Hug him for me, huh?"

"I will. Bye." She clicked off her phone and dug out a tissue. She should have brought a box. So many things to decide. Her phone began to play "Heigh-Ho, Heigh-Ho." Business call.

Ah, Carole Bergstrund from the preschool project. What a time for her to call. "Hello."

"I apologize for taking so long. We had to move the dates back a month for the opening, certification issues. Will that work for you?"

Will that work for me? Such a simple question. The instant war between her head and heart surprised and appalled Mona. She was getting the assignment of a lifetime, the very job to put her fledgling company on the map...and yet...Jakey, Mellie and Starbright, school, all the hassles that pop up out of nowhere. So many threads becoming all tangled. *Yes, but your dream...,* her head cried.

Yes, but there is only so much time and energy...

But I've been working so hard to make the career happen...

Mellie and Jakey need you. End of war.

Mona licked her lips and took a deep breath. She nodded to Ken, who had just walked in with two bobbing balloons. "Mrs. Bergstrund, there are problems, personal problems...Our grandson just came out of surgery, for one, and there—"

"Oh, dear. I hope it isn't, you know, serious."

"Serious enough. And there are other issues. The bottom line is..." Mona straightened her back and, watching Ken, said, "I am sorry, but I have decided I cannot handle your promotion at this time or a month from now. There is just too much going on, too many important issues, and..."

Ken looked dumbfounded. Honestly, wasn't he the one who had insisted all along that Mona could not juggle all this? Why was he surprised?

"We really like some of the ideas you brought to the table. Are you certain?"

"Thank you, but I believe this is for the best. I know the reputation of the other firm you've engaged. I'm confident they can handle the whole job, and they will do good work for you. Thank you again, but no, postponing the decision until later just doesn't seem right. You need someone who is fully available and fully able to concentrate."

"I'm very sorry to hear this, but I'm glad you are backing out right at the beginning and not when the project is rolling."

Mona said her good-byes and clicked off the call. "Ken, I had such big dreams. I just hope I am doing the best thing—for all of us."

Ken sat down beside her, holding the balloon strings in one hand and taking her hand with the other. "Dreams are the most fragile things of all. I see to some extent how hard this was for you. I'm proud of you. We pray for the best."

"That's what I told Mellie a couple of minutes ago. I think we need to say things like that to the kids more often. Right now she is feeling lost."

The nurse beckoned them from the doorway. "You can see him now."

They followed down a new hall and stopped at the door outside the ICU. "You will need to push this and identify yourself every time you want to go in. Mr. Sorenson, since you've got the balloons, how would you like to come first?"

Mona sat down in the chair by the wall. "Please don't stay too long, I want to see him, too."

"I know."

He returned a few minutes later sporting a wide grin. "He is tickled with the balloons. And asking for you."

When the nurse showed her the room, Mona paused in the doorway. Jake still had all the tubes as before. But he grinned when he saw her. *Thank you, Lord, You brought him safely through.* She crossed to the bed and kissed his forehead. "I love you, Jakey boy."

"Grampy brought me balloons." He spoke in a whisper, obviously with a sore throat from the intubation.

"I know. You sure look better than the last time I saw you."

He nodded, his eyelids already drifting closed. But he jerked them open again. "Don't leave me."

"Grampy and I will take turns."

"Mellie?" His whisper faded.

"She's at Aunty Marit's house."

He sort-of nodded and was asleep.

The nurse stopped beside her. "He'll probably sleep for a couple of hours now. He's doing well."

"Thank you." Mona rolled her lips together and sniffed. "Ken and I need to figure out how to do this."

"We have a sheet at the desk with information. I'll get it for you. That way you can stay close by, and we will call you if there are any changes. I know you live quite far away."

"I was hoping..."

"Once he is in a regular room, you or your husband can stay with him. We have chairs that fold out into beds."

"Thank you. We need to make some decisions. I'll be back later."

The nurse laid a hand on her shoulder. "Never forget you have to take care of yourself, too."

Right. She nodded, and after taking the offered paper, she headed for the exit. Life changed in an instant sometimes, and she was fast learning she didn't have control over it.

No control at all.

Chapter Twenty-Nine

Dear Mellie,

Thank you for your letter asking about your daddy, who is listed as MIA. I want you to know that we are doing all we can to find him, but we must keep all our efforts a secret because we don't want to put him in further danger. I promise you we will contact you immediately when we know more. Your daddy, Captain Steig Sorenson, is not only one of our top soldiers but a fine man. I know he loves you and your brother dearly and is very proud of you. Having your daddy gone to serve his country is terribly hard on families, and so we thank you for praying for him and all of us.

Sincerely,
Major George Paget

Mellie read the letter again and stared at her family. "He wrote to me. He read my letter."

"Let me see." Jake reached for the paper. His eyes grew even more round. "Look how—how important." He pointed to the army emblem and seal.

Jake had been home from the hospital for a week and was feeling better every day. He was still under restrictions, as in no running, climbing, swimming, lifting, and half the other things he wanted to do.

"I am in shock," Mona said. "To think Major Paget really answered Mellie's letter. He is the one who brought us the news about Steig. What a compassionate man."

"I'm glad I'm not in his position. Mine at the university was hard enough."

"Grampy, are we going to go to Chicago?" Jake reached for another pancake. Mona had been cooking some of his favorite things to tempt him to eat, but not his real favorite, peanut butter on top of the syrup.

"I don't know. You have another appointment with the doctor next week, and pretty soon, you need to get ready for school to start."

"What's get ready?"

"Registered, school clothes, school supplies." Mona ticked all the things off on her fingers.

His lower lip came out. "I don't wanna go shopping. They can go shopping." He pointed at Mellie and Mona.

"Sorry, Jakey boy, but you need to try the shoes on at least and maybe the clothes." Ken poured himself another cup of coffee and warmed up Mona's.

"Can I have coffee, too?" Jake held up his empty cup of hot chocolate.

He's been catered to for too long, Mona thought. Funny how quickly kids adapted to being waited on. Of course, perhaps it wasn't just kids.

"I think we could go up to the lake for a few days, get all the preparations for school done and run away from home." Ken glanced at Mona. "What do you think?"

"I think by then Jake will be able to go in the water.

What about the garden? Beans should be ready for canning and freezing."

"We could offer them to Marit. Her garden is pathetic."

"What's pathetic?" Jake asked.

"Sad. Not in real good shape."

"I don't want to miss another riding lesson." Mellie looked at Mona. "Only five more until school starts."

"We'll leave the day after a lesson." Mona returned Mellie's high five.

"Can Brit and the boys come?" Mellie asked.

"Let me think about it."

"That means no." Jake's pouty lip appeared again.

Ken stared at him. "Why do you say that?"

"Mommy always—"

"Jakey!" Mellie glared at him.

"Enough," Ken barked. "Remember, we talk about things here. Your mommy was part of your life, and we can't pretend it didn't happen. So Mellie, let it be. Jake, here in our house, 'Let me think about it' means just that. It probably means Grammy and Grampy need to talk about the idea before making a decision. That's how we try to do things here."

Mona nodded slightly, along with a lip rolling. She knew how hard the *try* was at times. Dreams of her own business still appeared, not only at night. But right now she appreciated not having extra pressure. How come a getting-well child took up so much time, for both her and Ken?

Ken got up and started clearing the table with Mellie helping—without being asked. "Your lesson is at three?"

She nodded, her eyes sparkling. "And Grammy is going to ride, too."

"And Grammy is really excited, too, huh?" Ken sent her

a teasing look. All because she'd mentioned she was more than a bit uptight about it.

Mellie studied her. "Grammy can do anything."

Mona reached for her with a big hug. "Thank you, honey. You make me feel mighty good. How about right after we clean up the kitchen, we go through your clothes to see what you need most for school. Jake, you after."

"I got lots of clothes." He slumped in his chair. "I don't wanna."

"We're just making lists today."

"I hate lists, too." He peeped from under his lashes and whispered, "Let's go ride bikes, Grampy."

"Not until the doctor says that's okay. Now get rid of that pouty lip, and after we finish here, we'll go down to the woodshop."

Mona patted him on the head after she stood. "I'll get the sun tea started."

Upstairs in Mellie's room, they laid all her clothes out on the bed and began sorting. School keepers, play keepers, summer, winter. Most of her pants were too short, as were the sleeves on shirts and sweaters. They tossed her winter jacket on the giveaway pile with the comment, "You need warmer gear here. We get lots of snow and cold."

When Mellie's lists were done, they attacked Jake's room and did the same, then called him up to try a few things on. He did so with a grump and charged back down the stairs.

Mona had listed all the sizes, too.

"I never did it like this before." Mellie motioned around the room, then picked up a blue sweater. "Daddy really likes this one. He called me Princess sometimes." She smoothed the sweater down her front. "I know this is small, but can I keep it?"

"Of course you may." Mona tipped up Mellie's chin with one finger and looked directly into her eyes. "You keep whatever you want that reminds you of him, okay?" They both looked at the framed picture of Steig in his dress uniform that sat on her chest of drawers, along with one of the three of them. Mona felt the sting of tears and heard a sniff from the girl at her side. "We're going to get through this, honey, we are."

Together they put back the keeper things and took their lists downstairs to tack on the cork message board on the door to the garage, right next to the calendar.

Mona studied the calendar. "Since we are riding today, how about we go shopping tomorrow? Get this done quick. What do you think?"

"The next day is the doctor. Do I have to go?"

"Nope. And I suggest that we swing by the library on our way home from riding. Sorry we didn't get to that before."

Being on a horse felt far better than Mona ever dreamed it would, not that she'd dreamed of riding. She leaned forward and stroked the golden neck of Bruna, the only Fjord horse she had ever ridden.

"Okay?" Miss Dixie asked.

"I most certainly am. This saddle . . ." She shook her head. "When I was a child, we sometimes rode the horses at my uncle's farm. We would pretend we were in horse shows, and I used to want to ride English, but Uncle Frazier didn't have an English saddle. So thank you." She squirmed around to settle deeper into this English hunt seat.

"We'll get your leg grip strengthened as we go. She responds well to legs. She is also voice trained. Remember to hold the reins separately, not like you were used to."

Miss Dixie adjusted the reins slightly. "Sit up straight, and keep your weight on your heels. You will need to buy boots with a heel if you decide to keep this up. We can switch Mellie to English, too, if you'd like."

"We'll see."

With a young man working with Mellie in another round pen, Mona and her teacher worked in a larger corral. By the end of her lesson when she dismounted, her legs were shaking.

"I thought I was in pretty good shape after all we walk and bike ride."

"This uses your muscles in a different way. So how do you feel about it?"

"Pure delight. Any suggestions on where to buy boots and helmets?"

Miss Dixie gave her the business card of a store in Madison. "They'll take good care of you and not try to sell you the store. For Mellie, we might have some boots in the office that will fit her. We have a boot swap for families—well, actually, other gear, too, but this is what you need right now."

On the way home, they stopped at the library and got Mellie a card of her own. They left an hour later with both of them carrying books. Mona had found one titled *Riding English*. Mellie had one on caring for a horse and several other horse stories.

"Thanks, Grammy." She hugged the books to her chest. "Maybe tonight we can do a lesson on drawing?"

"I'm sure we can."

"Can I come with you to the doctor?" Mellie asked when Mona tucked her into bed that night.

"Certainly, if you want, but you said you didn't want to."

"I changed my mind. I can read and draw all the way

there and in the waiting room and back." She sucked in a deep breath and let it out with a smile. "That might make Jake feel good, too." She closed her eyes and clasped her hands. "Dear Jesus, thank You for Grammy and Grampy and riding and drawing and reading and Jakey and my cousins. Most of all, please take care of my daddy and bring him home safe. And soon. Amen."

"Amen, indeed," Mona whispered. *And thank You for these children.*

School shopping took Mona back in time, making her realize she'd missed this part of family life. Even though she'd gone sometimes with Marit and the kids, this was different. She'd printed out the shopping lists and gave one to Mellie, too.

"I'm glad Jakey didn't come. He really can be a pain."

Mona smiled at her granddaughter. "Boys can be like that at times. He will have to try on the shoes, though, but not until we get back from the cabin."

"Good thing."

Jake was easy to shop for, all but the shoes. While they got most of the school supplies and his clothes at Target, they'd combed three stores to find cute things for Mellie. Mona had forgotten that a ten-year-old girl might have a hard time making decisions, especially when she would be going to a new school and didn't know anyone there— yet. She and Jake would be attending a different school than their cousins because of where they lived. At least the kids were registered. Ken had taken care of that while she stayed at the hospital with Jake.

They chose a sandwich shop in the mall and were seated by the window. Sitting. What a joy plain old sitting could be.

"Daddy hates shopping about as much as Jake." Mellie twirled her straw in her milk shake.

"Maybe that's where Jake got it from." Mona felt like she'd been run over by a Mack truck. How could shopping be so exhausting? She didn't remember being this tired. *You were younger then. And depression does that to you for months. You should know that by now.* That nagging voice inside didn't help. And she usually hadn't tried to cram all the activity into one day.

"Are we really going to buy riding boots?"

"Not today."

Mellie giggled. "I know that. Did you know that Brit found a summer horse camp on the Internet?"

"Really?"

"Uh-huh, actually Aunt Marit found it when Brit asked if she could go looking. They don't let her search the Internet for stuff, either."

Steig had asked them to keep the kids off the Internet without supervision and they totally concurred. She was glad Marit and Magnus felt the same.

The waitress set their hamburgers on the table. "Anything else I can get you?"

"Not now, thanks." She turned back to Mellie. "Let's say grace and have at it."

"I'm starved." She shut her eyes. "Thank you, Lord, for good food and nice clothes and for making Jake better again, amen."

"Good girl."

Eating out with her granddaughter promised to be a good memory. After she recovered.

"Wouldn't it be perfect if when we got home, the officer had called to say Daddy was on his way home?"

"That it would be." The comment caught Mona by surprise. Did Mellie think about her daddy all the time?

Chapter Thirty

"I don't wanna get putty." In the backseat, Jake had that lip out again.

"Too bad, sport. I'm not going to leave you out here in the car alone. Come along inside." Ken unlatched the child seat restraints and swung Jake to the ground. "Besides, shopping in clothing stores is boring, but hardware stores are fun."

Jake followed him into Cramer's Hardware, still pouting. "They're *not* fun. I don't wanna." He raised his head. "I smell popcorn."

"Yep. The store has a carnival-style popper, and they offer their customers free popcorn. I suppose they figure if you spend longer in the store eating popcorn, you'll buy more."

Rather than search all the aisles with little grumpy-pants, Ken just asked an employee. Smiling, she led him directly to a shelf of various kinds of putty and wood fillers. He never ceased to be amazed at the arcane knowledge these salespeople had of every item in their store. Millions of items, if you count nails and screws.

Brian was right, overkill of choice. Ken was carving basswood, and here was basswood-colored repair putty, along with oak, maple, cedar, and mahogany putty, as well as a couple exotic wood names he didn't recognize. He got the small can, thought again, and got the larger one. If his life was going to go as it had been, he'd need a lot.

"Okay, Jake, let's get your aunt's furnace filters and..."

"Don't wanna get furnace filters!"

"...and then get a couple bags of popcorn."

"Don't wanna get pop—" Jake paused and closed his mouth.

Ken already knew where the filters were; he bought many. He grabbed four one-inch twenty-by-twenties—two for Marit and two for him—tossed them in the shopping cart, and continued on to the gaudily painted popcorn maker. From inside the glass cabinet, Ken retrieved a bag and handed it to Jake, then got himself one. "Over here." He led the way to the display of patio furniture and sat down in a surprisingly comfortable wrought iron patio chair.

Jake sat down in the chair beside his. "This is good."

"I agree. They salt it well, and I think they put that artificial butter-flavored stuff on it. We just won't tell your aunt." He waited a few moments. "Okay, Jake. What's this business about 'I don't wanna' all the time? You don't even think before you say it."

Jake glanced up at him, looking a little guilty, and shrugged. "I dunno."

Ken figured he would say that, and no doubt it was the truth. A five-year-old has trouble articulating thoughts. "So what do you think about when you're not thinking about anything? For instance, when you're building with Legos, you're thinking about what you're doing and what you're going to do next. But like when you're riding along in the car, and there's not much going on?"

That shrug again. Jake carefully concentrated on his

popcorn, so Ken gave him the time. Finally, "I guess mostly about Mommy and Daddy. I'm scared Mommy won't ever come home again. I'm hoping she'll miss us so much she'll come home and quit fighting with Daddy, and she won't yell at us anymore. But if she comes home, she'll go to the wrong house, in Texas where we don't live anymore."

"Jake, that's pretty deep stuff. Think about anything else?"

"Daddy. Mostly Daddy. I'm scared Mellie's right. She thinks he's dead and he's never gonna come back. She's just saying she thinks he's alive because that's what you and Grammy want to think. She doesn't want to make you quit hoping, you know?"

"That's very thoughtful of her."

"She loves you muchly." Jakey looked up at Ken. "So do I."

"And you already know Grammy and I love you as much as a kid can be loved."

"Yeah, I know." He had most of his popcorn gone already. "Can we stop for ice cream?"

"Isn't your tummy full?"

"The ice cream will melt down around the edges so it doesn't take up any space."

This kid was going to be an engineer. Ken better start saving up for the tuition to MIT. It wasn't cheap.

They did indeed stop at the ice cream parlor for a single dip each. Ken ruminated on their conversation as they ate their ice cream and then drove home. No doubt Marit would say that Jake was handling the situation age appropriately, acting out his fear and anger. Ken would say the kid was wise beyond his years. Probably they both were right.

He would relate the whole afternoon to Mona tonight

when the kids were in bed, so that she would know about Mellie's little subterfuge.

His shirt pocket began beeping. He pulled into a drugstore parking lot, checked the screen, and answered. "Hey, Sandy."

"Gerald wants us to meet with his firm's attorneys. He just called. Tomorrow, eleven at their office."

"Probably wants to give us the final bill. All right, see you there." What more could happen now? From the tone of Sandy's voice, he felt this did not bode well.

The next morning in the conference room of the eminent law firm Ross, Vorstein, and Schumacher, Ken could not feel lower if he were lying facedown in the basement. Beside him, Sandy looked just as low. Across from them at the huge mahogany table sat Gerald and the senior partner in their law firm, Henning Ross.

Mr. Ross raised his hands in a gesture of helplessness and let them flop. "Since I'm mentoring Gerry, he brought your problem to me. I worked on it; the whole board ended up working on it. You might say it became a challenge for us, to find a way to reverse the university's executive board decisions. We could not find a remedy of any sort. Your university lawyers covered all the possible loopholes."

"And my department—my former department—is now without any funding at all."

"Save for a nickel here, a dime there, yes. Basically, it's dead. I begrudgingly give the devil his due; the university's legal staff is top-notch."

"But they acted illegally!" Sandy exploded. "Surely we can sue or something."

Mr. Ross drew a deep breath. "They acted clandestinely, but no closed meetings. They acted unethically but short of actually breaking any laws."

Ken knew well that unethical and illegal are two different things. And if the whole board of Ross, Vorstein, and Schumacher, attorneys-at-law, could not find a way to change the situation, there almost certainly was no way. The bean counters and profit people had won. The department Ken had worked so hard his whole career to build was toppled. Permanently.

And there was nothing he could do to save it.

"I'm sorry, Ken. I am so sorry." Sandy blew her nose.

"Don't be. You did everything humanly possible. Never apologize for doing your best."

A faint smile whisked across Gerald's face. "How many times did I hear that!"

Ken smiled slightly himself. "It worked, didn't it?" He looked at Ross. "How much do we owe you?"

"Postage. Four dollars and eighty-seven cents."

"No, I mean the whole bill. All of you did your best for us; those were billable hours."

Mr. Ross dropped forward, elbows on the gorgeous table. "Dr. Sorenson, we hired Gerry here provisionally because he seemed, well, rather timid. Mild mannered. When you're defending in court, you cannot appear meek. But his education at Stone was the very best we've seen in a new hiree. He knows his stuff, and he can think quickly, inside or outside the box. And when he has to be forceful, he steps right up to the plate—excellent self-confidence, good presence. He attributes all that to you. You helped him get financing, you encouraged him, you built his self-esteem, you pushed him. This firm has a crackerjack employee who will soon become a junior partner, and it is because of your efforts." Mr. Ross sat up straight. "It's the least this firm could do. I'm just sorry we couldn't do more."

What could he say? "I'm grateful. Immensely grateful for all you did."

Sandy spoke up. "You may not realize the gift you just gave us, Mr. Ross. The legal expenses were coming out of Ken's pocket, not the university's; naturally they would not financially support his crusade. I was going to try to help him with that. I thank you, too."

The man smiled. "We rather thought that. Gerry told us the kind of person you are." He stood up and extended his hand. "God's blessings on your retirement, Dr. Sorenson."

Ken stood and shook. The man's hand was warm and firm. "Thank you. Blessings on you as well." He reached for Gerald's hand. "You make me proud, young man. Thank you for all you did. Blessings on your career."

Mr. Ross looked at his watch. "Eleven forty-five. Gerry, you might as well take these two to lunch. Put it on the company card."

"Thank you, sir. My pleasure." Gerald led the way out.

Ken's brain was mush. Less than mush. He was getting hit on all sides by too much of too much. Now this last door, open just far enough to admit a tiny glimmer of hope, had slammed shut. His academic life. His career. Everything he had cared about. Gone.

They rode the elevator in silence; they walked a long hall between oil paintings of beautiful landscapes in silence; they crossed the sumptuous atrium in silence.

"Where shall we eat?" Gerald asked as he pushed out the huge front doors.

Ken didn't want to eat. He didn't want to talk to anyone or make nice. "Not one of the food services at the university."

"I agree. You know all the restaurants and cafés around here," Sandy said. "You pick."

"Let's go to the Boulangerie. It's in this next block, and they have lunches to die for."

Oh, let's not! Ken's heart screamed.

Shut up and cooperate! his rational mind snapped back.

And a sudden realization almost stopped him in his tracks. This was not just sadness he was feeling; this was a moment of full-blown depression. He recognized the symptoms from Mona's bouts of depression. Ken Sorenson, ever the optimist, the guy who could see an answer to whatever problem needed answering, was in the throes of a genuine, debilitating depression.

And another realization burst in on him. This despondency and feeling of worthlessness was what Mona had dealt with and dreaded and fallen prey to her whole life. Although his head knew that her depression was an illness, an imbalance beyond her control, his heart had always thought of her spates of depression more or less as an inconvenience for them both. Not the devastating woe that would suddenly engulf her.

What could he do to make it up to her? Apologize? For what? Ignorance?

He would tell her about this revelation, of course. It certainly opened his eyes. Perhaps the best course was simply to ask her how he could help ease his burden and hers. His depression would run its course, probably; he was naturally rather ebullient. But hers had to be beaten into submission. Every time.

"Here we are." Gerald held a door open for Sandy and Ken.

They entered a carefully manufactured mock-up of a Parisian sidewalk café, with recessed lighting and the kind of tables and chairs a person expects of a place like that. A smiling hostess in a beret led them to a cozy table in a corner. Frankly, all the tables in here were cozy or tried to be. Ken instantly disliked the place with its phony airs. He and Mona had dined in a real Paris sidewalk café. This wasn't it.

He sat down and a menu was plopped in front of him. *Wait.* Another thought grabbed him. Was his dislike of this café his actual opinion, or was it the depression intruding? Mona had once said that what she thought and what her depression dictated were different things, and often things she liked when she was "normal," so to speak, did not appeal to her when she was depressed.

Now he could not even trust his own feelings.

A server came for their drink order, a slim fellow in a white shirt and a beret. Sandy requested herbal tea, so Ken said, "For me as well, please," without really giving it any thought. He did know he had never cared for herbal teas. Did depression also lead you to make poor choices? He would ask his resident expert, Mona.

He read down the menu, but none of the words registered. And yes, he could read the French fluently. His inattention had to be something else. When the server returned, pencil in hand, he pointed at random to a selection and sat back.

Sandy asked, "How was your trip to Chicago?"

"Fell through. Jakey got sick."

"Oh, I'm sorry. Is he okay now?"

"He will be."

That disappointment and all the others washed over him, a tsunami of negativity. He wanted to show the children Shedd Aquarium, with its centerpiece Caribbean reef, its amazing fish and jellies...Steig and Marit had loved Shedd. Ken wanted their children to know its wonders, and now that dream was shattered. And the Field Museum with its Tyrannosaurus Sue. And all the other things that delight and were now out of reach.

Their meals came. Sandy and Gerald enjoyed an easy camaraderie, but then, they had been in frequent contact during this whole ordeal. Ken ate what he had ordered, but it was virtually tasteless. Well, it wasn't, not really; more accurately, he had lost his taste for food. He recalled that during severe bouts of depression, Mona lost the desire to cook or eat out or anything.

He learned another thing: He really did not like herbal tea, not even with sugar in it. They used turbinado sugar here, crystalline brown stuff, not white, cheery *real* sugar.

Gerald and Sandy made light conversation. Ken moped.

Sandy frowned. She looked at her watch. "It's not still noon, is it? I'm afraid my watch stopped."

Gerald glanced at his wrist. "Twelve twenty."

"Oh, dear." She stared at the cute little candle glass in the center of the table. "I have to get my hair done at one. I'm meeting Arch Tarkensen and a fellow from the University at Madison who's in town at the moment. Their School of Medicine and Public Health. Arch thinks I'm perfect for a position that just opened there."

"Arch Tarkensen, the headhunter?" Ken smiled. "Give Arch my best when you see him."

"I shall. Gerald, I'm sorry that I'll have to eat and run. This was a lovely luncheon."

He was grinning. "My cousin went there; she's in public health. Great school. You'll love it. Break a leg or whatever the appropriate encouragement is."

"Thank you!" She was grinning, too. Obviously she wasn't depressed.

Ken found himself annoyed by people who were not depressed, and he never had been before. What a strange attitude. What a strange thing, depression. It penetrated every fiber of your being.

Sandy left fifteen minutes later. The server came around to refill drinks, picked up her plate, and disappeared.

Ken felt Gerald staring at him and glanced that way. Yes, the callow young man was indeed staring at him. "What?"

"I know Ken Sorenson. You are not Ken Sorenson. What's going on?"

"Everything. Nothing." Ken grimaced. "The world or what's left of it."

Gerald was still staring. Silently. Intently. At ease. And suddenly the weight of that world was too much for Ken's shoulders to bear. He found himself unloading on this young man, and he really had had no such intention. He didn't mean to; it just poured out and poured out. He even admitted what his heart had been saying all along—*my son is dead somewhere*. And he ended the lengthy litany of woe with, "And now my lifetime legacy is wiped out. All I worked for is gone."

"Bull shoes."

It was Ken's turn to stare. Never once in the years he had known him had Gerald ever used even a minced euphemism for a bad word. As an attention grabber, it sure worked. "So what is your take on it?"

"I can't address how taking in your grandchildren has destroyed your retirement, or at least altered it radically. I've never been there, and I learned I still don't really click with people older than I am; I can sympathize, but not empathize. But I can speak to your legacy because I experienced it firsthand. I say you're completely wrong."

"The department is dismantled. For all practical purposes, it does not exist anymore."

"Remember Blowser Romney?"

"Blows— I do. The kid with his hair dyed green."

"Met up with him at the class reunion. Rumor has it his animated movie will be nominated for an Oscar, and it hasn't even been released yet. *His* movie. He's the executive producer and artistic director. Remember Ann Morris? She had such a hard time learning anything, and you got her help for dyslexia. She runs a clinic for dyslexics now, and she's talking about opening three more in Wisconsin."

"I remember she blossomed once she got her reading and writing under control."

"Brant Richards, Harry Loggins, Joe Rose, Becky Winthrup. They'd be flipping burgers or something if you hadn't helped them stay in school. All of them except Becky are making six figures now. Becky's take-home is only about eighty-five thousand, she says, but she's getting a raise in a year."

"How would you know all that?"

"We got together after the reunion. We're sort of a subset of the graduates, the people you more or less pushed through college, who had a personal hand in getting us through. Becky calls us the Sorenson sodality." Gerald leaned forward. "And me! You salvaged me, Dr. Sorenson. That's what it was, a salvage operation. And next year I'll be the youngest junior partner ever at Ross, Vorstein, and Schumacher."

Ken stammered something, but he couldn't really think what to say.

"Dr. Sorenson, your legacy was never the student re-sources department. It was the students. Us. We who could not have succeeded without you. We are able to give something back to the world because of you."

"I-I-I am at a loss for words."

Gerald's voice softened. "Mrs. Jensen will almost cer-tainly get that position at Madison; apparently that's how your Mr. Tarkensen works. People trust his choices. And you trained her to see the students' real needs and to handle all the minutiae to help them get through school. You showed her what an effective department is all about. Stone University lost one of its greatest assets, but the School of Medicine is gaining it. Your legacy, as you call it—your influence—hasn't changed; it just shifted to a new site."

Was this kid right in his assessment? Did he see what Ken had failed to see?

Steig. Steig was gone. Or maybe not.

Ken and Mona would have the retirement they dreamed about, but it would be different.

Two abandoned children, trying to pick up the pieces, faced a stable future and bright life ahead, even if at a cost to Ken. And they were certainly more important than trav-eling on a retirement cruise or something.

And his legacy, or rather, just one small part of it, sat at the table beside him.

Much to his own astonishment, he found himself dis-solving into tears.

Chapter Thirty-One

"You all ready?" Mona handed Jake and Mellie their lunchboxes.

"Grammy, I can't find my pencil box." Jake held up his pack.

"Did you take it out for some reason?"

"You had it in the family room, remember?" Mellie shook her head. "I'll go find it," she announced wearily. "I told you to put it back."

"Bus leaves in five minutes."

"You're not a bus." Jake frowned at Ken.

"I'm a bus driver today." He looked at Mona. "The school bus does come by here, doesn't it?"

"Two blocks over."

"Here." Mellie stuffed the pencil box in her brother's backpack. "We're ready. You're coming, too, aren't you, Grammy?"

"I am." While they had met the teachers and been to their classrooms, today everyone was a volatile combination of excitement and fear.

Jake hugged Ambrose and petted Hyacinth. "You be good while we're gone."

"Out the door, Jake. The others are in the car already."

He stood and gave Ambrose one more pat, hefted his

backpack on one shoulder, and trudged out the door. "I'd rather go fishing with Grampy."

"Sorry, the fish will wait for you." She closed the door behind them. "Hustle so we aren't late."

At the school, Ken parked and turned to the kids in the backseat. "You know the way now?"

"You come with me, please?" Jake fumbled with his seat belt.

They all got out of the car and walked up the sidewalk to the front door. They could hear kids playing in the fenced area behind the school. Ken held the door open and patted Jake on the head as he went through. Mellie grinned up at him, but even she did not have her usual bounce.

"Thank you."

"Have a good first day," Mona told her as she headed down the hall to her classroom while they walked with Jake to his in the other direction.

"Even smells like the first day of school," Mona said, looking around at the decorations.

"Okay, Jake, here you are." Ken stopped them at the door to his classroom.

"You'll come pick us up?"

They both nodded. "We'll be waiting by the car for you."

"And we can go out for ice cream?"

"Yes. That's what we said, to celebrate your first day at a new school." Ken stepped back. Several kids walked around them to go through the door. The bell rang.

"Time to go in."

Jake nodded, grabbed his pack strap, and went on in. His normal bounce got left at home with the critters.

Mona and Ken waved at the principal and, dodging

kids, returned to the car. "How about we stop for a latte for you and a mocha for me?"

"Good idea, I think we earned it." Mona flopped back against the seat. "I don't remember other first days of school being this wearing."

"We were younger."

"You were at work. I did all the first days."

He grinned at her. "Probably that's why I don't remember."

"We didn't take any pictures for Steig!"

"We'll play it over this evening. When he finally gets on his e-mail, he's going to be blown away. Oops, poor analogy."

She sent him one of her looks. "For sure." Staring straight ahead, she said softly, "He is missing so much." She thought back to former first days. Steig was the dragger sometimes, too, but only the first day. Marit would badger him along. But once he'd really met his teacher and realized how many of his friends were in his class, he was set to go. "You remember when Steig brought the guinea pig home for the holidays. Every time we opened the refrigerator door, that little pig shrieked to high heaven."

"Didn't Marit bring home hamsters? And one got loose?"

Mona chuckled. "I was so afraid the cat would catch it before we did." She was quiet again. "Maybe having our grandkids here like this will help keep us younger."

"Or make us old before our time. Drive-up window or go in?"

Jake chattered all the way home that afternoon and remembered more at supper, so he kept on. Mellie answered questions but volunteered little. Mona and Ken swapped looks of awareness and concern.

"Now, make sure your backpacks are ready before you go to bed, so we aren't hunting for stuff in the morning," Mona said, looking directly at Jake, who nodded. "After we get the kitchen cleaned up, I thought we should go for a bike ride."

"Yes!" Jake pumped his arm. "Come on, Ambrose."

"Wait! What did your grammy say?"

He stuck out his lip. "Clean up the kitchen." He drained his glass of milk and set it on his plate. "Whose turn to clear the table?"

"You and me, pal, while Grammy and Mellie load the dishwasher and the other stuff." Ken pushed back his chair. "I think we better get that chores chart made and on the message board." He paused. "Did either of you have homework?"

The kids both shook their heads.

Mellie seemed more herself when they were pedaling down the river path. They all laughed when two squirrels played tag across in front of them.

"Ambrose wants to chase them." Jake grinned up from his own bike. He could ride a lot faster now.

That night when tucking Mellie into bed, Mona said, "You seem pretty quiet. Did something happen at school?"

"We have to write about our summer."

"Okay, that's not unusual."

"Can I write about Daddy leaving?"

"If you want to, I don't see why not."

Mellie sniffed. "Grammy, I miss him so much." She looked at Mona through tear-filled eyes. "Do you think he will ever get to read all my letters?"

"I am thinking that the first thing he will do is call us,

then Skype us, and then he will read all the letters and open the packages, and every man in his unit will be so jealous that they will wish they had kids like you and Jake." Mona ignored the burning in her nose and eyes.

"Really? Oh, Grammy, I pray every day that he will come home, but sometimes I forget to think about him and then I…" Mona grabbed a tissue off the bedside table. "Thank you."

"You're welcome. Remember we have riding lessons tomorrow after school."

"Oh, I do. I'm so glad you decided to ride, too. When are you getting your boots?"

"Maybe we'll go on Saturday, what do you think?"

"Just us?"

"Just us."

After she and Ken had swapped rooms for the goodnights, Mona headed for the kitchen to make the tea. "Would you please light the citron candle out on the deck? Too soon it will be too cold to use the deck anymore, so let's take advantage of it." Hot tea rather than iced felt better now that the nights were cooling off more.

"What a day!" Ken sank down in the lounger and stared out at the river. "How many quarts of beans did you get canned?"

"Only ten, a canner full, but thanks to your slicing, we did, what, four more pints for the freezer? When I think of all the canning and freezing my mother did…" She sipped her tea. "We'll be doing tomatoes soon." To this point, they'd eaten or frozen the ripe ones, but the vines were hanging red now.

"Like tomorrow."

"You know, I enjoy this so much more with you helping me. Well, the kids, too."

"They've been a big help, both in the garden and in the house. I'd forgotten how much our kids did, too."

"Right, and they developed great work ethics because they helped us." He swatted a mosquito. "One thing I like about fall is the death of the mosquitoes."

She told him what Mellie had asked her. "Sometimes I wonder if we should talk about Steig more. You told me what Jake said, and I know how much he is on my mind, and Mellie is so sensitive. I don't want to..."

"To?" he asked after the pause lengthened.

"To—to create an obsession, I guess is what I mean. I want her to be a normal little girl with all little girl things, not grow up so fast, like some of the others I've seen. Teenagers at ten instead of thirteen and up."

"That's a concern all right. She's had far more to deal with than most kids."

"Evening is coming so much sooner." Mona watched a bat swoop across the deck. The maple trees were starting to turn color along the river path, and the weeping birch hung golden. A squirrel jumped to the deck rail, bringing Ambrose to his feet with a low growl. The critter flicked his tail and leaped from the rail to the oak tree. Such peace out on their deck. They didn't use it often enough but enjoyed the moments like this when they did. She glanced over at Ken, and he held out his hand.

They were two weeks into the school year when Mellie flew into the house. "Grampy, I got a big favor to ask you."

Ken looked up from the cucumbers he was scrubbing at the sink. "What is it?"

"We are having a program, kind of a show-and-tell, about dads and what they do, and since Daddy can't come, would you please come and tell what you did at the university? You could wear your suit and—and I would have to introduce you. I have to have a speech ready to do that."

"When is this program?"

"On October thirteenth. We'd have to practice and everything."

"Of course I will. Thank you for asking."

"I wish Daddy was here, but..." She hugged his waist and heaved a sigh he had heard too often. He wrapped an arm around her shoulders and hugged her back. "I am honored to be part of your show-and-tell."

"Grampy, I'm hungry." Jake dumped his backpack on a stool at the counter, saw his grandfather's raised eyebrows, and went to put it in the basket with his name on it in the laundry room. "Where's Grammy?"

"She had a meeting at the church. She should be back soon. Okay, what do you want for a snack?"

"Peanut butter sammich. I'll get all the stuff out." Jake turned to Mellie. "You want one, too? With jam?"

"Yes. I'm going to change clothes first." She grabbed her backpack and headed for the stairs. "Blueberry jam."

"Grampy, you want one, too?"

"You know, that sounds good. I think there might be some chocolate milk in there, too."

"Do you know that we ride the chipmunk bus?"

"'Cause it has chipmunks on it?" Ken winked at his grandson.

"Nope. I think they shoulda named it the shark bus." Jake had decided he liked sharks.

"But all the others are named after animals, and a shark is a...?" He waited for Jake's answer. They'd been reading all about sharks.

"A huge, mean, hungry fish. And they live in the oceans, not in our fishing lake."

"You are so right."

Ken finished scrubbing the cucumbers, keeping an eye on Jake at the same time. "You've gotten real good at sammich making, buddy."

"Grammy taught me." Tongue between his teeth, he finished spreading the jam on top of the crunchy peanut butter and laid the other slice on top. He even cut them in half, put them on plates, and set them on the kitchen table.

"Wow, Jake, you did a good job." Mellie, now in playclothes, slid into a chair. "Did you even pour the chocolate milk—without spilling?"

"I only spilled a drop, and Grampy mopped that up."

After they'd nearly finished their snack, Ken asked, "Any homework for today?"

Both the kids nodded. "I have to read ten pages of my chapter book and twelve spelling words." Jake shook his head. "Spelling is hard."

Ken looked at Mellie. "You always have homework."

"I got most of it done at school today so I can draw for a while. And I have a book report to finish."

"For tomorrow?"

"Nope, for Wednesday." Mellie, like her aunty Marit, always liked to get things done early. "Did you mail the packet to Daddy?"

"Grammy did."

"Did she get oil rubbed into her boots?"

"I don't think so."

"Just think, Grampy, if we had horses of our own, we wouldn't have to drive clear out to Clauson's."

He leaned over and tousled her hair. "You are always thinking, that's for sure."

"I think you'd like to ride, too, if you tried it. And nothing smells as good as a horse."

"They stink!" Jake insisted. "And when you come home from riding lessons, you stink like a horse."

Ken raised a finger to cut her off before she countered his accusation. "Put your dishes in the dishwasher."

"Don't you like horses, Grampy?"

"Sure, they are a great animal. But I've never owned one, nor ridden one, and I really have no desire to. Sorry, but I just don't. How come you never come fishing with me?"

She shrugged. "I went fishing once with Daddy, and I guess I just..." She paused. "I don't hate it, I..."

"No desire to go fishing again?"

"If you want me to, I would go."

Jakey burst in with, "No! That's for Grampy and me."

Ken shrugged. "See, we don't all have to like all the same things. Fishing is not Grammy's favorite thing to do, either, but she'll go if I insist." *Not that I've insisted for many years.* He smiled to himself. Ever since she got pregnant the first time, she'd not gone fishing. The waves made her so sick, they just came in. Ah, the memories; he'd not thought of that one for a long time.

Later that evening after supper, they were all sitting in the family room with the adults watching the news. Mellie sat curled in a corner of the sofa, reading one of her library books while Jake created a shark with his Legos on the floor. The screen shifted to a large plane where a casket, draped in an American flag, was wheeled out and lowered as six men in full uniform stood saluting. While the announcer told a bit about the soldier being brought home to be buried in the Arlington cemetery, Mona heard a sniff and then sobs.

Mellie dropped her book, bailed off the sofa, and threw herself into Mona's arms. "Oh, Grammy, that could be

Daddy." Her sobs drowned out the announcer. "That's what they'll do if they find him dead."

"Mellie, honey, but that is not your daddy."

"I know, but it...could be."

Oh, Lord, how do we handle this? Please help us. Ken knelt beside Mona's recliner and hugged them both, including Jake, as, with Legos going in every direction, Jake threw himself at them.

Chapter Thirty-Two

So here was Ken in a suit and tie again. Mona smiled inwardly as she watched him drive. Once his retirement took hold, so to speak, he had pretty much gone to casual unless he was ushering at church, which was only once a month. But today he was a speaker at Mellie's school Career Day, telling an auditorium full of children what it was like to be a professor. He was asked to dress in his everyday work clothes, which included his attaché case. And Mellie was to introduce him.

Ken looked grim. "This morning Mellie asked me if I was nervous about being in front of all those people. I said no, I speak to groups all the time. How about her? And she said she didn't care. Everyone else was introducing their fathers and her father was dead."

"At least she admits out in the open what she's been thinking all along. What a sad way to cure stage fright. Did Jake say anything?"

"No, but he didn't contradict her, either."

They pulled into the parking lot of Mellie's school.

"Crowded already," Ken commented. "Are parents invited, too?"

"Yes. Two children from each class were chosen to represent their class. In the fourth grade, Mellie is one, and Little John Marsh is the other. He will introduce his father, a fireman, and Big John says he's going to be wearing his full bunkers. Then he's going to turn it into a teaching session, especially for the little kids."

"Teaching session?"

"He says he's going to put on his survival mask and oxygen tank. He'll explain that is what he wears when he enters a burning building. Then he'll stress how important it is for a child to not be afraid of that scary costume and run to the fireman, not hide."

Ken smiled. "Is he going to blow his whistle?"

"I think so. Children are supposed to run toward that sound, not away from it."

"Wait till they find out how ear piercing that whistle is." Ken shook his head. "Quite a showstopper. Being a professor is going to look pretty lame compared to a fireman."

Mona laughed. "Maybe you could put on that welder's mask you use for face protection when you are turning something on your lathe. Explain that professors aren't in a white shirt all the time; they have a life."

He pulled into a parking slot and turned off the motor. "I have. A wonderful life, full of blessings." He twisted in the seat to look at her. "And you are the greatest blessing by far. You serve Jesus, you raised fine kids, and you made an ordinary house into a warm, loving home. You made my life, Mona. Thank you." He drew her into a long, leisurely kiss.

When he sat back, Mona clung for a moment. "And I have you to thank for so many blessings. For staying with me when the depression makes me such a sour apple to live with. Not every victim of depression has that kind of support. And for being such a fine Christian father to our kids and a great provider." She dug into her purse. "Now

I have to fix my lipstick." She grinned at him. "And that's wonderful."

Together they strolled inside. Ruth Holmstead, the principal, stood outside the big double doors to the multipurpose room, greeting people as they entered. Mona noted that she knew most of them by name.

"Mr. and Mrs. Sorenson. Welcome!" She smiled at Ken. "You look quite natty, professor."

"Thank you. I hope to impress children who like to dress up and wear a tie."

She laughed, but then she sobered. "Mellie does not seem to be especially excited about this; I thought she would be. In fact, that's one reason we chose her. And in September, when we were putting this program together—we do it every year, you know—she was certain her father would be back in time."

Mona nodded. "She has convinced herself her father is dead, not MIA."

"I'll make sure Lori knows about that. Thank you. As her teacher, Lori is concerned, too." She waved an arm. "Presenters are asked to sit on the aisle. You will follow a mechanic named Hugh Larsen. He's—"

"My mechanic." Ken grinned. "It will be an honor. The world can do without professors, but we can't get along without mechanics. I might even add that to my little speech."

They settled into aisle seats. Mona looked around the gymnasium that had a good-sized stage with heavy curtains and a long bank of lights overhead. The deep blue curtains were drawn with a lone microphone in front. And yes, under Mona's feet was the room-sized tarp they put down to protect the floor. Under that tarp, she knew, basketball keys were painted, and a volleyball court was outlined. When Steig and Marit were growing up, the school had a dedicated theater-like auditorium that was way too small. This huge room seemed to hold everyone comfortably.

"Good grief, the parking lot is full. I had to park out on the street." Marit slipped in beside them and put down her purse. "I am so excited for Mellie. Just think, maybe this will open doors to her mind about teaching or speaking or all kinds of things."

"I take it you've not heard that she wants to be a horse trainer like Miss Dixie? We could soon be sitting in bleachers watching horse shows."

Marit frowned at Mona, then shrugged. "Lots of time yet."

Since the front rows were reserved for lower-grade students, the back rows quickly filled with families and left the bleachers for the upper grades. As the students filed in, the noise level rose exponentially.

The magic hush happened when Mrs. Holmstead walked out to the microphone. She waited for complete silence before welcoming everyone. "Let us stand for the Pledge of Allegiance." She turned to the American flag off to the right of the stage. She placed her hand over her heart as did everyone else and began, "I pledge allegiance..."

By the end, Mona had the burning eyes and nose again. Both the pledge and the national anthem did that to her every time. When they all took their seats, she dug in her purse for a tissue. Ken patted her knee and turned his head enough to smile at her.

"Again, I thank all of you families for coming today. I know some of the parents had to take off work; we appreciate your support and dedication. I want to introduce sixth grader Brandylin Willkinson, who will be our MC for today." She turned to the left. "Brandilyn."

A tall girl strode out on the stage and took her place behind the microphone that did not even need to be lowered for her. "Thank you all for coming and welcome to this Career Day, where our relatives will be sharing what they do for a living and how that makes a difference in our town. I made a list of all the participants because I did not want to forget anyone." A chuckle rippled over the audience.

"But before we begin, I want to introduce our AV specialist, sixth grader Andrew Paine. He'll make sure everyone can speak into the mic." A redheaded boy, shorter than she, made his way out, tapped the mic, made certain those in the back could hear, and left the stage.

Mona leaned close to Ken. "She sure is doing a good job." He nodded.

They listened to a woman talk about being a doctor and a man tell about his life as a nurse. Another man owned a gas station, and he said he helped the town by keeping their cars on the road and fueled. The audience laughed at that one. A business owner spoke, as did a man and woman who owned and operated a restaurant that often ran specials donated to local sport teams. So many people, each making a small difference that added up to a huge difference.

When Hugh Larsen stepped out onstage, Ken left Mona's side. Some of the younger children were getting squirmy and restless.

Marit leaned close to Mona. "I like the way the teachers make sure they behave. This can be pretty boring for little ones."

"Just wait until the fireman blows his whistle."

With his daughter standing beside him, Hugh completed his presentation by waving a monkey wrench.

Brandylin announced, "Our next student is new to our school this year, fourth grader Mellie Sorenson." Mona and Marit clapped hard. Andrew lowered the mic so that Mellie could speak easily and grinned at her before he left the stage. Mona got out and aimed her iPad, watching its screen so she could film their segment.

Mellie stepped up to the mic and did not seem at all nervous. She licked her lips, but she often did that. "My father, Captain Steig Sorenson, is in the Army Special Forces. He has been deployed to Pakistan." She looked as if she might say something else, but then she said simply, "He's not here. So instead, today I am introducing my grandfather, Dr. Ken Sorenson, who just retired from being dean of students at Stone University. He will tell you what it is like to be a university professor and why it matters." She turned to smile at her grandfather and moved aside, giving him the mic.

Ken stepped up to the podium casually and set his attaché case down beside him. Andrew rushed out and began cranking and twisting to get the mic up high enough.

Marit wagged her head. "Right down to the briefcase."

"Show-and-tell. He wants to tell about the research aspect. He'll show everyone a tomahawk because most archaeologists are professors, and a resin cast of a baby dinosaur skull because most paleontologists are professors."

"Ah. My father the showman."

Mona heard the big doors behind her swoosh open. Latecomers, no doubt.

Ken turned his head from side to side, nodding, to address the whole room. "Thank you, Mellie, and thank you,

Brandylin. To most people, being a profess—" He stopped cold. His mouth dropped open and he stared.

Mellie screamed and kept screaming.

Mona swiveled to see who had just entered.

Captain Steig Sorenson.

Steig. Steig! Steig! He…Steig! Oh God, thank You! Steig!

ThankYouGodthankYouthankYouSteigGodthankYou. Mona's brain spun so hard she felt faint.

In his camo fatigues, he jogged down the aisle toward the stage.

Mona's legs lifted her out of her seat without being told to. Her feet propelled her toward the stage.

Ken and Mellie had both leaped down off the stage, and now Steig was wrapping his arms around them both. Jakey bolted across the room to slam into Steig, and now Mona was there, hugging, laughing, crying. She could feel her son's strong arm pull her to him. Then he let go of her to pick up Jakey, who wrapped himself around his father's neck. *Steig! Oh GodthankYouthankYouthankYou.*

Mrs. Holmstead moved back to the mic. "I am sure this will go down in our school's history as the most incredible day ever. We had no idea this was coming. It is a surprise to all of us, and it could not be a more welcome surprise. All I know is that Captain Sorenson was deployed last summer and later listed as missing in action."

Mona stepped back a little so that Marit could squeeze closer.

Mrs. Holmstead mopped her eyes and blew her nose. She continued. "Friends, let us thank Captain Sorenson for his service to our country." She clapped.

The audience applauded. Some of the fathers stood up,

and then all were on their feet, clapping wildly, a standing ovation.

Mona's heart and brain were both still in a tailspin. Many questions, but they would come later. Who cares? Questions and answers were no longer important to her.

Steig was home at last.

Steig was home.

Chapter Thirty-Three

M ona brought out the tray of coffee, hot chocolate, and sweet rolls and set it on the table in front of the sofa. She settled into her favorite chair beside Ken in his. Steig sat in the middle of the sofa with children plastered tightly against him, one on each side.

Steig leaned forward and retrieved a mug of coffee. "Thanks, Mom. So as soon as my plane touched down, I tried to call you and tell you I was on my way, but I couldn't reach anyone."

"Our phones were turned off so they wouldn't ring during the presentations," Ken said.

"The door was locked, and you left that note for Marit: 'Gone to school Career Day. Your green beans are in the shed.'"

Mona smiled. "I didn't know she was going to get off work and come to the presentation until she walked in."

"My driver was putting my duffel on the porch. I told him, 'Get back in!' and he drove me right there."

"Wow!" Mellie's eyes widened. "You have your own driver?"

"One of the perks of being a captain, sweet."

Ken wagged his head. "No communication from you at all. We didn't know what to think, and then we were told MIA."

Steig lost his happy smile. "I'm sorry. I really am. I promised to Skype, and it never happened. The mission was top secret. The first thing the bad guys do is try to wangle information out of the family. We didn't want anyone to know who I was or where I went or what I was doing or who my family was for your protection. My immediate supervising officer—my handler if you will—was the only one who knew about the operation. As far as Major Paget knew, I really was MIA. And incidentally, the mission is still secret. I was in a zone where American military is never supposed to be. So I can't discuss it, but it was nowhere near Pakistan. That's just where I shipped out from."

"Real cloak-and-dagger. Sounds like something you only see in the movies." Ken smiled. "We're proud of you. But I probably don't have to tell you that."

"Thank you." Steig gave Mellie a squeeze. "So how is school?"

"Great. My teacher says my reading is awesome."

"You tested eighth grade a year ago."

Mellie nodded. "Now I'm adult level." She shrugged. "Mostly."

"Wow. That's great." Steig groped around in a side pant leg pocket and hauled out a folded-up piece of paper. "So you can read this, right?"

She unfolded it and smoothed it out on her lap. She studied it a moment, frowning as only a serious ten-year-old can frown. "These are...are these discharge papers? It says honorable discharge."

Mellie passed the paper to Ken. "I have to say, our mission was completely successful, but I nearly died accomplishing it. Dumb luck that I didn't." He smiled at Mona. "Or the power of prayer. It was a wake-up call, so to speak. Do I want to keep going in the army, or do I want to be a father and raise the kids? The kids don't have a mother, and maybe next time I wouldn't be so lucky. I talked to my base financial officer, and he worked out an early retirement where I still get full benefits."

"Do you regret your choice?" Ken handed the papers back to him.

"No. Well, sort of. I loved my work, and I'm going to really miss it. Cloak-and-dagger is exhilarating. Addictive even. It's an adrenaline rush like no other. But the kids are more important, so I grabbed my chance. I'll go to Washington, where I'm going to be decorated for my service, me and three other guys. Then it's over."

"What's decorated?" Jake asked.

"Where you get a medal and an award."

"Which medal?" Ken asked.

"Medal of Honor." Steig said it so offhandedly.

Mona clapped her hands over her mouth to keep from crying out loud. The highest award the armed forces can give. Her son.

Thank You, God! Her heart and soul were still ringing with *Thank You!*

Most of all, best of all...

Steig was home for good.

Reading Group Guide
Discussion Questions

1. Which character did you most closely relate to and why?

2. What surprising things have happened in your life that forced to you to change and grow?

3. In the novel, Mona struggles with worry. Do you identify with this problem? What helps you to overcome it?

4. What advice would you give to this family to make times of change easier to manage?

5. Ken has difficulty making the transition to retirement. Have you ever struggled with a major life change, such as changing jobs or moving to a new place? What was the hardest part? What about the experience was rewarding?

6. We are encouraged to set goals and make plans, but what do you do when things happen to cause

those goals and plans to be dumped or at least put on the back burner?

7. Though Mona and Ken had raised two children, they found it challenging to transition back into the role of being parents to their grandchildren. Why do you think that was?

8. We always have the choice to turn to our Father for help but often we don't until we are totally struggling. Or drowning. How can we help each other turn to Him first and learn to thank Him and praise Him even in the hardest times?

9. Depression attacks so many of us, making daily living such a struggle. If this has happened to you, what did you learn from it? And how do you keep it from attacking again?

10. What do you think the characters learned about themselves and each other by the end of the novel? Did you take away anything from their experiences that might help you in your own life or help someone you care about?

Contemporary novels that celebrate love and family by Lauraine Snelling

Someday Home

"A wonderful tale of fresh starts, resilience, loss and love in this perfect summer read."
—*RT Book Reviews*

When Lynn Lundberg's husband passes away, she struggles to adjust to life without him in their big, family lake home—but she doesn't want to leave the place where they made precious memories. So she opens her home to two female tenants, each of whom brings along her own unique crises. Will these women be in over their heads, or find friendship to last a lifetime?

Heaven Sent Rain

"Snelling's story has the potential to be a big hit."
—*RT Book Reviews*

Scientist Dinah Taylor's life becomes increasingly complicated when she meets seven-year-old Jonah Morgan and his dog. As their friendship grows and the child faces a series of trying events, Dinah must decide just how much responsibility she's capable of taking on.

Wake the Dawn

"Snelling's description of events at the small clinic during the storm is not to be missed."

—*Publishers Weekly*

Physician's assistant Esther Hansen struggles to run an ill-equipped smalltown clinic during a devastating storm. But she is both tested and finds healing when a grieving border patrolman arrives with an abandoned baby.

Reunion

"Inspired by events in Snelling's own life, *Reunion* is a beautiful story."

—*RT Book Reviews*

Kiera Johnston is shaken when she uncovers the fifty-year-old secret that she was adopted, and soon after her teenaged niece's pregnancy is revealed. Will love be enough to hold the Sorenson family together in spite of these challenging truths?

On Hummingbird Wings

"Snelling can certainly charm."

—*Publishers Weekly*

Gillian Ormsby arrives in California to care for her ailing mother with plans to return to New York as quickly as possible. But as her friendship with her mother's neighbor Adam develops into more, Gillian considers trading professional success for a renewed and rewarding sense of family.

One Perfect Day

"[A] spiritually challenging and emotionally taut story. Fans of Christian women's fiction will enjoy this winning novel."

—*Publishers Weekly*

Only days before Christmas, the tragic loss of a child devastates one mother but offers another the miracle she's been praying for. The gift of second chances made bittersweet, can these mothers find hope in knowing that the spirit of each child lives on?

Breaking Free

"Reminding us that love can spring forth from ashes, that life can emerge from death, Lauraine Snelling writes a gripping and powerful novel that will inspire and uplift you."
—Lynne Hinton, author of *The Last Odd Day*

Maggie Roberts gains a renewed sense of purpose through working to keep a horse from being discarded. But her reason for living is threatened when a local businessman offers the horse a permanent home.

Available in trade paperback and ebook formats wherever books are sold.